LARA'S STORY

Diane Merrill Wigginton

ALSO BY DIANE MERRILL WIGGINTON

Angelina's Secret

Book 1 in the Jeweled Dagger series

A sweeping and engaging historical romance, Angelina's Secret has emotion, action, suspense and above all, an epic and timeless love. Filled with heroic, dashing pirates and brave, beautiful ladies, this is a fantastic read.
—blueink reviews (starred review)

Isabella's Heart

Book 2 in the Jeweled Dagger series

Isabella's Heart is a fun and imaginative tale of romance with
strong themes of family and loyalty.
Wigginton has created a unique series, following the mother-daughter link
of strong, thrill-seeking women.
-foreword reviews

Olivia's Promise

Book 3 in the Jeweled Dagger series

Olivia's Promise by Diane Merrill Wigginton, is yet another awesome book by this author. I read it very quickly — it was like eating good ice cream, I enjoyed it that much. Olivia's Promise is an excellent read, very hard to put down. I gave it Five Stars!

—International Writers Inspiring Change

International Writers Inspiring Change award: Diane Merrill Wigginton

"Most Inspiring Author of the Year 2017" for the Jeweled Dagger series

Other books by the author:
A Compromising Position, The Magician Killer,
and The Secret of One-Eyed Cogburn

www.dianemerrillwigginton.com

JEWELED DAGGER PUBLISHING COMPANY

www.jeweleddaggerpublishing.com

© Copyright 2026 by Diane Merrill Wigginton

All rights reserved.

ISBN: 978-1-946146-90-8

Designed by Fine Design

First Edition:

January 28, 2019

Follow Diane Merrill Wigginton at

https://www.facebook.com/share/15x6K6nniw/

https//www.goodreads.com/author/show/8355606

https//www.amazon.com/Diane-Merrill-Wigginton/e/B00MS5NV38

DEDICATION

I wish to dedicate this book to all those who
have endured difficult times in their lives.
Know that you are not alone,
for we are all called upon to do the difficult things in life.
No one is exempt from it.
That is what brings about a change in us.
It was because of difficulties I suffered when I lost
my brother and father in 2011 that I was able to fully realize
my dream of becoming a writer.
That was the catalyst that propelled me forward,
giving me the courage to publish my first novel.
Change is good, but it can also be painful.
I encourage you to embrace it, don't shy away from it.
Heartbreak is inevitable; we all must go through it.
Heartaches are also what makes us
compassionate as well as human.
A broken heart can be put back together again
and sometimes beat better than it did
before the pain broke it.

Table of Contents

1

APRIL 27, 1854
PHILADELPHIA WHARF

Lara's Story

Every question begins with a quest for answers, and every testimony of what is true begins with a test of one's resolve. I am reminded of this simple formula as I stand here on this boardwalk, looking out to sea. Each life is a journey, defined by turns we take or the roads we choose or those which fate chooses for us. Some of us move from one place to another, along a well-worn path or the path less taken; it really doesn't matter much as long as it leads you home again.

Memories of my home involuntarily flash through my mind as Mama's words come back to me like a sounding board that has followed me my entire life. She would often tell my sisters and me, "Don't ever make yerself smaller to satisfy the needs of another." Mama was always insightful and perceptive when it came to her children.

Oh, how I still miss her so, even to this day. I smile to myself, wishing my ears could hear that beautiful, rhythmic sound of Mama's voice again, just one more time, as a terrible memory of the last day I saw her alive flashes through my mind and I vigorously shake my head to dispel the thought.

When a heart breaks it does not break evenly—cleaving in half exactly down the middle. It breaks, jagged and rough, cutting one to the very core of the soul. And while things may appear perfectly normal to the naked eye, beneath the surface lies the real tragedy— fragmented and splintered beyond reconciliation. Heartbreak is not an innocuous pain, easily excused like a stomachache. It is more

insidious, spreading throughout ones' system like an infection. Merely closing my eyes to the pain does not eliminate it in the least.

Just breathe in, then breathe out and move forward, I remind myself. This simple little mantra is something I taught myself so many years ago, and it has gotten me through more than a few dire situations.

I was born Lara Flannigan, on the twenty-first day of April, in the year of our Lord, eighteen hundred and thirty-three. Mama liked to tell me it was a beautiful spring morn, the day I was born, which would have been an unusual occurrence for that time of year.

Mama also said, "I knew ye were special and destined for greatness the moment ye took yer first breath, don't ye know, 'cuz the sun poked out from behind the clouds with yer first breath of life. Why 'twere like the Heavens above truly recognized that an angel had been born to me," she teased.

If truth be told, I believe Mama told this exact story to each of her six children. But I loved hearing it nonetheless.

I was the sixth child of the seven children born to Rory and Laurel Flannigan, and I was named for my Da's mother. Our days were long and our lives were hard, but our nights belonged to us. I never knew life could be anything other than what I had experienced. My world was very small in those days, so I never missed the things I didn't have.

I am an Irish immigrant and I came to America at the tender age of thirteen, a disillusioned child, harshly mistreated by the very people entrusted with my care. I tell you this not to solicit your sympathies but to impart knowledge and gain your understanding, for I was a pitiful, angry child who was unaware of how many things in my life were about to change.

People meeting me today might say that I was more fortunate than most. Yet they would have never heard my story nor have known that I suffered in silence. I did not wear my pain like a badge of honor, but kept it deep inside of me, hidden away from the prying eyes of others.

Fear has made me keep my story to myself. I was afraid of the repercussions from the actions I took in the name of survival when

my whole world fell apart. Furthermore, I feared the behavior of peers—those who would use the circumstance of my birthplace and subsequent difficulties to hold me back or bludgeon me with my story like a weapon.

For many years I have pushed from my thoughts memories of home and all that happened there. And yet, every now and again I indulge myself with less painful memories of the past that push their way to the surface, and I give myself permission to embrace them—loving, bold, nostalgic memories that are impossible to forget. This is especially true today as I find myself waiting, yet another day, for a ship to come in, one that I thought would never arrive upon these great American shores.

Oh, I have everything a person could ever desire. Enough food to ward off hunger for a lifetime. Good health, a beautiful home, fashionable clothes, and the love of my family. I truly have every comfort one could want at my disposal, yet still, I long to recover the missing pieces of myself torn from me the day I left my native land of Ireland—a loss that can still be keenly felt whenever I lay my head down upon my pillow at night. And even though I am far from familiar old haunts, I swear I hear the land beckoning to me in my dreams, calling from across the ocean, summoning me home to the cliffs of Dunmore Head on the westernmost shores of Ireland. Closing my eyes now, I can still recall the smell and taste of the breeze on my tongue and the tangy feel of the salty island sea air as it mixes with the sweet scents of wildflowers growing along the craggy cliffs.

The memories grab hold of my soul, leaving me longing for home, even more this day.

"Ireland," I whisper, as it all comes flooding back to me—the green grassy moors waving in the gentle breeze like waves on the ocean. I can still feel the way the grass tickled my bare feet when I walked upon it.

In my mind's eye I can see the ancient moss-covered rocks and hills that seem to roll on forever and the overwhelmingly familiar smells of home assault my senses and kindle even more longing inside me—peat moss burning in the hearth, earthy smells of fresh mud coming

from our simple thatched roof dwelling built from wattle and daub that plastered the rocks and boulders in place to form walls, rain leaking upon my head in the middle of the night whenever a storm blew in just right, and sweet earthy tones mingling with the bitter as they played across my tongue whenever I chewed on a blade of grass.

Vivid, sweet memories wash over me, transporting me back in time as I see myself as a little girl, sitting in the middle of a field of tall grass, watching with fascination as the wind blows the grass to-and-fro. Then I see myself laughing and playing among the cliffs with my best friend Jamie. There are so many precious and sweet memories that I have denied myself for so long.

I swallow hard to push down the lump that forms in my throat. I can recall every ridge, crag, twig, and moss-covered rock that littered our unyielding plot of land.

Many afternoons were spent upon those cliffs basking in the glorious sun after bathing in the ocean with Mama and my two sisters. Alana loved tickling me just to hear me laugh while I lay upon the warm rocks, soaking up the last glorious rays of sunlight. A cool breeze would kick up, washing over my skin and chilling my flesh with its gentle touch. Those were the days I thought would never end, and it is those same sweet memories that now make me mourn the loss of them all the more.

I shake my head quickly, dispelling any more memories of the past as I hold back more tears, attempting to keep them from escaping. Swiping at the lingering few that trickle down my cheeks, I feel anxious and frustrated all at the same time.

Please do not mistake my tears for weakness, for tears can express many different emotions and convey more than mere words. One should never assume that there is only one reason to shed tears. There are tears caused by overwhelming grief and pain and tears of contrition. There are tears of joy and love, or tears of annoyance caused by situations that are beyond one's control. My tears today are a culmination of many different emotions that are simply too hard for me to put into words.

Coming back to reality, I take a moment to compose myself. Drawing in a deep breath, I turn away from the people walking by me who have stopped to stare. Quickly wiping away fresh tears as I attempt to dispel my complicated thoughts, I notice a man staring at me from across the street and I realize it's my fiancée. Suddenly I find myself wondering how long he has been standing there watching me as he steps down into the street and crosses over to me.

"Lara, my love, let me take you back home so you may warm yourself by the hearth. It really is far too cold today for you to be standing out here waiting for that blasted ship to come in. Watched pots never boil and all," he teases. "Why, this is the third day this week—"

"The fourth. But who's counting?" I inform him tersely, turning away slightly in hopes that he doesn't notice my reddened eyes.

"Have you been crying?"

"Don't be ridiculous. A piece of ash flew into my eyes and caused them to tear up," I lie.

"Both of them? Let me see," he insists, forcibly turning me to face him.

"I've already removed it." I slap at his hand. "Now stop fussing over me and leave me be. Don't you have someplace other than here to be? Like work?"

"Not today, darling. I've taken the day off. When you are the boss, you can do that sort of thing," he gloats, then smiles broadly.

"Seems someone has developed a rather high opinion of himself," I playfully reply, trying to distract him from his original concern. "Now off with you. I can assure you that I am made of heartier stock than you give me credit for. I'll be fine," I retort, and lift one brow when he gives me one of his questioning looks that says he doesn't quite believe a word coming out of my mouth. "Surely, you know that I am not leaving this spot before the ship docks. I would not take the chance of missing it, you know. You, of all people, know why this particular ship is so special to me." I stubbornly lift my chin. "You couldn't pry me away from this spot if you tried."

He throws his hands up and replies, "I know, darling, but I had to try. So why don't I stay and keep you company?" Then, with a patient smile, he jokingly mimics a thick Irish brogue while adding, "Because I have a feelin' in me bones, don't ye know, that today is the day," sounding utterly ridiculous while doing so.

"Oh, aye, ye have a sharp tongue on ye today, sir," I tease. I look up and down the street to ensure that no one is paying attention to us before standing on my tippy toes to kiss him on the mouth. I truly love this man standing before me, with all of my heart. And on a day like today, I marvel at my good fortune, and even at fate itself, for bringing us together. If truth be told, I feel even more blessed that I am still alive.

I look up and catch him studying me out of the corner of his eye. I see a look in his eyes that proclaims that his mind is working overtime and I know he wants to say something but is holding back.

"What is it, darling?" I quietly ask, looking off towards the vast ocean for any sign of the ship.

He continues to gaze down at me a moment longer before turning his attention to the activities on the docks. Then, without another word, he takes hold of my arm, leading me over to a nearby bench. I notice a basket sitting on the ground next to the bench with a blanket resting on top.

"I was hoping you would help me pass the time as we wait by telling me a story of when you were a little girl growing up in Ireland," he suggests slyly, giving me a quick side-long look.

I smile awkwardly before taking a seat just as my knees give way because of his unexpected request. Unfolding the blanket, he places it across my lap before taking a seat next to me. All the while his eyes never directly meet mine, even though he knows I am searching his face.

Pulling the blanket up a little higher, I turn away to hide the fresh tears that spring to my eyes. Looking out to the ocean's horizon again, I lift a hand to block the brightness of the sun. I am certain he doesn't

fully understand what he is asking of me because, if he did, he would never have asked.

The raw nerve he hits with his simple request drudges up so many emotions—sweet and precious memories intermingle with dark and painful flashbacks. I realize he does not truly understand that he is asking me to journey back to a time fraught with difficulty and pain. To a time full of memories and traumatic experiences from my childhood I have deliberately boxed up, knowing that I dare not examine them too closely for fear they will be my undoing. These memories are the most precious yet devastating parts of me. He has no way of knowing his request is equivalent to opening up Pandora's Box. I have worked hard to hide that part of myself from the world…and from him.

Closing my eyes, I sit quietly with my thoughts and memories for a moment, allowing them to flood back to me as fresh and raw as the day they happened. So many things have happened to me since Ireland that putting words to them is difficult. And yet all the memories are still there, just beneath the surface, waiting for me to bring them up and give them life.

As I begin to speak, details I had long ago pushed away come rushing in. "Some may have considered us poor, without means to sustain ourselves, when I was a child. Others speculated that we would never amount to anything—my brothers, sisters, and I—but they would have been wrong. In my eyes, they were the ones who were lacking in substance and means. They were the ones poor in heart and poor in spirit. They were the ones who would never amount to anything because they could never have imagined, for the life of them, what we as a family had. In my heart, we had everything that was important. We had each other," I whisper. "I discovered at an early age that if your heart isn't right, you can never be truly happy. I had loving parents that counted their children as their most precious and prized possessions, or so I thought, and we looked out for one another, offering love and support to each other."

Memories wash over me like the ocean, whirling and swirling about me, pushing me back across the Atlantic, hundreds of miles away. Back to a more innocent time, so many years before, when my

life was carefree. "Every day was an opportunity for an adventure, and every night was filled with joy, laughter, and dancing as my large, boisterous family gathered around the warmth of our humble little hearth," I say with a sad smile.

"Nothing smells quite like Ireland." I choke back another sob as I catch myself thinking about my mama, so bonnie and light before—well, before the tragedy.

Thinking of my family always makes me sad, but I will not pull away this time. *No, not this time!* I tell myself.

2

The Carefree Days,
Before It All Went Wrong

When I begin to speak again, I barely recognize my own voice as the floodgates of emotions open up wide, pouring out feelings and thoughts in my mind's eye so quickly I can scarcely contain them all.

I find myself back in Dunmore Head, a part of the Dingle Peninsula, in Kerry County, Ireland. It was May 1846, and I was twelve years old standing in the cooking area of our modest, two-room home. Mama, my two sisters Alana and Caitlin, and I worked together, preparing a special meal for Da's birthday. He didn't like a fuss made over his day because, he said, "It was a waste of time." Yet Mama felt differently about the matter and told us on more than a few occasions that Papa was full of malarkey.

Alana, who was eighteen and looked so much like our mama—tall and fair, with dark auburn hair and hazel green eyes—was promised to Newel Cummins from the next township over. They were to be wed in August, and preparations for her special day had already begun. The beginnings of a wedding dress hung on a hook in the corner of the room and the glow of young love shone on her bonnie cheeks.

My other sister, Caitlin, was fifteen and nearly as tall as Alana, but looked more like Da with her darker skin and chestnut hair that shone with red tones beneath her dark tresses. She had eyes fringed with beautiful, full lashes and, of my two sisters, was the most striking.

Although my two sisters were very different in appearance, they were aligned in their allegiance to one another and did everything

together. They stood in the corner of the room mixing dough for the sweet bread and rolling it in raisins and nuts before allowing it to rise. Then the bread would be baked and drizzled with a sweet glaze while it was still warm.

My mama and I worked in tandem to prepare Da's favorite soup—potato and fish. We made it from a creamy broth combined with diced potatoes and onions from our garden and whatever fish my oldest brother Colin happened to catch that morning.

Mama, who was always so beautiful and fair in my eyes, and once considered to be the prettiest lass in the county, was beginning to show her age. Her curly red hair, once vibrant and bold, was beginning to streak with gray. Hard work, coupled with time, had taken its toll, marring her once smooth, supple, alabaster skin with brown spots and fine lines around her eyes and mouth.

I often asked Mama why she smiled so much. Her answer was always the same. She'd say it was because she had been lucky enough to tame the rebellious heart of my Da, the most handsome man in three counties. Then she would add that he had blessed her life with six wonderful children who brought her life meaning and joy. Da stood just a little taller when he heard Mama say it.

Mama loved to laugh, finding happiness in the little things life gave to her. In fact, I truly can't remember many times in her life when she wasn't laughing or smiling about one thing or another.

Colin, who was nearly twenty years old and the oldest son of Rory and Laurel Flannigan, was decidedly, might I add, the pride and joy of our Da. Oh, he claimed he loved us all the same, but we all knew Colin was his favored child because he was the firstborn. Tall and strong, Colin was the spitting image of Da, with his shiny black hair and dark brooding eyes fringed with beautiful thick lashes that drove the girls in our humble little county crazy. My brother Colin was also selfless. He felt an obligation to stay on and help the family, even past the proper time of marriage. Da couldn't till and grow enough potatoes, while supplementing our meager income by working in town from time to time, without Colin's help. And it was important to our survival that Da earn enough money to sustain our large brood.

Da's family had emigrated from Spain and planted themselves in the small peninsula to populate the islands in the 1500's. His skin was brown, but not as dark as the Spaniards because his family had integrated with the locals. Mama and Da made a striking pair, one dark and the other fair. I felt I was the beneficiary of this blessed union, with my dark auburn hair that lit up in the sunlight like a bonfire, and fair skin unmarred by freckles like other redheads I knew. And although I had light skin, I was blessed with the ability to turn a pleasant shade of tan when I spent any time in the sun rather than blistering and turning bright red.

My other brothers, Mick (or Micky as we liked to call him), who was seventeen, and Michael, then fifteen, were a mixed bag of light and dark, but Da's dark eyes and thick lashes prevailed throughout the three boys, unlike my sisters and myself.

Some people would make off-handed comments, calling us poor, but we were anything but poor in my eyes. We were your typical Irish Catholic family with too many mouths to feed, but somehow we got by. Da and my brothers found work in town and occasionally hired on at one of the neighbor's farms as hired hands, tending to the crops or milking cows when they were needed. The pay was meager at best. Still, it was enough to get us through the hard times until the potato crops were ready to harvest. We could survive most anything with potatoes to fill our bellies and fish in our pot.

We lived in a small, two-room house made from rocks, mud, and grass for the walls, and a thatched roof fashioned from dried sedge and heather, tightly woven together for a roof. Most of the time the water ran off when it rained, but not always. And though the accommodations were meager at best, Mama and Da worked hard to make the small home feel cozy, warm and filled with love. Mama was the heart that pumped life into each of us as well as the glue that kept us all together. I believe this was because of the love she had for Da, and that is what kept her going when life was difficult. My parents had a love that was very single-minded, putting the needs of the other above their own needs. I never heard them speak a harsh word to one another or to any of us. Only words of love and encouragement were spoken under our roof.

I could always count on Mama to make me feel better if I scraped my knee climbing over rocks or running down a hill too fast. I would come in limping with tears rolling down my cheeks and find her humming to herself as she was washing or milking the goats. And before I knew it, I would be laughing and humming alongside her as I helped her with the rest of her chores.

We rented twenty acres of unforgiving, rock infested land, which we all diligently worked side by side—all, that is, except Mama. She was the only person exempt from working in the fields, but that didn't mean she had it easier than the rest of us. In my opinion, she worked harder—washing and mending clothes, preparing all the meals, and taking care of the household and all of us young ones.

Once, after a particularly long, hard day, I complained about there being too many rocks to move, only to look down and see Mama's work-worn hands, cracked and raw from the lye soap she used to wash our clothes. Placing her hands in her apron when she noticed me staring, she told me that the stones on our land were magical rocks and that they would protect us from all of life's harsh storms. I didn't truly believe her at the time, but it made me laugh and I never again complained about how hard the work was.

Most nights we gathered together after supper to enjoy one another's company. Da and Colin played their fiddles, Mama sang, and the rest of us clapped along. Sometimes the older siblings taught us younger ones how to dance an Irish jig or whatever was popular at the time. Life was so sweet. I remember thinking to myself that I never wanted it to change. I was blessed beyond anything my young mind could imagine.

We had family surrounding us and potatoes in the cellar—which was really a deep hole in the ground that Colin and Da dug, with a board standing over it to keep us from slipping in. Summer was just around the corner. I had everything I could ever need.

"But sometimes, things have to come completely undone before they can be put back together the way they are meant to be," Mama would say.

That evening, as we celebrated Da's special day, Mama had been quiet. She shied away from the festivities, clapping along to the music rather than singing gayly as she normally did. The fact was, I had noticed a difference in her during the past two months and I was becoming concerned.

Mama, also famous for saying, "Sometimes the seeds of happiness are sewn into the clouds of darkness," seemed to have a dark cloud following her. Truth of the matter was that I had never truly known what a dark cloud looked like until I came into my thirteenth season. And yet, somehow, I could sense a storm coming, sitting out there in the distance, just beyond the horizon, ready to drown out our happiness.

I felt the change coming in the air. Call it a sixth sense if you must, but nothing could have prepared me for the squall that was headed my way, or should I say our way. All of our lives were about to change in a very dramatic way.

Mama was pregnant and not exactly thrilled with the prospect of another mouth to feed.

3

AUGUST 10, 1846

The Day My Childhood Ended

Months passed and spring turned to summer. Micky had badly injured his leg while clearing the field of rocks and boulders in late May. He was using an old board as a lever when it snapped in half, causing the boulder to settle wrong, rolling over his leg and severely breaking it in two places.

Da went to fetch Doctor Griffin, who was little more than an animal doctor, but he was all our small township could afford.

Doctor Griffin came to set my brother's leg, and it was a horrible thing to witness. Afterward, I observed the doctor's face and it said more to me than his lips dared to speak in front of the family. He looked very grim before he and Da stepped outside to talk. Mama was fussing over Micky, trying to make him comfortable, so I wandered over to the small window near the door to listen to the outside conversation. I could hear every word. Doctor Griffin told Da that he highly recommended removing Micky's leg. That was the first time in my life I'd heard Da cry out loud.

Colin and Michael picked up the slack without complaint as Micky fought a terrible fever for more than a week. Then one day his fever seemed better and we thought the worst of it was over. But we were wrong. Micky suffered horrible pains, often crying out in the middle of the night from the infection that settled into his leg. By the end of June, Micky began to use the crutches Da made him. Each day, he would put a little more weight on the injured leg, until one day he didn't need the crutches any longer. Unfortunately, Micky was left with a permanent limp. He never complained or let on that his leg still

pained him. Yet, I could see it in his eyes; every time he stood up or tried to walk, he grimaced. But at least he still had his leg.

Micky refused to let his circumstance get in his way or slow him down. I really looked up to him after that; he was the strongest man I had ever known, besides Da, of course.

Mama's mood began to improve as the months passed. She was never one to brood over things that she couldn't control and had come to accept the inevitable. As her belly continued to grow, she became slower, plagued by back pains and aches in her legs that she'd never had with any of her previous pregnancies.

When Mama complained that she was too old to be having more babies, Da made sure he told her she was still the most beautiful woman he'd ever seen—that she was even more beautiful now than the day he'd first laid eyes upon her. This would make Mama blush and she would say he was full of stuffing, which always made us girls laugh.

Alana took over running the household as well as planning her wedding that was quickly approaching.

"Mama, let me do that for ye," I pleaded.

"Hush, child, I'm capable now," she protested. "Off with ye. Go on now. Go outside and play! I'm no invalid."

"But, Mama, I wanna' help."

"Then be off with ye, and get out from under me feet," she insisted, swooshing the broom at me for emphasis.

"Go on, Lara, do as mama says," Caitlin added, stepping through the doorway after hanging the washing on the line. "I saw Jamie O'Brien and his little sister waiting for ye outside by the barn."

My desire to help suddenly vanished as I ran toward the door, leaving it standing wide open behind me. "Thanks, Caitlin," I hastily called over my shoulder in my rush to go play. A satisfied smile played across my lips.

Jamie O'Brian was my best friend in the whole world and lived on the next parcel over from us. He was only a few months older than me

but he always seemed so much older. We had been playmates since the day I could walk. Several inches taller than me, Jamie had hit a growth spurt three months before and shot up straight and tall like a weed in the field. He wore his rich chestnut hair slightly longer and wild these days, on account his mother was over-burdened with children and never had time to cut it. Two sets of kind blue eyes smiled at me from across the yard as Jamie and his ever-present shadow stood by his side.

Katy, Jamie's younger sister, was a sweet girl and, never one to be left behind, she went everywhere he did. Although eight years younger than us, Katy was attached to Jamie's hip from the day she was born. The O'Brian's were also a large family, but his mother passed on the responsibility of looking after the newest baby to each of her children. So, when it came Jamie's turn to look after a sibling, he took his responsibility to heart and never left Katy behind. They were inseparable.

"Good morrow to ye, Jamie," I called out my greeting. "Miss Katy, so good to see yer well today."

"Good morrow to ye," they called back in unison, pushing off the side of the barn wall, which was nothing more than a smaller version of our humble home. It housed the livestock consisting of six chickens, three goats, and one large sow that was ready to birth piglets any day now. Although some looked upon us as poor, at this point in time, we felt that we had everything we could truly need. My Da was a very smart, hardworking man. It was one of the things that impressed me the most about him.

"Wanna go on a treasure hunt?" I asked, turning in the direction of the bluffs as I began to walk.

Jamie called back. "Only if I can be the pirate!" he insisted, catching up quickly to me as Katy brought up the rear.

"And I want to be the princess," Katy cried as she was forced to run to keep up, taking ahold of Jamie's hand with a large grin. She loved playing the helpless maiden.

I smiled, knowing that we were free to run the hills and bluffs or walk down to the ocean's edge and put our feet into the cool water for the next few hours. It had been a blistering hot day and I, for one, felt like my insides were melting. "Perfect! Race ye both!" I called out my challenge over my shoulder as I took off running, giving myself a head start with a carefree laugh.

"Ye are an unscrupulous cheat, Lara Flannigan," Jamie shouted, quickly pulling Katy behind him.

I laughed even harder when I looked over my shoulder and found him running to catch up as I stood at the cliff's edge preparing to traverse the steep slope. Then I paused a moment and sniffed the air. A strange smell assaulted my nose and I took a brief moment to analyze it.

"What's wrong?" inquired Jamie breathlessly as he and Katy finally caught up to me.

Pushing my concerns aside with a shake of my head, I headed down the cliff's trail with another volley of giggles as Jamie and Katy followed. "Nothing, silly," I shouted, racing down the steep trail. "Now hurry up, I hear the water calling out to me." I turned my attention back to the trail ahead of me. "First one to get wet, wins!"

"I'm goin' ta enjoy plunderin' treasures from ye today, ye fair weathered friend," Jamie protested, causing me to laugh that much harder.

Suddenly Katy squealed, slipping on a pebble, as she slid farther down the trail in the dirt. "I'm fine," she called out when I stopped to see what had caused her to scream.

"I got ye, Katy, me girl. Never fear," her ever-doting brother assured her as he lifted her up and dusted her off. "I would no' let ye fall."

Katy's little face beamed with joy. "I know, Jamie. I was no' afraid."

Racing the rest of the way down the trail, I lifted the hem of my already too short dress, trying to prevent it from getting saturated when I ran into the water. Then, momentarily lost in my own triumph, I threw my arms into the air and did a little victory dance, dropping

my skirt into the water anyway. "I be the winner, Jamie O'Brien. Ha! Take that you scurvy pirate!"

Carrying Katy the last hundred feet, Jamie deposited her in the water next to me. "Only if ye like to win by cheatin'," he proclaimed, unperturbed by my gloating.

Kicking water at him, I screamed as he and Katy began pelting me back with the cool, refreshing water. The battle continued until the three of us were completely soaked through. Then, finding several long sticks on the shore's edge, we began to play in earnest. Jamie was Captain Longfellow, the notorious one-eyed, peg-legged pirate who happened upon the fair maiden, Lady Katherine Cornwell, the beloved princess of the land. And I, of course, was the other fair maiden, set upon by the infamous pirate captain who took me prisoner. I was from the far-off land, yonder, across the bay, and forced into servitude. His wish was my command.

We had many small skirmishes that required more water play and a few hideous battle cries. Then there were the pleas for help from Lady Katherine Cornwell, who was eventually relinquished by the dreaded pirate. I, too, won my freedom and all was well with the world once more.

We hunted for seashells, dried ourselves in the sun, then headed back up the steep cliffs, happy and exhausted by our vigorous play. Jamie had to pull Katy up the last few feet and I brought up the rear as we reached the top of the cliff. Sticking my nose into the air once again, I noticed the strange smell was back.

"Do ye smell that?" I questioned, sniffing the air.

"What do ye think it is?" Katy asked, bringing her hand up, blocking the bright sun from her eyes.

"It smells like somethin' rottin'," Jamie exclaimed, wrinkling his nose up as he pulled his sister behind him.

The three of us continued to walk towards home, but the smell only got stronger. Then, I saw my Da and brothers standing in the middle of the field scraping at the ground and searching about for something.

Curiosity got the better of us and we drew nearer to see what they were doing.

Jamie called out his greetings, "Good day to ye, Mr. Flannigan."

Strangely though, my Da didn't seem to notice us as he kept his head down.

"What's the matter, Da," I yelled before noticing the condition of the crops. "Jamie, have ye ever seen such a thing?" I turned to him.

"What is that?" Katy uttered as the three of us made our way through the blackened, rotting field of potato stems, curled over and withered on the ground.

I heard Da exclaim, "Ruined! Every stinkin' last one of them's ruined!"

The three of us came to stand next to Da, Micky, and Colin, who finally looked up at us. "What is this, Da? What has happened to the crops?"

"Blight!" he cursed, then spit on the ground as if just the mere mention of the word made him sick. "It's all rubbish. Every stinking last bit of it," he snapped, throwing his shovel down and walking away in disgust.

Slowly picking up the discarded shovel, Colin said, "It's not even fit to feed to the pig." Turning his back to us, he trailed after Da. "Come on Micky, let's go," he called over his shoulder.

My heart sank as I realized the putrid stench was rotting diseased crops dying a terrible death. Even though I didn't yet fully understand the implications of that word, *blight*, I soon would.

4

NOVEMBER 10, 1846

The Glue That Held Us Together

Alana married Newel Cummins on the twenty-first day of August in a quiet ceremony attended by close family and friends. The small celebration afterward was subdued. We served fish soup, bread, and wine.

Due to the devastating loss of potato crops throughout the region, many who would have attended Alana and Newel's wedding didn't come.

Shortly following the wedding, Newel and Alana moved in with his parents. He was a blacksmith by trade, but, being the youngest of four siblings, he helped his folks work their land when he could.

Widespread disease devastated the fields in the surrounding towns. People lost entire crops and, subsequently, their entire years' worth of income in one mighty blow. The word in town was that the loss had been greater in the western region of the country than anywhere else, which is exactly where we lived.

What followed in the months to come was so devastating, no one saw it coming. The Government set up public workhouses so people with no resources could labor at the most menial and repulsive tasks possible to human kind. Men, women and children cleaned out public toilets, collected the dead, and moved rocks for road construction for little pay. But, to the destitute, next to nothing was better than absolutely nothing.

Many people sold everything they possessed, bit by bit, to survive the first winter. The second winter would be an entirely different story.

All of the workhouses opened their doors but were ill-equipped to cope with the overwhelming influx of people pouring in looking for shelter. Soon, the overcrowded conditions caused disease to run rampant, exacting a human toll that was beyond any one's wildest imagination. The already distressed populace of commoners was dying off by the cartful.

Dysentery, black fever, yellow fever, and starvation devastated our country in the months that followed.

Our family was more fortunate than most; we had a few livestock and the sea to sustain us until aid could be sent from England. "Surely, they will recognize our plight and do something about it," I overheard Mama saying to a neighbor one day.

But the relief never came and there was never enough work to go around for all those who were in need. Maize, known as Indian corn, was a cheap substitute for potatoes and became the main staple of the poor. The only problem was people didn't have money to pay for it.

October came and went and the weather turned from bad to worse. Da and my brothers were gone for weeks at a time, staying near town so that they could obtain work. They would camp outside or find shelter where they could, refusing to stay in the workhouses. They took any job, no matter how demeaning, so they could put food on our table.

Returning home, Da and the boys had been back for two days when disaster struck our home. Da had been worried about us girls when he was gone. He especially worried about Mama, seeing how she was heavy with child. It was the 10th day of November, and Da proclaimed earlier that morning that it was time to clear the fields of any infected plant material. He had decided to store everything in the barn and incinerate the mess once the rains stopped.

Mama was nearing her time and I could see the concern in her eyes that November morning as she served me the last bowl of boiled maze, along with what little goat's milk was left, to make the concoction go down a little easier. She looked so very frail and thin to me as she served me.

We were rationed one meal a day, but I suspected that mama had been forgoing even that small luxury when she could, to ensure that Da and my brothers had enough to sustain them.

"Mama, I'm no' really hungry this morn," I offered, even as my belly gurgled and complained loudly. "Won't ye please eat me breakfast?" I pleaded.

"Silly child, I already had me portion before any of ye awoke." I could tell she was lying, even as she shoved the bowl back at me. "Now eat and then ye can help with the chores."

"But Mama—"

"Hush child and don't waste yer energy," Mama insisted, straightening her spine as she closed her eyes to the pain in her back.

The rain was coming down in a gentle mist and I was mesmerized by the water dripping from the thatched roof, absently spooning mush into my mouth, when I heard Mama cry out in pain before doubling over and falling to her knees.

Jumping to my feet, I rushed to her side and knelt down beside her. "What's wrong, Mama?" I cried, completely forgetting about my hungry belly.

Taking several deep breaths and blowing them out, she tried to smile but failed miserably. "Go fetch yer Da and tell Michael to get the midwife," Mama insisted through gritted teeth, grabbing at her stomach again as a whoosh of liquid spilled out between her legs. I hesitated a moment. "Hurry child!" she screamed.

Running out the door and headlong into the rain without a coat for protection, panic drove me forward. I was oblivious to both wet and cold. I just needed to get help for Mama.

I was certain my Da and brothers heard me coming long before I could make out any of their faces through the rain that matted down my hair and flopped it into my eyes. I screamed at the top of my lungs as I reached the field where they were unearthing the rotting potatoes and throwing them into a cart.

I saw Da drop his shovel first, then Colin set the cart he was pushing down on the ground. Michael and Micky carried their shovels with them as they all came running.

"What is it, Lara?" Da cried, gripping my shoulders, somehow knowing the answer to his question before I uttered a single word.

"Mama," I cried breathlessly, unable to get the rest of it out. A look of fear crossed his face and he turned and ran towards the house.

I grabbed ahold of Michael as he turned to leave as well. "Mama wants ye ta fetch the midwife. Oh, and tell Alana the babe's comin'. She'll want ta know."

Nodding his head, Michael turned, running in the opposite direction as the rest of us, and I ran to catch up with Micky.

As we got to our home, the boys hovered just outside the doorway, afraid to go any further. When I stumbled through the door, I didn't see Mama where I left her when I ran to get help. Soaking wet and dripping all over the floor, I grabbed a blanket off the nearest bed as I quickly walked to the next room where I saw Mama in bed with Da and Caitlyn by her side. Caitlyn saw my questioning eyes and explained, "I found her sprawled on the floor when I came in from milking the goat and helped her to bed."

"What'll we do, Caitlin?" I asked when I reached Mama's side, trying to be as quiet and inconspicuous as possible so I wouldn't be ordered to leave.

Just then, Mama looked up and saw me. Taking a couple of deep breaths, she said, "Come here child, ye're old enough to help. Fetch the clean blankets and gown for the babe when it comes." She pointed her finger to the corner of the room.

Running to do her bidding, I placed the items on a chair near the bed.

"I need ye to gather the water and put it on ta heat," Mama insisted with a reassuring smile. "That's a good girl." I believe the task was more about giving me something to do, rather than being particularly useful at the time. I ran from the room to do as I was told.

Laying the blanket over a chair I walked out into the rain to fill the pail with water, and I remember I felt afraid. I had spent my entire life on the farm and I'd witnessed many animals give birth and yet I was unsure of what to expect when it came to a human birth.

When I returned to the house with the pail of water, Da was trying to coax fresh moss and sticks to catch on fire in the hearth. I carefully poured the water into a kettle and swung it over the fire that quickly sprung to life.

"Ye're a good girl, Lara. So much like yer mama, ye are," he mused, sounding melancholy as he stared into the fire. "Best get out of those wet clothes before ye catch yer death. Then ye be no help to anyone."

"Straight away, Da," I muttered, stepping behind the makeshift curtain to remove my soaked dress and undergarments. Something in his voice told me he was scared, but I didn't know why. Taking one of Caitlin's hand-me-downs off the hook, I slipped it on and was still buttoning it up when I rushed into the next room to see what Mama wanted me to do next.

Caitlin bathed Mama's forehead and cheeks with cool water and a rag. Mama was soothed by this as she rolled to her side and reached out to take my hand. "Come closer child, let me look at you," she called softly, waiting patiently while I complied.

Kneeling on the ground next to the bed, I was grateful she was no longer crying out. "What can I do, Mama?"

"Just lookin' into yer eyes is enough. Now don't be scared," Mama insisted, trying to reassure me, when a grimace crossed her face as another wave of contractions racked her frail body. "Caitlin, get yer Da."

"Yes, Mama," she replied, quickly walking out of the room to do as Mama instructed.

Da rushed into the room and I stood up, getting out of his way as he squatted down on the floor. "I sent Colin to get the Doctor," he told her while grasping her hand.

"The midwife should be good enough. I don't need Griffin."

Shaking his head, Da kissed Mama's hand. "Not Griffin, my love. A real doctor from the next town over."

Tears of gratitude shone in her eyes as Mama shook her head. "The babe will be here before he arrives. Besides, we can no' be affordin' him."

"And I can no' be affordin' ta lose ye," Da exclaimed, wiping tears from her eyes with the back of his dirty, work-worn hand.

"Ye'll no' go losin' me, when I be right here, always, Rory Flannigan," Mama said, gently reaching out a hand and laying it upon his heart.

Then Da leaned over, gently touching his lips to hers. The tenderness between them made me smile.

Moments later, Michael came through the door with Mrs. O'Keefe, a happy woman of considerable girth. Mirna O'Keefe was a hearty woman, having given birth seven times herself. Rumor was that she had delivered the last baby herself, tying off the cord, then feeding the baby, and still managed to serve her family their evening meal on time.

That was three months ago and she was already back to midwifing.

"Good day ta ye, Mrs. Flannigan," Mrs. O'Keefe called out, blowing into the room like a great storm off of the ocean as she assessed the situation and took charge.

Attempting to get up, Mama cried out in pain again. "If'n ye be claimin' it's a good day," she retorted.

"Bit of a rough morn' then?"

"One might say," Mama replied.

With a jovial tone, Mrs. O'Keefe began, "Then let us see what we can do ta change that."

Da quietly left the room with one last look back before closing the door. A few minutes later, Alana came in and walked over to where Caitlin and I were standing beside the bed.

"I was worried I'd missed it," Alana whispered as she leaned over toward us.

Mama screamed when Mrs. O'Keefe asked her to lay on her back. "Won't be much longer girls. Yer Mum is close," she announced triumphantly. "Alana, dear, get behind yer mum and help her ta push when I tell ye. Caiti, ye go fetch yer sharpest knife and ye, me girl, will take the babe from me when he comes."

All of us moved as one to do as we were instructed by Mrs. O'Keefe. The midwife pushed Mama's gown up even higher as soon as Caitlin returned. A strange look played across her face for just a moment and then it was gone.

"Is there always so much blood?" I innocently blurted out.

With one quick look in my direction, the midwife quashed any more outbursts from me about what was and was not normal. "Hush child and get the blankets ready."

Silently bobbing my head, I did as I was told.

"Now push, Laurel. Push hard!" Mrs. O'Keefe stressed, narrowing her eyes as Mama grunted, giving it all that she had.

Helping push from the back, Alana whispered encouraging words into Mama's ear. "Push Mama. Ye can do it."

"You can do it, Mama," I cried excitedly, stepping over to take her hand.

"Almost there, Mama. The babe's nearly 'ere," Caitlin blurted out, tears shining in her eyes.

Fifteen minutes passed and still very little progress had been made. "Take one last solid breath and push with all yer might, Laurel," Mrs. O'Keefe bellowed, her voice shaking with emotion.

Laying back against Alana, Mama looked completely spent. "I can no' do it. I have nothin' left," she cried, tears streaming down her face. "There be no more in me." The words trickled from Mama's mouth.

"Ye can no' give up now, Laurel Flannigan! That horse left the barn long ago," Mirna scolded. "Now buck up and push!"

The look in Mama's eyes was like the light had all but gone out. Shaking her head, she cried out as another contraction doubled her over. "Please, Mama! Yer almost there," I begged. "Ye can no' give

up, Mama. I can see the babe's head," I said, stepping behind Mrs. O'Keefe to cheer Mama on.

Alana pushed her forward and with one last mighty breath, Mama pushed with every ounce of reserved strength she had, and the baby spilled out into Mrs. O'Keefe's arms. Wiping the baby vigorously with a towel, Mrs. O'Keefe declared, "She's a wee lass!" Then, hanging her upside down, Mirna gave the baby three solid smacks to the back and I heard a small whimper followed by a robust cry.

Taking me by surprise, Mrs. O'Keefe placed the baby girl into my outstretched arms and handed me a blanket. "She has red hair, just like us, Mama," I proudly announced, wrapping the blanket around my baby sister the moment the cord was tied and cut.

I was looking at the baby, marveling at her tiny, perfect features, when I realized everyone had gone completely quiet. Turning, I saw a strange look on Mrs. O'Keefe's face before turning to look at Caitlin and then Alana. The three of them looked stricken.

Mama had become very still and she looked ashen. Blood was oozing out as the midwife reached around me grabbing for anything she could get her hands on to stem the flow of blood.

"Laurel, wake up!" Mrs. O'Keefe yelled, mercilessly shaking Mama, trying to wake her. "Someone get yer Da!" she shouted when the three of us stood frozen in place, paralyzed by fear.

I stared blankly at the tragedy that was taking place before my eyes. "I said for you to move, girl! Now!" she bellowed, grabbing my arm and squeezing it hard then shoving me toward the door.

Grasping the baby to my chest tightly, my legs and arms shook so badly that I feared I would drop her. Yet I still obediently made my way to the door and opened it. My eyes locked on Da's as he came through the front door carrying an arm full of fresh wood. I could no longer contain my tears. "Help her, Da. Please! Ye have ta help Mama," I cried, dropping to my knees, still clinging to the baby girl, who began to whimper again.

Dropping the wood where he stood, I heard him choke back a sob as he stumbled past me. "No, no, no, no—" he repeatedly said, dropping to his knees beside Mama's bedside.

Mama gradually opened her eyes, gave a lopsided smile and reached her arms up. "Let me see her," she insisted weakly. "I want to hold me girl."

I watched as Da slowly turned his head and nodded for me to bring the child. Taking the baby from my arms, he placed her next to Mama and pulled back the blanket to reveal her delicate little features. She was so very tiny and frail, just like Mama.

Alana, Caitlin, and I made eye contact, and a silent message passed between us. Something was very wrong with Mama.

"Look at the baby's graceful little fingers," Mama marveled, brushing the baby's cheek with the back of her boney, work-worn finger. "Will ye christen her Grace for me?"

That was the moment Da lost control. A sob slipped through his lips and he laid his head upon the pillow next to Mama's, unable to contain his grief any longer. After a few minutes, he finally lifted his head, wiping his eyes and nose with the back of his hand and leaving behind a dirty smudge upon her pillow. Then, finding the strength to speak, with a loud sniff he insisted, "Don' ye talk like that, Laurel, me love. Ye will be right next ta me when we christen our baby girl Grace."

Mustering up strength, Mama lifted her hand and stroked her husband's glossy black hair. "Promise me, Rory. Please," she pleaded weakly.

He began loudly sucking in and then blowing out air through his mouth until he regained control. Then, slowly, he exhaled and squared his shoulders, gazing upon his wife's face before nodding his answer. "Anythin' for you, love. Just do no' leave me. I beg ye," he pleaded pitifully.

"Tell her every day how much I love her," Mama continued as the tears began to roll down her face, pooling into her ears. "Will ye do this for me, Rory?"

"Laurel—" Da raised his voice slightly in warning.

"Promise me, Rory Flannigan," Mama persisted.

Staring into Mama's eyes, he relented, "I will. But, Laurel—"

Mama reached her hand out again and softly touched the side of his face, causing him to fall silent as she continued, "I have loved ye from the first time I lay me eyes on yer sorry excuse of a face, Rory Flannigan. The day ye pulled me hair in class and then walked me home from school," she smiled wistfully. "Remember?"

"How could I ever forget? Ye were the prettiest girl I'd ever seen. And ye're still the most beautiful girl I've ever laid me eyes upon, Laurel Flannigan. That truth will never change in me eyes. Not ever!" he fiercely proclaimed, leaning down to kiss her lips. Then, slowly standing, he lifted the baby girl in his arms, still holding Mama's gaze before nodding his head and stepping back a pace.

"Alana," Mama whispered, slowly turning her head to the side so that she could see my sister's face.

Wordlessly, Alana leaned over, kissing Mama's cheek, her tears spilling onto her face.

"I need ye ta help yer Da with the wee babe. He's never been any good with 'em."

Stroking her cheek, Alana could no longer contain her grief. "Oh Mama, I love ye so," she softly cried, bravely trying to choke back her sorrow as she covered her mouth, then turned away.

Gently touching Alana's hand that still rested on her cheek, Mama tried to comfort her oldest daughter as she turned to Caitlin. "Caiti, me sweet girl, take care of yer Da for me," she whispered with sadness, somehow knowing that her time on earth was short. Turning her head so she could look at Da once again, she continued. "He will be no good without me."

I looked over to see Da clasping baby Grace even tighter to his chest while silent tears slipped down his dirt-streaked face. He gasped for air, quickly inhaling then exhaling several more times as the baby began to squirm and then cry softly.

Da was trying to be strong for Mama, but it was painfully apparent that he would soon lose that battle.

Mama tried to lift her head to look for me. "Lara, where's me Lara?"

Stepping forward, I kneeled beside her. "I'm here, Mama." I grasped her thin fingers, cradling them to my lips. "Oh, Mama, I'm so scared."

Squeezing my hand with more strength than I thought possible, she tried to sound stern. "I have no time for ye to be scared, child. I have so much to tell ye and I need ye to promise me ye will be strong and listen."

"Anything, Mama," I murmured softly.

"Promise me, Lara, that ye will make somethin' of yerself. Ye hear me? Ye make somethin' of yerself. I want ye to be strong and live. And if that be no' enough to keep ye goin' when things get tough, then live for me—" Mama said as a tear rolled down her cheeks. "When your life gets tough, remember I will always be with you. Remember everything I've taught ye…"

My eyes followed Mama's line of sight as she gazed up to one corner of the room. "What is it, Mama? What do you see?"

"Can't ye hear them?" she asked, a smile lighting up her face. "There's angels in the room," she began, "and they are glorious."

"Mama, look at me," I pleaded, turning her face towards me.

"Can ye no' see them? But no', of course ye can no' see them. They did no' come here for…for ye—" Her words dwindled down to a whisper before ending abruptly.

"Mama! Mama!" I cried, gently patting her cheeks and shaking her as the life drained from her eyes right in front of me. "Mama!" I screamed, shaking her shoulders harder, even though I knew in my heart that she was gone. Yet my childish mind could not accept what was happening. Laying my head down upon her chest, I could no longer feel it rise and fall. Quickly lifting my head again, I cried, "Mama, come back. Come back to me! I love ye! Mama!" I shouted with a shrill whine as I buried my head in her chest once again and roughly pulled her to me.

I heard gasps and my sisters' sobs.

A mournful cry sounded from the corner as Da collapsed to his knees and cried out for Mama.

Suddenly, the door to the room crashed against the wall and Colin stood there frozen in place, the doctor standing just behind him. He had a look of complete shock on his face, which quickly gave way to despair as he seemed to crumble where he stood. As the doctor pushed past Colin, I saw Michael and Micky, who had been standing under the eaves of the house trying to stay dry, step behind him as all three brothers entered the room together, only to see that their mama had just died.

Mirna O'Keefe looked very pale and shaken as she silently stood up and moved out of the way, making room for the doctor, who rushed to Mama's bedside. The stricken look on his face as he saw the bloody scene told me that there was nothing more he could do for her.

Da was inconsolable as he made his way back to Mama's bedside, kneeling down next to me, still grasping baby Grace in his arms. "Laurel! Laurel, me love," he croaked as disbelief settled into the deepening lines of his face.

"I'll take the baby," Mirna said softly, not waiting for Da to respond, but removing Grace from his grasp before walking quietly from the room.

Colin lifted me to my feet by the shoulders, even as I tried to shake him off, and walked me from the room as well. He sat me down in a chair next to the midwife who was suckling the baby to her breast. Tears freely flowed down her plump cheeks as she tried to comfort the fussy baby with soft shushing sounds, rocking her back and forth in her arms.

I felt numb as a bone-chilling coldness spread through my body and I had to remind myself to keep breathing in and out for fear that I too would die. *Everything will be alright if you just keep breathing in and out,* I told myself.

Shock and disbelief shrouded our home as we all tried to process the inconceivable fact of what had just occurred.

Mama was gone.

5

Mama's Funeral

Mrs. O'Keefe helped Alana and Caitlin prepare Mama's body, washing and dressing her before laying her out on the bed she had shared with Da as if she were merely sleeping.

Before leaving, Alana kissed Da on the cheek and took baby Grace with her, telling Da she had a neighbor who'd lost a baby boy, two days before, and would have milk to feed baby Grace. I don't even think he heard her as he sat in his chair, staring into the empty hearth where the fire no longer burned.

Da appeared to be a mere shell of the man he had been, bereaved and unable to sleep or eat. He sat in his chair staring into our hearth for three days. I would hear him crying in the middle of the night when he thought we were all asleep and my heart would break all over again. He seemed to be willing himself to die but his body wouldn't cooperate.

The potato famine became so rampant that people became conditioned to be cold and unfeeling. Forced to carry their family members out to the street and watch as they were loaded onto carts and dumped into mass graves without coffins, the only way people could cope was to become detached. They had learned to turn a blind eye to the suffering of their neighbors.

Yet, close friends and family members gathered in our small parish church to pay their respects to my mama. The formal funeral was such an unusual occurrence that many who showed up were there merely out of curiosity's sake as well as a need to experience normalcy, if only for an hour.

I don't remember much that happened at the services that day, but what I do recall is the Priest, Father Timothy, standing before the small congregation with his book opened to a certain page as he tried to bring comfort to us all. He began, "The Lord is my Shepherd; I shall not want. He maketh me to lie down in green pastures: He leadeth me beside the still waters. He restoreth my soul: He leadeth me in the paths of righteousness for his name's sake. Yea…" he said hesitantly, his voice cracking, before beginning again. "Yea, though I walk through the valley of the shadow of death, I will fear no evil: for thou art with me." The Priest's words caught in his throat and a small sob escaped his lips as he slammed the book closed.

Pulling a well-worn handkerchief from his robe pocket, he wiped his eyes, then blew his nose loudly before folding the handkerchief up with purpose and shoving it into his pocket. "These simple yet powerful words, which are meant to bring you all comfort at this time…don't!" he said raising his voice to a loud cry. "They no longer bring me much comfort, either." Looking down at the ground, he wiped a stray tear from his cheek with the back of his hand, then lifted his eyes up to study the congregation. "And yet, you all sit here mourning the loss of a great woman, Mrs. Laurel Flannigan. You are poor and hungry, wondering when it will all end. And while I do realize you cannot feel His great love for you in this moment, let me assure you all that He is here with you and does love you. Each and every one of you! Many of you are suffering greatly, feeling as if you have fallen into a deep pit, and have become lost and alone in the vast darkness and you are unable to find your way out! I implore you…Nay! I beseech thee. Hear my words. Put your trust in Him, your Heavenly Father, and His Son. They will lead you from out of the darkness and into the light. And yes, He will even lead you into greener pastures, for which you have been promised. Your suffering will end one day and your loyalties will be rewarded. This I do promise you," he concluded.

For the briefest moment, my spirits were lifted up and I felt lighter. My heart did not feel so broken as the quiet weeping that had been all around me subsided. Father Timothy's words had struck a chord deep inside of me.

Yet as his sermon ended and we all stood to follow the casket outside into the light drizzle to lay Mama into the ground, the feeling quickly passed.

After the graveside services, a modest lunch was served. We'd given two chickens to the priest to perform the ceremony and they were used to make a large pot of soup, which was served up for all to enjoy. A few of the women who knew Mama well provided the bread for the meal. Mama was so well loved and respected by our neighbors and community that there were those who were willing to make the huge sacrifice.

A ball of sorrow and anguish knotted at the back of my throat, leaving me with a numbness that went deep. Food held no appeal as I sat in my chair with a bowl of half eaten chicken soup and a piece of bread resting in my hand. That's when Jamie walked into the room and stood over me, waiting for me to notice him. I looked up into his large sad eyes, then looked around for Katy, but she wasn't with him.

Placing the rest of my bread in the pocket of my coat, I pushed the soup aside and stood as he wrapped his arms around me. "I'm so… I'm so…" Jamie cried as he tried to console me while his own tears fell upon my shoulder. "I'm so sorry, Lara," he repeated.

The floodgates of my sorrow opened up, unrestrained, and the waters rushed out as Jamie tightened his arms around me. His own tears dripped down the back of my neck. "Oh, Jamie," I sobbed, "it hurts so."

"I know," he soothed. "Just let it out," he added, placing a handkerchief into my hand while he held me tightly until I ran out of tears.

Blowing my nose, then wiping my tears away, I looked around again for his sister. "Where's Katy?" I asked, bewildered by her absence.

A different kind of pain shone in his eyes as he attempted to hold back his grief. Finally, tears began spilling from his large brown eyes and he shook his head, unable to speak for the longest time. Then, when the words did finally come, they stuck in his throat. "Katy—" he choked out before burying his face in my hair, sobbing and repeating her name over and over again. "Katy, Katy, oh my Katy," Jamie cried, unable to say anything more.

I felt sick. Disbelief filled my mind and I clung to him. I could feel him slipping from my arms as his legs gave way and we both slid to the floor together. Our worlds had been turned upside down. Loved ones had been savagely snatched from us, far too soon, and our innocence had been stolen.

I was left feeling spent and weakened as I wiped my nose before handing James back the handkerchief he'd lent me.

"Oh, Lara, what am I goin' to do without her?" Jamie cried, blowing his nose before looking up.

The words of my mama came back to me in that moment. *Sometimes things must come undone before they can be put back together again in a different way.* But somehow, I did not feel repeating her words would bring Jamie any comfort. "Ye can choose ta give in ta the darkness, Jamie O'Brien, or ye and I can choose ta walk through it, coming out of the other side. Either way, we can no' choose if we experience it," I concluded, sniffing loudly before swiping the last of my tears away with the back of my hand.

Still clinging to my free hand, Jamie nodded his head. A few more tears spilled down his cheeks as he bravely gulped back all those painful emotions. He got to his feet and pulled me up. Without saying another word, Jamie put his arm around me again before leading me to the food table, where he picked up two glasses of water and handed me one. Silently, he stuffed two pieces of bread in his pocket, retrieved a bowl of soup, and walked over to join his family.

Slipping a couple more pieces of bread into my pockets, I looked around for my Da. The day was gloomy, just like my mood, as the rain continued to fall. I stepped to the back door of the church and looked out. Da stood over Mama's grave, seemingly unaware of the wet or cold as he bowed his head.

Pushing the door wide, I was about to join him when I noticed a man walk up to him and begin to speak. I couldn't hear what they were saying, but I knew it wasn't good. Da looked up suddenly, glaring

at the man. Then, Da's face contorted as he yelled, quickly looking around as if he were searching for someone. Our eyes locked and he appeared to be even more haunted than before. I felt frozen in place as he turned his back to me. I knew Da was furious about something as he continued to vigorously argue, using his hands while vehemently shaking his head and fist at the stranger. And just when I thought for sure Da was going to punch the man in the face, things got real quiet and the other man grabbed Da by the collar and pulled him in close. Suddenly Da pushed the man away and raised his voice again before the man turned and stared at me. An involuntary shiver ran up my spine and the hairs on the back of my neck stood on end. The man turned back to my Da and said something that made his face turn white, then pulled a piece of paper out of his pocket, shoved it at my Da, and handed him some sort of writing implement I didn't recognize. Angrily, my Da scrawled something on the paper, which the man quickly grabbed. After stowing the paper back into his pocket, the man looked over his shoulder at me one last time, then, donning his fancy hat, walked away.

I felt sick to my stomach as I watched Da crumble, falling to his knees in the mud. He hunched his shoulders and began to weep. Intuitively I knew that whatever they had been discussing, it had something to do with me. *What could have made him so angry and then so sad that he would kneel down in the mud like that?* I wondered.

I was about to join him when Da stood up and began walking down the road towards our home. Jamming his hands deep into his pockets, he never looked back at me, but simply walked away.

As I stood there staring after Da, wondering what had just happened, Alana and Newel came over, carrying baby Grace. She was completely bundled-up to protect her from the drizzling rain. Grace laid in my sister's arms, so peaceful and content, it made me mad.

"Do ye want to carry yer baby sister part of the way home?" she asked, offering the child to me.

Bringing my eyes up to meet hers, I tried to be civil, but fear I failed miserably in that moment. "No, I would no' care ta hold my baby

sister!" I asserted belligerently, turning my back to her to search the road for any sign of Da.

Turning back around, I observed Alana's face as it registered her shock, as if I had struck her physically across the face with my bare hand. It was at that very moment Colin rushed up behind me, slipping his arm around my shoulders and pulling me along with him as we hurried to catch up with Micky, Caitlin, and Michael.

"What was all that aboot?" Colin questioned, smoothly rolling his tongue around the last word.

"I simply did no' wish to hold the child is all," I insisted, sounding petulant, even to my ears.

Throwing his hands up in front of him as if he were defending himself, he teased, "All right, all right! Don' go bitin' me head off, ye wee beasty," and pulled back as if he feared I would truly hurt him. When I turned and tried to punch him, he put up his fists as if he were in a boxing ring and began dancing around me. "Do ye wish to fight," he questioned, "because I'm pretty good at boxing." Then he grinned, a grin shadowed by sadness.

Throwing another punch, I completely missed my mark when Colin ducked and dodged easily away from me. "Don' ye go callin' me a wee beasty, Colin Flannigan!" I warned, unshed tears of anger shimmering in my eyes, "or I swear, I'll hurt ye like ye've never been hurt before!"

"All right, all right, fine!" he conceded, slipping an arm around my shoulders, forcing me closer to him. "I'm sorry ta have teased ye so, Lara. Today has been hard on us all, and ye have to know in yer heart that 'twas no' her fault."

Glaring up at him, I murmured, "What was no' her fault?"

Softening his words and his tone, Colin pulled me to a stop and turned me around to face him as he leaned his head in close to mine. "The wee baby, Grace. She did no' kill our mother."

Defiantly shaking free from him, I stomped off, skirting just out of his grasp as he reached out to stop me. I had no desire to hear what he had to say regarding my baby sister. I blamed her for taking

my mama from me and no one could tell me otherwise. "If no' for her, Mama would be here with me today. I want nothin' to do with that baby!" I screamed over my shoulder before running off down the road, completely ignoring Colin's cries for me to stop.

"Lara, Lara!" Colin repeatedly called, trying to catch up to me. I was hurt and angry and there was nothing anyone could have said to change that fact. Mama was gone and she wasn't coming back.

Even the sea was turbulent and rough as I passed by on my way home, and the clouds hung so low they touched the water. The tide shifted and turned, smashing against the rocks like an angry woman ranting against the world, mirroring my own mood. The water sprayed above the cliffs, unable to find any other means of escape, while the wind blew the spray sideways before it returned to its original source, only to blow in a different direction upon hitting the cliffs again. I was angry at the world and would have struck out at anything and anyone who didn't have the good sense to stay out of my way. Something heavy and cold had settled in my heart and it wasn't going away any time soon. Throwing myself upon the bed I shared with my sister, Caitlin, I cried myself to sleep.

The next morning, I sat up in bed, pulled the forgotten piece of bread from my pocket, and began nibbling on it. There was no sign of Caitlin and I figured that she must have come to bed late and awakened early to do the chores.

Stuffing the last bite of bread into my mouth, I stood up and stretched, then pulled an apron from its hook, tying it around my waist and slipping my worn boots on. Then, grabbing a ribbon, I stretched again and allowed a large yawn to escape my lips before stepping out from behind the curtain separating the girls' sleeping area from the rest of the house.

I stopped short when I saw Da sitting at the table staring out of the window. He looked as if he had been sitting there the entire night. He had fixed his red-rimmed eyes upon me the moment I stepped out from behind the curtain.

"I was hopin' I would no' 'ave to wake ye," he stated. "I need to go to town, and ye 'ave ta go with me. Get yer coat." Then he stood up and walked out the door without saying another word.

It seemed like a strange request to me, but Da appeared to be in no mood to argue. He would normally have taken one of the boys with him when he went to town and I couldn't imagine why he would want to take me instead. Slipping my coat on, I ran my fingers through my hair and quickly braided it, tying the blue ribbon around the end. Then I ran the rest of the way to catch up to him.

We walked for a long time in silence until I could stand it no longer. "What do ye need in town, Da?" I questioned, more to make conversation than anything else. An awkward silence settled between us, and I looked up to see tears shimmering in his eyes. "What is it, Da?"

Wiping his eyes with the back of his hand, he cleared his throat and tried to smile. "Ye are so much like yer dear…mother," he coughed, trying to clear his throat. Then, with a sharp inhale of air, he tried to choke back his emotions.

Taking hold of his hand, I lovingly looked up into his face, "I love ye, Da."

Bringing his free hand to the pit of his stomach, he nearly doubled over as he swallowed hard, choking back another sob, then stopped in the middle of the road. "What is it, Da? What's troublin' ye?" I demanded, touching his wet cheeks with my fingers as I searched his eyes.

Quickly inhaling and exhaling, a slight sound of pain escaped from the back of his throat. Then Da stomped his foot and straightened up. Suddenly, he reached out and pulled me to him, squeezing me so tightly I thought he would crush my lungs. "Please forgive me, Lara," he pleaded. "I need ye to forgive me…" He kissed me on my forehead before standing up again and pulling me quickly behind him.

I felt even more confused by his words and strange behavior as I was forced to run just to keep up with him. What had he done to me that he needed forgiveness for? He had never hurt me before. He was

my Da. He loved me and took care of me. "Slow down, Da. I can no' keep up."

"I won' be able ta go through with it if I slow down," he muttered, refusing to look at me.

"Go through with what?" I demanded between breaths. "Where are we goin'? Da! Stop!" I screamed, pulling back on his arm.

"We can no' stop. We are late," he insisted gruffly, reaching out to take hold of my arm, yanking on me again to follow.

"Da, I don' understand."

"I know. So, hush child and walk," he persisted, pulling me after him.

Doing as I was told, I attempted to keep up when suddenly I realized we had missed the road that would take us into town. "Da, we're goin' the wrong way," I pointed out, looking up to see his jaw set and his eyes staring straight ahead. Then, pulling back with earnest, I dug my heels into the ground.

Swinging me around to face him, he brought his face down to mere inches in front of me and ground out each word. "Stop it, Lara. Just stop! I am doin' this ta give ye a chance. There be no other way. We've no more food. We will all starve. Do ye understand?"

"No, Da. No, I don' understand," I cried, feeling suddenly scared. "Why are ye doin' this? Where are we goin'?"

"The bill came due. The landlord needs ta be paid or we will all be turned out into the street," he said harshly.

I think that my young mind comprehended what he was trying to tell me, but my heart wouldn't accept it, so I blurted out, "How Da? How are we goin' ta pay the bill?"

"Ye Lara! Ye're goin' ta pay the bill," he yelled, exasperated by my naive questioning. "I was given a choice, Lara," he added, "which is no choice a'tall."

I could hear the frustration and anguish in his words, but I also knew in my bones that what he was planning to do wouldn't end well

for me. "I still don' understand, Da. Please, Da, stop. What are ye tellin' me?"

"I know ye don' understand, Lara, me girl. That's why this is so unfair," he whispered. "Unfair to be sure, sweet girl," he sobbed as his face took on a look of resolve. Clenching my arm again as he hurried down the road before he lost his nerve, he said, "And that is why I truly am sorry."

"Sorry for what, Da?"

Setting his jaw, I could see the muscles working as he clenched his teeth and tugged on my arm even harder when I tried to dig my heels in the ground again. Then as we came around a small hill, I noticed a man sitting in a cart pulled to the side of the road. He had his back turned to us before hopping down from the seat. Turning to face us, I recognized him as the same man I saw Da arguing with at the funeral. Suddenly I became desperate and began tugging harder at my coat sleeve, trying to free myself from Da's tight grasp. I suddenly had a sinking feeling in the pit of my stomach.

"Let go of me!" I screamed. "Please, Da, I won' cause no more trouble, I swear it," I pleaded, still struggling to pull myself free and run in the opposite direction. But Da's grip was relentless. "No, Da! I don' want to go with that man!" I screamed. "No! No! No!"

Giving me a stern look, he brought me around to face him again, gripping me by both shoulders. "Hush now," he demanded, shaking me harshly before softening his tone when I fell silent. "Hush, child."

Burying my face in his chest, I clung to him, my tears wetting his shirt as I begged him not to send me away. "I will no' eat much. I promise. And I will do more chores," I cried desperately, burying my face in his chest again. "Please, Da, please don' send me away. I will die."

Da roughly pulled me away from his chest, forcing me to look him in the eye. It was then that I saw the tears swimming in the shiny, dark brown pools of his own eyes. "Lara, me love. I don' wan' ta send ye away. But I have no choice," he gently said, kissing my forehead and clasping me to his chest tightly. I could hear his heart hammering

against his ribs. "Of all me wee babes, you be the most like her." He choked back a sob, squeezing me even tighter. "And as much as it tears me heart out of me chest, I have ta send ye away. I truly hope that one day ye can find it in yer heart ta forgive me."

I could hear and feel the pain in his words as he clung to me that last time. Those were the last words my Da would ever say to me.

Peeling me off of him, he handed me over to the man as I cursed Da's name while kicking in an attempt to free myself. I was inconsolable and screamed out his name over and over again as I watched him walk away. Helplessly, I stood there as Da disappeared from my life forever.

My grief was twofold that day as a piece of my heart died. My Da faded from view as the landlord secured me to the cart, tying my hands with a rope to prevent me from escaping and running away from him.

I still feel the sting of that moment—the last time I ever saw my Da. The pain is still so raw, so devastatingly deep, that I've trained myself to look away from his memory whenever it threatens to surface.

6

Sold into Servitude

I was sold into servitude by my Da—simply handed over to Lord Henley, our landlord, for a mutually agreed upon price.

I became the sacrificial lamb—the payment for rent and overdue taxes that had come due for our property. Just like that…my freedom was stripped away from me. I could not bend my mind around this simple fact. The reality was not made any more palatable by the passing of miles as I drew farther away from the only home I'd ever known with each passing minute.

Soft and paunchy around the middle, Lord Henley's brown eyes had an unnatural yellowish tinge to them where they should have been white. His very short, cropped hair was swept forward to hide the fact that he was balding, and his discolored, yellowed teeth showed years of abuse and wear. Soft, pale hands told me that the man had never done an honest day's work in his life. Everything about him caused me to cringe with revulsion.

About two hours into our journey, Lord Henley pulled the wagon over, parking it in front of a tavern. Handing me two pieces of bread, a wedge of cheese, and a cup of water, he excused himself before stepping through the nearby tavern doors, "For some libations to warm the gut," he said, then added in a stern voice, "If you run away, I'll throw your family out into the street without a second thought!"

I quickly removed the rope, found a place to relieve myself, and fell asleep in the back of the cart. I jolted awake when I heard his guttural sounds as he emerged from the smoke-filled establishment, blurry eyed and staggering. He climbed into his seat, softly singing to himself, and I could smell the alcohol on him from where I sat.

"Glad to see you listened and stayed put, girly. How's about you come sit up here next to me and keep me company?" he asked with a lewd smile, lifting his brows and wagging them suggestively.

Glaring at him, I made a noise deep in my throat that expressed just how I felt about the offer before turning my back to him. He let out a hearty laugh and clicked his tongue, slapping the reins at the same time and sending the horses into a trot.

It was another few hours before we reached his home just before dark. I was spent, keeping an eye open, ready to bolt if he made a move to accost me. At one point, he nearly drove us off a cliff when he fell asleep. I was forced to reach over the seat back to grab the reins and bring the cart to a halt. Then, placing the leather straps back into his hands, I shook him until he stirred and quickly sat back up as if all was well with the world.

In hindsight, I should have pushed Lord Henley off the cliffs when I had the chance and been on my merry way. But I wasn't a vindictive person, so I obediently stayed just as I was told, like a loyal dog. I told myself that I was doing this for my family's sake. But if truth be told, I was scared.

Lord Horatio Henley pulled up to a stately front porch with a massive front door that fronted an immense three-story mansion. It was surrounded by a huge, manicured yard. I was momentarily awe-struck as I gazed at the seemingly numberless windows and I had to push my jaw closed as I climbed down from the back of the cart.

Servants seemed to appear from everywhere. A young boy of about fourteen ran out, taking hold of the horses' leads, keeping them steady for Lord Henley as he teetered a bit climbing down from his seat. Nearly toppling over twice, Horatio finally steadied himself enough to slide down to the ground. Then he slapped the boy twice on the side of his head. "I thought I told you to hold the horses steady for me so I don't fall," he groused.

"I'm sorry, my Lord. It won't happen again." The boy cowered and ducked, avoiding being hit a third time.

Something told me that this wasn't the first time Lord Henley had come home inebriated.

"Good lad," Henley said as a burp, then a hiccup, escaped his lips. "Come along, girl. No time to be shy. The Missus will want to look at you," he added, gesturing with his hand for me to follow him as he walked towards the door without turning around. I guess he'd forgotten all about me supposedly being tied up in the back of the cart.

I followed behind him as he stumbled up the steps to the porch, then he turned around and sat down on the third step. "Go on in, girl. I think you can find your way. I'm just going to sit here a moment until the world stops spinning." He burped and hiccupped again.

Silently bobbing my head, I made a wide arc around him, climbing the steps before letting myself in the front door. I was starving and could smell the evening's supper wafting through the house the moment I stepped through the threshold. My stomach started growling, reminding me that I had barely eaten a thing in two days.

"Hello," I tentatively called. "Is anyone here?" I said a little louder, making my way towards the back of the house where I could hear dishes gently clanking together. "His Lordship sent me," I added as a young woman came around the corner, pushing a cart full of dishes.

"Oh," she squealed, grabbing at her chest. "You startled me. Who are you and why are you here, child?" she demanded.

"Lara, Lara Flannigan," I stammered, eying what was left of dinner, smelling the air as my stomach made another loud gurgle.

With a heavy sigh, the young woman continued, "I'm asking you to explain why you are in this house, child."

"His Lordship told me ta come inside," I indicated, waving towards the front door. "We've been travelin' since early this morn—"

Just then an older woman came around the corner and interrupted me. "Marie, who is this?" she asked with an incredulous tone.

"That's what I've been trying to get at, ma'am," Marie politely smiled before turning back to me.

"I'm Mrs. Henley and this is my home. What are you doing here?" Her voice was now terse and demanding.

Exhausted, hungry, and scared, I jammed my hands into the pockets of my coat and began to cry. "I don' know, ma'am. My Da brung me down the road and gave me ta the man who brung me here."

Immediately, the woman's voice changed. "You poor dear. Why, you're nothing but skin and bones," she soothed, looking as if she were about to put her arms around me but then thought better of it. She wiped her hands down the front of her skirts. "I will find my husband, but for now, Marie, show the girl to the kitchen and get her something to eat," she ordered before turning and walking towards the front door. "Oh, and get her a bath and be sure to wash her hair. We wouldn't want to bring anything into the house that didn't belong," she said pointedly.

"Yes ma'am," Marie called back, bobbing her head and dropping into a quick curtsy. "Come with me, Lara Flannigan," she demanded the moment Mrs. Henley was out of earshot. "One more thing for me to do," she complained under her breath, shoving the cart roughly down the hall.

Obediently following Marie, my mouth continued to water and my stomach felt like it was twisting in on itself. I truly hoped that she was going to let me eat before she made me take a bath. I felt like I would faint away in the middle of the hallway from hunger before I had a chance to taste anything.

"We have extra dresses and aprons upstairs in the closet. I'm sure we can find something more suitable that will fit you," Marie said, pushing the cart into the kitchen. "Bobby, Mary, Ann, this is Lara Flannigan. Lord Henley lugged home another stray. Make her feel welcome and get her something to eat. She's half-starved by the sounds that her stomach's been making."

"That is all well and good but where do you think you are going?" the woman who appeared to be the cook complained, before taking another sip of her soup and dunking her bread in the bowl.

"I'm off to prepare a bath for our new arrival. Bobby, be a love and put more wood on the fire for me," Marie ordered, stopping at the back door to pick up a bucket. "I know I promised to help with the dishes this evening, but would you be a dear, Mary, and take care of them yourself? Ann, can you help me?" Marie called over her shoulder.

Scooting her chair back quickly, scraping it on the wooden floor, Ann jumped up immediately to do as Marie asked. "Yes, ma'am."

The cook muttered under her breath, "Why I otta—I'll—who does she think she is anyway?" Mary blustered as she grumbled under her breath, gathering up the dishes to carry them to the sink. "I'll show her, *dear*. Why, she can take her *dear* and—" Mary continued grumbling but stopped short when Marie stepped back through the doorway.

"What's that, Mary? Did you say something?" Marie questioned, glaring at Mary's back.

Feigning a smile and a happy disposition, Mary twirled around as if she were dancing while she carried the last of the dishes to the sink. "Oh, don't mind me, I was simply singing a happy little tune, ma'am."

The man, who must have been Bobby, scoffed and shook his head in disgust. "Women," he muttered, before carrying his dishes to the sink. "If you need me, I'll be in the pantry," he informed them all. "Welcome, Miss. I hope you find your stay here a happy one." He turned, smiling at me before disappearing down the corridor.

Ducking my head, I said shyly, "Thank ye, sir."

"Well, sit down," Mary ordered. "I can't serve you while you're standing in the doorway."

Removing my coat and quickly sitting in the nearest empty chair, I watched as Mary placed a bowl of split pea soup and two pieces of bread in front of me. I wanted to pick the bowl up and drink it down while Mary took her sweet time fetching me a spoon and napkin, but I controlled my baser instincts and waited for her to set the utensil before me.

I was so hungry that I didn't really taste the soup as I spooned it into my mouth, one spoonful after another, using a piece of bread to wipe the bowl completely clean before popping the last morsel into

my mouth. I was about to wipe my mouth with the sleeve of my dress when Mary glared at me, stopping me dead in my tracks. Embarrassed, I looked around for the napkin she had placed before me and used it to wipe the excess soup from my mouth.

"Would you like more?" Mary asked.

Immediately raising my bowl up to hand it to her, I accidentally burped and smiled sheepishly. "Yes, please."

With hands on her hips, Mary took the bowl from me and filled it up again, handing me another piece of bread. I waited for her to turn her back to me and slipped the crusty bread into my coat pocket to save for later. This time, I ate a bit slower, lapping up the thick peas until I felt like my stomach would burst. I began to think that living here would not be so bad after all. I had a full stomach and someone to prepare my bath for me. How bad could it be?

"All right, Lara Flannigan, your bath awaits," Marie called to me from the doorway. "Well?" she added impatiently when I didn't immediately jump up. "Come along. Don't doddle."

Getting to my feet, I grabbed my coat and quickly followed her up the back staircase to the servants' quarters. Leading me down the hallway to the last room on the left, she opened the door and announced, "This will be your room, and you will be expected to keep it as neat and tidy as you find it right now."

Waiting for me to enter, then closing the door behind us, Marie walked over to the cabinet and pulled out a nightdress, which she laid before me on the bed.

"There will be no fraternizing with the men in this household," she admonished. "You will be expected to do your share of the work and do as you are told by Lord Henley and his wife. You also need to always remember that you are at the bottom of the ranking here, and as such, you need to know your place. I am the head housekeeper and you need to clear everything through me," Marie stated with a haughty tone. "And I won't tolerate any backtalk or sass! Do you understand me?"

"Yes, ma'am," I whispered, removing the piece of bread from my pocket as she looked over my clothing with a critical eye.

"Now, let's get you out of those rags and cleaned up," she smiled, satisfied that she had put me in my place as she examined my coat. I could see by the disdain on her face that she did not approve. "We will see if it can be salvaged once it has been washed, but I wouldn't hold out hope. Now, as for you, I believe we will find a pretty young woman under all that grime."

I tucked the piece of bread under the pillow as I pretended that I needed to sit down to remove my boots. Then, smiling sheepishly, I felt embarrassed by her implied criticism of my wardrobe. Shyly slipping off my hand-me-down dress, I crossed my arms in front of me before slipping into the small tub that allowed water to come to hip level.

Marie roughly scrubbed my skin, wet and soaped my hair, and then poured a mixture of cold and hot water over my head to rinse the bubbles. Standing back to examine her handy work, she pronounced me suitably clean.

Holding up a bath sheet in front of her, she waited for me to stand up, then wrapped it around me. "I trust you can properly dress yourself if I leave," she stated as she stepped to the door.

"Yes, ma'am," I answered, lowering my eyes to the floor.

"Good." Nodding toward the bath sitting in the middle of the room, she continued, "I'll have Bobby remove that for you in the morning. You'd better get a good night's sleep. There will be plenty of work for you to do tomorrow." Without further words, Marie closed the door behind her, leaving me alone with one half-burned candle and my thoughts.

For the first time in my life, I was completely alone. My hands and knees began to shake and I quickly sat on the edge of the bed as tears trickled down my cheeks. Once the floodgates were opened, the tears would not stop. There was no one to comfort me or tell me that it would be alright. No one would be there to tell me that everything

would work out for me in the end. Even the comforting words of the Priest the day before at Mama's funeral seemed like a distant memory.

The reality of my situation sank deep into my soul. There would be no words of wisdom delivered at just the right moment or strong arms to wrap themselves around me by my Da to make me feel safe again. I even longed for the irritating teasing by my older brothers that would leave me feeling frustrated or annoyed. Never again would there be silly antics by Jamie to make me laugh or forget my cares when I was feeling down. I was utterly and completely alone for the first time in my life and I cried myself to sleep, lying atop the covers of my small, lonely bed.

7

The Lord and Master of His Home

I awoke to Ann knocking on the door. "Wake up, sleepy head. You'd better hurry and dress or you will miss breakfast," she called through the closed door.

I sat up, wiping the sleep from my puffy, swollen eyes and then I remembered where I was. The pain in my heart began to hurt all over again. Looking about for my clothes, I suddenly realized that Marie must have taken them the night before. Opening the cabinet doors, I found a slip, black dress, starched white apron and my boots. Slipping them on, I glanced in the small mirror sitting on the dresser and saw the frightful state of my hair. Opening the top drawer, I found a comb and brush and ran them through my tangled tresses, tying them back with the ribbon I had worn the day before. I noticed a little white cap resting on top of the dresser, which I placed on my head, tying it beneath my chin.

Taking a deep breath, I stepped into the hallway and cautiously made my way downstairs. The kitchen was abuzz with activity. Everyone from the night before sat around the table, along with the young man who had held the horses for Lord Henley when I first arrived the day before.

"Lara, this is Ryan. He is the stable boy, farm hand, and whatever else Lord Henley needs him to be," Marie informed me. "Ryan, Lara Flannigan, our newest addition to—well, I'm not sure of her title. His Lordship hasn't exactly been forthcoming with the details." She smiled stiffly. "Well, sit down, Lara. It won't do having you stand there gawking at everyone. Sit!" she insisted, sounding slightly perturbed.

"Yes, ma'am," I replied, scooting into the same chair I'd occupied the night before as Mary placed a bowl of porridge and a cup of strong tea in front of me. Staring at the bowl, the memory of the last time I had eaten a bowl of porridge hit me. It was the day Mama died. Tears flooded my eyes as I shoved a spoonful into my mouth. Nearly gagging on it, I forced myself to swallow the lump in my throat along with the mouthful of porridge.

Ann, who was sitting next to me leaned over, "Are you all right, Lara?" she inquired.

Keeping my head down, I nodded and took a sip of tea. Then, as I reached for a piece of toast, Ann passed the jam without being asked to, then patted the back of my hand. I was comforted and touched by her concern.

"Perhaps Lara can help me scrub the floors today. I could show her around and help her get familiar with the house," Ann suggested, turning to look at Marie.

Pulling a watch from the pocket of her starched, high-collared, black dress, Marie checked the time and absently answered, "Yes, perhaps that would be best." She stood up, bringing her eyes around to Ann's. "Then maybe we will receive further clarity from his Lordship as to what we are to do with her," she concluded, stiffly smiling before excusing herself from the table.

"Don't forget to bring your dishes to the sink when you are finished," Mary called out from the other side of the table. "I'm the cook, not the maid," she quipped, eyeing me in particular.

The clock in the hallway chimed seven times and everyone scooted their chairs back from the table, stood up, gathered their dishes and deposited them in the sink.

Taking another piece of toast from the plate in front of me, Ann tucked it into my pocket, then stacked my dishes with hers. "We had best get started," she prodded, walking the dishes to the sink. "Thank you for the lovely breakfast to fortify me, Mary," she beamed at the cook before turning back to me. "Come along, Lara, we wouldn't want to be late."

Obediently I stood and followed Ann from the room; glancing back over my shoulder I saw Mary staring after me. She gave me a stiff smile before turning back to her dishes.

Opening a closet door halfway down the hallway, Ann retrieved a rag, a duster, and a metal bucket with a lid on it. Humming to herself, she checked to make sure that I was still following closely behind her before continuing up the stairs.

"We will begin with the upstairs rooms and work our way down. How does that sound to you?" she asked cheerfully before turning around to stare at me when I didn't immediately answer.

"Good," I replied with a shy smile.

"Excellent. I will show you how to clean the chamber pots and you can have something to do while I dust and make the beds," she chirped cheerily.

I had the distinct feeling that I was not going to like the chore Ann didn't want to do, and now knew the real reason she insisted that I shadow her. I was getting the jobs Ann didn't like doing.

Quietly knocking on the door before entering, Ann kept her head down, trying to be as invisible as possible when we entered Mrs. Henley's room. Mrs. Henley was in the dressing room talking with Marie and we could hear every word.

"What am I supposed to do with her?" Marie questioned.

Mrs. Henley sounded disgusted with the entire matter and tried to brush it aside. "Just do your best, Marie. His Lordship will grow weary of his new plaything soon enough. Then we can ship her off to a nunnery like the rest of his Lordship's broken toys."

"But this one is so young," Marie interjected, sounding genuinely concerned.

Mrs. Henley scoffed, sounding indifferent. "We have all taken our turn on that pony ride, my dear. You were just more fortunate than the rest of them in that you never conceived. Now, don't concern yourself with Lord Henley's extracurricular activities. I know I won't."

I had a sick feeling in the pit of my stomach and I jumped when Ann gently touched my arm, causing me to drop the empty chamber pot on the floor with a loud *clank*. I cringed before quickly picking up the pail.

Rushing from the changing room, Mrs. Henley and Marie stood in the doorway staring at us. "I was not aware you were in here, Ann. How long have you been…uhhh…tidying up," Mrs. Henley inquired suspiciously, bringing her eyes around to me.

Dropping into a quick curtsey, Ann ducked her head and stammered, "Not long, ma'am." Her lie was unconvincing.

I must have looked like a trapped animal because Mrs. Henley glared at me, squinting her eyes down until they were mere slits on her face. "I don't believe you."

"Apologies," Ann said, taking me by the arm and pulling me with her as she backed out of the room. "I am terribly sorry for disturbing you, ma'am. We will come back later to finish up," she added, quickly closing the door when she realized that Mrs. Henley was advancing on us.

"Come on, we need to make ourselves scarce and quick," Ann insisted, pulling me around the corner as she tucked us both behind a set of curtains just as Mrs. Henley's door opened.

"Where did they go, Marie?"

"I will handle this, Mrs. Henley," Marie assured her, heading down the hallway in the opposite direction.

Ann put a finger to her lips, warning me to stay completely silent until we heard Mrs. Henley's door close and Marie's footsteps disappear down the hallway.

"That was close," she whispered with a conspirator's grin, pulling me out from behind the curtains. "We will go to the children's room and hopefully when we are finished, she will have forgotten all about us."

Pulling on Ann's arm, I forced her to look at me. "What did Mrs. Henley mean when she said, *we have all taken our turn on that*

pony ride? And who is she plannin' to send ta a nunnery?" I asked suspiciously, narrowing my eyes at her.

Laughing nervously, Ann tried to brush the question aside. "Oh, she weren't talking about nothing that concerns you—"

"Why do I no' believe you, Ann?" I blurted.

"Come on, we have work to do if you want to eat again today," Ann insisted, turning her back to me and walking down the hallway. Resting a hand on the door, she waited for me to follow.

A young boy with curly brown hair and bright, brown eyes was sitting in the middle of the room on the floor playing with metal soldiers as we entered.

"Did you come to play with me today, Ann?" he squealed happily, looking at us with anticipation.

Smiling indulgently, Ann got down on the floor and picked up a couple of his pieces with a giggle. "I wish we could stay and play with you, my sweet boy, but we must tidy up today."

"Oh—," he cried disappointedly. "Ever since Nanny Tess left, I've been so lonely."

"I know, Duncan, but I can't today. Maybe tomorrow. Now cheer up. I brought Lara with me. Be a good lad and say hello to her," she insisted, straightening her skirts as she stood up.

"Hello, Lara. Do you want to play with me?" he whined, coming over to take a hold of my hand and lead me to his battlefield.

"Well, I don' know. I'm new and have ta do as Miss Ann tells me ta," I said shyly.

"Oh, please, please, please, Annnnn," he begged. "Can she play with meeeee?" Duncan whined long and loud through his nose.

"Perhaps I will let Lara play with you for a few minutes, while I tidy up your room. But only if you are a good boy," Ann asserted with a wry smile as she turned to me. "But you have to be quiet."

Eyeing her warily, I wanted her to know that I was not forgetting about our previous conversation. Pulling my eyes downward to Duncan, I smiled. "I will stay to play for a little while. But I need to

help Ann first," I relented, stepping to the side of the bed to help Ann straighten it.

"Hooray!" Duncan loudly yelled.

"Duncan!" she scolded, "you must be quiet or you will give us away," Ann warned. "And then we will not be able to stay."

"Hooray," he loudly whispered, pulling me to the ground.

"Where is your sister?" Ann inquired.

Absently pointing towards the door to the adjoining room, he explained, "Cora is brushing her hair." Duncan rolled his eyes. "She said she was too busy to play with me today. I wish I had a brother instead of a dumb old sister," he lamented. "Girls are so boring."

"Hey, I'm a girl," I pointed out indignantly as I knelt down in the middle of the room.

"I didn't mean you or Ann, of course," Duncan interjected, looking very sincere as I sat next to him. "You are a huge improvement over my dumb old sister."

"That is a very big word for a little boy," Ann laughed.

"I'm almost six. I'm not a little boy," he corrected.

"Oh, well, pardon me. I didn't realize I was speaking to such a mature young man," Ann teased. "Next week you will be telling me how you are all grown up and unable to play with me."

"I will never be too old to play with you, Ann," he insisted. "I love you."

"Oh, you do now?" she laughed.

"I think you're pretty," Duncan said pointedly, turning to me and placing a kiss upon my cheek.

"Hey!" I protested, making him laugh with glee.

"Cheeky boy," Ann scolded, chasing Duncan around the room amidst his squeals of delight.

Suddenly the door opened and Marie stood in the doorway, glaring at the two of us. "His Lordship would like to speak with you," she said, looking directly at me. When I hesitated she became impatient,

walking over and lifting me up off of the floor. "He doesn't like to be kept waiting."

"But…but I—" I stammered.

Ann set the pillow down and moved towards us as if she intended to come as well. "Not you, Ann. You will resume your duties," Marie ordered while dragging me from the room.

Duncan curled his legs up, tucking his head into his knees, making himself into a ball. When I glanced back, Ann looked frightened for me.

While being dragged down the hallway to the other end of the house, I could feel Marie's hand shaking. She looked mad but I didn't understand why. "You do as you are told and no back talk. He doesn't like back talk," she instructed, taking me by the shoulders when she stopped outside a large wooden door and faced me. "And whatever you do, don't scream. He really detests it when someone screams."

"But, Marie, why would I need ta scream?" I naively questioned.

"I have said too much already. Just be a good girl and do as you are told," she insisted, turning around and tapping three times on the heavy wooden door.

"Enter," his Lordship called out from behind his desk. Marie hesitated a moment before opening the door, dragging me into the room behind her. "Thank you, Marie. That will be all," Lord Henley said, dismissing her as he stood up and stiffly stepped around the desk to show her out.

Without much protest, Marie stepped out of the room, then turned around as if she wanted to say something just as Henley closed and locked the door in her face.

I could feel my knees knocking together as he turned to face me with a strange smile on his lips. "I like to introduce myself to the people living under my roof and really get to know them," he began. He walked over to a cabinet, opened it, and pulled out a crystal decanter and two glasses. "How old are you, Lara?"

I could feel an inkling of fear rising up from inside of me as a scream tried to form on my tongue. But then I remembered Marie's words and

swallowed hard. "Thirteen, sir. Why did you lock the door?" I timidly asked, taking two steps back and bumping into his massive desk.

He grinned and walked towards me with the two glasses after partially filling them with an amber liquid. Stopping a mere foot from me, Lord Henley offered me one of the glasses, which I declined, waving it off. With a shrug of his shoulders, he tipped the glass to his lips and downed the contents before leaning over to set the glass down on the desk next to me with a wry smile.

"Are you certain you wouldn't want to try some?" He raised a questioning eyebrow. Looking up at him I shook my head. "Suit yourself," he added before sipping from the other glass. "So, tell me, Lara, have you ever had a special friend?"

I thought his question queer and opened my mouth to say so when he placed a finger on my lips and shushed me. "I can see by the odd look on your face that you have not," he interrupted. "So, I will explain it to you." He downed the remaining liquid from the second glass, then, slowly leaning forward to place the crystal glass on the other side of me, his smile turned lewd.

Now standing so close to me that I could feel the heat coming off of his body, he reached up and untied the strings of my cap, allowing it to fall to the ground. "You have the most beautiful red hair. I don't want you to hide it from me," he insisted, pulling the ribbon and letting my hair spill free.

I felt my breakfast sour in my stomach and the hair on the back of my neck and arms stood on end. Instinctively I knew what he had in mind for me. I didn't know how I knew, but somehow his intent was clear.

Panic set in and a kind of madness took over. Frantically, I felt around Henley's desk, searching for some way to defend myself. I did not dare question what I would do after I found the object. I just knew that I had to have something. Anything. Now!

With his face so close to mine, the stench of his fetid breath made me gag as I continued to pull away from him. He growled in frustration, grabbing me by the waist to hold me still just as my hand landed on something solid. A paperweight sat upon a stack of papers. It felt heavy in my hand and I lifted it up, swinging the weighted object at his head the very same moment his lips touched mine. The blow was a shock to his vanity, especially when I hit him a second time. I raised my hand to hit him a third time when he dropped to the floor like a stone.

Staring at the solid piece of stone in my hand, I noticed it was in the shape of a large bullfrog, which seemed fitting at the time because it reminded me of his Lordship. A giant toad. Quickly placing the offending paperweight back on the stack of papers, blood and all, I looked at my hand that was shaking uncontrollably and saw that it was splattered with blood. I needed to gather my wits about me and forced myself to take several deep, slow breaths to stop the shaking. Removing the handkerchief from his front pocket, I wiped the blood from my hands.

I stopped to check if he was still breathing, but my fear got the better of me and I panicked. *I have to get out of here,* was all I could think. Not wasting another moment, I reached into Lord Henley's front pocket to retrieve the key to the door and found a few coins as well.

I was always taught never to take anything that didn't belong to me, but I felt the coins might come in handy, so, clutching them in my hand, I quickly made my way to the door. Placing the key in the lock, I turned it and paused to look over my shoulder one last time. I wanted to see if he had stirred. But Lord Henley still laid in the same position as before, a pool of blood forming around his head, and I felt certain that I had killed him. This only heightened my panic and made my course of action certain. I had to get away. I needed to run as far as possible from here and not look back. No matter what.

"Bloody hell. What have I done?" I whispered to myself.

I took one last deep breath to bolster my sagging nerves before pushing forward with what came next. I knew, even at my young age, that killing a highborn, for any reason, was a hanging offense, so I had to run. There was no other choice. But where would I go? I couldn't go home. It was too far, and besides that, it would be the first place the authorities would come looking for me. I continued to think as my

hand rested on the doorknob. I would find a town where no one knew me and I would hide there for as long as it took for the authorities to stop looking for me. I would get lost and live on the streets and pray that the law never caught up to me.

Turning the knob, I opened the door and stepped into the hallway, closing the door and locking it behind me.

"What happened? Are you all right?" Marie blurted out as she came down the hallway as if she had been waiting for me.

A small cry of surprise escaped my lips. "Ye startled me," I said, tucking the key into my pocket before turning around to face her. "He told me to tell ye that he was no' to be disturbed," I stated as calmly as I could while avoiding direct eye contact.

"Did he hurt you? Oh, you've forgotten your cap. I'll go back in to fetch it for you," Marie asserted, reaching for the doorknob.

"No!" I uttered suddenly, then fumbled for what to say next. I took Marie's hand in mine and led her away from the office door. "He seems moody and said he did no' want to be bothered again," I added with a nervous smile. "I would no' go in there if I were ye. There be no telling what he will do if someone were to disobey him."

"Perhaps you are right," she said, looking nervous and unsure of herself as her eyes wandered back to the door. "Are you sure he didn't hurt you? You look a little flushed and flustered."

"He told me to get a new dress. He even gave me a couple of coins. See," I added, digging into my pocket and producing two coins, which I held out to her for examination.

"He never gave—" she began to say. "Well, aren't you a clever girl. He must really be impressed by you to be so generous," Marie mused, forcing a smile.

I awkwardly smiled back as I looked down again and stuffed the coins back into my pocket. My heart beat wildly in my chest and I was glad she didn't know me well enough to sense that something was off. Every second I stood there talking with Marie was another second wasted. My opportunity for a clean escape was narrowing. I had to escape before Lord Henley's body was discovered.

"Pardon me," I added anxiously, heading for the back staircase. Looking over my shoulder one last time, I saw Marie hesitate as she looked towards Lord Henley's study door one last time before deciding to continue on her way.

8

The Great Escape

Breathe in, breathe out, and just keep moving, I kept repeating in my head as I hurried down the back staircase and out through the servant's door. Once outside I turned and headed for the barn, where I found Ryan saddling a horse.

"Where are ye off ta?" I inquired, trying to sound casual.

"Oh, I didn't see you there, miss." He jumped back a step or two, clutching at his chest as if I had startled him. "His Lordship asked me to take a look at a couple of horses in the next township over and tell him if they are worth the price the farmer is asking for them," Ryan replied as he continued to saddle the horse. "What are you doing out here?" he asked, peering over his shoulder at me.

Stepping closer to him, I replied, "Looking for someone to give me a ride ta town. Do ye think ye could help me?"

With a friendly smile, Ryan patted the horse's neck. "Only if you don't mind riding double. I don't have time to hitch up the buggy for—"

"I don' mind at all," I cut in, taking a step towards him and the horse so Ryan could give me a boost up. "The quicker the better. *" Just as long as I get as far away from here as possible,* I added to myself.

Looking slightly startled for a split second, Ryan obliged me by helping me into the saddle before he walked the horse out of the barn, then hopped up behind me.

"Ye're very kind ta help me," I gasped as he kicked the horse into a trot.

"How did you get permission to go into town?" Ryan questioned, quickly grabbing a hold of my waist when I slipped as the horse began to trot faster.

"His Lordship insisted I get a suitable dress ta wear. Says mine is little more than rags." I rambled off my story, looking over Ryan's shoulder to check to see if anyone was coming after us. I slid down close to him, trying to hide myself in front of Ryan as we rode away from the house. I hoped to make myself as small as possible in case someone looked out of one of the upstairs windows and saw him riding away so they wouldn't know that I had gone with him.

"Are you all right, Lara? You seem awfully nervous."

My heart was banging against my chest so hard I was certain he could hear it. "I'm fine," I assured him with a forced smile, before turning back around. "I'm just no' use ta riding on a horse."

"I won't let anything happen to you. I swear it," Ryan proclaimed gallantly before squeezing my waist a little tighter. "Your life is safe in my hands."

"I hope so," I muttered under my breath.

"Did you say something?"

"Oh, no," I answered. "I did no' say a thing."

A while later we came upon a work crew of men and women clearing rocks from the road. It was hard, grueling work, and it broke my heart to see the men and women struggling with such heavy labor. There were adolescent children mixed among them, working alongside the adults with their malnourished, underdeveloped bodies, straining to lift the burdensome rocks. But the most disturbing thing was witnessing the children, like unflagging birds, thin, emaciated and gaunt, following behind their parents with a look of anticipation in the hollows of their sunken cheeks and eyes.

I wanted to pick up each child and lend them at least some meager comfort by telling them that everything would work out for the best in the end, even if it was a lie. Because everything was not going to work out for the best or be alright. It would never be alright, ever again. The world had turned upside down and I was about to become a sad

statistic myself. I had just killed someone and would spend the rest of my life looking over my shoulder, waiting for the law to catch up to me. I would not be able to show my face at the workhouses or find employment if there was any to be had. I was now a fugitive.

I bowed my head to say a little prayer, truly hoping that it would reach my mama's ear and that she would be sure to get the message to the right person way up there in heaven. *Mama,* I silently began, *if ye be watchin' over me, I need help. So, if ye have any pull whatsoever, I need a miracle, Mama, and quick. Amen.*

"Are you in trouble, Lara?" Ryan inquired. "You're shaking like a leaf."

I found myself wanting to trust him, yet he was a stranger that I just met yesterday. His loyalties had not yet been established. Part of me felt it would be best to keep things to myself, but my tongue had a mind of its own. Once I opened my mouth to speak, I couldn't stop myself. "I lied to you, Ryan, and I truly am sorry. I did no' have permission ta leave today," I replied, "His Lordship, his lordship—"

"Did he lay a hand on you?" he demanded. "Why, that sick—" Ryan fumed, stopping himself from saying anything more as he breathed in and out rapidly.

Turning my head to look at him, I could see conflicting emotions in his eyes. "He tried ta, but I stopped him," I said quickly, turning around in the saddle to lay a calming hand on his chest.

"How, Lara? How did you stop him?" Ryan demanded.

They say confession is good for the soul, yet I was still afraid to open up fully to him. "I hit him," I said timidly at first. "Please, Ryan, ye have ta help me," I begged. "Please don' turn me in. I'm afraid they will hang me for what I did. Please, Ryan," I pleaded pitifully.

Pulling the horse to a stop, Ryan said, "I would never turn you in, Lara. You're just a kid. Besides, he deserved whatever he got," he added with a satisfied grin. "He's been getting away with terrible, unspeakable things for too long if you ask me. Did anyone see you leave his study?"

"How did you know it happened in his—" I began to say, then realized that if Ryan knew what Lord Henley was capable of, the others did too. "Marie saw me comin' out of his office, but I locked the door before she got there. See," I added, pulling the key from my pocket and showing it to him.

Taking the key from my hand, Ryan threw it as far as he could. "No evidence, no crime," Ryan concluded as the horse began to move forward again.

Suddenly pulling the horse to a stop again, Ryan took a long hard look behind us. Then, turning around, he smiled and said, "Change of plans." Bringing the horse about, he cut across the moors, holding on tightly to me as he galloped the horse for a fair distance. "I need to take you to a different town. Not the one I was headed to, but rather someplace they won't think to look for you. Eventually, they will check every town, but if you keep moving—"

"I think I killed him," I whispered, as fear and frustration took hold of me.

"You what?" Ryan stopped the horse again.

"I think I killed him, all right!" I repeated while casting my eyes downward. "I think I killed him and I am going to hang."

He looked ashen as the blood drained from his face. Quickly recovering, Ryan kicked the horse in the side and we were off again. "Not if I have anything to say about it."

"But you will hang, too," I pointed out.

Ryan laughed. "Only if we get caught."

"But, ye have a job. Are ye no' afraid ta go hungry?"

"Na. I've been saving my wages so I could afford a ticket back to England," he answered. "I can't stand that old codger, and this is the excuse I needed. I'm going to go home, Lara. I only wish I had enough money to take you with me."

"So, ye will no' turn me in?" I questioned.

"Absolutely not! As far as I'm concerned, his Lordship got exactly what was coming to him," Ryan said with a wink.

"Even if I accidentally killed him?" I questioned softly.

"Even if you did it on purpose," he added.

After that, there was no more talk of what may or may not have happened or who got what they deserved. We rode the rest of the day, stopping to water the horse and stretch our legs. We rode all night through the cold rain until we reached Ennis, in Clare County, just before dawn.

It was very early as we passed the workhouse, where bodies were already laid out for the death carts to pick up. The atmosphere felt hopeless and I shuddered, not only because I was cold, but because I could not fathom how my life had taken such a turn. One moment I was happy and carefree with a loving family surrounding me, and the next I'm running for my life, a fugitive from the law.

"You should be safe here for a while," Ryan announced, trying to sound confident as he stopped in front of the local church. "If you don't call attention to yourself and stay out of sight, you will be fine. Besides, I doubt anyone will come looking for you here. If they figured out that you left with me, they will be looking in Tipperary or Cashel," he added, pushing wet hair out of his eyes.

I tried to smile. "Thank ye for helpin' me. I don' know what I would have done without ye," I whispered, knowing it was time for us to part ways.

Lowering me to the ground, Ryan nodded his head. "I just wish I could do more for you, Lara Flannigan."

"I will be fine. Ye do no' have ta worry yourself on my account," I assured him, trying to sound stoic as I tipped my chin up bravely.

As he rode away, Ryan called over his shoulder, "Don't forget to keep moving."

"I won't," I called back, walking up the steps of the large white church. "Safe journeys ta ye," I called out to him.

Waving farewell to me without turning around, Ryan continued down the road at a slow, steady pace until he disappeared around a row of buildings. Walking up the steps and giving the set of heavy, wooden doors in front of me a shove, I was unable to make them

budge. There was nothing more for me to do but sit down and wait for them to open. Propping myself against one of the doors, I pulled my knees up to my chest for warmth and fell asleep. The next thing I remember, I was being violently shaken awake.

"You cannot stay here," the nun bellowed harshly, pursing her lips together as she stood up, crossing her arms over her ample chest and glaring down at me.

Quickly getting to my feet, I could feel my resolve instantly dissipating as I stood before this frightening woman who loomed over me. "But, sister, I have nowhere else to go," I whined helplessly. "I be far from home and need sanctuary."

Shaking her head, she backed away and turned to reach for something on the other side of the doorway. Producing a broom, which she wielded like a weapon in front of her, the nun once again advanced on me. "We cannot take in every stray that comes around looking for a free hand out," she said, shaking the broom at me menacingly.

"But I'm just a child," I protested, grabbing her sleeve as she turned her back to me.

Tersely ripping the garment from my hands, the nun turned on me, knocking me viciously in the side with the broom. "So are all the others who beg at these doors. Now go away before I send for the authorities and have you removed," she hissed.

Backing away, I turned and ran down the steps. "Ya be pure evil, and I'll never step foot in yer lousy church again," I screamed at her before disappearing around a corner.

My hands and legs shook uncontrollably as my heart raced in my chest and, for a moment, I thought I would pass out. The last thing I needed was trouble from the authorities. Peering around the corner at the nun, I watched as she continued to stare after me for a few minutes before going back to sweeping the steps where she happened across another sleeping vagrant who dared to seek solace at the stoop of her precious church. I continued to watch as she rousted the poor unsuspecting indigent and, in that moment, I made a vow to myself

that I would never again step foot in another church for as long as I lived.

Cold, hungry, and scared, I wandered the streets looking for something to eat. Gingerly stepping around people who were sleeping or already dead—it was difficult for me to tell the difference—I made my way from one dismal alleyway to the next. People slept in the streets, put there by unsympathetic landlords and overcrowded workhouses riddled with disease. The Irish government was so ill-prepared to cope with the overwhelming numbers of unfortunate souls that many were forced to seek shelter wherever they could find it.

Turning up my nose at the stench of the alley, I suddenly realized that there was a different smell in the air—a smell that brought me great comfort and left me longing for home. It was the smell of fresh bread baking. I was so hungry at this point that my stomach ached. Reaching a hand into my pocket I pulled out the piece of crusty bread from the day before and the four coins that I'd stolen from Lord Henley.

Looking up, I suddenly noticed a man leaning against the wall, intently watching my every move. He was a scrawny, scruffy individual, who must have been a robust man at one point in time, by the way his clothes hung on him like an empty sack of potatoes. He was eyeing me and my dried-out piece of bread when he got to his feet and took a step towards me. I felt scared and threw the stale bread at him, then ran as fast as I could the other way, cramming the coins back into my pocket as I went. I glanced over my shoulder when I reached the end of the alley and saw the man, without a tooth in his mouth, gnawing on the crusty bread I'd thrown at him.

Turning from the sad scene, I followed my nose to the bakery, confident that at least today I would not go hungry. I also realized that I needed to be more careful about flashing around what little money I had.

Waiting for the bakery doors to open for the day was excruciating as the smell of freshly baked bread floated through the air. My stomach churned and rumbled as I peered around cautiously, making sure that no one was watching me. When the bakery owner turned the 'open' sign around in the window of the store, I crossed the street and stood near the door for a moment before entering.

"I don' think I've ever seen you before," the woman behind the counter commented as she took a closer look at me. "Oh, ye poor dear, ye're drenched ta the bone, ye are."

My mouth began to water. "I'll be fine once I have somethin' ta eat," I assured her, eyeing the freshly baked breads and pastries on display, trying not to lick my lips and drool on the counter in front of her.

Stepping behind the counter, the woman smiled pleasantly, dusting flour from her sleeve. "I'm Mrs. Murdoch. Welcome to my shop." She continued casually probing for answers. "Did yer mum send you?" She sounded suspicious, eyeing me as she decided whether I was there to buy something or just browse.

Unable to lie straight out, I looked away while nodding my head, breathing in deeply to fully appreciate the delectable smells of the breads. "I would like a loaf, please."

"A whole loaf, then?" she mused, scratching the side of her face. "Do ye have any money?"

With anticipation, I eagerly nodded and presented a coin from my pocket to show her. "Please, I'm awful hungry," I moaned.

Mrs. Murdoch laughed, taking the coin from me as she placed the warm loaf of bread in my outstretched hands. I must have made an involuntary noise expressing my delight because she chuckled again. "Let me get ye some change, my dear, and something to dry yerself. Wait right here for me. I'll be just a moment."

Tearing into the loaf of bread like a hungry beast, I filled my mouth, hungrily devouring each bite. A happy moan passed my lips as I tore into the loaf again, shoving even more into my mouth this time as I filled my cheeks and chewed with difficulty, wiping crumbs away with the back of my hand.

"Oh, my, you were hungry," Mrs. Murdoch exclaimed as she walked out from the back room. Then, noticing my face turning red from embarrassment, she smiled pleasantly, placing an old blanket

around my shoulders. "This is all I could find, my dear. I can no' imagine yer sweet mum sendin' ye out in the rain without a coat. Ye really should be more careful or ye might catch yer death."

A small bell jingled as a patron came through the door and Mrs. Murdoch looked up to see who it was. "Good day ta ye, Mrs. Scott. What can I be gettin' ye this fine day?" she cheerfully greeted, giving my shoulders a tight squeeze. "No hurry to return that old thing, child. Use it as long as ye need," Mrs. Murdoch said as she turned away from me to see to Mrs. Scott.

Tucking what remained of the loaf of bread under my arm, I pulled the blanket tightly around my shoulders and headed for the door. Stopping in the doorway I turned, making eye contact with Mrs. Murdoch. "Thank ye, ma'am."

"My pleasure, child. Come back anytime. Tell yer mum hello for me," she added, turning back to her customer.

Tears formed in my eyes; in that moment I wished with all my heart that I could tell my mama hello from Mrs. Murdoch.

9

I Turn 14

The Lowest Point of My Life

Winter came in with a vengeance, taking its toll upon me and the good people of Ennis who had been hit especially hard by the continuing famine. Many died during the cold, wet months of November and December, leaving many to wonder if their miseries would ever end.

I was left severely malnourished and emaciated by the months of little to no food. But I never lost heart or felt like giving up. I still got up each morning with a feeling of purpose and with the utmost confidence that the famine had to end sooner or later. Yet there were many who believed the world had come to an end. They were the ones who lost their faith and simply sat down on the side of the road or in some filthy alleyway to wait for death to take them. My heart went out to them and I often wondered what it would take to cause me to give up like that.

It hadn't taken Mrs. Murdoch long at all to figure out that I was living alone on the streets. But instead of banning me from her shop, she continued to invite me back, even after my money was completely gone. She was always so kind and respectful, giving me her unsold, two-day old bread to distribute among those who were truly destitute like me.

I would eat my fill, stashing a piece or two aside for the days when I couldn't find anything else to eat, and then I would give the rest to my friends, the Marshes, and others in our small encampment.

I'd taken up residence just outside the city, away from the main streets of Ennis, where people were less violent with one another. The area was occupied by folks much like myself, displaced by circumstances beyond their control. The Marsh family was one of these families. Mr. Marsh had recently lost his wife to starvation, exacerbated by a case of yellow fever that she'd contracted when they were living in a workhouse. Mr. Marsh and his five children had become my extended family. The oldest daughter, Audrey, had also contracted yellow fever while in the workhouse and was left extremely weakened by the disease and unable to exert herself without becoming severely short of breath.

The Marsh family had left the workhouse months before when Mrs. Marsh and Audrey became ill and happened upon me by chance as two men were attempting to take undue advantage of me. Mr. Marsh hit the two men in the back of the head with a large club that he'd found, rendering one man momentarily unconscious and the other man severely injured as Mr. Marsh screamed bloody murder at them when they limped away. Ever since that day, we watched over each other, forming an alliance to share everything and anything we had. In turn, we kept an eye open for scavengers who might try to harm any of us in our small community.

One night, around the campfire, Mr. Marsh broke down and told me of his family's experiences while at the workhouse. He said that there were many diseases that had run rampant through the festering hellhole of a workhouse and that when his wife and daughter, Audrey, became sicker, they were told to leave. He had no choice but to move his family outdoors, exposing them to the elements. In the end, he realized it had been the right choice, but it had cost him dearly. He lost his beloved wife a week later and nearly lost his oldest child, Audrey.

It was Audrey's job to watch over her two youngest siblings while her father and two brothers, Jon, thirteen, and Eli, fifteen, went off each day seeking work to feed the family. I helped with the younger children when I could, giving Audrey time to rest and get stronger.

Audrey called out to me as I left for the bakery that day. "Be careful, Lara. Are ye sure ye would no' want to wait for me, Da or one of the boys ta accompany you?"

Waving her off, I called over my shoulder, "Nay, Audrey. There be no call to worry so. I'll be back before ye know it," before bringing my hand to my chest as I began to cough.

A raspy cough had settled in my chest two days prior, making it difficult for me to catch my breath.

"Are ye sure, Lara? I don' like the sound of that cough," Audrey fretted.

Clearing my throat, I pulled on the collar of the coat that Mrs. Murdoch had given me, trying to fend off the severe chill I felt. "Don' fuss so, Audrey, and keep the fire warm. I'll be back soon," I called back, bracing myself against the sudden cold breeze that kicked up as it blew through the worn-out coat I was wearing. The extra layer of Audrey's coat would have been nice but would have left her vulnerable to the chilly air. Shoving my hands deeper into the pockets, I turned and left, keeping an eye out for potential danger. Cautiously looking around from the safety of the tree line, I stepped out into the open at Main Street.

I was already dreaming of how good it would feel to fill my belly with Mrs. Murdoch's pastries when a cart came barreling down the road, forcing me to jump out of the way and into a muddy ditch.

"Hey! Watch where yer goin', you dunderhead!" I ranted, climbing out of the ditch and dusting off the dirt from my coat. Flexing my right knee, I began to cough into my hand. Then, raising a fist into the air, I began another boisterous rant expressing my great displeasure at the rude behavior of the driver. At that, I started to cough again, gasping for air when the raspy cough took my breath away.

As I straightened up, my head began to spin. It had been three days since I'd eaten more than a mouthful of rubbish and I could feel myself getting weaker.

Walking past the steps of the church where I had been chased away by the nasty nun my first day in town, I crossed myself to ward off

the bad memories that flooded my mind. Deciding to cross the street to avoid a possible run-in with the despicable woman, I noticed two rough looking men sitting on the steps, watching me with interest.

Quickly ducking my head to avoid direct eye contact as I passed them, I crossed the street again, praying the entire time that I was wrong about their abnormal interest in me. As I reached the corner, I turned back to see if they were still looking in my direction and noticed that the two men were no longer sitting on the steps of the church. They had vanished and for a moment I found myself wondering where they might have gone. But the smell of fresh baked bread pulled my attention back to what was really important to me at the moment—my stomach.

I had been feeling the need to be especially cautious as of late; starvation had been so rampant among the people living on the street that they had turned into animals. They would stab one another over a piece of tack or a stale crust of bread. Desperation caused people to do crazy things to survive, and it made it more difficult for me to sneak the bread out of town that Mrs. Murdoch gave me.

Word of Mrs. Murdoch's generosity had spread through town and, from time to time, someone would be waiting outside of her shop when they saw me go inside.

Quickly walking to the bakery, I pulled the hood of my old coat up to cover my red hair so that I wouldn't be so easily recognized. I stood across the street from Mrs. Murdock's shop, looking up and down the street to make sure that I wasn't followed.

Ushering the last patron out of her shop, Mrs. Murdoch turned the 'open' sign around, and still I waited across the street, pretending to examine something of interest in the mercantile shop window. When I was certain that no one was watching me, I crossed the street and softly knocked on her door, then waited for her to let me in.

"Come in, child, come in! It is getting cold, and ye must be frozen ta the bones, ta be sure," she remarked with a smile, stepping outside to look around. She was aware of just how dangerous the streets had become. "I have some hot tea for ye ta warm those weary bones of yers."

"Ye be too kind, Mrs. Murdoch," I exclaimed, rubbing my hands together to warm them, when I began to cough again.

"Aye, that does no' sound good," she pointed out, pouring me a cup of hot tea as promised, placing it down on the table before me. "No good t'all. When was the last time ye had a hot meal, child? Why, yer nothing but a sack of bones," she added, walking to the counter and retrieving a particularly large sweet bun she'd set aside. "Here, eat this. It will put some flesh on those bones of yers."

"I'll be fine, Mrs. Murdoch. Now don' you be worrying about me. I be strong as an ox, don' ye know. But I won' go turning down a cup of hot tea and sweet roll, ta be sure," I laughed, tipping my cup to her, and then dug into the sweet roll.

"Promise me ye will come back if ye get worse, and I will make ye a poultice for yer chest," she ordered, stepping to the counter and placing two loaves of bread in a bag for me to take, making it easier to carry. Then, bringing two more sweet buns over before sitting down across from me, Mrs. Murdoch poured herself a cup of tea.

"My friend Audrey has recovered and is doing much better," I informed her. "The bread you gave me the other day really helped her," I added, then coughed into my hand again as my lungs spasmed.

With a sympathetic smile, Mrs. Murdoch chuckled. "Well, that is marvelous to hear. It warms me heart to hear your friend is feeling better," she said while pouring more hot tea into my cup. "Have some more, child. It will warm yer insides right up."

I happily drank it down, grateful for the warm liquid in my belly. "Yes, ma'am, and thank ye again. Why, I think I'm feelin' a wee bit better already," I lied, forcing a smile to my lips as I patted the bag of bread she'd laid before me. "And this will go a long way ta helpin', Mrs. Murdoch." Then, not wishing to wear out my welcome, I finished my tea quickly and got to my feet. "Thank ye again for yer kindness. I don't know what I'd of done without you all these months."

Tears filled Mrs. Murdoch's eyes as she walked me to the door. "It is me pleasure, Lara, my dear. Try ta stay warm, child," she admonished, hesitating a moment before she opened the door to let me out.

Tucking the bag of bread beneath my coat, I turned with a smile and off I went. Fortified with two sweet buns in my belly and another one in my pocket, I walked a little taller as I rounded the corner. Not even the cold weather could dampen my spirits.

Retracing my steps back to the church, I stood on the opposite side of the road waiting for a death cart to pass me before I crossed. Something akin to a sixth sense tugged at my insides as I stood there waiting. I felt this odd feeling crawl up my spine causing me to feel tingly all over. It was like cold fingers were touching my skin, causing the tiny hairs on the back of my neck to stand on end. I tried to push it aside, telling myself that I was just being silly, but the strange intuitive feeling persisted.

I turned to have a look behind me when I caught the sight of a pair of filthy hands just before they grabbed ahold of me by the scruff of my coat, dragging me backwards into the alley. I screamed for help but was quickly silenced by the perpetrator's dirty, callused hand clamping down over my mouth.

"Looky what's we got us here, Tully. Dinner!" the man laughed as he dragged me over to his friend leaning against the alley wall with his arms crossed over his barrel-like chest. The man didn't look to me as if he had missed many meals as of late.

The man named Tully pushed away from the wall, snatching the precious bag of bread that I'd been hiding beneath my coat. "Well, ain't she sweet ta bring us somethin' ta eat," he chuckled, running his fingers through my hair with his filthy, dirt-smeared hand.

Panic set in and I began to struggle. "Give me that back. It does no' belong ta ye!" I screamed angrily, hoping to draw attention to myself.

Easily lifting me off of the ground, the man behind me squeezed me so tightly that the tea and sweet buns I'd just eaten began to come back up. I gagged and swallowed hard to keep them down. "Stop it! Help! Somebody help me!" I yelled, causing the man behind me to drop me suddenly so he could deliver a brutal kick to my side when I landed on my knees.

Tully smirked. "Ain't no one goin' to help you, girly," he laughed, and pushed me back down on all fours when I tried to stand up. "Hey, Billy, what do ye reckon we should do with her?" he asked with a smirk, giving me another vicious kick to the stomach.

Doubling over from the pain as I dropped back down to the ground on my knees, I lost the battle to keep my recent meal down. Then, rolling over and clutching at my stomach, I pleaded for mercy. "Please, leave me be," I moaned.

"I think we should have some fun with her, Tully," Billy exclaimed, kicking me in the leg and laughing when I cried out in pain.

"Please, give the bag back. It belongs to me," I cried weakly, slowly getting to my feet only to be pushed back down again from behind by Billy.

Holding the bag above my head, Tully began to taunt me at the same time he delivered another brutal blow with his foot, propelling me backwards and knocking my head against the brick wall.

"Please," I feebly begged, touching the back of my head and feeling something sticky on my fingers when I pulled my hand away. "Ye keep the bread, just let me go," I said as small flashes of light danced before my eyes. I feared that I would pass out and worried what would happen to me if I did lose consciousness.

Gathering the collar of my coat in one hand, Billy loomed above me menacingly. "Thank ye for yer generosity. And to shows ye that we ain't completely uncivilized, we plans on showing ye a good time," he laughed, exposing a row of blackened, stained teeth as he grabbed for the hem of my skirts.

Frantically fighting him off, I winced in pain every time I moved. "Please, stop," I cried as unshed tears of pain, frustration, and anger welled up in my eyes. "Stop it! Please, stop! I beg of ye!" I desperately screamed while holding down my skirts.

"Hey, you there!" a man yelled, stepping into the alleyway. "Unhand that child this instant, before I call the authorities!"

Balling up his fist, Billy punched me in the jaw, delivering one final humiliating blow. "We was done with her anyway, governor," he

smirked, before looking over his shoulder at the man. Then he gave me one last intimidating glare. "We will see you later." He snarled the words in my face before spitting on the ground next to me. "No harm done here," Billy insisted, raising his hands into the air to indicate that he was leaving. Then, with an innocent smile as if he were guiltless of any wrongdoing, he slapped Tully on the back. The sound of their laughter echoed in my ears, adding further insult to injury as they walked away with my precious bread tucked beneath Tully's arm.

Closing my eyes to the pain, I laid there in my pitiful state, in that filthy, garbage riddled alley, softly crying. Great sadness had come to my home months before, uninvited, and now it had followed me here. Life didn't get much lower than that. My will to continue living had finally been taken from me and I could no longer see the purpose in fighting for survival. You either reject the darkness or you embrace it, and I decided, in that moment, to embrace it.

"Oh, Zane, she's just a child," I heard a woman cry, and then I heard steps running towards me. I didn't even bother opening my eyes or acknowledging her existence as she bent down to examine me. "Quickly now, you need to help her up, darling."

"Don't touch me! Leave me alone!" I objected sourly, turning away from the couple who'd stopped to help me in my hour of need. I had lost the most important element of survival…hope. I no longer needed anyone's help, ever again. I was giving up.

Why can't they see that? I thought to myself.

I had decided, in my young, childish mind, that I would lay in that dirty, filthy, rat-infested alley until the moment I drew my last breath.

No one would miss me. My short, sad, pitiful life had come down to this one, defining moment and this is the way it would end—alone and destitute, in a stinking alley! I couldn't quite believe the injustice.

"Perhaps we should find someone to help her, Charity, my love," the man suggested, trying to pull his wife away from my side. But she refused to be deterred from her mission of mercy. Placing a gentle hand upon my arm, she asked, "Is there someone we can inform of your condition? Some family member or friend we can locate for you?"

"No," came my bleak reply. "There is no one," I concluded, turning my head slightly to look up at them both.

Charity leaned in even closer. "Oh, you poor, dear. Don't be afraid, we won't hurt you. We have come from America to help your people. Won't you let us help you?"

"No!" I said sullenly. "I am beyond yer help."

"Dear child, no one is beyond help," she assured me in a soothing voice, placing a gentle hand upon my bruised cheek, causing me to wince in pain. "Can my husband go find your mother for you?"

"No!" I said, pushing her hand away, defiantly glaring at her. "My mama is dead."

"Come along, Charity. She obviously doesn't want our help," Zane said, tugging at his wife's shoulder.

"Nonsense, darling, the child is merely traumatized," she stated matter-of-factly, turning back to me with a patient smile. "What is your name, my dear?"

Giving her a leery look, I jerked away from her when she reached a loving hand out to me. "Lara. Lara Flannigan," I answered sullenly, staring suspiciously at her outstretched hand while pulling away.

"Well, Lara Flannigan, I'm Charity Roscoe and this is my husband, Zane Roscoe. We want to help if we can. Is there any member of your family we can contact for you?" Charity coaxed, refusing to be put off by my bad disposition and angry glares.

"No—" I began, grabbing at my tender side, unable to catch my breath, when I suddenly began to cough. When the coughing subsided, I continued, "I do no' have any family."

Looking up at her husband with a profoundly sad look in her eyes, Charity glanced back at me, then stood up and pulled her husband aside to discuss something privately.

Becoming somewhat disinterested, I laid my head back down on my arm with a loud sniff. Then, scrubbing my hand across my tear-

streaked face, I gave them a suspicious glare just as I saw the man named Zane vigorously shake his head. I could see his lips mouth, "No." His wife gestured with a stern nod in my direction, then continued to make her opinion known to her husband. The strain of keeping my eyes open was giving me a terrible headache so I decided to close them, rolling over to turn my back on the couple.

Grabbing my sore jaw, I settled in, pulling the collar of my coat up against the cold. I began to pray, as I'd been taught my entire life, that the pain in my head would subside soon and that it wouldn't take long to die. And yet, I had precious little faith that such a simple prayer would be answered since not one of my prayers thus far had been.

I felt a slight tap on my shoulder and slowly rolled back over, giving the woman a contemptuous look as she kneeled on the filthy ground next to me. "I thought I told ye to leave me be," I admonished.

Unperturbed by my foul mood and ill manners, Charity, smiling sweetly and with the patience of Job, said, "I understand, Lara, really I do, but I cannot in good conscience leave you here to die. It just doesn't sit well with me."

"Of course, ye can," I added bluntly, rolling back over and turning my back to her again, mistakenly thinking that I'd ended our conversation. I adjusted my coat, trying to make myself comfortable once more, when she tapped me on the shoulder again.

Now I was irritated and turned on her, quickly sitting up to glare at the woman, which proved to be a mistake. I grabbed my throbbing head, pursed my lips together and cursed beneath my breath as the sudden motion caused me severe pain. I would have cursed out loud if not for knowing the effort of doing so would cause me further pain.

Mrs. Roscoe's sweet smile never faded. "I know this is going to sound crazy to you, but I want to take you away from here and give you a home," she said.

"I am no' a puppy ye can pick up and take with ye," I quipped.

"I realize that, Lara—" Charity began to say when her husband interrupted her.

"Come along, darling, I told you this was a bad idea."

Still unfazed by my foul temper or her husband's insistence, Charity persisted, brushing her husband's hand away as he attempted to pull her to her feet. "Can I tell you a story?" she asked, "I know you will think me odd, but I believe that you are the child in my dreams."

Suddenly, my interest was piqued. Never one to turn down the chance to listen to a good story, I decided to listen to this odd woman who came all the way to Ireland from America to help my people.

"A few months ago, I was lying in bed and I had this strange dream. It was strange because I had never had a dream like this one before." Noticing that she had drawn me in, Charity paused and asked me, "Would you like me to continue?"

"Well, I be listening to ye," I added curtly, bringing a hand up to cradle my throbbing head.

"In my dream, Mr. Roscoe and I came to a foreign land that was very green to help people that were starving to death. Oh, it was so vivid!" she exclaimed. "Anyway," she continued, clearing her throat and blushing as she looked at her husband, continuing only after he gave her an encouraging nod and a smile. "We had come to give aid and feed the starving people of the land." She paused and looked deep into my eyes. Then taking a deep breath as if telling me something very personal, she continued. "In my dream, I saw a lot of people suffering and very bad things were happening to them. The streets were full of bad people, much like the men my husband just ran off. Well, anyway, things just went from bad to worse, no matter how hard I tried to change them. I felt so disheartened and saddened by what I was seeing, and then I thought to myself, if I can't change things, then why should I even try? Do you know what happened next?" she questioned.

"Why ask me? It's yer dream."

With a patient smile, Charity continued, "Then a voice came to me in my dream, and it told me to go anyway—that I would make a difference in the life of one family, and by doing so, I would change the course of everyone concerned, including my life. Then it told me that the life of one child depended on me doing the right thing.

I believe that child is you, Lara Flannigan," she concluded, laying a gentle hand upon my shoulder.

I looked down at the hand resting there on my shoulder, then back up to her face. "And somehow, out of all the orphaned children living on the streets, ye picked me?" I questioned with disdain.

Reaching for his wife again, Zane tried to pull Charity away while nervously looking up and down the alleyway. "You tried, Charity."

Refusing to be put off by the belligerent look in my eyes, Mrs. Roscoe gently patted her husband's hand, which now rested upon her shoulder. She smiled up at him, and as if fortified by his presence, she turned back and smiled so angelically at me, I had to blink.

"Dear Lara, I know without a shadow of a doubt that I was sent here to meet you and save your life. The only thing I'm a little fuzzy on is how I am going to convince you that I was sent here for you. It takes real strength of character and faith to reach your hand out and accept the help of complete strangers. I cannot even imagine what you have been forced to endure, living on the streets by yourself. The things you have had to witness..." she hesitated. "I truly am sorry that you've lost your mother and family, Lara. Such a burden like this should never be put upon the shoulders of a child. My heart goes out to you. And yet, my real fear is that you will refuse to take the lifeline I offer to you. I want to give you a home," she continued, looking up at her husband as she spoke. "We want to give you a home and a family, dear child. A place to call your own. I fear that if you don't take my hand and come away with me now, you won't live to see another day."

How could she possibly have known I was giving up? As I continued to gawk at her, a sudden, sharp, piercing pain struck my heart. The thought of never experiencing all the things that I'd once dreamed of as a child was pressing down on me. An overwhelming, abrupt pain penetrated deep as Mama's dying words came flooding back to me all at once, "I want ye ta make something of yerself. I want ye to live, if no' for yerself, then live for me." Tears filled my eyes and ran down my dirty cheeks.

Recognizing the weakness and vulnerability now showing in my eyes, Mrs. Roscoe inched closer to me. I could tell she wanted to throw her arms around me, but she stopped when she saw me pull back and stiffen my back, hitting the wall behind me. "Oh, child, please don't focus on all of the things that have gone wrong in your short, tragic life. Instead, focus on all the things that can go right," she implored. "I know you are broken down and fear this nightmare will never end. Don't lose heart, Lara Flannigan. Stop consulting your fears, I beg you. Instead, think of the possibilities. That is the only way you will be able to see the light that waits for you at the end of the very long and dark tunnel you have been in. I am here so you can begin to live again. And isn't that what you want to do, my sweet girl?" she smiled. "Won't you let me help you live again?"

The chink in the armor was made, opening up just enough to allow hope to invade my heart, even for the briefest of moments. I fell into her outstretched arms, unable to hold back the pain and sorrow any longer. She had given me back my hope, if even the smallest of a sliver of it. Crying like a newborn baby, I knew, without a shadow of a doubt, that Mama had sent an angel to save me, and her name was Charity Roscoe.

Mama was watching over me when she guided me to Mrs. Murdoch, who kept me from starving to death on the mean streets of Ennis. Which, in turn, helped me to survive long enough for Mrs. Roscoe to cross an ocean from America to save me from a fate worse than death: disillusionment, despair, and despondency. Mama saved me from giving up when that was all I wanted to do. Mama re-established my faith in humanity by sending Charity and Zane to save my life. There was a remedy for utter despair and hopelessness after all, even when it came at the lowest point in my life.

"Now, there, there, my sweet Lara. Everything is going to be all right," Charity soothed as her words penetrated my heart. Patting my back, I sensed her looking up at her husband as she continued, "You are going to be just fine, sweet Lara. Just fine indeed. I'm here now. I won't ever leave you alone again. I promise," she assured me, smoothing my matted hair with her fingers as I continued to cry on her shoulder.

10

JULY 3, 1847
THREE MONTHS LATER

Settling into My New Life

I do not recall much of our journey to my new homeland in America; I was very sick, weaving in and out of consciousness for most of the voyage. I was out of my mind with fever and unable to hold down anything more than water or broth for weeks. I don't care what people say about developing sea legs, because it's a lie. The rolling and pitching of the rough ocean waves caused me further distress and I was miserable.

My native home and all that I held dear was becoming a distant memory with each passing hour. Several weeks into the voyage I found myself letting go and submitting to the reality of my situation. Some people might say that holding onto what you want takes strength, but it is the letting go of old dreams that requires the real strength. Sometimes you have to let go and trust that everything will work out. In the end, I wielded my shield of hope like some kind of weapon, telling myself that if I managed to survive the ocean voyage, after everything else I'd been through, then I would be the true victor.

Upon arriving at the port of Philadelphia, I was immediately detained and sent to quarantine at Lazaretto hospital, eight miles south of the city, on the Delaware River. In the wake of the yellow fever epidemic of 1799, the city's Board of Health had deemed it necessary to build a quarantine station. The hospital had continued operating and serving its purpose to protect the citizens of Philadelphia and surrounding townships from any further outbreaks of deadly diseases carried to their shores by European immigrants. The Lazaretto hospital was a ten-acre Georgian-style complex, dominated by the large, four-story, red brick building housing the hospital's offices. The staff resided in their own quarters on the grounds. The physicians and quarantine master each lived in individual but identical two-story houses on either side of the massive hospital building. They also had a large building on the grounds that served as a kitchen and mortuary. There was an area for gardening and a burial ground as well.

I remained hospitalized in the main building for six weeks, recovering from some undetermined disease that I'd picked up while living on my own in the streets of Ennis. The doctor said my condition had been further complicated by my prolonged malnutrition and long ocean voyage.

Charity looked concerned over the doctor's diagnosis, and even blamed herself for a portion of my illness, even though I assured her I was grateful for her taking me in. Keeping her word, Charity never left my bedside and nursed me back to health, watching over me both night and day to ensure I received the best care possible.

A very generous contribution to the hospital's private funds earned me a private room, furnished to Mrs. Roscoe's specification, which included an extra bed for her to sleep in. Her husband, Zane, came by each day at one o'clock like clockwork to check on us both and to encourage my progress. During this time, I learned a lot about the couple who had taken me in.

Mrs. Roscoe told me stories of her childhood and of how she and her husband had met. She spoke in great detail about their life together, explaining that Mr. Roscoe was a very successful, well-respected businessman of society and that he owned a thriving carriage shop. She spoke of her greatest heartbreak—her inability to bear Mr. Roscoe children. They had both prayed for many years to have children, but were unsuccessful in their endeavors and had only recently given up all hope of a family of their own since Charity was now forty-five years old.

She told me again about her dream of traveling to Ireland, but this time she added things she had left out before—details that hadn't seemed pertinent when she was crouched over me in that filthy alley,

trying to convince me she was meant to be my new mother. She told me how close she and Mr. Roscoe had come to returning home without finding me, and that they had been on their way back to the ship when they'd turned down the wrong street and happened upon me being accosted in the alley.

"We were being led to you by an angel," she said with tears in her eyes.

I was brought to tears by her story and the heartfelt gratitude she expressed to me. Her words and actions drove home to me her sincerity and genuine gratitude for stumbling upon me that day.

I can't tell you how wretched I felt when an image of my own sweet mama popped into my head. I felt like such a traitor to her even as I rejoiced in my good fortune and gratitude toward the Roscoes for saving me that dreadful day. Then, as memories of a faraway family I'd left behind haunted my every thought, I wondered to myself if I would ever see them again in this lifetime.

Days passed quickly and my strength slowly returned. I was released from the hospital on the twenty-eighth of September with a clean bill of health. Charity had a new dress brought to me in the hospital and anxiously hovered over me as I unwrapped the box. Removing the top of the box and pulling back the tissue paper, I reverently touched the supple material of my new outfit. I had never worn anything brand-new before, and certainly nothing as fine as this.

"'Tis mine?" I whispered, still not believing my good fortune.

"Yes. Of course, Lara. Please tell me you like it," she prodded nervously as she studied my reaction.

"Aye!" I quickly answered. "I've never had nothin' so fine afore."

She helped me into the petticoats, then tied something around my waist that had metal rings sewn into it that stood out, away from my body and legs. She called it a hoop skirt and said it would keep my skirts held out in a perfect, circular, poof. Then, helping me slip on a white blouse, she pushed my hands out of the way and quickly buttoned the front. Pulling up the dark blue skirt from the floor, she tucked the blouse down and secured the buttons in the back as she

admired the fit. Next, she pulled out a fitted coat, smiling as she held it out for me to slip my arms into.

"I know it will be a little big on you now, but only for a little while. I am confident we will remedy that problem with some hearty meals," Charity mused, standing back to admire the entire ensemble. "Oh, Lara, it is so beautiful on you."

I felt my face grow warm as I blushed. No one had ever fussed over me before, let alone what I wore. "Thank you, Mrs. Roscoe."

With a shake of her delicate head, she laughed and petite brown curls bounced as she moved. "Nonsense, Lara, and for heaven sakes, call me Mother," Charity added, wrapping her arms around me.

"Moth…Mother," I stammered while testing the way the strange word felt on my tongue as it awkwardly fell from my mouth.

"There're my girls," Zane announced, looking as if he would bust at the seams with pride as he stepped into the room grinning from ear to ear. "My, don't you look like a proper young lady of society," he added, removing his hat and placing a kiss upon his wife's cheek. "And since we are handing out titles, I think I would like to be called Papa, if that is all right with you, Lara?" he added, giving me a questioning glance. "Since we will soon be a family."

Shyly I nodded my head, returning his smile. It all felt so unreal. One moment I was ready to give up and wait for death to take me in some dirty alley in Ireland, and the next moment I was being showered with so much love and attention I could hardly take it all in. "Aye. It's a fine name for me new Da," I said, looking at my new family.

I saw tears well up in both their eyes as Zane cautiously stepped forward, unsure if I would accept his embrace. With a smile, I stepped into his arms, hugging his waist. I was more fortunate than most, there was no doubt about that.

Stepping back and removing a white handkerchief from his trouser pocket, Zane wiped his eyes. "There is so much dust in the air," he explained. Then, picking up Mother's cape, he placed it over her shoulders as he gave her an affectionate squeeze before picking up a second wrap and placing it over my shoulders. "Shall we go home and

get you settled into your new room? And let me assure you, it will be a step up from your last accommodations," he teased, taking hold of my arm and jauntily placing his hat upon his head with a wry smile. We all laughed and stepped into the hallway. Then, holding out his other arm for Charity, he waited for her to take hold of it before we walked down the hallway and out of the hospital together as a family.

We laughed and talked all the way home, pulling up in front of a large three-story brick structure in the heart of downtown. I found myself surrounded by people busily going about their business while calling out their greetings to Zane and Charity, who stopped to accept their warm wishes. People I had never met before cheerfully greeted me as well. Through all of this commotion, I couldn't pull my eyes away from my new home.

The beautiful structure was surrounded by a three-foot-tall white picket fence, with a curving courtyard that was surrounded on both sides by perfectly manicured lawns and hedges. Beautiful red, white, and purple flowers lined the front stoop. Three steps led up to a small porch, with a large window that looked out onto the busy street. A brass knocker in the shape of a lion's head stood out against the jet black painted large wooden door of the home. The brass door handle dwarfed my hand as I touched the smooth metal. *We never had anything like this where I came from,* I thought to myself.

I felt a hand come to rest gently upon my shoulder as my new parents concluded their conversation with their neighbors and stepped up next to me. Then, like magic, the door opened, and a tall, thin man stood in the doorway. "Welcome home, Sir, Missus," he said with a curt nod of his head. "This must be the new addition to the family I've heard so much about." He smiled, sweeping his hand in a grand gesture, inviting me in. "Please, do come in."

"Emerson, this is Lara, our daughter. Please see that the staff are all informed of the wonderful news," Mother ordered, showing me inside as she continued to rest her hand proudly on my shoulder.

The interior was even more impressive than the outside; the clean white walls contrasted with the rich wood tones of the furniture. An aroma of fresh furniture polish and flowers filled my senses as I gazed

at a large bouquet gracing the entry table while we walked through to the stairs. The stair banister was painted black like the front door and stood out against the stark white walls.

My jaw must have been unhinged from my mouth because my new mother took me by the hand and said, "Close your mouth, my dear, this is merely the entry. Just wait until you see your bedroom. You are going to love it."

Leading me quickly up the staircase behind her, she giggled like an excited school girl as she pulled me down the hallway. I had never imagined life could be so grand nor so much fun. The carpeted runners down the hallway stretched on forever as she showed me to my room. "Go ahead, you can step inside," she coaxed, grinning widely.

Cautiously placing my hand on the glass doorknob, I was concerned that it would break but soon realized that it was actually quite sturdy. I enjoyed the smooth way it felt in my hand as I turned the knob and pushed the heavy paneled door open. Gasping out loud, my jaw dropped open yet again upon entering my new room—it was nearly as large as my entire childhood home.

"Do you like it?" Mother inquired, sounding a bit uncertain when she saw the look on my face.

"Like it?" I answered, still feeling shocked that this was mine as I stepped even further into the room. There was so much to admire that I was unsure of what to look at first. "Aye, I love it," I sighed, trying to take it all in. "I've no' seen anythin' so grand." My voice was filled with awe as I contemplated all around me.

With a gleeful cry, Mother hugged me. "I knew you would be happy here," she exclaimed, squeezing me so tightly I could hardly breathe. "Sarah has put everything away for you and she will help you to get settled in." She pointed to a young woman standing off to the side. A slight, petite person, Sarah had delicate features, large blue eyes, and blond hair that she had pulled back into a knot at the back of her head.

"I did no' see ye there. Wait, what things?" I questioned, puzzled by Mother's words. I'd never had anything of my own before so how could Sarah have put them away for me?

Smiling patiently, Mother walked over to the wardrobe cabinet and opened the doors wide to reveal that it was filled with dresses in many different colors and styles. My eyes teared up and suddenly I was overcome with emotion. My mind was having difficulty comprehending so much all at once and I began to spontaneously cry.

"Oh, now I've gone and done it," she fussed, quickly coming to my side. "Zane warned me that I would befuddle you by giving you too much all at once."

Through the tears, I managed to babble the words, "Thank ye, Mother."

11

Lara Turns 15
Making New Acquaintances

The Roscoes had friends in high places to facilitate my adoption in a matter of weeks rather than months. My adoption was made official three weeks after being released from Lazaretto Hospital. My new name became Lara Ann Flannigan Roscoe. Mother added the Ann after her mother, who had died fifteen years earlier. And I was permitted to keep my family surname as part of my full name for sentimental reasons, of course.

As the months wore on, we settled into a comfortable rhythm. Papa hired private teachers to guide me through the integration process. One teacher taught me reading, writing, and mathematics, while another taught me world history and proper pronunciation of my words. Sarah and Mother gave me instruction on the subtleties of Philadelphian society while Papa cheered me on. He would occasionally bring me treats or little treasures and trinkets to make me smile when he noticed I was struggling or looking overly burdened by all my lessons.

My speech and pronunciation of certain words held me back some, as my jaded peers were more than happy to point out. They refused to garner me the least bit of grace as they ridiculed me for being born an Irishman and a girl to boot. I tried to ignore their hurtful barbs and discourteous behavior, yet it was difficult pretending that I was not hurt by their words, especially when I longed for a friend to call my own.

There were days I wanted to give up, but I told myself that I made a promise to Mama that I would make something of myself and I was not about to go back on my word. I'd been blessed with a second chance at life and was determined to do something with it. I had a beautiful home, plenty of food to fill my stomach, lovely clothes to wear, and attentive parents who loved me very much. What more could I ask for besides the obvious—companionship.

On these lonely days, my daily affirmations were not enough to keep me from longing for a simpler time with my best friend Jamie by my side to splash with me in the waters beneath the cliffs of Dunmore Head.

"So, who truly cares what a bunch of over-indulged, rich, spoiled socialites think of me anyway?" I would tell myself. But the truth was, I cared, and maybe I cared a little too much. That is why it hurt so badly when my peers snubbed and ignored me as if I didn't exist. And, as grateful as I was for everything my adoptive parents did to ensure my success, it couldn't keep me from becoming melancholy or morose when memories of home drifted across my thoughts. The only good thing to come from all of this was that I felt motivated to work twice as hard as anyone else. With that hard work came clarity, and as I pushed these memories aside, I was able to put all of my efforts toward learning as much as I could. This made my parents proud.

One particular day, Papa surprised me by inviting me to accompany him to the carriage shop. He sweetened the bargain by promising to take me on an adventure complete with a picnic lunch. Thrilled by the prospect, I could barely contain myself during breakfast.

We ate a quick morning meal of toast, poached eggs, sausage links, and dried apricots, then donned our hats and coats and walked out the back door. The Royal Carriage House stood directly across the street from our home, distinguishable by the wooden sign hanging above the storefront depicting a red prancing carriage horse with a gold crown hovering above its head. Our shop sat between Bauer's Bakery and Drake's Mercantile store, both owned and operated by second generation immigrants. As we paused to take in the scene, we noticed several immigrant workers heading toward the industrial section of town which held promises of work.

Recently, Philadelphia had become a safe haven for the large influx of immigrants coming from England, Germany, and Ireland. Immigrants flooded the American shores as they escaped their land's potato famine and political unrest. Much of Ireland's economy had been crippled by the great famine, and there was little to no chance that the country would recover from the devastating loss any time soon. The flow of European and Irish immigrants from the European continent reminded me of the time I watched rats fleeing a sinking ship off the shores of home after a particularly rough storm. It was an unsettling sight to behold and even if I wanted to, I couldn't look away as I watched everyone scurrying along with the rats searching for dry land.

I had often overheard the talk of promises of work in Philadelphia, whispered by neighbors or muttered by weary men as they trudged past our door. At dawn, I would peek out the window and see men already lined up along the streets, their shoulders hunched against the morning chill, their breath clouding in the air. They spoke of the mills, the ironworks, the shipyards—always with that same flicker of hope that maybe today would be their day. That today would be the beginning of a better life. But by evening, when some returned with blistered hands and empty pockets, I understood what those promises truly meant. The work was harsh, the hours endless, and whatever coin they earned was scarcely enough to keep hunger from the door.

I had heard people say that the less-skilled Irishmen found work digging the canals along the Schuylkill and Delaware rivers. When I traveled with my family through towns like Conshohocken, Norristown, and Bristol, I saw the rough canal camps myself— clusters of men with shovels and picks, their clothes caked with mud. It was clear why so many had been drawn there; those towns seemed to spring up overnight along the riverbanks, promising a kind of work that asked for nothing more than strong backs and willing hands.

As we continued across the street, hand-in-hand, and entered the carriage house through the large wooden doors standing wide open

that allowed the excess heat from the iron forge to escape, I saw men busily working like bees in a hive. They were fashioning wagon wheels, carriage bodies, and undercarriage pieces and putting them together in sections.

A young man standing with his back to us was pumping the bellows of the forge, causing the flames to leap and jump in the furnace. He wore a pair of heavy gloves to protect himself from the intensity of the heat as he held onto a piece of metal with a pair of large metal clamps. The outline of his muscles bulged through the thick shirt he wore to further protect his skin from burning as he stood close to the heat. Pulling a piece of metal from the fire, he brought the large anvil down, pounding out the metal to form a ring for a wagon wheel. As he dunked the red-hot metal into the water, it hissed and sputtered, sending water vapors into the air in a rush of steam. Papa called out to him, trying to catch his attention, but he didn't react immediately.

Taking a step closer to the young man while pulling me along with him, Papa yelled over the sound of the anvil as it struck the metal so he could be heard over the noise of so many men working with hammers, wood, and steel. "Roman, my boy, let me introduce you to my daughter, Lara."

Looking over his shoulder, Roman pulled down the red scarf resting across his face to protect him from the heat of the furnace. He smiled broadly when he saw us. Setting his tools down and removing his gloves, he walked toward us with an effortless gait. "Good to see you, Mr. Roscoe. What brings you to the shop today?" he asked, giving me a quick once-over. "And who might this lovely young lady be?" he questioned, as if I were a young child who needed to be patronized.

Yet, regardless of the fact that I felt slighted by his tone, I couldn't stop staring at his eyes. They were such a deep blue that I was reminded of the ocean of home on a clear day. I was fascinated by the long, dark lashes that fringed his eyes, which made them seem even bluer. He was the most beautiful man I'd ever seen and when he spoke, the timber of his voice was so rich and smooth it felt as if little butterflies were dancing about in my stomach. I couldn't decide whether I enjoyed the feeling or not; in the end, the entire experience left me feeling rather queasy.

"Roman Blackthorn, this is my daughter, Lara. Lara, Roman Blackthorn, my new apprentice," Papa introduced proudly, gesturing between us with his hand.

The two of them must have thought me quite daft as I continued to stare at the young man's outstretched hand for an awkward moment. "It's a pleasure to make yer…your acquaintance…Mr. Blackthorn," I finally acknowledged, smiling shyly as my cheeks flushed bright red.

For the first time in my life I was genuinely embarrassed by my Irish accent and tried to hide it with all my might. But there it was, following me around like an obnoxious albatross around my neck.

With a most gentlemanly bow, he smiled broadly. "The pleasure is all mine, Miss Roscoe," he assured me before turning his full attention back to my papa as the two men began to discuss business. In essence, I was being dismissed.

I took a few halting steps backwards while continuing to admire Roman's profile. He was a very handsome man and I found myself wondering if he knew it. Towering over me by a good foot or more, he appeared to be around eighteen or nineteen. He had very broad shoulders, narrow hips, and those eyes—I just kept coming back to those eyes—were so blue I could have drowned in their depths. I felt my entire face flush crimson and I was thankful neither one of them was paying me any attention. I tried expressing an air of indifference, clasping my hands behind my back as Roman looked over at me while he talked with Papa. I smiled pleasantly and turned away quickly, hoping he hadn't noticed me staring at him.

I felt momentarily irritated by the fact that the two men were talking business, cutting into my time with Papa and his promise of taking me on an adventure. But at the same time, I was relieved. Taking a deep breath, I took this as my cue that I was dismissed and had free reign to look around. Papa had never brought me to the carriage shop before even though we lived directly across the street. With my hands tucked into my coat pockets, I wandered through the spacious shop, observing men working on different vehicles.

Two men were working on an axle that had been broken on a delivery wagon. They looked up as I passed by, quickly dismissing me as they returned to repairing the axle. Another man had his back to me, meticulously sanding the wooden fittings of a rig's harness. Two men stood near a partially finished body of a two-seater Surry and a closed-door coach discussing when they were going to apply the final coat of sealant over the glossy black varnished paint. For the most part, people ignored me as I wandered through the shop.

It would have been a merry little wonderland to a child, which I clearly was not. There were so many places to hide or stash away in, with half-finished carriage bodies in various stages of completion and pieces and parts hanging along the walls or in bins, just waiting for the opportunity to be used. There were so many stalls that served different purposes, and I found it was all very magical and fascinating. It was then that I spotted a set of stairs at the rear of the building.

"Where do those lead to?" I wondered to myself out loud as I ventured towards them. Looking over my shoulder before proceeding up the stairs, I murmured, "What harm would it be to anyone if I explored above the staircase?" Lifting my skirts with one hand, I held onto the railing as I climbed the stairs. "I was promised an adventure, and this will surely qualify," I mused, checking to see that no one was paying me any mind. The staircase twisted back around on itself at the landing as I tip-toed my way up the remaining steps. At the top was a long corridor running the entire length of the building. To my right was a row of closed doors, and to my left, a large wooden door that stood open.

After checking to see that no one was about to stop me, I stepped onto the landing and walked towards the open door to look inside the room. Realizing that it was a spacious office, with a large desk near the window looking out onto the street, I stepped into the room. Running my hand across the solid surface of the heavy wooden desk, the wood felt warm to my touch where the sun came through the window. A variety of papers lay strewn across the majestic desk. A dark leather chair had been pushed back and turned to face the door as if the last occupant had left in a hurry. An inkwell and quill set sat neatly upon a polished silver tray in the middle of the desk, and a hand-drawn

portrait of Mother in her wedding gown was prominently displayed on the corner of the desk. I smiled as I looked around. Papa's office was warmly furnished, and I could see a clear view of the house when I looked out the window. Mother sat in an upstairs parlor having tea with two women from one of her societal clubs, and I thought how lovely it was that Papa and Mother could be apart, and yet, were still so close in proximity.

A wood-burning stove sat opposite the desk in the far corner of the room, and in between was a richly furnished sitting area that included a leather couch, two chairs, a coffee table, and a large red and gold rug, making that part of the room feel more like our living room rather than an office. Bookshelves filled with leather-bound books and ledgers lined the wall behind the desk. Two stone sculptures also sat upon the shelves. One was of a man on the back of a warhorse, his sword raised in the air, and his horse reared up in the air as if he too were ready to fight. The other was of a woman accepting a handful of field flowers from a man down on one knee. I found it odd, the two completely opposing depictions of the human condition sitting upon the same bookshelf.

Stepping out of the office and back into the hallway, I noticed another sitting area. This one was more casually furnished than Papa's office, with two high backed chairs and a settee. I glanced at several opened books sitting on a small table next to one of the chairs, and then continued on my way exploring the second floor. Passing by more closed doors, I made my way down the hallway, stopping at a door that was cracked open. Curiosity bid me to look and I pushed the door open a bit wider, where I saw a modest kitchen with a wood burning stove, a hearth, and an iron pot which hung from a hook near the still smoldering embers. Tables, chairs, and a food prepping area were near the middle of the room, and an indoor sink was along a wall. It was clear that this room had everything necessary to prepare meals.

Suddenly realizing that the men who worked here at The Royal Carriage Shop also lived here, I gasped. I felt as if I had been peering in through a window where I should not have and backed out of the door, hurrying down the steps as quickly and quietly as I could. Halfway down the staircase I came face to face with Roman Blackthorn. I could

feel the rush of color start in my chest, crawl up my neck, and begin to blush bright crimson in my cheeks again. I forced a smile, mumbled something about Papa's office, then continued down the stairs. I even forced myself not to look back when I reached the bottom landing and felt his eyes following me as I hurried away. I walked with purpose towards the last place I'd left Papa and found him talking with another employee, giving him some kind of instructions.

Looking up once he saw me, Papa smiled. "I was wondering where you'd wandered off to," he remarked, standing next to a very handsome four-seater, horse-drawn buggy that was ready to go. "Have you explored enough to sufficiently satisfy your curiosity?" he teased.

Nodding my head and forcing a smile, I didn't slow down, but quickly climbed up into the carriage and settled in. "Aye," came my simple reply.

"Well then, that must mean we are ready to set off on our adventure," he said, turning back to the other man. "Thank you, George, for agreeing to handle that matter for me." Papa shook the man's hand before climbing up beside me and tipping his hat to George. "I should be back later this afternoon with the parts."

A large basket sat between us on the floor and it looked as if it held enough food to feed a small army. I smiled as Papa slapped the reins and clicked his tongue. "Giddy up, boys," he called out as he turned, giving me a rye wink. "Are you ready for some fun?"

With one last look in the direction I last saw Roman, I looped my arm through Papa's and smiled up at him. "Aye…I mean, I truly am, Papa. Where are we off ta…I mean to?"

Raising his hand to wave to a tall, well-dressed man passing by, Papa turned his head from side to side and maneuvered the rig into traffic as we crossed the street heading towards the Wharf. "We are going to meet a gentleman by the name of Tom Dossier. He owns a shop that makes the leather harnesses we use on our carriages and rigs. After that, I was thinking we could stop off and have a picnic in the park near the Wharf."

"That sounds lovely, Papa. Then afterward, could we go by the sweets-shop?" I asked, lifting a questioning yet pleading eyebrow in hopes that I looked adequately sincere and innocent so that Papa would have no choice but to indulge me.

"Are you sure you want to simply go by the sweets-shop? I was thinking it would be much more fun to go inside, rather than simply pass by it," he teased. "I'd really like to sample Samuel's newest creations and maybe a few of my favorite pieces, rather than simply smell them as we pass by," Papa added with a chuckle.

"Oh, Papa, ye are so much fun," I laughed with delight.

I had discovered the joy of chocolates and hard candies when I was recovering in the hospital. Papa would bring me sweet treats as a bribe to get me to eat a little bit more each day so that my strength would return faster. His ploy worked so well that I begged him to take me to Shane's Confectionery shop every time we were out and about town. It was kind of our little secret. I loved picking out delicious treats, and Papa loved to make me smile.

The storefront resided at 112 Market Street and was run by a gentleman by the name of Mr. Samuel Herring, a delightful man with very kind eyes. He loved surprising people with the unusual high-quality candies he created. The hard ribbon candy was as beautiful to look at as it was to eat. It looked like fancy ribbons with its 'S' shape and lovely red and green stripes running through it. But my most favorite treat of all was the buttercreams with their soft, creamy chocolate centers that melted in my mouth and caused my tongue to water every time I thought about tasting the delightful confections.

"Oh, Papa, I can't wait."

With a wink and a laugh, Papa slapped the reins again, causing the horses and the rig to move a little faster. "Then I'd better hurry before all the best candy is gone for the day," he laughed heartily, throwing his head back. "Because I really like those caramel candies Mr. Herring makes."

I gave an enthusiastic nod. "Me too, Papa. Me too."

<h1 style="text-align:center">12</h1>

<h2 style="text-align:center">My Heart Goes Out to All
The Poor and Downtrodden</h2>

After visiting Mr. Dossier's leather shop, Papa and I made a beeline for Shane's Confectionery store to sample some of Mr. Herring's latest creations. Stepping through the doors, we were set upon by the many delightful aromas. Sugar, butter, and chocolate wafted through the air, making my mouth water.

The white walls were lined with sky blue cabinets that reminded me of a robin's egg. Cream colored paint outlining the intricate scrollwork of the carved cabinets added interest to the display. Glass jars sat upon the glass display cases, allowing patrons to further admire the confectionary delights safely while they were kept out of reach of small children and grown-ups alike.

We ate our fill of samples, trying everything from chocolates with nuts to chocolate covered caramels. The two of us in a confectionary store was a serious undertaking and Mr. Herring half-jokingly suggested that we consider moving into the upstairs apartment and paying rent, for which Papa replied, "I will take it under advisement." We all laughed and tried another sample.

Shortly after sampling everything we could in all good conscience eat, we purchased enough caramels to keep us happy for a couple of weeks—which in our case would translate to exactly three days. Papa tucked the large box safely under his arm as we left, along with the samples we hadn't gobbled up yet. He placed the box next to the picnic basket before we drove away. The only thing left on our to-do list was to find a perfect spot to have our picnic lunch.

Passing by the wharf I noticed a new ship had come in. "Oh Papa, can we please stop a moment and watch the people coming off the ship?" I pleaded while flashing him a large smile.

Pulling the carriage to a stop not far from the immigration gate, we watched intently as people filed through the final inspection lines and out the gate to their new homeland. My heart went out to them and I was reminded, in vivid detail, of the day I was escorted from the ship on a stretcher and sent to the hospital. I had been so afraid that I would be rejected and sent back to Ireland, forced to live on the streets again, I could scarcely breathe as they carried me through the gates and loaded me onto a carriage Papa hired. The less fortunate who arrived ill and didn't have loving family to assist them were transported by rickety old carts that were fashioned with tarps wrapped around them to protect the general populace.

I noticed a few immigrants looking around, fear and bewilderment reflected in their gaunt, unwashed faces. There were many who arrived looking half-starved and bereft. They couldn't hide the expression of disillusionment at the sight of such a large city. The sheer size of the buildings with multitudes of people rushing past at such speeds, hurrying off to their important lives, was enough to befuddle any small-town folk. Why, the number of people to contend with alone was enough to cause someone from a small village to rethink their decision to move here. I still have those feelings of being overwhelmed by it all from time to time.

I heard loved ones calling out to their kin waiting just beyond the final barrier that stood between them and their freedom. I felt my heart beat a little faster and wondered how I could simply stay seated, doing nothing, while my own countrymen continued to suffer the indignities of society because of where they came from. They traveled such great distances to make a better life for themselves and their family, only to get to the American shores with two strikes against them and half-starved. It was all too much to bear.

I turned to leave when I noticed a woman gathering her meager belongings as she stepped forward, past the inspection line, with her two small children clinging to her skirts as if they were hanging on to

her for dear life. This was the final straw, the catalyst that propelled me forward into action. Her children were so thin and emaciated from the long journey across the ocean that I could no longer endure it. A pitiful look filled their eyes and their cheeks were so very hollow—as if they hadn't eaten a meal in more than a week. The look of fear and helplessness struck me so deeply that I found I could no longer sit idly by and do nothing.

"Oh Papa, we must do something to help her," I gasped, quickly climbing down from the carriage with our picnic basket clasped tightly in my hand.

Setting the brake, Papa tried to halt my progression, but I was too quick for him. "Lara, Lara, wait!" he called, trying to disentangle himself from the reins so he could follow me.

My eyes never leaving the woman's face, I called over my shoulder, "I have to do something, Papa. I must help the children!"

My heart crumbled as I drew nearer and saw the condition of her skirts, so thread barren and thin that it was a miracle they hadn't come apart in the children's bony hands.

Walking straight up to the lady, I smiled and asked, "May I be of assistance to you?" as she stood on the wharf looking up and down the busy street. I could see the indecision in her eyes and added, "Yer children are lovely," certain that my Irish brogue and red hair would put her at ease. Her eyes lit up with recognition as I continued. "Please know I mean ye no disrespect, but my papa and I have eaten our fill of our lunch and wondered if ye and yer wee bairns would like the rest of it?"

I could see indecision cross her delicate features again and recognized the look of one who had suffered mistreatment at the hands of strangers. Setting the basket down in front of her, I lifted the top and pulled out a sandwich. It had been lovingly wrapped in a cloth napkin to keep it fresh. As I unwrapped the bundle of ham and cheese on bread, the children's eyes came alive. They could no longer hide their hunger and turned loose of their mother's skirt to each reach a spindly hand out and take half of the sandwich. Then, reaching into the basket again, I pulled out a second sandwich for their mother and held it out to her as I stood up.

I could tell by their dress that they came from my homeland. "My name is Lara Flannigan Roscoe and this is my Papa, Zane Roscoe. Which county do ye hail from?"

The woman's eyes lit up with relief as she began to speak. "Forgive me, miss," she whispered, tears filling her eyes. "It's just, no one has spoken kind words to me or me bairns…" Her voice faltered and her lower lip quivered. Taking a deep breath, the woman tried to speak again, but she was overcome by emotion as she continued to hungrily stare at the sandwich in my hand.

"Please, ye must be so very hungry after such a long journey," I coaxed, offering up the bundle to her again.

Taking the sandwich cautiously from my hand, she took a tentative bite, savoring the taste while she slowly chewed. I heard her belly grumble loudly and remembered in great detail what it felt like to be so hungry. Unwanted memories flooded my mind and I had to push them aside. When I looked down at the children again, they were eyeing the opened basket.

I chuckled, then looked up at Papa standing behind me with a strange look on his face. He nodded and handed me the bag of our precious uneaten samples from Shane's Confectionery store. "I thought you could put these to good use," he said with a smile. Nodding my head in agreement, I took the bag from him, breaking the ribbon candy into three bite-size pieces and handing them each one.

"My name be Eliza McBride," the woman finally said, "and this is me son, Timothy and me daughter, Sarah.

My heart swelled and I reached into the basket again, pulling out two hard boiled eggs that had already been peeled. I watched as Sarah and Timothy's eyes lit up.

"I noticed you looking around. Do ye have family meeting you?" I questioned, as I stood back up.

"I received a letter from me husband. He be a-workin' in a shipyard. He sent passage for us," she replied while pulling out a letter, still in

its envelope, from her pocket and handing it to me. "But I don' know where to find him."

"He's probably still working," exclaimed Papa. "They don't release the workers from the shipyard until dusk," he explained, pulling a pocket watch from his pocket and checking the time. "May we give you a lift to your residence?"

"Ye've already gone out of yer way. I would no' be any more troublin' ye," Eliza insisted.

"No trouble at all," I spoke up. "Right, Papa?"

"No trouble at all," he smiled, already reaching down to retrieve the woman's bundle of clothes wrapped inside of a blanket and tied with a rope.

"And here is the address on the envelope," I said, showing Papa.

Looking slightly embarrassed, Eliza tried to take the pitiful bundle of rags from Papa's hands. But he simply smiled graciously and gestured towards the carriage parked just a hundred feet away on the street. I helped the children climb into the back of the carriage, then climbed up next to them as we settled in for the ride. Mrs. McBride looked nervous as if she had never ridden in a carriage before.

I hummed Irish tunes to the children and fed them another piece of candy as we rode forty minutes out of our way to deliver the McBride family to their destination. Waving goodbye to our new friends, I snuggled up next to Papa as we drove home. My heart felt full as we rode together in silence for a few miles.

"Tell me, my beautiful daughter, what made you pick them out of everyone else who was getting off that ship?" he asked, giving my shoulders a tight squeeze.

"I'm not sure, Papa. Maybe it was the forlorn look in Mrs. McBride's eyes. I remember feeling that way once upon a time."

"Forlorn is it?" he questioned with a genuine smile. "Could that be one of your new words?" Papa teased, trying to lighten the mood.

Elbowing him in the side, I laughed. "Oh Papa, why do you tease me so?"

Pulling me closer, he kissed my forehead. "Did I tell you how proud I am of you? You have a very kind heart, Lara, my dear," he declared with a grin.

"Thank you, Papa. I think you're pretty special too," I bantered playfully, giving him another gentle elbow to his rib.

"Are you hungry?" he asked as he heard my stomach grumble loudly.

"Starving!" I answered dramatically.

With a flip of the reins, he made the horses trot just a little faster. "Wonderful. I know the perfect place to eat. It will be our little secret."

"My lips are sealed," I replied, locking my lips with an imaginary key and tossing it from the carriage. "I really love spending the day with you, Papa."

"And I love spending the day with you, too, Lara my girl," he said, flashing me a proud look.

Pulling into the carriage shop an hour and half later, we both felt a difference in our relationship. We had turned a corner and forged a new bond, one that had become somehow stronger that day by our shared experience.

I stood off to the side looking out of the window as Papa finished up some paperwork when Roman walked into the office. He and Papa were discussing one of the carriages Roman had been working on when memories of Da came to me as I watched the two men talking. I wondered if he'd survived the terrible famine that took so many lives back home and if he ever thought of me. Would he be proud of me like my new papa was?

Papa and I didn't eat much that night because we were still full from the late lunch we'd consumed. Yet that didn't dampen the lively conversation that evening as we discussed our day and everything we'd done. I was working up the courage to broach a topic that touched a chord deep within my heart. Ever since meeting Mrs. McBride and her children earlier, my mind had been turning over and over trying to come up with a way I could help others less fortunate than myself.

"Mother, Papa, I was wondering if I could talk to you about something," I began tentatively.

"Of course, Lara, anything," Mother replied, putting down her piece of buttered bread to give me her full attention. "I was wondering how long it was going to take you to bring up the matter plaguing your mind this evening."

A shy laugh escaped my lips as I began. "I was wondering if it would be alright with you if I did something for the people coming to our country," I began. Then, taking a deep breath, quickly continued, "So many of them looked half-starved today and it bothered me."

"Well, that depends," Papa interjected.

"Depends on what, Papa?"

"Well, Lara, it all depends on what you have in mind to do," Mother answered for him.

"I want to feed them," I said, hurrying through my explanation before they could stop me. "I was thinking I could serve them some bread, cheese, and maybe a dried piece of meat as they disembark the ship. You know, like a sandwich. Kind of like a first meal. So many of them are hungry and haven't had a decent meal for days, maybe even weeks." Then, shaking my head, I moaned, "Perhaps it's a stupid idea," unsure it would even be possible to do.

"And how do you intend to fund this little venture of yours?" Papa inquired.

"Well, I was thinking that over as well and I think I know of a way," I began slowly. "I thought that maybe I could petition business owners, much like yourselves, well-to-do, of course, who wouldn't mind giving back to their community by donating a little something to the cause to help those who are less fortunate," I rambled. "Then I can find out when the ships are due in and maybe Mrs. Burnett, our cook, who is a wonderful cook, by the way, could teach me how to bake bread. I could prepare everything the day before so that it would be ready when people get off the ships," I hurried to explain until Papa stopped me by holding up his hand.

"But what about your studies?" he asked calmly.

"I promise not to neglect them," I assured him. "And I will work twice as hard as anyone else. I swear it!" I added quickly, then crossed my heart.

Mother and Papa both looked at each other as if they were pondering the matter over for a moment before they both smiled broadly. Turning to me they simultaneously said, "It's a marvelous idea."

"I for one think this is a most worthy cause, Lara," Papa added as he puffed out his chest proudly. "How can we help?" he asked, nodding towards Mother.

"Yes, how can we help you?" Mother chimed in.

I clapped my hands excitedly together. "We can make a list of people you both know. And then Mother, perhaps you could accompany me when I ask for a donation."

"Of course. Why, I would never let you go by yourself," she said, "you are far too young."

With an understanding smile, I continued, "Papa, you are very good with numbers and bookkeeping," I noted. "Perhaps you can teach me how it is all done. That way, if anyone should ask, everything will be properly accounted for, and we can kill two birds with one stone. I will learn accounting skills and mathematics as well."

"Oh, isn't this wonderful? We have a family project together," Mother said gleefully. "This is going to be so much fun."

"I will go along with it, just as long as your studies don't suffer," Papa stated emphatically.

"I agree with Papa," Mother said, nodding her head and looking serious when Papa looked at her, then grinning at me from ear to ear the moment Papa turned his back to her.

Jumping up from my chair, I rushed around the table to give them both a great big hug. "You have made me so happy," I squealed.

"And we could not be prouder of you, Lara," cried Mother as they both squeezed me tightly between them.

"I am the luckiest girl in the world."

Papa held me and Mother at arm's length. "No, Lara, we are the lucky ones," he proclaimed, tears shimmering in his eyes. "We have been, since the day we found you. You have blessed our lives."

"Oh, Papa," I cried, and my heart swelled. "I love you both."

13

The Magical Age of Sixteen
And a Debutante is Born

I was a girl on a mission, collecting money and donations from prominent business owners throughout Philadelphia. I named my charity *Laura's Helping Hands* after Mama; I often felt her hand still guiding my life. I even created a motto for my organization, *We feed the needy, lifting them up, one hand at a time.*

I also started a coat drive, asking people to donate gently used coats for children and adults of all ages. We distributed them among the poorer neighborhoods. I had a volunteer force of six people, not including myself or my parents. I was finally feeling good about who I was because I finally had a purpose: I was fulfilling the promise I'd made to Mama.

I'd turned sixteen, and the debutante season was upon us. Much like the European courts of London, the season began in April and went through June. The wealthier families of Philadelphia would gather for lavish balls thrown in honor of the young women of eligible marrying age to introduce them into society. Eligible young men of good breeding were invited to peruse the young ladies being introduced and take their pick.

Of course, this tradition did not sit well with me and I had a lot to say about the barbaric custom—young ladies vying for the same eligible bachelor and trying to outdo each other with lavish dresses and hair designs, fancy bobbles and combs and such. I preferred a much more civilized approach to courting and made sure my parents

knew my opinion on the matter. I assured them both that I would be perfectly happy sitting this season out, skipping it all together, but Mother wouldn't hear of it. So, I did the next best thing and chose to wear a simple dress that wouldn't draw too much attention to myself.

Oh, Mother tried her best, parading lavish dresses before me for weeks. Some were very intricately designed, mostly white gowns with hand beading. It was apparently the trend that season, yet I chose a dress that I'd fallen in love with the moment I set my eyes on it. And it was definitely not white, but instead a most magnificent shade of blue. It reminded me of the ocean off the coast of my native land, and instead of making my red hair look garish, it highlighted it to perfection and complimented my green eyes. The design was simplistic, made of refined silk with capped sleeves, a scooped neckline, and a fitted bodice. The entire dress flowed gracefully as I walked and it made me feel like a princess when I wore it. Mother ordered long white gloves that reached beyond my elbows and dainty little slippers with a small heel commissioned from a cobbler she knew well. They were dyed to match my gown to perfection.

The fact that I got my way with the dress was the only thing that made the entire ordeal bearable.

The time for the debutante ball quickly approached and everything was ready. I slipped out of the house and across the street to visit Father in his office so I could escape the fuss of all the final preparations taking place in our home. We would be hosting the evening's festivities and I felt as if I were in the way every time the staff turned around.

Even the noise of pounding hammers against steel and anvils could not make me turn back. I ducked past Roman Blackthorn, careful to keep my head down. He was speaking to Mr. Oliver about a carriage they were working on when he noticed me and gave me a nod. I returned his acknowledgment with a shy but slight smile as I rushed past him and marched up the steps with purpose.

I recognized the smell of cigar smoke before I'd reached the top landing. One of the two men standing in the doorway saying their farewells to Papa was a prominent business owner I knew well. I beamed my brightest smile when he turned around.

"So, we will see you in a week with the final specs for your new design, Zane," Mr. Taylor was saying to Papa when he noticed me. "I was hoping I would run into you before we left," his voice boomed as he smiled broadly at me, pulling a wallet from his front coat pocket.

"Mr. Taylor, it is always a pleasure to see you, sir. How is your lovely wife, Hannah?" I smoothly asked as he opened his wallet.

"She is in very good health, Lara, thank you for inquiring. I was going to stop by the house to deliver my donation for your charitable foundation personally, but you have saved me the trip," he added, popping his cigar back into his mouth and squinting his eyes as cigar smoke wafted into them. Then, placing a stack of money into the palm of my hands with a chuckle, he patted the side of my arm.

"Mr. Taylor, this is a very generous contribution to the cause, sir. Thank you so very much and I promise to put it to good use," I assured him.

"I have no doubt that you will, my dear. You keep up the good work. Your efforts have not gone unnoticed by the community," he proclaimed.

Not to be outdone by Mr. Taylor, the other gentleman also opened up his wallet and pulled out a signed script. Then, placing it on top of the stack of bills in my hand so that the dollar amount would not be missed, he proclaimed, "This is a small donation to tide you over. I will be sure to send a proper amount over to you on Monday morning."

"Thank you, sir! You have no idea what this means to me and those it will help," I said, trying not to cough from the amount of cigar smoke floating into my nose and eyes as he stood close to me.

"Well, my girl, I have heard of the fine work you have been doing in the community and it is entirely my pleasure. You just come back and see old Uncle Owen when you need more," he said boastfully, making sure his voice carried as far as possible. "You wouldn't know this my girl, but your father and I go way back. Isn't that right, Zane?" he insisted, slapping Papa on the back.

Papa laughed and winked at me. "That's right, Owen. All the way back to when we were both still wearing dresses and drawers."

"Oh, don't remind me, old man," Owen chuckled, slapping Papa on the back again. "I am Owen Reed, dear girl, and that makes us family. Your father has boasted about you to me for over a year now," he added, taking my hand in his. "Your father sings your praises every time he can." His gregarious voice boomed as he cupped my hand with both of his. "Remarkable, Zane, just remarkable."

"Thank you for your generous contribution, both of you. I don't know what to say," I sighed, smiling up at him and Mr. Taylor.

"Just say you will keep doing good things with the money. The world needs more people willing to help," Mr. Reed said with a wink.

"Yes, of course I will, Mr. Reed, and with wonderful philanthropic-minded gentlemen such as yourselves, how could I not?" I answered back with a wink of my own, flashing them both another large smile.

"Call me Uncle Owen, dear girl. I insist. Your father and I are like brothers," he explained. "Why, your papa and I grew up in each other's homes. We were inseparable as boys. Isn't that right, Zane?

"That is the truth of it."

"See there, darling, that makes us family, and I would do anything for family."

Uncomfortable with the instant familiarity, I tested out Mr. Reed's new title. "Of course, Uncle…Owen," I replied.

"Well, we will see you both this evening," Papa asserted, walking the men to the stairs then watching as they walked down the steps. "You are quite the little entrepreneur," he blurted out as he walked back into the office to find me standing by the window looking out. "Shouldn't you be home getting ready for the ball?"

"I have time," I absently answered over my shoulder, placing the large sum of money in his hand. "Would you mind adding this to the account, Papa? Besides, if I hadn't been here, those two very generous gentlemen may not have been so generous. I think they did it to impress you."

Shaking his head, Papa chuckled. "They really are good men and you should be home getting ready. I'm sure Mother is looking for you as we speak," he admonished, peering out the window towards

our house. "See, there's your mother right now, and she appears to be frantically searching for someone," he concluded, turning to give me a stern look. "There will be many eligible young men attending tonight. Don't you want to look your best?"

Quickly peering out the window towards the house before turning my attention back to him, I whined, "Oh, Papa, must I?" while wrinkling up my nose at him.

Placing both hands on either side of my head, he pulled me towards him and gently placed a kiss upon my forehead. "It means the world to your Mother," he persisted, walking me to the door before giving me a slight push in the right direction. He raised his hand, waving the bills around in the air. "I'll just put this money in the safe. Then I will enter the amount in the ledgers before I join you and Mother at home. Now run along, before your mother has both our heads on a pike."

"Yes, Papa," I obediently replied as I reluctantly walked down the stairs. "But don't be long," I called back up to him as I made my way to the landing.

"I won't," he yelled back, "I promise."

That evening the house vibrated with activity and excitement as the festivities were getting underway. The other young debutantes waited upstairs, cloistered away with me in the parlor. The house began to fill with guests who gathered downstairs, awaiting the magical hour of nine o'clock to chime on the grandfather clock, at which time the young ladies would be announced one by one.

The girls reminded me of a gaggle of geese as they excitedly chattered amongst themselves, barely making sense as they preened and giggled mindlessly. I was content to watch them from the corner, observing their movements and facial expressions, which all seemed quite foreign to me as their lips moved but nothing of real substance seemed to emit from them. Then a young woman strolled up to me and sat down. Her dark chestnut hair glowed in the candlelight as her deep brown eyes seemed to be looking straight into my soul. She had

a sober constitution compared to the rest of the young ladies and I felt an immediate kinship to her when she introduced herself to me.

"Hello, my name is Eloise—Eloise Blackthorn—but my friends and family simply call me Ella," she added, reaching her right hand out to me.

It took me a minute to gather myself and I stared at her outstretched hand before I took a hold of it, then replied, "I'm Lara—"

"I know who you are," she interrupted. "My brother told me you were pretty, but he neglected to say just how beautiful you actually were."

Taken aback by her forwardness, I was left speechless by her bluntness. Retrieving my hand quickly from her, I replied, "You're Roman's, I mean, Mr. Blackthorn's sister? The young man who is apprenticing for my Pap...I mean Father?" I corrected myself as I stammered.

Smiling broadly, Ella showed off a row of brilliantly white teeth. "Yes, Roman is my brother. He is leaving for University in a few days, so technically, after tomorrow he will no longer be apprenticing for your father. I think you and I are going to be best friends," she quipped. "You're nothing like I expected and certainly nothing like the others," she added quickly, looking over her shoulder before turning her attention back to me.

"The others?" I questioned.

Turning, I looked at the girls gathered in their respective circles, enthusiastically talking as if they were in their own little worlds. Each of the three circles was directed by an individual who kept them engaged, like a bunch of chickens pecking at the ground. "No, I am definitely not like them," I answered, scrunching my face up in horror at the thought of it. "They are too self-involved."

"Definitely not like you," Ella smiled, wrinkling up her nose. "That's why I know we are going to be good friends. I don't subscribe to that kind of circus side-show either," she laughed. "I like your dress. It isn't like anyone else's."

Looking around again as if seeing everyone for the first time, I realized Ella was right. My dress was definitely very different from anyone else's. First off, it wasn't white, blush, or pale pink. Nor was it puffed out with a large hooped skirt and dozens of petticoats to make it stand out around me by two feet. My dress was simplistic and sported only three petticoats to give it enough 'swoosh' to sway without showing off the outline of my legs. I found that too much volume was difficult to sit down in and annoyed me when I walked. The smooth, silky material felt rich to the touch when my fingers brushed the surface, and I liked that its deep, lustrous blue called to mind the rolling waves of the Irish Sea.

With a whimsical smile, I pursed my lips together and looked back at Ella. "I suppose that makes me an outcast too and the reason why the other girls haven't bothered to talk to me, even though they are in my home."

Drawing even closer to me as if she were about to tell me a secret, Ella giggled when she turned to look at the other girls again. "They aren't talking to you because you are the prettiest one here and they are terribly jealous," she concluded. "See how they keep looking over here every so often?"

Taking a closer look now, I leaned forward so our heads were very close together. "You know, I can't say that I really paid much attention before, but now that you mention it, I do see what you are saying." I quietly added, "It is very strange of them. Wouldn't you say?" I pointed out a particular group of young ladies in the middle of the floor. "Especially that group."

"That would be Mary Rogers. She has been after my brother since the day she could walk. Oh, and that young lady next to her, with the blond hair, is her best friend, Mariam Kinney. Mariam's father is a doctor. A very good one from what I've heard. Then there is Jenny, Trisha, Jaclyn, and Charlotte." Ella pointed them out one by one. "I would watch my back with that group of ladies. They can be particularly ruthless," she said with a shudder.

"What makes you say that?" I asked, giving her a curious look.

Ella gave Mary Rogers a distasteful look as the young woman turned back to her hen circle. The slight went unnoticed by everyone but me. "Once, Justina Smith had the audacity to smile at my brother," she explained. "Then she committed the unthinkable."

"The unthinkable?" I questioned.

"Justina spoke to Roman at a social event we all attended and the very next day there was a vicious rumor floating around polite society that Justina and Samuel Moore had done something inappropriate together in the library."

I gasped. "Oh, how dreadful."

"Oh, it was awful and I dare say, I would not repeat a word of that dreadful rumor because not one word of it was true," Ella said, gripping my arm. "But it didn't matter because it was too late to salvage Justina's reputation by then. She was ruined. Justina was sent away to school and her family was disinvited to social events and eventually had to move away, I'm guessing from the shame of it all."

"Oh," I gasped again, then turned to look at Mary Rogers' group where she stood in the middle of her little close-knit circle, seeming to be giving detailed instruction to the girls of who they were to associate with and who they were not. "How awful!" I exclaimed, bringing my eyes back to Ella's. "Was anyone ever punished for doing such a despicable thing?"

"No," she answered sadly, as if it was just the way things were handled then. "And even though a few people knew the entire truth of it, Mary's father made a large contribution to an organization that was popular at the time, as if, somehow, that made up for his daughter's spiteful behavior. A month later, the entire matter was swept under the rug, so to speak, and everyone went on with their lives. That is, everyone but the Smiths," Ella concluded with disgust.

"Well that is just wrong," I snapped. "I could never be friends with someone like that!"

Ella shrugged and took a deep breath. "It is very naive of you to believe that you or I could make a difference when someone chooses

to commit a traitorous act against another. It is just the way of the world," she lamented, "and there is nothing you or I can do about it."

"People like that get away with such terrible behavior because no one is willing to stand up and confront them," I added with a sigh of anger.

"Ladies, ladies, may I have your attention, please!" Mrs. Lyons said loudly, clearing her throat and clapping her hands together to get our attention. "We are ready to begin."

"Let the three-ring circus begin," Ella whispered sarcastically. "Lions over here, leopards and tigers over there," she spoke out, "and who could forget the clowns." She pointed towards Mary Rogers' group and loudly blurted, "Someone queue up the clowns," drawing the attention of everyone in the room. Then she smiled broadly, giving me an auspicious look before winking as she stood up, pulling me to my feet and squeezing my hand reassuringly. "Watch your back or you just might find a knife sticking out of it come the morning," she chuckled. "Mark my words."

I squeezed her hand in response as we stood together at the back of the room. "Very sound advice, my friend. And I think you were right, we are going to be the best of friends."

"I'm glad Roman didn't tell me just how beautiful you really are before I met you. Because I might have disliked you on principle, without giving you a chance," Ella quipped before leaving my side to take her place at the front of the line.

The young ladies were lined up alphabetically by last names, but for some reason, I was put at the back of the line, behind the Williams' sisters, Candice and Margaret. The dance cards had been filled out earlier as young men lined up to write their names on the cards of the young ladies they desired to meet and dance with. If a young lady's card was filled up by the time a young man reached the front of a line, the man was encouraged to move on to their next choice. Now that all of the debutantes were lined up at the top of the staircase, their names were announced one by one as the young ladies descended and received their own personal dance card.

I could see everything that was happening from my vantage point at the top landing. Men and women mingled as the debutantes searched through the lines of their dance cards that were now tied to their wrists, looking for the names of the most eligible young men of society. Some of the ladies that went down before me seemed excited as they saw who had signed their cards. Some ladies didn't hide their disappointment well at all, and still others could have played poker with the best of them. Then my name was announced and I walked down the stairs and was greeted by Papa, who smiled and tied my dance card to my wrist.

"I hope you have a lovely time," he said, patting the top of my hand as he wrapped it around his arm. "I just need to borrow you for a moment. The newspaper man I've been telling you about is here this evening and has requested a moment of your time. The truth is, he asked me to pick out the most fetching young woman in attendance this evening, and I told him that I knew the perfect candidate," he teased, giving me a wry grin.

My cheeks flushed red and I laughed. "Oh, Papa, you really need to stop teasing me."

"Why? Because I tell the truth?"

"No. Because I'm getting too old to be teased."

"You will never be too old for me to tease, of that I am sure. You will always be my little girl," he added somberly.

Zane Roscoe stood up a little taller that evening with pride as he marched me over to Edward Harper, the newspaperman, and his photographer. Edward Harper was a slight man with thin, narrow features and very large spectacles that sat midway down his nose.

"This must be the lovely Miss Lara Roscoe I've been hearing so much about," he stated jovially as he walked up and took my hand, giving it a gentle shake. "There has been a lot of talk about you and your charity benefiting the immigrants," he continued when he saw the skeptical look on my face.

Shaking his hand, I graciously smiled. "Then there has been much ado made over nothing," I suggested.

Making a sound in the back of his throat that said I was wrong, Edward Harper was quick to point out, "I've been trying to get past your father for months now so that we could tell the world about your extraordinary story—a young lady adopted by one of Philadelphia's wealthiest families."

Then he dramatically held up his hands, making a frame of me in the air as if he were painting me into a picture, hoping that I would grasp his vision and get excited by all the fuss he was making over me. Then, giving me his most engaging smile, Mr. Harper continued. "Once orphaned and abandoned, forced to live on the mean streets of Ireland as a child, a girl comes to America and starts a non-profit charitable organization to feed immigrants from her homeland," he blurted out.

"Sir, please," I admonished, looking around to see that no one was staring at us. "May I remind you that we are at a respectable event? I do not wish to be a spectacle nor do I wish to draw unwanted attention to myself. This evening isn't about me! It is about all these lovely young ladies who are being introduced into society," I reminded him, sweeping my hand towards the others. "They too have come of age, just like me. I am merely one of many young women here tonight. So, I am going to have to insist that we make this evening about them as well—"

"But, but—" he began to stammer, cutting me off.

"Papa, I think the young ladies would all enjoy seeing their picture in the newspaper," I stated emphatically, then turned to glare at Mr. Harper. "And if you are not going to involve them as well, Mr. Harper, then I believe we are finished here," I concluded, turning to leave.

Taking my hand before I could escape, Papa attempted to smooth things over. "You heard my daughter, Mr. Harper, this evening is also about the other young ladies."

"But, sir, we had an agreement—" Edward began to argue when Papa cut him off by holding up his hand.

"I believe my daughter Lara has made her wishes very clear. She does not wish to discuss the matter of her charity work this evening.

That does not, of course, mean that she wouldn't be willing to sit down with you at a later date and tell you about her organization. After all, good publicity can only help bring attention to your organization, my dear," he added pointedly, looking at me before turning back to Mr. Harper. "It just means that she feels this evening is about the young ladies of Philadelphia and not herself alone. An admirable quality, wouldn't you say, Mr. Harper?"

Forcing a smile to his lips, Mr. Harper knew when he was beat. "Yes, of course," he relented. "Might I ask for a moment more of your time and indulgence, Miss Roscoe. I would like to take one picture of you and your father before I gather everyone else for a group shot."

I hesitated a moment before giving into Mr. Harper's reasonable request. After all, I could see Papa's point of view and knew it meant a lot to him that we take a picture together. "Of course. It would be my pleasure. And I apologize if we got off on the wrong foot, Mr. Harper. It's just that I don't wish to, well, you know, stand out. You understand, don't you?"

"Of course, Miss Roscoe, and you are right. I should have been a little more sensitive to your feelings. Perhaps another time. For the organization's sake, of course," he added, trying to sound happy even though I could tell he was disappointed by my answer. Sweeping his hand in a wide arc, he pointed to the spot he wanted us to stand. "Might I get you both to stand over here?"

Papa nodded. "We would be happy to."

"Thank you again for your understanding," I said, knowing in my heart that I would never sit down with Mr. Harper to discuss my personal story. The emotional aspect of what happened to me in Ireland was still too raw and my story wasn't something I wished to have plastered on the front page of the newspaper for the world to gossip about. Nor did I wish to be the subject of pity by women and men pointing and regarding me as that poor little orphaned child rescued by the Roscoes. Oh no, I thought to myself, when I sat down with Mr. Harper to discuss my story, I would insist that the subject matter be strictly centered around my organization and nothing else.

The rest of the evening went by like a blur, with one dance partner blending into the next. My card had been filled with eligible young men, themselves curious about the young orphan girl from Ireland adopted by the Roscoes. I smiled politely and avoided answering their intrusive questions by distracting them with questions of my own.

Ella Blackthorn proved herself worthy of the title 'best friend' when she swooped in and rescued me from a particularly unsavory young man. She taught me a very valuable lesson that day. It was the art of avoidance. She knew I was definitely out of my depth when it came to him. She had glanced at my dance card and knew exactly when I would need saving.

Just as this young man was joining me for his assigned waltz, Ella walked up and took me by the hand, distracting him with her dazzling smile. "If you will excuse us for a moment," she demanded without any real sign of remorse, much to the young man's chagrin. "This may take a while, so let me apologize to you beforehand," she blurted out. "Oh, and you may want to look for someone whose dance card isn't full at the moment. I think I saw Jenny Baker was available," she called over her shoulder as she whisked me away to the refreshment table.

Turning to me, she whispered, "You're welcome, by the way."

"For what?" I inquired, leery of her motives at first.

"Billy Daily is intolerable," she sighed, then raised a delicate eyebrow. "He will rest his hand inappropriately low, if you know what I mean. Not to mention the fact that he is a terrible dancer." Looking down at my feet, she added, "He will step all over your toes and mark up your pretty slippers." Shaking her delicate head, causing rich chestnut curls to bounce about her face, she made a sound of disgust deep in her throat. "His parents truly wasted their money on dance lessons."

Pulling her to a stop, I forced her to look at me. "Thank you, Ella."

"For what?" she asked.

Wrapping my arms around her and pulling her near, I whispered, "For being my friend."

"Don't be silly," Ella added with a wink, "we girls with something more than fluff between our ears really have to stick together. Then, perking up suddenly, she smiled. "Oh. Hi Roman. I didn't realize you would be in attendance this evening. Save me a dance?"

Tweaking his sister on the cheek, he playfully replied, "Anything for my favorite sister."

"I'm your only sister, you dunderhead."

"Is that any way to speak to the one person who will save you from these simpletons?"

I turned quickly to find azure colored eyes intently studying me. "I didn't see you here earlier," I remarked tentatively.

"I've only just arrived and hope that I'm not too late to commandeer a spot or two on your dance card, Miss Roscoe," Roman entreated sweetly.

Pushing me towards her brother, Ella slipped the dance card easily from my wrist. "She is free and at your disposal for the evening, Roman," she declared with a wide grin.

"But what of the others—" I began to argue.

"You leave them to me," she insisted, pulling a spare dance card and pencil from her sleeve as she began to write Roman's name in several slots. "I will take care of any disgruntled gentlemen."

"But don't you have obligations yourself?"

"Why do you think I came prepared with several extra dance cards?" she laughed as she brandished her secret pencil at me. "Just have fun you two."

Allowing Roman to lead me onto the dance floor, we blended into the crowd, ignoring the dirty looks from Billy Daily and his partner, Mary Rogers, as they waltzed past us.

"I truly hope my good name is not besmirched come the morning," I murmured when I saw the look Mary was giving me.

"What was that?" Roman questioned.

With a shake of my head, I uttered, "It doesn't matter. So, I hear you are off to University soon."

"Yes, that's correct," he answered, gazing down at me with a strange look in his eyes. "You look very grown up in that dress," he added pensively.

A nervous laugh escaped my lips before I answered. "Thank you, but I don't feel any more grown up than I did yesterday."

"That color truly brings out the green of your eyes. I guess I never really looked at them closely before."

Feeling suddenly shy, I felt the color flush my cheeks and wanted to change the focus of our conversation away from me. "How long will you be away to University?"

With a knowing smile as if he understood my discomfort, Roman cleared his throat before answering. "A year, maybe longer. It really all depends."

"What does it all depend on?" I questioned.

"On how quickly I learn everything I need to learn," he chuckled. "I hope I won't be gone any longer than necessary."

"Why is that?" I asked curiously.

"Because there are definitely some excellent opportunities here that I have not yet explored," he whispered.

Somehow, I felt he was talking about something other than business opportunities.

14

MARCH 15, 1851
TWO YEARS LATER

A Teacher and Her School:
Making a Difference

Ella Blackthorn and I became inseparable in the months and years that passed. We took many of our lessons together, learning Latin, mathematics, history, English, French, and especially how to be a proper young lady.

We loved to give our tutors fits by outsmarting them whenever possible, correcting their words and generally challenging their teaching efforts. Yet, in the end, we studied hard and buoyed one another up when one of us was feeling low.

I had heard of a woman by the name of Sarah Worthington King Peter who'd established an industrial art school in her home. She was helping women without the means of support learn how to take care of themselves by teaching them a trade. I was curious, and so I arranged for us to attend one of her classes.

Papa hired a driver to take Ella and me out to Third and Spruce Streets where Sarah conducted her art classes. She had converted one of the spare rooms on the third floor of her home into a studio. Upon arriving, we were ushered into the brightly lit room on the upper level and we introduced ourselves to Sarah. She then turned and introduced us to each of her students in attendance.

Emily Sartain was a young woman who looked to be in her early twenties. She wore her hair pulled back into a tight knot at the back of her head. She gave us the briefest of smiles, which didn't quite reach

her eyes, before quickly glancing away. Her sober brown eyes seemed to immediately hood over as she shut us out of her private little world. Emily withdrew into herself as if we were no longer there, and my heart went out to her.

Jessie Wilcox Smith was a woman who seemed to be in her middle twenties. A thick, blond braid circled her head and her deep blue eyes looked up shyly before quickly darting away as she went back to working on her wood carving project.

Alice Barber Stephens was a heavier-set woman with pleasant, round rosy cheeks who appeared to be a little older than the others, perhaps in her early thirties. She glanced up from her carpet weaving to smile, showing off darkly stained teeth from years of tea drinking.

Elizabeth Shippen Green was a bone-thin woman, with raven hair, which she wore twisted atop her head. Little curly wisps escaped the hairpins, causing her to nervously fidget with the hairs as she brushed them back into place. Darkened circles ringed her dark, midnight colored eyes, making her look older, but I guessed she was probably a bit over twenty.

Finally, Sarah introduced us to Alice Neel, a petite woman less than four and a half feet tall with auburn hair and sweet amber eyes. Her complexion was pale, almost white in color. Her eyes dodged between us and I could tell she had lived a hard life which took away any youthful glow she might have had at one time. I tried to determine her true age but found it impossible to do.

My heart went out to each of these women, somehow pushed aside by society as if they no longer mattered. Yet I could tell by the warmth with which Sarah spoke of each, that in her eyes these women did matter, each and every one of them. Sarah Worthington King Peter had made it her mission to make sure that each one of them felt remembered in some small way.

At four o'clock the class came to an end, and one by one the ladies filed past us, smiling and thanking Sarah for the time she devoted to them. Then they each donned hats and coats and left. Ella sat quietly next to me and I could tell she had been profoundly moved by the women. When they had left, she stood and removed a hanky from

her beaded bag. Then, walking over to the window, I joined her as we watched the women hug, pair off, and walk home in different directions.

Mrs. Potts, Sarah's housekeeper, came in with a tray of tea and freshly baked shortbread. "Please, won't you both join me?" Sarah gestured to the loveseat directly in front of her.

"Of course. It would be our pleasure," I answered, leaving my friend who was still standing at the window quietly blowing her nose.

"It feels like I have something in my eye," Ella exclaimed. "I won't be but a moment. Where is your washroom?" she asked, turning towards the open doorway.

Sympathetically, Sarah gave a knowing smile before she said, "Mrs. Potts will be happy to show you the way. Thank you, Mrs. Potts."

Nodding in acknowledgment, Mrs. Potts led the way out of the room and down the hallway.

"Sarah, tell me a little about yourself and how you started this school of yours? How did you know you wanted to make it available to these particular women?" I asked, trying to fill the awkward silence while learning something about my hostess.

"Well," she began, "I was born on May 10, 1800, in Chillicothe, Ohio. My father was Thomas Worthington, an Ohio Senator. I married my first husband, Edward King, the son of the New York Senator, Rufus King, in 1816 and we moved to Cincinnati, Ohio in 1831. We had two sons before my husband died in 1836." Sarah paused while pouring out the tea when she heard me gasp.

"I am so sorry to hear of your loss," I expressed sympathetically.

"Oh, you are a dear, but my story is far from over," she assured me. "I believe that sometimes tragedy strikes to make us appreciate what we have when the turbulent waters of life are calm," Sarah mused, then continued to pour out the tea. "I also believe that when we tell of our sadness, healing can take place. Cream and sugar?" she inquired.

"Yes, please," I replied, still pondering her profound words.

Handing me a cup of tea after stirring it for me, she continued. "Now, where was I? Oh, yes. After Edward's death, I moved to— Miss Blackthorn, feeling better?" Sarah inquired when Ella entered the room.

With a shy smile, Ella answered, "Yes, thank you. I think I got the eyelash out of my eye," and took a seat next to me.

With an understanding look, Sarah poured Ella some tea and asked, "Cream and sugar?"

"Just sugar, please."

Handing the cup to Ella, Sarah continued. "I was just telling Miss Roscoe—"

"Oh, please, do call me Lara," I blurted out.

With a gracious smile, she replied, "Of course, and please, you must call me Sarah. My entire name is quite a mouthful," she insisted, to which we chuckled a bit. "After Edward's death, I moved to Cambridge, Massachusetts to be closer to my boys, who were attending Harvard University. After they graduated I decided to settle here in Philadelphia, where I met my second husband, William Peter. He is the British consul to the city. I've always been politically minded," she said, passing around a plate of shortbread cookies, "because of who my father was, I suppose. I felt it such a waste to squander the opportunities I was given, so I started this school. I've always loved art and felt it was my duty to help others less fortunate than myself. By combining my love of art with my desire to be useful, I established The School of Design for Women. My goal is to teach women without a means of supporting themselves a trade so that they may lift themselves up as well as the next generation of women," Sarah concluded.

I wanted to stand up and give her a standing ovation. In my eyes, she was amazing. "That is an incredible story and you should be pinned with a medal," I gushed.

"Oh, no, my dear. I do what I do out of a sense of duty and love. I do not want recognition or glory," she insisted, shaking her head. "If just one person stands up with the desire to make a difference, and

that person inspires the next person to do the same, and so on and so on, can you even imagine what that future would look like?" Sarah's entire countenance lit up.

"I'm sold," Ella chimed in, passing her teacup back, ready for a refill.

"That makes two of us. Where do I sign up?" I queried, placing my cup down on the tray Sarah held out to me.

Pouring three more cups of tea, Sarah paused and looked up. "I hear you have already been helping. What is the name of your charity again? Helping Hands? Angel—"

"Laurel's Helping Hands, after my mother, who passed away when I was just a girl," I explained. "And if there is ever a time that you need our help in any way, Ella and I would be happy to help or assist you with your program. I hope you know you can call on us. We are willing and able to help. I want you to consider us friends to your cause."

"Yes, we would love to help," Ella blurted out enthusiastically.

Looking genuinely touched, Sarah smiled. "You are extraordinary young ladies in your own right, and you are to be commended for your valiant efforts."

Ella quickly answered, "Oh, we don't do it for the recognition, Mrs. Peter, I mean, Sarah. We simply wish to be of use."

"I understand," Sarah replied, reaching the tray back towards us with full cups of tea, "I am just so very honored to know the two of you."

"And we are honored to have the privilege of knowing you, Sarah Worthington King Peter," I replied, tipping my cup of tea to her.

Ella and I spent a pleasant hour and a half talking of social matters and politics, knowing we had met a kindred soul and that we were in the presence of a truly great woman.

15

The Great Exhibit of All Nations

Papa had heard whisperings for over a year and a half of preparations being made for an extraordinary first-ever event happening in Europe. He learned that it was to be billed as The Great Exhibition of the Works of Industry of All Nations, and that it would draw people from all over the world to display unique and innovative products that furthered the industry of their country.

Recognizing this once in a lifetime opportunity, Papa determined to press forward with new designs for his carriages, incorporating features that would make them ride smoother, accommodate more people, and provide more comfort in inclement weather. Some of the design features were made so that the everyday family could afford a carriage, while others were tailored to appeal to the wealthiest of society.

We had all looked forward to making the journey, but Papa was especially excited for his carriages to be part of *The Great Exhibit.* He couldn't wait to see all the other modern innovations and to converse with the great minds from around the world.

The voyage across the Atlantic had felt endless. Weeks at sea left me restless, pacing the narrow length of our cabin until I thought I might lose my wits entirely. Papa insisted we were fortunate—our two-room quarters were larger than most, yet they were still cramped and airless compared to home. The only relief came when the captain allowed passengers on deck. I would walk back and forth, no more than a few hundred feet, before turning again, the horizon stretching

endlessly on all sides. Each morning, I marked the days in my little journal, counting down until London.

When at last the ship anchored on English shores, my heart leapt. Even through the fog of travel weariness, the very air smelled different—coal smoke and damp stone mingled with the scent of budding spring. We rode through the streets of London in a hired cab, my face pressed eagerly to the window. Every corner seemed alive with motion: hansom cabs rattling across cobbles, ladies in silks strolling with parasols, and children hawking papers with cries that echoed through the smoky air.

But nothing—nothing—could have prepared me for the Crystal Palace.

From afar, it appeared as a glittering mirage rising out of Hyde Park, its vast glass walls catching the sun and transforming it into a thousand dazzling shards. As we drew closer, I craned my neck until it ached, trying to take in the sheer enormity of it. The structure seemed to stretch on forever, a palace spun of glass and light. My breath caught. "It looks as though it could touch the sky," I whispered, though whether to myself or to Mother I scarcely knew.

At the grand entrance, a painted placard announced in bold letters:

The Great Exhibition of the Works of Industry of All Nations

The Crystal Palace

Designed by Joseph Paxton

Completed in Nine Months

Beneath it, smaller writing boasted the dimensions—"1,851 feet in length, 128 feet in height"—numbers that staggered me as much as the building itself. Papa, with scholarly enthusiasm, pointed out how the cast iron frame supported the sea of glass panes, but I hardly listened. All I could think was how the sunlight poured straight through the walls and ceiling so that the entire place seemed lit from heaven itself. Inside, trees rose up toward the vaulted roof, their green

branches framed in glass, as though nature itself had been captured and displayed.

Crowds pressed around us the moment we stepped inside—ladies in bright silks, gentlemen with polished canes, tradesmen in plain coats—people from every walk of life surged shoulder to shoulder, their voices blending into a constant hum of anticipation. The air was warm with the mingling of perfumes, pipe smoke, and the faint tang of oil from some nearby machine.

"Papa, look!" I tugged at his sleeve as a group of children squealed at a set of whirring gears that powered a cotton spinner. The contraption clicked and whirred, drawing threads into neat spools. A placard announced its origins, but Papa needed no help explaining. "All the way from Manchester," he declared to no one in particular, his chest puffed out with pride for his nation's industry. "You see, Lara, this is how cotton becomes yarn—every revolution of those wheels draws the threads tighter."

Nearby, a tall gentleman with a German accent was explaining to his companion how the Trophy Telescope worked. I lingered, listening, my eyes widening as he described its lens—"eleven inches in aperture, sixteen-foot focal length." Though the numbers meant little to me, the reverence in his voice stirred my curiosity.

Everywhere I turned, something new captured my attention and fueled my imagination. A diamond, so large it glittered like frozen starlight, lay encased in glass. I leaned close enough to see my reflection sparkle back. A sign named it the Koh-i-Noor—"Mountain of Light"—and whispered tales from onlookers told how it had come from India itself.

Not all marvels shone with jewels. One placard boasted of "Mr. George Jennings' Retiring Rooms," and the laughter of two boys told me why. "He charges a penny!" one exclaimed, still clutching his coin. Mother pursed her lips, scandalized at the thought of paying to use a lavatory, while Papa only chuckled.

Yet, even amidst all this splendor, Papa's gaze kept straying to his own exhibit. He had spared no expense to bring three carriages across the sea, each polished to a shine that reflected the glassy glow of the

hall. He smoothed his hands over the lacquered wood, his eyes alight as he spoke to anyone who would pause long enough to listen.

The Landau stood first, its padded leather seats facing one another invitingly. Papa explained how it was built for society folk who wished to converse while riding through the park. He pointed out the folding hood that could be drawn up in bad weather. His tone grew almost reverent as he described the new undercarriage springs—the fruit of three years' labor—that promised passengers a smoother ride than any they had known before.

Beside it stood the Surrey, doorless but sturdy, its rigid top gleaming beneath the hall's light. I watched a pair of ladies run gloved hands over the fine leather stitching, nodding in admiration. Papa's eyes gleamed. "Hand-crafted," he told them proudly.

Last was the Trap, nimble and light, the sort of carriage that an ordinary family might afford. "Popular with the masses," Papa explained, patting the seat affectionately, as if it were a faithful horse. I thought of how different these carriages were, yet each bore the mark of his skill.

As we stood admiring, the crowd ahead thickened. Murmurs swept through the hall like a sudden breeze. I followed the turning of heads and saw the reason: a ripple of movement, the slow advance of guards in scarlet. At their center walked a small woman whose presence seemed to command the entire space.

"Mother," I whispered, my heart leaping, "it's the Queen."

Queen Victoria moved with a poise that belied her height, her pink gown billowing with each step, a blue sash gleaming across her chest. Behind her trailed several ladies and three children, their slippers and bows immaculate. The crowd parted reverently as she approached, smiles and curtsies blooming like flowers in her wake.

To my astonishment, she stopped directly before our booth.

"Mr. Roscoe," she said, her voice crisp and clear even over the hum of the crowd, "I have heard of your carriages."

Papa bowed deeply, his voice uncharacteristically hushed. "Your Majesty does me great honor. May I present my wife, Charity, and our daughter, Lara."

Mother curtsied so low I feared she might topple over as she tugged me down beside her. My knees trembled as I lifted my gaze to meet the Queen's. Her brown eyes burned with intelligence and something warmer—curiosity, perhaps.

"That shade of blue suits you, my dear," she said to me suddenly, her lips curving into the faintest smile. "Always wear it."

Heat flooded my cheeks. Somehow, I found the courage to reply, "Thank you, ma'am. And I was just thinking how your gown becomes you."

Gasps rippled from those nearest, but the Queen only laughed, a sound bright and unrestrained. "A cheeky one," she declared. And before I could quite comprehend it, she pressed a lace fan into my hand. "It grows warm in here. Share this with your mother, child."

My heart thundered. The fan trembled in my fingers as I stammered my thanks, hardly able to believe what had just happened.

The Queen turned her attention back to Papa, and I drifted into a daze, catching only fragments of his practiced speech about springs and undercarriages. It mattered little. All I could think was that the Queen of England had spoken to me—*to me!*—and left her fan in my keeping.

That day blurred after her departure, though I remember the ribbon Papa received with so much pride and triumph as he took first place for his designs. I remember wandering among telescopes and telegraphs, among machines that whirred and hummed with promise. But most of all, I remember the feeling that lingered in my chest long after the crowds dispersed and the doors of the Crystal Palace closed.

We stood, all of us—every nation gathered under glass—on the edge of something vast and new. The world was changing, rushing forward on wheels and gears and light. And I, Lara Roscoe, had been there to see the beginning of it.

16

Shall We Dance?

Mother and I had returned from the Great World Fair in Europe without Papa only two days before. He'd stayed behind to oversee the exhibition and address the many carriage orders he'd received as a result of the exhibit. At least that was his excuse for sending us ahead. I believe he wanted to stay and converse with other forward-thinking men of his generation; it seemed to excite Papa and fill his mind with possibilities.

Upon our arrival home, we discovered several invitations to Independence Day parties sitting on the entry table. Independence Day was widely celebrated in Philadelphia and there were some who began preparations a year in advance for the special day of celebration.

I was surprised to find three letters waiting for me when I returned and took them to my room to read. All three were from Ella Blackthorn, keeping me abreast of what had been going on while I was away. Mariam Kinney had suddenly become engaged to Edward Clark, of the shipping industry Clarks, and Jenny Baker was sent abroad to England for school quite suddenly. "At least that is the story that was circulating," Ella added in the letter she wrote to me. Charlotte Wade was sent to live with an aunt in Iowa and Trisha and Jaclyn were no longer associating with Mary Rogers for some strange reason.

Apparently, everyone was gossiping about the matter, having their own idea of what happened, but no one really knew what had truly taken place to cause all of these young ladies to suddenly disassociate with one another. And the people directly involved with any incident had been sent away. That is, except for Mary Rogers.

"It is all very salacious," she stated in her letter. Ella was like having my own personal newspaper reporter, filling me in on all the pertinent issues upon my return. Her last letter was dated just five days prior and said that she had a surprise for me when I arrived home and hoped that I arrived in time to attend the Independence Day party at the Rogers' home. I thought it an odd statement to make since we, or that was, Ella and myself, had made a pact not to associate with Mary Rogers. But it seemed that the Rogers' party was not to be missed.

Quickly running down the stairs, I found the mail and various invitations still laying on the entry table. Mother hadn't felt the urgency to reply to any of them yet, so I took the liberty. Quickly, I weeded through the envelopes until I came across the one I was searching for, with a large gold embossed 'R' on the front of the envelope. Tearing the flap open, I removed the gold embossed lettered card and read: *Your family is cordially invited to attend the Annual Independence Day Soiree at the Rogers' home on July 4*th*, from 6 p.m. until midnight. Come dance, eat, and be entertained. Many exciting surprises await you. Please R.S.V.P. before July 1*st*.*

Taking out pen and paper from the writing desk in the sunroom, I wrote our acceptance note and apologized for the late reply, explaining that we had only just returned home from Europe the night before. Then I crossed my fingers that Mother would happily go along with me on this one and that my note of apology would be sufficient. Dispatching one of the houseboys immediately, I gave him an extra coin so that he could stop by the bakery on his way home and purchase a treat for himself if he waited for a reply.

I rubbed my hands together as I watched the young man tear out of the kitchen door. I truly loved it when a plan came together, and if Ella insisted that I had to attend the Rogers' party, then by golly, I was going to be there. I was not yet sure what Ella had up her sleeve or even what her endgame was, but if Ella thought it important, I was not going to let her down. Besides, I was fairly certain that there would be some fun to be had at the festivities.

First, I would take Mother her tea and toast so that I could tell her of the wonderful party we were going to attend that evening, then I

would pick out a dress. There was no way on God's green earth that mother would say *no* to a party.

"No! Absolutely not!" she contested. "We are not attending the Rogers' Soiree," Mother unequivocally stated, putting her foot down.

"But Mother," I whined, "I've already sent a reply accepting their kind invitation. And besides, everyone who is anyone is going to be there tonight. Ella, I mean, Eloise Blackthorn, swore to me that it would be fun. Come on, Mother, please," I begged, with a contrite expression.

"I can't stand that woman!" she blurted out.

"Who, Mrs. Rogers?" I asked, trying to sound disconcerted, already knowing full well that mother couldn't stand Audrey Rogers. "Don't you tell me that we need to be charitable in our hearts towards everyone? Why, that attitude of yours doesn't seem very charitable at all to me," I countered.

"Lara Ann, don't you go using my own words against me," Mother scolded, shoving another bite of toast into her mouth and chewing it as if she wanted to take my head off instead. "You know full well that this is a different matter altogether!"

"Why Mother? Is it because Mrs. Rogers has always been sweet on Papa?" I chided. "He won't even be there, so there is nothing to be concerned about." I turned the tables on her to make my point. And sure, it was devious, despicable, and duplicitous of me to do so, but I really wanted to find out why Ella wanted me to attend that party. "The two of you were friends once, Mother. Couldn't you be the bigger person and take pity on Audrey Rogers? After all, look who she is married to."

Letting loose with a large sigh, Mother looked at me over the rim of her tea cup as she sipped it. "I'm not going to win this one, am I?" she conceded.

Trying to keep the smugness from my expression, I shook my head.

"No, I'm afraid not."

"Fine, on one condition," Mother interjected.

Smiling back at her because I knew that I had just won, I replied almost gleefully, "Anything, Mother."

"If I am not enjoying myself by the time they serve the food, we are coming home," she declared.

"Before the fireworks?"

"Before the fireworks!" Mother replied sternly.

Taking a deep breath then letting it out, I surrendered. "Fine," I glumly exclaimed, as we shook on it, which concluded our formal agreement. "But I am telling you right now, you are going to have fun."

"Don't count on it," Mother retorted, pouring more tea into her cup. "Will you send Maggie up? I think I will get dressed now."

"Of course, right away, Mother," I answered with my hand on the doorknob.

"Oh, and Mother?"

"Yes, dear."

"Thank you," I said softly.

With a smile, she replied, "You're welcome."

I thought the evening would never come as I readied myself for the party. The oppressive heat was beginning to lift as we arrived at the Rogers' home just after 6:30. I was dressed in a white, button-down blouse and a lightweight, navy blue skirt. Mother wore an all-white, lightweight cotton dress with a red sash tied around her perfectly slim waist.

We stood in the Rogers' welcoming line and I could hardly contain myself as I looked around for my friend and partner in crime. Finally, it was our turn to greet our host and hostess. Mother was polite and distant when she greeted her old friend Audrey Rogers and I could see how it hurt Mrs. Rogers by the look in her eyes. Mother barely acknowledged Audrey before moving on to Mr. Rogers and shaking his hand, saying a few polite words, then moving on.

I tried to make up for her slight by complementing Mrs. Rogers on her lovely dress. "You look quite stunning this evening, Mrs. Rogers. I do love your gown."

Perking up slightly, Audrey's dour expression changed. "Thank you, my dear. That is very kind of you," she added. "And might I say that you look very comfortable. Maybe I should follow suit and change. This gown is far too warm for a day like today."

"Thank you for your generous invitation. It really was a very nice surprise upon our return home to find it waiting for us," I explained.

"I heard that Mr. Roscoe took first place for his carriage design," she continued pleasantly. "Please give your father my most heartfelt congratulations when he returns."

"I will be sure to do that, Mrs. Rogers," I answered, shaking her hand as I moved down the line to her husband. "Mr. Rogers," I cheerily greeted while placing my hand into his outstretched hand. "It truly is a pleasure to meet you."

"And you as well. Miss Roscoe," he replied. "I was happy to hear of your father's success across the waters in Britain."

"Your acknowledgment is most appreciated, Mr. Rogers, and thank you for opening up your lovely home to my mother and myself."

"The pleasure is all mine. I hope you both will have a lovely time," he added, "and if you don't, I want to hear about it."

I smiled and moved on when I heard Mr. Rogers lean over to his wife as I walked away and say, "now that is a lovely young woman," as if he were trying to make a point about something.

Spotting Mother talking to the Wrights, I turned to my left and made my way out to the backyard where I saw young men and women dancing around a bonfire. The orchestra was playing something lively as I searched the crowd for my friend Ella. Retrieving a glass of cold lemonade from the refreshment table, I took a seat to wait for Ella, knowing that my good friend considered it *gauche* to be anything but one hour late to any event. She called herself *fashionably* late to everything.

The smoke from the bonfire tickled my nose as I tapped my toes to the tempo of the music. I was becoming hypnotized by the rhythm of the song they were playing in conjunction with the flames as they shot up into the evening sky.

Then suddenly I was startled back to reality when a pair of delicate fingers wrapped themselves around my eyes. "Guess who?" Ella called out excitedly, turning loose of me almost immediately.

With a start, I leaned over so that I didn't spill lemonade on my dress. "Ella," I squealed like a young girl, rising from my seat and turning around to face her, only to come face to face with Roman, who stood directly behind his sister with a smirk on his handsome lips. His confident air stopped me short as piercing eyes bore into me.

"You remember my brother, Roman?" Ella said smoothly when she saw the smile suddenly fade from my lips.

"Yes, of course. Mr. Blackthorn, how have you been?" I asked, extending my hand to him.

Looking down at my outstretched hand a moment as if he were somehow offended by the formality, Roman clasped my hand with both of his hands in a familiar way. "Miss Roscoe, what a pleasure it is to see you again. Please, let us not stand on formality. You have called me Roman before."

"Yes, thank you, Mr.—"

"Roman," he interjected, sweeping his hand towards the chairs in front of us. "How is your Father?"

Ella took the seat I'd been saving for her as Roman pulled a chair over closer to me.

"He is well. Thank you for asking," I finished, unhinged by his sudden and unexpected appearance. "However, he is still in Britain, at the fair, showing off his new carriage designs."

Pulling a chair even closer so that he could face me now, Roman continued to engage me. "I heard he won accolades for his new undercarriage design. Good for him."

"Yes, Papa was very honored by the recognition."

"I will have to stop in and congratulate him when he returns," Roman replied, still staring at me intently.

"I'm sure he would like that. What about you?" I began trying to draw the attention away from myself. "Tell me what you have been doing with yourself since we last parted."

"I'm going to get some refreshments. I won't be a moment," Ella informed us as she quickly jumped up, then looked over her shoulder at me with a large grin on her face before she rushed off.

Roman looked up at his sister suspiciously. "Now, what do you suppose that was all about?"

"I think your sister is playing matchmaker," I said very matter of factly.

"So, you caught on to her as well?"

Shaking my head, I chuckled, "How could I have possibly missed it?"

We both laughed and suddenly I didn't know what else to say.

"Would you like to dance?" Roman asked, gesturing towards the people dancing around the bonfire.

"I'd love to," I replied, placing my hand into his, allowing him to pull me from my comfortable chair and lead us down to the edge of the bonfire. It was then that I caught Ella watching us from the refreshment table as we began to waltz.

Looking down at me, Roman smiled, then turned us around, deftly guiding us through the steps. "You are very good," he complimented, his tone taking on a husky, deep quality.

Looking up, I noticed his expression was somehow different than the last time I'd seen him—more intense as he continued to study my face. "Thank you," I replied, feeling self-conscious.

"So Ella tells me that the charity you started before I left for school is going well," he said after a long pause. I could tell he was searching for things to talk about. "Helping Hands—"

"Laurel's Helping Hands," I corrected. "It's named after my mama, who died when I was very young." Then I added. "And yes, we have

been able to make progress in helping the less fortunate, although the needs are so much more than what we can meet."

"One doesn't usually see that kind of commitment from young ladies of a certain—"

"Breeding? Decorum?" I countered.

Smiling patiently, he continued, "I was going to say *echelon* of society, but have it your way," he interjected with another brilliant smile, showing off his white teeth.

"I think we established long ago that I am nothing like the other young ladies of Philadelphia society. My life took a different path than theirs," I confessed, confidently looking up into his probing eyes.

"I think I would like to hear your story sometime," Roman said, holding me a little tighter as he spun me around the bonfire again. "I have the feeling that it would be a very interesting tale."

Feeling my stomach do a little flip, I bit nervously at my bottom lip as I looked around for a way out of this conversation. "There really isn't much to tell," I insisted, suddenly avoiding direct eye contact with him.

"Perhaps someday you will deem me worthy of hearing it."

"Truly, it is not that interesting a story at all," I persisted, praying that the band would stop playing and I could make a polite excuse to flee his hold. And yet, another part of me wanted to keep dancing with him the whole night through. The way his blue eyes bore into me, I felt like he already knew my entire story, including all of the sordid details that I'd never revealed to anyone before.

"Forgive me, Miss Roscoe—"

"Lara, please. I believe we have stepped beyond the boundaries of formality."

Moving us outward, towards the edge of the dancers, Roman pulled me with him as he continued to dance us to the rhythm of the music before coming to a stop away from the others. "Forgive me, Lara, if I have made you feel uncomfortable. It was not my intention. It's just that—"

Crackle! Crackle! Crackle! Pop! Snap! POP! Firecrackers sounded next to our feet, causing me to scream and jump into Roman's arms. A group of young men laughed out loud from behind a tree before running off. They had thrown a chain of lit firecrackers at our feet. My ears were now ringing and it took me a moment to fully realize what had happened.

"You're safe, I have you," Roman soothed, running a hand down my trembling arms while pulling me even closer to him. He continued to make little shushing noises while I buried my face into his chest. I heard him swear under his breath. I could tell that he was looking around for the culprits. "I have you, Lara. I won't let anything happen to you. Why, you're shaking like a leaf."

Slowly pulling away from him, I suddenly felt embarrassed by the entire incident and my reaction. Then I felt him smooth a stray hair from my face, tucking it gently behind my ear. "I will be fine," I shyly replied, forcing a stiff smile to my lips.

"You're still shaking. Let me get you something to—" he insisted, slipping an arm around my shoulders in an attempt to shelter me from further harm as he moved us towards the house.

Stepping away from his grasp, I turned. "That won't be necessary, really," I insisted as I interrupted him. "I'm fine now. Truly I am. The noise merely startled me," I quickly added. "Thank you for the dance. It was quite lovely." I smiled, then made my escape, deliberately walking away from Roman. I took off towards the garden, which was on the far side of the yard, then dashed into the carriage house before he had gathered his wits about him enough to follow me.

Holding tightly to my chest, I waited for my frantically beating heart to slow to a normal rhythm before I could take a proper breath. That's when I heard a strange noise coming from the far corner, near the stack of hay. The carriage room smelled of fresh hay and horse manure. A lit lantern hung from a post on the other side of the room. Stepping around several obstacles, I quietly made my way towards the noise that was becoming louder and more intense as I drew nearer. That is when I noticed someone in the parked carriage looming over the body of another person. The young woman was calling out the man's name over and over again in a raspy voice and I took her cries as from someone in need of help.

Rushing to the rescue, I picked up a pitchfork. "You there!" I shouted. "Unhand her or I will run you through!"

Two startled figures scrambled to cover themselves and the young woman screamed, "Stop!" throwing a hand up to shield herself. "Go away, please," she pleaded.

"Mary?" I gasped, quickly turning my back to them both. "I thought you were being attacked."

"I'm fine. Get out of here. Now!" she shouted, greatly perturbed by my interruption.

Turning back around, I grabbed the lantern from the post and held it in front of me. "If you are fine, why were you making those awful noises?" I questioned before it dawned on me what the two of them had been doing. "Mary!"

"Just leave me alone!" she shouted at me again.

"I am not leaving you here with that, that—" I stammered, searching for the right word to use as the frightened young man ran past me holding his pants up with one hand. "Mary Rogers, how could you?"

Haughtily stepping down from the carriage, she smoothed down her skirts and straightened her blouse while buttoning her top few buttons. "How could I?" she snorted indignantly. "How could you not know the difference between a woman being attacked and a woman in the throes of ecstasy?"

"If *that* is your definition of ecstasy—fumbling about with some young man in the back of a carriage, in your own family's carriage house—then perhaps you and I differ greatly," I snapped. "And let us not forget, that same young man cared so little for you—or your reputation—that he vanished rather than stay and defend your honor, Mary Rogers!" My voice cut like glass. "Have I overlooked anything? Because if I have, do enlighten me—"

"You are missing something all right, Miss Roscoe. You're missing the point. Because I really don't give the slightest care of what you

think of me. Oh, and if you tell anyone about this, I will destroy you," she hissed viciously.

"Me? You're going to destroy me?" I laughed, annoyed by her declaration of war. "Miss Rogers, I would look at where you are perched before you start slinging around more mud."

"I will just say that I found you in the carriage house with some young—"

I gasped out loud at her audacity just as a masculine voice came up behind me in the dark, interrupting Mary's venomous rant, "I dare say, I wouldn't finish that sentence if I were you, Miss Mary Rogers. I just saw a half-dressed Billy Daily beat it out of here as if his pants were on fire. Why, he nearly ran smack dab into me before I stepped out of his way. Can't say that the man who was behind me fared so well," Roman declared, stepping out of the shadows and into the light. Mary's father stood directly behind him with a very solemn glower on his face.

Her entire countenance melted and tears instantly sprang to her eyes as she began to convey to her father the convenient lie that never had the chance to leave her mouth. "Father—"

Throwing his hands up, Mr. Rogers bellowed, "Save it, Mary! I don't care to hear any more of your lies."

"But Daddy," Mary whined as she turned to me with eyes that said she wanted to put a knife in my back.

Reaching out, I pulled two pieces of hay from her disheveled hair as she passed by me. "You had some hay—" I weakly explained, as if removing them would somehow help her case.

The moment they were out of earshot, I turned to Roman and asked, "What do you think will happen to her?"

He smiled, "Something that should have happened a long time ago, I suspect," he chuckled.

I slapped his arm. "Don't laugh at her."

Shocked, Roman tilted his head to one side. "Don't tell me you feel sorry for her."

"A little," I answered tentatively.

"She is a beast!" Roman stated emphatically.

"Perhaps you are right, but I still feel sorry for her," I mused with a sad smile on my lips as I looked up into his deep blue eyes that were searching mine. We could still hear Mary's pitiful pleading for leniency from her father.

"Come on, let's get out of here before people begin to talk about us," he insisted, taking my arm and leading me out of the carriage house. "Ella said she has a surprise for us."

"I love her surprises," I quipped. "What is it?"

"I don't know. She wouldn't tell me," he laughed.

"Then we'd better hurry."

17

The Fortune Teller Sees All

Mother was having a wonderful time at the party and had made amends with her old friend after Audrey apologized for wasting so many precious years fighting over nothing.

Ella had seen her opportunity to speak with Mother about taking me on an adventure, assuring her that we would be on our best behavior and that she and Roman would have me home no later than 12:30.

After receiving Mother's less than enthusiastic blessing, we were off. Climbing into the carriage with Roman's assistance, I attempted to pry information from Ella about where we were going, but she continued to remain tight-lipped about our final destination.

The rhythmic clip-clopping of the horses' hooves on the cobblestone street was relaxing to me. Yet after a few minutes, I noticed the sound had changed as we pulled off the main street onto a dirt road. I was becoming very curious about our destination while still trusting in Ella's good judgment as we ventured deeper into the darkened woods.

Suddenly, through the trees, I could see a large bonfire burning in a camp and the smell of cooked meats prepared over an open fire reminded me that I hadn't eaten yet. Sounds of music, singing, and people clapping drifted to us upon the sultry air.

"What have you gotten us into, Ella Blackthorn?" Roman questioned, sounding slightly skeptical in the darkness.

"Just be patient you two, we are nearly there," Ella assured us.

"I hope they are serving food because I am famished," I stated as I leaned forward to get a better look at our surroundings. "What is this place?"

"You'll see," Ella answered cryptically.

I could tell that we were near the banks of a canal, but I had never been in this part of town so I really didn't know where we were.

"This better not be one of your crazy, hair-brained-ideas, Ella Blackthorn, or I will tan your hide myself."

Giving her brother a death stare, Ella picked up the horsewhip. "I wouldn't try it if I were you. I've learned to use this thing since you've been gone."

Throwing his hands up, Roman conceded, "All right, all right, I take it back," he laughed.

Putting the whip back in its holder, satisfied that her point had been made, Ella added, "Don't you ever threaten to spank me again, Roman Alister Henry Blackthorn the III."

Relenting, Roman again conceded defeat. "All right, Eloise Helena Gray Blackthorn," he teased, giving me a stern look when I snickered. "But if you use my full name again in front of anyone else, I will not be responsible for the outcome."

Ella laughed and stuck out her hand. "Deal! Do you want me to tell you Lara's full name?" she said with a wicked grin, showing her rows of white teeth.

Looking at me with an equally wicked grin, Roman nodded his head. "Of course."

"Eloise Blackthorn, don't you dare—" I scolded as she blurted it out.

"Lara Ann Flannigan Roscoe," Ella giggled.

Watching me fold my arms across my chest as if I were mad, Roman turned to me and said, "What's wrong with that? It is a perfectly respectable name. Not like ours."

"And just what's wrong with our proper names?" Ella blurted out, sounding slightly frustrated by her brother's disparaging remark.

Roman turned back to his sister. "Well, for starters, they are pretentious and long. Why couldn't we have been named something a little more plain, like John and Betty Blackthorn or Ed and Suzy Blackthorn?" he countered with a perfectly straight face. This only lasted a few seconds before they both melted into a couple of giggling kids. It was in that moment that I realized just how normal the two of them were when they were together, and I suddenly missed my brothers and sisters.

We were all giggling like school kids when we pulled into the camp. "Ella, have you taken us to a gypsy encampment?" I blurted out louder than I intended.

The music ceased and heads turned to stare at us. Under her breath, Ella shushed me. She turned, calling out to a woman who appeared to be in charge. "Madam Sabina, what a pleasure it is to see you again."

Roman and I looked at each other and then he shrugged and smiled. "When in Rome," he quipped as he climbed down and turned to offer me his hand. Meanwhile, Ella was negotiating with the woman she called Madam Sabina just as the music began again, so I couldn't hear what they were discussing.

People whirled past us, dancing strangely, yet somehow it was fitting. Women twirled and clapped to the rhythm and men danced around them. Several smaller fires burned throughout the camp as food was being prepared. My mouth began to water when Ella and Madam Sabina rejoined Roman and myself.

"You'd like to try?" Sabina asked with a thick accent, gesturing to the dancers.

"No, no, I couldn't." I waved her off. "I wouldn't even know where to begin."

Taking hold of my arm, she guided me over to a young man. "Caspian, show her how to dance," she ordered, and just like that, the young man took my hand and placed me in the middle of the dancers.

"Is easy. Just watch," he said as he clapped to the rhythm and stomped his foot. "Now you try but go in other direction than me."

I copied what he had done. Caspian smiled broadly and threw his arms up in the air. "She is natural," he yelled, and everyone smiled encouragingly, pausing mid-step to yell, "Oompah!" at once before returning to their dancing.

Taking ahold of my waist, Caspian suddenly picked me up, spun me around, and placed me back down on the ground as part of the next steps of the dance. I tried to copy what the women were doing on either side of me and, before I knew it, I was dancing like the others and having fun. When the song finally ended, everyone threw their hands in the air and shouted "Oompah!" again.

Caspian returned me to my friends, who were sitting on makeshift chairs made from logs, eating. I sat between Ella and Madam Sabina wishing I had a plate of food when Caspian quickly returned with one. "For you," he proclaimed gallantly, his thick accent somehow suiting his dark features and foreign dress. "Dancing makes you hungry, no?"

Rubbing my stomach, I smiled, "Yes, I am very hungry. Thank you, Caspian. You are very kind." My gratitude caused his cheeks to tinge a slight shade of red as he turned to go. Then, quickly glancing over his shoulder one last time, Caspian resumed his previous task of preparing food for the others in the camp.

As Sabina spoke she shook her arms in the air. Her bracelets loudly jingled and clanked together, making the most marvelous noise. "He is good boy, my Caspian. Very strong!" She emphasized the word by bending her arm back and making a muscle as her eyes shone with pride. Then, with a lift of her chin, she directed our attention to twin girls who appeared to be around eighteen. "Lena and Neela are also mine. So pretty those two."

"They are lovely," Ella agreed.

"They must make you very proud," I added. "The way you look at them is the way my—" I began to say before thinking better of discussing something so personal in front of a complete stranger and my friends.

"When you are finished, we meet in my trailer," Madam Sabina insisted, her sharp eyes searching my face. "I will not take no for

answer. Come to trailer." She pointed out a brightly painted wagon that was her traveling home. "We talk where's quiet. You make sure she gets there, da?" she said, looking at Ella.

"Of course I will," Ella assured her.

I waited for Madam Sabina to walk away, out of earshot, before I confronted Ella. "Ella, what does Madam Sabina mean when she said, *we talk?*"

Ella shrugged her delicate shoulders, avoiding direct eye contact with me as she dug into her plate of food, pretending to suddenly be starving.

Meanwhile, Roman, who had been very quiet this entire time, decided to speak up. "Ella, is this one of your hair-brained-ideas I'm always warning you against?"

Ella looked up suddenly. "No!" she cried defensively. "It's just that Madam Sabina is marvelous and I wanted my best friend in the whole world to meet her, face to face. That's all!"

"Is that truly all there is to it or do you have something more sinister in mind? Like the time you dragged me along with you to that gathering at the Moore's and—"

"Don't be ridiculous, Roman!" Ella cut him off nervously, fidgeting with her plate before deciding she was no longer hungry, placing it upon the ground. "And I thought we agreed never to bring that matter up again."

"I believe you were the one who insisted I never bring it up again. I don't recall stating that I would never use it against you," Roman heartily laughed, which only threw fuel on the fire.

"Roman Alister Henry Blackthorn the III!" Ella raised her voice as the flames from the campfire reflected off her angry eyes.

"Yes, Miss Eloise Helena Gray, sassy pants, Blackthorn, what may I do for you?" he teased.

Clenching her fists by her side, Ella growled, "You are insufferable."

"Don't make me get a bucket of water and douse the two of you. Let's keep things civil, shall we," I interjected before placing my plate

next to hers on the ground, deciding that I had had my fill as well. "Well, let's go see what Madam Sabina wishes to talk about," I said with a sigh, getting to my feet and dusting off the back of my skirt.

"Really?" Ella jumped to her feet.

"Sure. You and Madam Sabina have piqued my curiosity," I exclaimed, eyeing the colorful trailer in question. "What harm can there be?" I added soberly.

Taking ahold of my arm, Ella lifted her chin to Roman. "Hum!" she sniffed. "Now that's the spirit," she cheerily said, practically skipping us both to the trailer's steps. "I've taken care of everything," Ella insisted, pushing me towards the door.

Nervously turning back around when I reached the door at the top of the steps, I questioned anxiously, "Aren't you coming in with me?"

"Don't be ridiculous, Lara, my dear. This is about *your* life's path, not mine," she announced, sounding very cryptic. "I will be right here waiting for you when you are finished." Ella pointed at the bottom step, then added, "Go on, she doesn't bite!"

I was about to change my mind when the door opened and Madam Sabina took ahold of my hand. "Come in, come in, my dear. I've been expecting you. I've been waiting a long time for your visit." She took my arm and dragged me through the doorway before shutting it behind us.

Skeptically looking around her little trailer, I asked, "What do you mean, you've been waiting for me? Ella surprised me just this evening with our visit. I had no idea that you existed before we drove into your camp."

"Oh, but I've known of you for a while, now," she announced very mysteriously. "I had the dream and knew that you would come to me one day. And here you are!"

I felt my stomach clench and suddenly I wanted to escape, but Madam Sabina was between me and the door. There was one way in and only one way out and that was through her. The smell of burnt sage and something else I couldn't put my finger on lingered in the air. Several lanterns hung on either side of the small round table in

the middle of the room, lighting the small space. A patchwork quilt covered the modest bed at the back of the trailer, and a small cabinet built into the framework had a mirror on the door, separating the two living spaces. The two wooden chairs were pulled out as if she had been expecting company.

"Don't worry. You will receive the answers you have been seeking," she insisted while gesturing to the chair on the other side of the table. "Please, sit. Let me guide you."

Not wanting to make a fuss, I obediently sat down in the chair and put my hands in my lap. "I don't really know what it is you think I am seeking."

"Oh, child, your eyes have been closed for too many years and you have been walking around in the fog for too long," Sabina said ominously while shuffling a very large deck of cards. The music drifted through the wooden walls of her trailer and shadows danced in the dark. I could feel my heart beating wildly in my chest as a finger chilled my skin.

"Clear your mind and take deep breath, letting it out slowly. You are like cornered mouse," she smiled reassuringly.

Sweeping back a stray piece of gray hair and tucking it behind her ear, she ordered, "Now, give me your hands," and placed the deck of cards in my hand. Then Sabina folded my free hand over the top of the deck. "Shuffle, then place the cards into three piles."

Obediently doing as I was told, I mixed the strange cards around on the table for a minute then split them into three separate piles. Sabina picked up the first pile, dealing out the first three cards, placing them close to her, and discarding the rest. Then she repeated the act with the next two piles but added one card to each line to form a pyramid. Madam Sabina studied them and inhaled deeply before speaking.

"Poor child," she lamented before clicking her tongue and shaking her head.

Growing concerned I fidgeted in my seat. "What?" I queried. "What do you see?"

Looking up at me, Sabina pointed to the first row of cards. "This is younger you. Now I can see why your friend insisted on bringing you to me," she said ominously. "You carry much pain with you."

Defensively bristling, I objected, "I do not!" I blurted out, sitting up a bit taller in my seat. "I have a lovely—" I began to say.

With a patient smile she continued, "Dear child, I speak of things in the past. This is the *Death* card. Someone close to you died when you were but a child. Am I right?" she asked, not waiting for confirmation but continuing as if she already knew the answer. "This alone would be enough to scar one's soul, but then you add the *Betrayer*," she announced, pointing to the next card, "and your world falls to pieces."

Opening then closing my mouth, unable to say anything, I stared blankly at the card she was referring to.

With a smile, Madam Sabina moved on to the last card. "This is good card. It is the *Savior* card. Meaning someone saved you from this cataclysm. Yes?" Noticing the tears forming in my eyes, Sabina reached over, taking my hand in hers. "This is the past, child, let it go. Prison can take many forms," she said wisely, patting the back of my hand, nodding her head. "This is why you come to Sabina. We fix this," she continued, letting go of my hand to pour over the cards again.

I stared at the cards before me again and wondered what ancient mysteries they held to be able to say so much about my life as they had. The pictures were all so strange and foreign to me. I remembered whispers of such things in my small village back home, but I was far too young to understand what people spoke of. Yet now, it all felt so strange and real at the same time.

Moving on to the next row, Madam Sabina ran her fingers over the tops of the cards without actually touching them as her many bracelets clanked together, making a tinkling sound. Her head slowly tilted back and I noticed that her eyes were closed, then suddenly her hand stopped and hovered over a particular card. It was of a court jester wearing a funny hat, dancing about with a dagger behind his back.

"Quickly, child, shuffle the deck and pick out just one card and hand it to me," Sabina demanded, sounding frantic.

I mixed up the deck again, gathered it together, and pulled a card from the middle, handing it to her. She placed it across the other cards then looked at me. *"The Six of Cups,"* she said under her breath, "hum."

"Well?" I asked briskly, "what does it mean?"

"Someone from your past will bring back happy memories but will also dredge up past pains—tread lightly, child—for he sits near the fool and will help you heal the past but it will be painful," she whispered. "Draw another card!"

Taking the card from the top, I turned it over and saw a large red heart with three swords running through it. My eyes flew up to hers and saw the concern there before she could cloak her eyes from me. "This is bad, isn't it?"

I could see that she was choosing her words carefully before answering. "The *Three of Swords* or *Lord of Sorrow*—"

"That sounds really bad," I blurted out.

"Upheaval will disrupt your life but it is necessary to make way for the good that is to come." Pointing to another card, depicting a queen sitting upon a throne with a large gold coin in her lap and a basket of coins sitting next to her, Sabina quickly said, *"The Queen of Pentacles,* this is for you.*"

"And that is good, right?"

"Yes. That is good. She is a practical woman, using her good fortunes to help others. This may save you in the end," Madam Sabina explained, forcing a smile to her lips.

"Well, is there anything else good you can tell me?" I questioned, feeling overwhelmed by everything.

Wickedly grinning, she pointed to another card. "The *Chariot* next to the *Lovers* card is good."

The *Chariot* card had a king driving a chariot pulled by two lions, and the *Lovers* card depicted an Adam and Eve figure with an angel hovering between them.

'This means that you will be saved by a very strong man—someone who has admired and loved you from afar for some time now. Love at first sight, perhaps?"

Lara pointed to another card depicting a young woman wearing white robes and a green garland around her waist and head, petting a tamed lion. "What does that card mean?"

Grinning widely, Sabina chuckled, "That card means that you won't truly need to be saved because you possess the strength inside of you to save yourself." Then, pointing to the card next to that one, she explained, "The *Five Wands* means an unavoidable irritation will occur, but you will have the strength and ability to leave it behind you." Clapping her hands together, making me jump, Sabina placed her hand upon another card in the last row. "The *Page of Wands*. Someone who is trustworthy, reliable, and desires to bring you happiness if you will let him. He will have light eyes."

"What is that one?" I asked, pointing to a card depicting a king sitting upon his throne, a sword in one hand and scales in the other. "What does that card mean?"

Patting my hand as it rested upon the table, she said reassuringly, "The *Judgment* card simply means that the Day of Judgment is coming and that you should be prepared." Then pulling all of the cards together in a pile, Madam Sabina decided that she had revealed enough of my future for one night. "I wish for you to consult not your fears, child, but look to your unfulfilled potentials. You will be a great woman someday. It is here in the cards. You simply have to get beyond yourself. Frustration and pain are a part of everyday life. You are not excluded on that account. We all experience such things. Look to the future. Believe in the possibilities and stop dwelling on the failures of others. Searching for that which is beautiful is its own reward."

"But I am afraid," I pitifully whined. "What if I'm not good enough? What if I make a mistake and choose wrong?"

Standing up to signal that we were done, Madam Sabina took my hand and pulled me to my feet. "Everyone has fears, child. The trick is to not be paralyzed by them. You are young. You will do the right thing if you get out of your own way," she added with a yawn. "But now it is time that you go."

Showing me to the door, she opened it and gave me a hug. "We will meet again, someday soon," Sabina said wistfully. "For now, you go. I am tired and must rest," she concluded, shutting the door suddenly.

"Well, how was it?" Ella rushed to me, taking hold of my hand and pulling me down the steps as I continued to stare at the closed door. "Did she tell you about your future husband or how many children you will have? Oh, I know, did she tell you that you and I would grow old together? Best friends and all," she continued to babble as we all walked back towards the bonfire in silence.

"I wish to go home, Ella."

Taking ahold of my arm, Ella seemed to understand my reticence to speak on the matter any further and yelled over to Roman, "We are leaving," then turned back to me. "You know this was all just for fun, right? You can't take anything too seriously."

"I'm fine, Ella. It's nothing," I admonished. "It was all a bunch of nonsense, anyway."

"Well at least tell me what she said, Lara," Ella complained, "after all, we are best friends."

Forcing a smile to my lips, I climbed up into the carriage with Roman's help. "To tell you the truth, I didn't understand half of the things she said to me," I said over my shoulder. "Something about a new romance and having the strength inside of me to get through anything that was coming my way. She said a bunch of stuff like that. She probably says the same thing to everyone." The lie easily fell from my lips.

Anxiously, Ella shuffled up into the carriage beside me. "She didn't say anything like that to me," she complained. "She said that I would be married and have six children and live in a big house and have a best friend by my side as I grow old," Ella added impishly. "I wonder why she didn't say anything like that to you."

"Are you all right, Lara?" Roman asked with concern as he climbed up into the carriage and sat beside me.

Sitting up even straighter I forced a stiff smile to my lips. "I'm great. Can we go home now?"

"Of course," he replied, slapping the reins against the horses' rumps and clicking his tongue. "Giddy up, boys, we're going home."

The music mingled with the crickets and frogs as we made our way back down the narrow dirt road in silence. We had gone several miles before Ella couldn't stand the silence any longer and began to babble on about someone or something. I really didn't pay much attention to what she was saying, but I nodded my head every so often and said, "uh huh," in hopes that she wouldn't notice my lack of attention.

That's when she stopped to gaze over at me with an expectant look on her face and said, "Are you listening to me?"

"Of course, I am. You said something about Mrs. Marston stopping by the other day."

"That's right," she interjected, then continued with her story as I drifted back to my own thoughts.

Madam Sabina's words kept turning over in my mind. *Someone from your past will bring back happy memories but will also dredge up past pains...tread lightly, child, for he sits near the fool and will help you heal the past and it will be painful.* Then there was her warning about *Upheaval will disrupt your life but it is necessary to make way for the good that is to come,* that had me somewhat concerned. What did it all mean?

Feigning interest again as if I were actually listening, I murmured, "Uh huh, that sounds lovely," to Ella as I nodded, absently smiling as the fireworks lit up the night sky near the wharf while we made our way home. My mind was being pulled back across the ocean to a faraway land, and I was pondering whom it might be from my past that would soon be crossing my path, dredging up old memories and

turning my life upside down. A violent shiver caused me to shake all over and I wrapped my arms around myself to stop it.

Pulling the carriage to a stop, Roman asked, "Are you alright, Lara?" as he pulled a blanket out from under the seat.

Waving him off, I answered, "I'm fine, Roman. Thank you for your concern. It was a momentary chill, nothing more," I assured him.

"It really is a shame to miss all of the fireworks," Ella murmured under her breath, sitting on the other side of me.

I reached up to gently touch Roman's arm. "She is right, you know. It would be a shame to miss all of the fireworks," I said, staring into the depths of his eyes as flashes of the fireworks from the night sky reflected in them.

With a wordless nod, Roman moved the carriage to a better spot on the side of the road and set the brake. "But I insist you take the blanket," he persisted, placing it over my lap despite my earlier objection. I turned to watch with awe as another rocket shot up into the night sky, exploding into a cascading waterfall of deep red and bright green sparkles, like the branches of a colorful willow tree.

The three of us had been sitting in silence watching the fireworks display for a few minutes when a group of rambunctious youth began shouting next to us, then ran past us disappearing down an alleyway. I watched after them, remembering the day two men had accosted me in an alley years before, and suddenly shivered violently.

"Perhaps we should get you home after all," Roman leaned over to whisper near my ear.

Forcing a smile, I shook my head. "You worry overly much for nothing." Placing a protective arm around my shoulder, he gave me a reassuring squeeze then let go. "As long as you are sure?"

Dragging my eyes away from his penetrating gaze, I tried to sound casual. "Stop fussing over me like an old woman, Roman Alister Henry Blackthorn the III, before I'm forced to change your name to Mother," I teased. This made him chuckle.

"Now that tears it," he growled, sternly trying to sound serious. "There was no call for using my full name." Ella and I giggled like a couple of school girls.

Then Ella leaned forward and said, "Would the two of you just start courting already and stop dancing around everything!" earning her a punch in the arm from her older sibling. "Ouch!"

"Sorry," he mused, grinning sardonically as he retaliated. "I had a muscle spasm."

Glaring at Roman before turning back to the fireworks display, Ella pursed her lips together, looking terribly put out. "Spasm, my foot!" she grumbled.

A few minutes later the bells rang out throughout the town, signaling the end of the festivities as ten rockets were fired into the air simultaneously. Some of the rockets sprayed upwards in streams of colors, others fell gracefully down like a fountain, and several more burst outwards like sunflowers opening themselves up to the sun, or in this case, the enormous full moon.

I wondered to myself, once again, just who it would be from my childhood that would be stepping back into my life after all of these years. I allowed happy memories of my childhood to drift across my mind, going back in my thoughts to a happy time when I was young and vulnerable. A shiver shook me again as I looked over at my two companions. Ella was engrossed with the fireworks, a permanent smile etched on her lips, while Roman continued to study me with a strange look in his eyes. I couldn't tell what he was thinking and it suddenly made me uneasy. *How long has he been staring at me?* I wondered as he reached down, pulling out a second carriage blanket and wrapping it around my shoulders.

"You really should have brought a shawl. The nights can cool off so quickly, you know," he said, slapping the reins and calling, "giddy up boys," as he clicked his tongue.

"Thank you," I replied, even though the goosebumps running up and down my arms at this point had nothing to do with the coolness of the night air.

18

Papa Comes Home

July rolled into August as the sweltering months continued, and before we knew it September had come and still there was no Papa. We'd received two letters over the past month while he'd been gone, yet it was the most recent letter that we received which had us both very concerned. It was short and to the point. The letter let us know to expect him home the middle of September. Mr. Grayson, Father's trusted employee, had arrived in Britain to take up the reigns of the new carriage shop Papa was opening. The letter further let us know that he was on his way home just as soon as he could take care of a few matters. In this short note, Papa mentioned that he had taken ill while in Europe and that he had lost a bit of weight.

This, of course, sent Mother into a complete tailspin and she did nothing but worry about him until the moment he stepped through the front door at 3:05 in the afternoon on September 15th.

Mother gasped when she saw him. His clothing hung from his bony frame like someone who had been starved half to death. "Zane Roscoe, you will march yourself straight up those stairs and go directly to bed while I send for Doctor Sheridan," Mother ordered, her voice shaking with emotion. "Martha, send Boone to fetch the doctor, straight away," she called out with exasperation before turning back to Papa.

Good-naturedly, Papa kissed her on the lips. "Charity, my love, stop fussing over me. I am fine. Just missing a home cooked meal, that's all. With your loving care I will be fit as a fiddle in no time," he assured her, putting his arms out to greet me.

I had been standing behind mother, shocked by Papa's appearance.

"There's my girl," he cried.

"Oh, Papa, you are a sight for sore eyes. I have surely missed you," I sobbed, launching myself into his thin, feeble arms. "We were so worried when we received your last letter. Can I help you up the stairs?" I asked, taking hold of his arm without waiting for him to reply.

Mother took his other arm and the three of us slowly made our way up the stairs as Boone raced past and out the back door, letting the screen slam shut with a bang.

Doctor Sheridan was a longtime friend and physician to the Roscoe family. In just a few minutes, we heard the front door open and hastening steps coming up the staircase. Wasting no time, he went right to Papa's bedside as we stepped out of the room.

I sat in a chair in the hallway watching Mother wear a hole in the carpet as she paced back and forth in front of Papa's door. She was wringing her hands together, barking out orders to any staff who had the misfortune of coming too near her.

It felt like an eternity before Doctor Sheridan emerged from Papa's room with a grave look on his face. Mother was on him the moment he shut the door. "Well? What's wrong with him, Hank?"

With great patience, Henry Sheridan forced a pleasant smile to his lips. I could tell he had unpleasant news and I felt sick to my stomach. "Let us leave the patient to rest and go downstairs so that we can talk," he insisted, taking mother by the arm as he led her away from Papa's door.

Naturally, I jumped up from my chair and followed them as we all made our way down the stairs. At one point, I thought Mother was going to faint when she grabbed the railing. "Charity, have you eaten today?" Doctor Sheridan asked with concern.

"No, she has not," I quickly answered, taking hold of mother's other arm to assist her down the stairs.

"You won't be helping Zane if you fall ill yourself," he explained.

"Martha, is the afternoon tea ready?" I called to the housekeeper who was standing at the foot of the staircase looking very concerned.

"Yes, ma'am. Will Mr. Roscoe be having some as well?" she asked, frowning when she saw Mother's frail appearance.

"I think we will let him sleep for now. Maybe when he awakens in an hour or so," the doctor answered briskly, leading mother toward the sunroom. "But Mrs. Roscoe requires sustenance, immediately, if you would be so kind, Martha."

Racing back to the kitchen, Martha called over her shoulder, "Of course, sir. I will bring a tray in shortly." Then grumbled under her breath, "I told her she should eat something."

Seating Mother on the couch, Doctor Sheridan sat next to her, taking out his pocket watch and flipping it open at the same time so that he could check Mother's pulse. Grasping her wrist, his movements were sheer precision as he concentrated on the second hand. Then, ever so gently, Doctor Sheridan laid Mother's hand back into her lap. "It would seem that you are overly stimulated, Charity. I need you to calm down and take several deep, slow breaths."

Mother bristled at the doctor's patronizing tone. "Hank, we have been friends since childhood. I need you to tell me what is wrong with my husband. And for the love of all that is holy, Hank, don't sugar-coat it!"

"Oh, here she is, right on time. Thank you, Martha," I suddenly blurted out the moment Martha stepped into the room. "You can leave the tray. I will pour out the tea today." Turning, and trying to distract Mother and Doctor Sheridan, I asked, "Doesn't everything look delicious?"

"Indeed," Sheridan concurred, reaching for a plate and placing several finger sandwiches on it before forcing the plate into Mother's hands. "Eat! Doctor's orders."

"Then you will tell me what is wrong with Zane?"

"When I feel you have eaten sufficiently and you are ready to hear what I have to say," he admonished, "I will be more than willing to tell you. Minus the sugar-coating, of course."

"Here, Mother, just the way you like your tea, strong and hot."

Tearing up, she turned to stare at me a moment before obediently taking the cup of tea from my hand. "Oh, Lara, what would I ever do without you?" she sobbed.

I flashed her an assuring smile. "Thankfully, you will never have to find out," I replied, sitting down next to her when I noticed Doctor Sheridan pouring out his own cup of tea.

"Doctor Sheridan, how long have you known my parents?" I asked, trying to make polite conversation, giving Mother a moment to compose herself.

"Oh, child, that is a complicated question," he began. "I've known your mother ever since I was a young boy. She was the prettiest girl you'd ever want to meet. Always so sweet and kind," he murmured. "She is the reason I never married."

Blushing, Mother almost choked on her cucumber sandwich. "Henry Sheridan, you stop telling my daughter such stories."

Looking slightly offended and put out, Henry chuckled and winked at me. "It's true you know," he insisted. "When we were thirteen years old, I swore to my best friend, Joe Burrows, that when I grew up, I was going to marry her or stay a bachelor for the rest of my life." He crossed his heart and smiled at me.

Completely captivated by his story, I asked, "Then what happened? Why didn't you two marry?" I continued looking between Mother and Doctor Sheridan.

"Zane Roscoe happened," he answered without any real ire. "Your father moved in across the street from your mother," he gestured with his head. "The rest is history."

"But why didn't you just marry another pretty girl?"

"No one could hold a candle to your mother," he lamented, taking a sip of his tea before chuckling.

"Hank, you stop filling her head with your nonsense," Mother scolded as she took a sip of her tea to cover up the fact that she was blushing profusely.

"Don't listen to her, Lara. Your mother knows that I'm telling the truth," he continued, putting his hand to the side of his mouth as if sharing a secret with me. "Everyone in school knew I had hung my hat on her long before Zane Roscoe ever came along. But once she laid eyes on that handsome man, Charity was smitten and was lost to me—"

"You are so full of hooey, Henry Sheridan, and you know it. We all knew that Tessa Mathers was so in love with you and you broke her heart by chasing after the one girl that was already spoken for. That is the real reason he never married," Mother interrupted, taking another bite of her cucumber sandwich and chewing it briskly.

Giving me another wink and a smile, Henry Sheridan took a deep breath and set his cup of tea aside. "Who are you going to believe, Lara—?"

"Of course, she is going to believe her mother, Hank. Lara is a level-headed girl and can spot a storyteller from across the room," she chided. "And when someone is as prone to storytelling as yourself—"

"You have your side of the story and I have mine—" he interrupted.

I held up my hands, to stop their banter. "Alright, alright, you two. I'm sorry I even asked the question in the first place," I conceded.

Suddenly looking quite serious, Doctor Sheridan cleared his throat and prepared to get down to business. "We shall have to agree to disagree, my dear, Charity," he concluded. "Now for the real reason I'm here. Zane is suffering from pneumonia, which is bad enough, but what has me concerned is his weight loss. It has affected his heart," he grimly informed us both.

Mother gasped and her eyes filled with tears as she covered her mouth with the back of her hand.

"I'm not saying that he's a goner, by any means, Charity. I just want you to be prepared for the worst while hoping and praying for the best," he said, giving mother a serious look.

"What can we do for him besides hope and pray, Doctor?" I inquired, taking Mother's cup and saucer from her shaking hands before she dropped it. Pouring out fresh tea, I placed the warmed cup between her icy fingers.

"I will send a nurse over to attend to Zane around the clock," he offered, still staring at Mother. "And before you tell me that you don't need a nurse," he countered, putting his hand up to stem off any objections by Mother as she opened her mouth, "I just need to say that Zane will be ill-served by you if you pass away from sheer exhaustion, Charity, my dear. You and I are not as young as we once were. You will need help, my friend," Doc Sheridan added sternly, placing a compassionate hand of friendship over Mother's when she looked down to stare at the fresh cup of tea in her hands.

Wiping away a few stray tears that trickled down her cheeks, Mother straightened her spine as if she were trying to buoy herself up. "You are a good friend, Hank. A very good friend and you are right, of course. Neither of us can do the things we used to do. Thank you for your help," she concluded, placing the fresh cup of tea down on the tray in front of her as she got to her feet. "Tell the young woman that I will expect her for dinner this evening, and I will have a room made up for her to stay in."

Doctor Sheridan cleared his throat and, following suit, he placed his teacup next to hers on the tray. "I have written some instructions down," he said, pulling a piece of paper from his inner coat pocket and handing it to Mother.

"Thank you for coming so quickly, and please don't think me rude, but I really must see to my husband."

Taking a step back, Doctor Sheridan turned to leave. "I will pop back around to check on you both later this evening, with the nurse, of course."

"Of course. And thank you again for coming so quickly, Hank," Mother said stiffly, then turned to leave, which I thought odd. "Lara, be a dear and show the good doctor out for me."

"Yes, of course, Mother," I answered, jumping to my feet to do as she had asked. "This way, Doctor."

Retrieving his hat, coat and medical bag, the doctor walked with me to the door. Then I ran all the way up the stairs to Papa's room. I stood there with my hand still on the doorknob, frozen in place for the longest time as I watched my parents speaking quietly, their heads together. The room smelled of disinfectant, mustard seed, and various herbs, which had been made up into a paste for Papa's chest. He was complaining that his chest burned, but Mother assured him that it only meant the medicine was working. The two of them sat quietly talking in hushed tones as Mother sat on the edge of the bed, holding his hand, stroking his forehead with her free hand. I felt like a peeper, standing there watching the intimate exchange between them. They were truly meant to be together, there was no doubt in my mind about that. You could see the love and respect they had for one another, even after so many years of marriage. I felt simply awestruck by the love that was reflected in their eyes. I took a step back, softly closing the door behind me.

19

Crossing Paths with My Past

Roman Blackthorn was called to the house and I was asked to join him in Papa's room once the two of them had spoken privately. Upon entering the room, Papa smiled, and the hollows of his cheeks hung loose. It was yet another reminder to me that he had once been a vital, vibrant man. The dark circles beneath his eyes looked almost purple today as if someone had punched him in the nose. I caught my breath and fought back tears as I turned to close the door, giving myself a moment to compose myself.

The scent of illness and herbs mingled together in the room caused the air to feel heavy and thick. I forced a smile to my lips as I turned to face Papa and Roman, who stood up the moment I entered the room. He remained standing, then stepped aside to give me the chair closest to Papa.

"You're looking better today, Papa," I lied. "Mother said you wanted to see me," I added, trying to sound cheery as I took the offered seat."

"You should go into politics, my dear. You lie so convincingly, I almost felt better for a moment, hearing such sweet words coming out of your mouth."

My laugh felt forced to my ears as I continued, "Oh Papa, don't talk like that. You know that believing in something is half the battle to achieving your goals. You taught me that."

He tried to laugh but then grabbed at his chest, doubling over as a coughing spasm racked his body. Placing a clean handkerchief in his hand, I waited for the coughing spell to pass before handing him a glass of water. "I'm glad to know you were actually…listening to me all…" he stammered and cleared his throat, "these years."

Taking the glass from his hand and placing it back on the nightstand, I cried, "Oh, Papa, I always listen to you when you speak. I may not always do as you ask, but I listen," I teased, then looked up at Roman. "So, why did you ask for me?"

Looking very serious now, Papa took in several short breaths before speaking. "I've asked you both here because," he paused when Mother came into the room, "Mother and I have come to a decision," he explained, holding out his hand, waiting for Mother to join him. "I am going to take a step back from the business and turn the running of it over to you, Lara."

I felt shocked by his words as disbelief registered across my face. "But Papa, what do I know about running a carriage business?" I inquired anxiously. "I'm simply not prepared—"

"That is why Mr. Blackthorn is going to help you," Mother interrupted, speaking for Papa when he began to cough again. "He is an excellent businessman and he graduated top of his class. He has agreed to become a full partner, which is something your papa and Mr. Blackthorn had discussed in great detail before he left to attend University. He will purchase half of the business and teach you everything you need to know—" she added, stopping mid-sentence to pound on Papa's back several times to help him breathe better.

"But I don't understand."

"It is very simple, Miss Roscoe," Roman began, very businesslike even though we were well acquainted with one another and his sister and I were best friends. "I pay your family a fair market price for half of the business and you and I will become partners, at least until Mr. Roscoe is well again and able to return to work. Mr. Grayson will continue to run things in Britain, sending reports back to us, and I will help you learn all that you need to know or care to know about the carriage business."

With my mouth still hanging open, I stared between Papa and Roman, who stood before me with a placid look upon his face. I thought I would lose my mind, considering the unexpected news and all that had happened since Papa's return.

"Perhaps you and I could have dinner this evening and discuss matters?" Roman offered, taking my arm and leading me toward the door. "I could answer your questions and we could talk about the business as we eat."

"That would be an excellent idea," Mother quickly blurted out. "Oh, and please tell Martha I need her when you go downstairs."

"Would you like to change?" Roman suggested, giving me a critical look that said what I was wearing wasn't exactly appropriate for where we were going. "I'll come back around to pick you up, shall we say, in an hour?" he suggested, pulling out his pocket watch to consult the time. Then with a courteous bow before excusing himself, he added, "I will inform Martha that she is needed as I leave. That way you will have more time to ready yourself."

Wordlessly nodding my head, I watched as Roman walked down the stairs. Then, opening the door to my room, I stepped inside. "Sarah, I am in desperate need of your expertise," I called out the moment I entered.

At 6:30 on the dot, Roman returned, just as he'd said he would, to pick me up for dinner. He wore a black dinner jacket and trousers, a black and white herringbone designed vest, a white shirt with a midnight blue silk cravat, freshly polished black leather shoes, and a shiny top hat. The blue of his eyes stood out starkly against the contrasting colors and I was momentarily taken aback by how stunning he was. I was so awestruck by his elegance and ease of perfection that it took my breath away.

I'd dressed in an emerald green evening gown that swept to the edge of my shoulders. Although simplistic in design, with its fitted bodice and flowing skirts, the outfit was apparently dramatic, because I heard Roman audibly gasp when he turned around to greet me.

I wore my delicate teardrop emerald earrings because I knew they danced and sparkled, catching the light when I moved. Draping a white shawl over my arm, I smiled, offering him a gloved hand. My hair was swept up and when I looked up, I found him staring down at me intently.

"I hope that I am not overly dressed for this evening. I wasn't sure what to wear since you didn't tell me where we are going for dinner."

An appreciative gleam shone in Roman's eyes as he smiled even broader, taking my shawl from me. "You are a vision of perfection," he said, clearing his throat, immediately wiping the boyish smile from his lips. "Shall we," he added, trying to sound very businesslike as he offered me his arm.

"Yes, of course," I replied with a smile, taking his arm.

Making small talk all the way to the carriage that was parked on the street, Roman helped me up, then draped my shawl over the back of the seat and took his place beside me. With a wink and a grin, he slapped the reins against the rump of his beautiful chestnut mare and we were off, taking us down the street towards Elm before turning down another street which led us out of town, towards Canal Street.

This area of the city was operated by workers who ferried carriages from one side of the canal to the other. Driving onto the barge, Roman turned, stepping down to give the young man instructions as we began to move across the water. I was marveling at the young man's accent and trying to determine what part of Ireland he was from when we docked on the opposite shore. Stepping back up into the rig, Roman handed the ferryman his payment as another young man lifted the wooden barrier, allowing us to pass onto the shore.

As we began to pull away from the canal docks I heard someone laughing as he called out, "Clayton Brown, ye old dog," which struck a familiar chord in my memory.

Taking a moment to react when I recognized the voice from my childhood, I suddenly grabbed Roman's arm. "Stop!" I gasped. "Please!" I shouted, jumping down from the carriage the moment he pulled his horse to a stop.

Frantically running back the fifty feet or so to the docks, I called out, "Jamie? Jamie O'Brien, is that you?"

A scruffy, startled young man turned towards me and stared at me for a moment as I approached. "Lara? Lara Flannigan?" he questioned, squinting his eyes and looking at me as if he had just seen a ghost.

"Can it be?" he called, squinting and taking a step back, putting his hands up to keep me from coming any closer.

For a moment I'd forgotten propriety and nearly threw myself into his arms, but then, recognizing the horrified look on Jamie's face, I stopped abruptly, not sure of what to say next. Shock and disbelief coursed through me before I came to my senses.

Roman, who had followed me, gently touched my arm. "Is everything alright, Lara?"

"I don' believe me eyes," Jamie cried awkwardly as he forced a smile to his lips before removing his hat and scrubbing his dirty hands on the sides of his dirty pants. "Jamie O'Brien," he introduced himself as he offered his hand to Roman.

Hesitating a moment, Roman reached out and took hold of Jamie's hand. "Roman Blackthorn," he answered back. "It's a pleasure to meet you."

Not bothering to take my eyes off of Jamie, I offered an awkward explanation to Roman. "Jamie and I grew up together. He was my best friend when he and I were children."

"Well, then, Mr. O'Brien, it truly is a pleasure to meet you," Roman said graciously as I stood there, suddenly feeling ill at ease.

"I heard your voice and—" I began to say, stammering for words to explain. "I…well…have wondered for years what had become of you."

Putting his hat back on his head, Jamie looked at Roman and then back at me. "I arrived a couple years back, and have been livin' the dream ever since," he assured me, shuffling his feet while peering over his shoulder. "Look at ye. A right fine highborn ye've become now," Jamie pointed out as his words almost sounded accusatory, causing me to feel the sting of his rebuff.

Self-consciously I peered down at my gown and then back up to his eyes, unconsciously touching my earrings and then hair before answering. "Yes, well—" I faltered as if I was guilty of committing a terrible sin. Something in the pit of my stomach felt heavy and I could feel the color rising to my cheeks. "It is so good to see you again,"

I nodded, holding back the words I truly wanted to say to him. "I'm glad you survived," I babbled nervously as someone bellowed out Jamie's name in a deep, authoritarian tone.

"Get back to work before I dock your pay!" his foreman called out.

"I wouldn't want to keep you. I know you are terribly busy," I said, backing away.

Sensing my sudden discomfort, Roman gently touched my arm and led me away from the chance meeting that had turned into a train wreck. "It was good to meet you, Mr. O'Brien. I do hope that we have the opportunity to speak again," he added before clearing his throat.

With a nod and a wave, Jamie turned to hurry off, looking grateful to have been dismissed. Allowing Roman to lead me back to the carriage and help me back up into the rig, I couldn't help taking one final glance back over my shoulder, only to see Jamie standing there staring after us.

There were a million questions I wanted to ask Jamie, but I couldn't. Not now. Not in front of Roman, who was an outsider where I came from. He wouldn't understand the way we lived or what I had been through. How do you explain something like that to a person who came from privilege their entire life? Then, suddenly, a horrifying thought struck me. Was that how Jamie saw me? That strange look on his face. The way he'd been staring at me just now as if I'd become someone who no longer belonged in a world where small dwellings and poverty existed. Where little children played on beaches, creating adventures with their imaginations. I had become the outsider. But when had I become one of those people? An outsider!

In Jamie's eyes, I had become just like Roman—someone who didn't belong to *that* world any longer. My heart felt heavy and broken. I sat quietly in the seat next to Roman, nodding my head, mindlessly agreeing with everything he said, trying to buy myself a little time to think.

"Did you hear what I just said, Lara?" he asked.

Bringing myself back to the present with a shake of my head, I replied, "Yes, of course I did," I responded. "You wanted to know if

I was cold. And I answered you," I quietly replied, then thanked him when he draped my shawl over my shoulders. "Now, would you like to discuss something of importance this evening or would you like to continue prattling on about the weather?" I admonished.

Slapping the reins against his horse's rump, Roman gave me an appreciative grin as the horse sped up. "Now that's more like it," he chuckled, before launching into a well thought out plan for our newly formed partnership.

Dinner was filled with lively conversation, excellent food, and sips of sparkling wine. We discussed our commitment to the carriage shop and together we came up with a solid business plan. Yet, my mind kept going back to the docks and the look on my oldest, dearest friend's face. I couldn't shake the feeling that I had let him down somehow— as if I were a traitor for surviving and landing on my feet. I made a note to myself to search him out and talk with him. If anyone knew what had happened to the rest of my family, it would be him. After all, he had indicated that he had only just arrived on American soil a couple of years prior.

I formed a plan in my mind, telling myself that I would find the time to slip away and visit with Jamie O'Brien. Then I would know for sure what had become of my family.

20

Here's to Undying Friendships

A week passed, and I was beginning to feel like a trapped animal who was ready to chew its leg off just so it could escape. There weren't enough hours in the day to accomplish everything I needed to do. I was kept so busy with bookkeeping, carriage orders, and running Laurel's Helping Hands Foundation that the days disappeared like so much sand through my fingers.

Mother was keeping everyone on their toes, trying to manage the household and care for Papa at the same time; I had to finally step in and intervene before we had a rebellion on our hands.

There had been rumblings from the kitchen staff for days that Martha was getting ready to quit. The extra demands on her had stretched her to her breaking point.

Mother wouldn't allow the nurse to do her job and trying to do everything herself was leading her to reach the end of her very frayed rope. Mother had not been sleeping, and her nerves were stretched thin, along with everyone else's in the household.

I'd made a point of stopping by to see Doctor Sheridan the day before, begging him for a mild sedative to slip into Mother's evening tea.

That evening, after returning from Doctor Sheridan's, Martha prepared Mother's tea, and I slipped the powder into her drink, sweetening it with extra cream and sugar. Mother slept so soundly that when she awoke in the morning, she appeared refreshed and her step was somewhat lighter. I felt as if another crisis had been averted

and I went off to work satisfied that the house and all of its staff would still be standing when I returned.

The only matter that still needed to be handled was Jamie. I had to find a way to get away for a while so I could track him down and explain myself. I was standing at Papa's office window staring down at the street below while pondering this matter when Roman walked into the office, startling me from my daydream.

"Lara, I have an order of leather that needs picking up. Would you like to get out of the office for a while?" he asked, laying a receipt on my desk. "I really need to supervise the Greyson order today. It should be a pleasant ride for you," he continued, noticing the distracted look in my eyes when I turned to face him. "I can send Peter if you're too busy."

Quickly shaking my head, I said, "That won't be necessary. I can pick up a simple load by myself. Besides, I was looking for an excuse to get out of here for a while." I smiled, grabbing the leather rain slicker that Papa had given me from the coat rack on my way out the door. "I'll take the wagon if you can have someone hook the team up for me," I called over my shoulder as I hurried toward the stairs, only too anxious to be on my way.

"Already done," Roman called after me, following me as I practically ran down the staircase. "Are you sure you don't need anyone to come with you?"

"No, really, I'll be fine," I insisted again, climbing up into the seat of the wagon without assistance as Roman reached up to help me.

Picking up the reins, I slapped them against the rumps of the matching Clydesdales, barely looking to see if anyone was walking past the doors before I clicked my tongue and sped off.

"You remember how to get there, don't you?" Roman cried as I pulled away.

Waving to him over my shoulder, I turned and yelled back, "Stop worrying, Mother!"

Free at last—I thought I would lose my mind if I'd been forced to wait any longer—and not a moment too soon, I needed to make

the most of the time I was given. I would cross the canal and find Jamie, I thought to myself as I hurried the team along, nearly colliding with a carriage coming from the opposite direction. Looking over my shoulder to make sure that Roman hadn't seen me nearly crash, I let out a sigh of relief when I saw that he was no longer standing on the sidewalk looking after me. Forcing myself to take a deep breath and slow down, I continued on my way.

It felt like it was taking an eternity to get to Canal Street when in reality it likely took me the usual twenty-five minutes to maneuver through the afternoon traffic.

I drove the wagon up and down the street looking for my childhood friend until I spotted him coming across with several passengers on his barge. Cutting my team sharply to my right, I moved the wagon into position to be the next person in line for Jamie's floating boat.

Approaching the young man who was manning the toll, I paid him extra so I could be the only passenger to cross with Jamie, explaining that I was in a terrible hurry and couldn't wait for them to fill the barge up.

Pulling the straw hat from beneath my seat, I tucked my vibrant red hair beneath the hat and positioned it low over my eyes so Jamie wouldn't immediately recognize me. My right leg nervously jiggled beneath my dress as I impatiently waited for the people and wagon to disembark before pulling onto the barge. My heart raced the entire time and my mouth went dry. Before the other night, I hadn't seen Jamie in years, and I felt more like a complete stranger instead of his best friend.

I glanced over my shoulder when I heard Jamie curse under his breath. He'd pinched his finger while lowering the wooden arm. I saw him quickly look up at me, but his reaction made it seem as if he didn't recognize me. Jamie turned back around to tend to business as he pushed us off from the docks. I waited a minute before jumping down and walking to the back of my rig where he was standing. He was using a long pole to push the barge along as large ropes assisted our progress. Teams of horses were hooked up to the ropes on either side of the canal and, depending on the direction the barge was headed, a team would either pull the rope or back up, giving slack to the rope.

"I was a-wonderin' when ye'd show up again." Jamie acknowledged me without looking up from poling.

Chewing nervously at my lower lip, I held onto the railing to keep from toppling into the water. "Can we talk?" I asked tentatively.

His eyes were shining with anger when Jamie turned on me. "I thought that's what we were doin', unless I've been doin' it wrong all these years," he said, then turned back to vigorously shoving the pole into the canal.

Uncertain of what to say next, I removed the hat from my head, allowing thick red locks to spill down my back. Then, running shaky fingers through my hair, I turned to face him once again. "I am not sure why I am here, Jamie—"

"That makes two of us," he interrupted, sounding angry.

"What has happened to make you so angry at me?" I continued in rapid succession before he could interrupt me again.

When he continued to ignore me, I let out a heavy sigh. "We were so close, once. You and I were best friends, Jamie O'Brien," I added with a shrug. "My only friend, really."

Pulling his pole partway out of the water, Jamie turned back to me with such fury in his eyes I had to take a step back. "Ye left!" he barked.

"I what?" I questioned, taking a step towards him.

"Ye left and did no' come back," he answered, punching his words.

Finally, his meaning hit me like a punch to the gut. "I was sent away. I had no choice in the matter," I defended. "My own father traded me away to Lord Henley, our landlord, for the rent!" I slapped the straw hat against my leg as I fought to control the wall of emotions that particular memory brought up. Then, turning on him with even more indignation, I continued to let the words spill. "And where were you when I was fighting my way out of that man's palatial study when he attempted to force himself upon me? Where were you when I was

running for my life, scraping and fighting every single step of the way, just to survive, one more miserable day, so I could open my eyes the next day and do it all over again?" I demanded. "Where were you?!" I cried. "I'll tell you where you were—you pompous, pampered, dock worker. You were in your warm, cozy bed at home, with your loving family. That's where you were!" I concluded, poking my delicate finger in the middle of his chest before turning and marching back to my rig and climbing back up. "This was clearly a mistake," I said under my breath, loud enough for him to hear.

Staring straight ahead, I refused to look at Jamie again as the barge approached the docks on the opposite side of the canal. I could feel the painful fire of indignation, raw and hot, burning a hole in my belly. Straightening my spine, I sat perfectly upright, staring straight ahead, anticipating the moment someone on the docks would raise the wooden arm keeping my horse in place and allow me to pull off of Jamie O'Brien's barge and out of his life forever. I didn't care if it took twice as long to go around on my return trip, I would never set eyes on him again, as long as I had breath in my body, I told myself. He simply brought up too many bad memories from the past.

"Hold up, Eli," Jamie called out, stepping in front of my team. "I'm takin' lunch," he insisted, lifting the bar himself before turning and climbing up beside me on the bench seat. Then he took the reins out of my stiff fingers. "Cover for me," he called down to his friend Eli as he drove the team and wagon off the barge and onto the main road.

Silently I sat next to him fuming as I stared straight ahead like a statue, my back stiff and straight as a board. I scooted over to the edge of my seat as far away from him as I could and crossed my arms over my chest with a loud huff, refusing to acknowledge him further. Finally, Jamie pulled off to the side of a tree-lined drive by the waterfront and set the brake.

"I should never 'ave been so angry at ye. I realize now how silly it be. It's just, well, the other day when ye showed up with yer guy—" he quietly explained, searching for the right words. "Well, I thought ye were dead all these years, so ye can imagine that it came as quite a shock to me."

Tears of anger mixed with grief streamed down my cheeks before I roughly wiped at them with my hand. Turning, I found my repentant friend offering me a clean, but stained, handkerchief. Hesitantly taking it from his hand, I blew my nose and then slowly folded it up purposefully, three times, before speaking. "How could you ever believe me capable of leaving me home of my own volition, Jamie O'Brien, without so much as a word of good-bye to ye?" I countered. "Ye big, dumb…you and I were—" Tears began to run down my cheeks.

"I know," he interjected, "and for that, I beg yer forgiveness." Jamie reached out to take my hand in his.

After that, the floodgates broke wide open and I threw myself into his arms. "Oh, Jamie, I've missed you so much," I groaned in the crook of his neck. "I couldn't come home after I—"

Pushing me from him so he could look me in the eye, Jamie questioned, "Why could ye no' come home, Lara?"

I sat silently weighing my options for a few seconds before the words came bursting from my lips. "I killed Lord Henley, Jamie…I was a wanted person!"

Giving my shoulders a slight shake, Jamie looked at me with his mouth hanging open at first, then responded, "Lord Henley is no' dead."

My mind couldn't process his words at first and I looked at him with a blank look on my face. "What? What did you just say?" I questioned. "Why, yes, he is," I insisted. "I left him lying in a pool of blood on the floor of his office. The man was no' moving!"

"We all wondered how he got such a large scar on the side of his head. No one believed his wife, who insisted that he'd fallen from a horse."

"I hit him with a paperweight when he was trying to—" I broke off, diverting my eyes, embarrassed by the memory of that moment in time.

Placing a finger to the side of my chin, Jamie forced my eyes up to his and said emphatically, "It was no' yer fault, Lara. The man has always been a degenerate. There'd been whisperins' for years."

"And yet, there lies the rub, Jamie O'Brien," I asserted, renewed anger flashing in my eyes as I easily slipped back into my old dialect, "because me own Da turned me over to that deviant! A daughter he claimed to love!" I indignantly added.

"He's dead, Lara," Jamie blurted out quietly, casting his eyes downward. "Ye can no' speak ill of the dead," he advised, crossing himself and lifting his eyes up to heaven before gazing into my eyes to gauge my reaction to this new revelation.

Feeling as if I had just been punched in the gut, I began rapidly sucking in air through my nose and blowing it out again through my mouth. Then, climbing down from the rig, I found myself walking around in a circle before bending over suddenly and swallowing hard, unable to keep the bile from coming up. Afterward, I leaned my head against the rig and felt it jerk as Jamie jumped down to stand next to me.

"Lara!" he cried, bending over to rub my back. "I'm sorry. I should no' have told ye like that."

Reaching back to take his hand, I absently wiped my mouth with the handkerchief still in my hand before turning to face him. "I'm fine, Jamie. Just shocked, that's all. Yer news took me by surprise, nothing more," I said, choking back another sob.

When he wrapped his arms around me, I sobbed into his shoulder as I had the day we buried my mama, the same day Jamie had told me about Katie's passing. So many memories flooded my mind as I blew my nose again into the stained handkerchief.

"I'm so sorry, Lara, but there's more," he said hesitantly. I suddenly felt apprehensive, my breath catching in my lungs.

"There's more? I don' know if I can take any more bad news, Jamie O'Brien." I began backing away from him until my spine was against the wagon wheel.

Like ripping off a cloth bandage that has glued itself to the skin, Jamie continued, regardless of my objection. "After ye didn't come back, Lord Henley put yer family out on the street and had the house torn down. Micky didn't survive the harsh winter, despite Colin and Alana's best efforts."

I felt my legs wobble just before they lost all feeling and I fell to the ground. Disbelief and grief washed over me and I felt numb all over. I could not allow myself to feel the pain of Jamie's news. Not now. Maybe not ever. I feared that if I did, I would never stop crying. *Breathe in, breathe out, move forward.* The words kept running through my head like an endless loop over and over again.

"Lara!" he cried, dropping to the ground next to me and trying to wrap his arms around me. He stopped short when I put my hands up to prevent it.

"Please, Jamie, I beg ye, no'—" I muttered, bracing myself against the spokes of the wagon's wheel, shakily pulling myself up to a standing position. Then, pulling myself up into the seat of the wagon, I forced myself to stare straight ahead. I didn't dare say another word to him, for I was certain that if I did, I would shatter into a million tiny, little pieces of glass.

Jamie, sensing my fragile state, did not attempt to climb up next to me, but instead, stood on the ground next to the wagon, looking up at me. "Lara, I truly am sorry—" he began.

I cut him off as I raised a hand in the air. "Jamie O'Brien, don't you dare say it again!" I warned, giving him a look that stopped him short.

When we were children we had developed our own secret code—a way of communicating with one another without the need of words. Some people thought it eerie the way Jamie and I knew what the other was thinking, but I guess that is how it is with best friends.

I straightened my back, disengaged the brake, picked up the reins, and slapped them against the horses' rumps, quickly pulling away from Jamie without another glance back. I was mentally packing up my emotional baggage and placing it away neatly on a shelf in the

recesses of my mind. I couldn't think about what I had lost, even if it was years ago. To me, it felt like it just happened.

It was one thing to be angry with someone for what they had done to me years ago, and another thing to know that you would never see them again. The death of my father and brother Mick was beyond devastating. It was unthinkable.

Arriving at my destination, I retrieved the order I was sent to get, sitting silently as I waited for the wagon to be loaded with supplies. Then I signed the paperwork and left without even so much as a pleasant word of thanks to the foreman. I made sure to take the long way around, completely bypassing the canal district as I headed back to the carriage shop.

Sometime during my long drive home, it began to rain, but I didn't notice that I was cold and wet, drenched from head to toe. I must have looked like a drowned rat as I pulled through the tall wooden doors of the carriage shop when Roman greeted me. He had a distinct look of irritation on his face.

Pacing back and forth in front of me, he immediately held up a lantern, shining the light directly into my eyes, and I could tell that he was anxious about my late arrival. I put my hand up to shield my eyes from the glare of the light while pulling hard on the reins to keep from running into him.

"I was about to send out the Cavalry to search for you," he declared, sounding somewhat put out and not waiting for my reply before asking the next question. "Was there a problem? Was the order not ready when you arrived?"

Eric Brown, one of Papa's most loyal employees, ran towards the team, taking hold of the horses' reins so that I could climb down. I answered with little emotion. "I am fine. Thank you for your concern, Mr. Blackthorn, but there really is no need to make such a fuss on my account. I needed some time to myself, so I took the long way around and skipped the canal crossing so I could think. That is all."

Energetically waving an arm in the air, Roman stepped in front of me, halting my progression to the office to drop off the invoice slips.

"No need to make a fuss?" he questioned, taking ahold of my arm. "I was worried sick about you, Lara Roscoe. You cannot imagine the terrible scenarios that went through my head as I imagined you—"

"If you honestly spent your day pacing the floors, concerned over my welfare, you wasted your day," I interrupted. "I am fine and quite adept at taking care of myself."

Taking a step back as if I had slapped him across the face, Roman looked startled. "What has happened?" he asked.

Swallowing hard to keep my emotions in check, my mind continued to repeat my simple mantra, *breathe in, breathe out, move forward*, and I dared not deviate from it for fear that I would fall to pieces. Taking a deep breath, I pursed my lips together. "Nothing is wrong, I assure you. It has just been a rough few weeks, so I beg your forgiveness for my abrupt manner, but I truly need to put these invoices away before I can go home."

Looking slightly bewildered, Roman nodded his head after a few seconds. "Of course. I didn't mean to be so insensitive. I am the one who should be apologizing to you." He sounded slightly sarcastic, waving his arm in a large arc.

"I am truly very tired, and as you are well aware, drenched," I stated, looking up at him. "I really need to get home to check on Mother and Papa."

"Yes, of course," Roman demurred, looking repentant as he stepped aside, allowing me to continue on my way toward the stairs.

I didn't dare look back. I could feel his eyes staring after me as he called out to Eric. "We'll unload in the morning, Eric. Go home. I'll see you tomorrow."

"Thank you, sir," Eric replied, sounding relieved. "Goodnight to you both," he called out as he stepped past us on his way to the carriage house doors.

While slowly climbing the stairs to the office I caught sight of Roman out of the corner of my eye. He was still standing in the same spot I had left him, and I wondered if he intended to wait for me to

come back down. Stopping on the landing to look at him, I said, "I will lock up if you like."

"I would feel better if I walked you across the street and safely home," Roman replied.

"It isn't necessary, Roman, really. I can cross the street by myself. I've been doing it for years."

"I wish to discuss a matter with your father if he is still awake," he responded, adding, "I insist."

I felt this was just a ruse to keep an eye on me, but I nodded my head anyway before continuing up the stairs. I was feeling frustrated by his scrutiny. I needed time to process the devastating information Jamie had given me earlier. How was I to do that with Roman scrutinizing my every move?

Quickly dropping the paperwork off on my desk, I braced myself for more of Roman's prying. Why couldn't he just let me be instead of trying to ascertain what was wrong with me? Taking a cleansing breath and blowing it out, I checked my reflection in the mirror on the wall, then blew out the lantern and carefully made my way down the stairs.

After securing the large wooden doors to The Royal Carriage House with a padlock, Roman offered me his arm. I hesitated before taking it. "Ella stopped by earlier," he began pleasantly. I could tell that he was searching for things to talk about. "She said to tell you that she missed you and wanted to know if you were free Saturday evening. Seems she has a surprise for you," he added with a smile as he wagged both eyebrows at me. "She said it would be quite the adventure. So, what should I tell her?"

Pondering Roman's words a moment as we crossed the street, I opened the back door and took in the aroma of freshly baked bread and stew. My stomach loudly gurgled, a reminder that I hadn't eaten a thing since breakfast.

Facing him, I forced a smile and somberly said, "Tell Ella that I would be delighted to join her for a little adventure. I just need to have a hint as to what she wants me to wear." With a large sigh, I made my way to the kettle still hanging near the fire. "Could I offer you some?" I asked, lifting the lid and breathing deeply. "Martha makes the most wonderful stew."

"No, thank you. I really must be getting home," Roman insisted with a stiff smile.

"But I thought you wanted to discuss something with Papa?" I argued, turning to see his hand already on the doorknob.

"It's late and I am sure he is sleeping by now. Besides, it isn't a very pressing matter and can keep until tomorrow."

I almost blurted out, *I knew you were lying*, but chose instead to take the passive route. "Well if you are sure—" I exclaimed.

"Positive. I will see you in the morning, Miss Roscoe."

"See you in the morning, Mr. Blackthorn," I countered as I reached for a bowl and spoon, suddenly ravenous despite my bedraggled state.

21

OCTOBER 25, 1851
SATURDAY

The Silver Slipper Dance Hall

Ella Blackthorn sent a simple note that morning, telling me to wear something less high society and more country bumpkin. To say that I was somewhat confused and intrigued by her cryptic message was putting it mildly. I wore a simple dress that I'd worn to the boat docks to greet immigrants as they stepped off the ships. It was a deep blue, almost black, long-sleeved gown that was fitted at the waist and made of a soft cotton. The modest neckline was rounded with a white lace collar.

My emotions were still quite raw from my conversation with Jamie only days before and, truth be told, I was looking forward to seeing my good friend Ella again. She could always distract me from my problems. Ever since Papa had returned home from Europe, my world had been turned upside down. Running a business left precious little time for socializing.

I tried keeping myself busy in hopes that my mind would be so overwhelmed with work-related issues that I wouldn't have time for any other thoughts. Yet memories of my life before coming to America had been pushing their way to the forefront of my mind.

Unfortunately for me, work seemed to end too soon each day and the nights seemed to linger on too long. The house had become depressingly quiet and somber since Papa's return. I could hear the grandfather clock in the hallway marking time as I paced the floor of my bedroom each night. I'd decided that it was not healthy for me to be alone with my thoughts. That was one of the main reasons I was so grateful for Ella's invitation to distract me, whatever the adventure.

Ella arrived to pick me up promptly at 6:30 as she had said she would in her note and, to my surprise, she was driving the carriage herself.

"Where is Murphy, your driver," I inquired as we approached the small surrey.

"There wasn't room for him and you, so I left him home," she quipped with a giggle.

"And why do you have that look on your face?"

"What look?" she asked, trying to sound quite innocent.

Pointing at her face, I declared, "That look!" I narrowed my eyes at her and swirled my finger in a circular motion in the air as we continued to walk towards the surrey. "The one that says 'I'm about to involve you in something lewd, salacious, and underhanded.' "

"Oh, now you are just being ridiculous, Lara Roscoe," she retorted, her voice pitching higher at the end.

Climbing into the carriage, I quickly turned on her. "That, right there!" I pointed out. "That's how I know you are lying. Any time your voice pitches like that I know your words are pure fabrication."

Bringing her hands up on either side of her body with her palms opened and facing towards the sky, she gave me one of her famous shrugs. "Why, I don't have the slightest idea of what you are blathering on about, Lara Ann Flannigan Roscoe," Ella said coyly, gathering the reins up in her hands and clicking her tongue. "Are you sure you are feeling alright?"

Facing forward with a rather sullen glower, I felt my brows crease together. "You're taking me to one of those underground places where men fight bare-knuckled in one of those no-holds-barred establishments, aren't you?" I accused.

Shaking her head, Ella chuckled as she turned to me. "Now, what makes you think I would take you to one of those disreputable places?" she scoffed outright. "I've been to one of those bare-knuckle-brawl

places before and let me tell you, they are despicable. The men beat each other to a pulp for a fistful of cash and bragging rights."

"Ella Helena Blackthorn!" I gasped, "You did not frequent such a place!"

With a self-sufficient, satisfied smile, she turned to me with a wink and giggled before turning her attention back to the street. "I certainly did. Wouldn't lie about a thing like that. Never did get the blood stain out of my pretty white dress," Ella answered matter-of-factly. "Note to self, never wear white at one of those places again," she stated as if she were alone.

Clicking my tongue at her and sighing heavily, I crossed my arms over my chest. "If that is what you have planned this evening, you turn this rig around, this instant, Miss Blackthorn, because I will not be stepping foot into one of those establishments," I scolded with a stubborn glance.

With a sound deep in her throat as if she were disgusted with my statement, Ella made a sour face and waved me off. "Don't get yourself all riled up. I would never take you to a place like that. You are a refined lady, after all," she added with a proper highborn British accent.

"Oh, stop it, Ella, I'm not that out of touch. I do know what goes on in the world, after all," I scolded, slapping her arm. "You make me out to be such a prissy,"

"Well, you are after all," she teased.

"I am not!" I argued. "It's just that I've already experienced that side of life, first hand, and I don't ever care to experience it again."

Looking repentant, Ella touched my leg. "I'm so sorry, Lara. I didn't know. You've never told me before."

Looking away quickly to hide my eyes that suddenly teared up with the memory, I answered, "I know."

"You could tell me, you know," she encouraged, sounding sincere in her request.

Shaking my head to dispel the negative thoughts, I turned back to face her. "Maybe another time. Now, why don't you tell me where we are going tonight? I was looking forward to having some fun this evening, not bringing you down with my sad stories of home."

"Well, if you are sure—"

"Absolutely, positively sure!"

With a wicked smile, Ella sat up straight and giggled. "It's a surprise, dear friend. Besides, I want you to have plausible deniability if this all goes sideways."

"What?" I gasped, suddenly scandalized by Ella's statement. "Tell me that you aren't considering involving me in the robbing of a bank."

"Oh, nothing that derelict or despicable, I assure you," Ella replied with a lilt of amusement. "How could you even think such a thing? Besides, neither one of us lacks for anything, least of all money."

I gave her a playful shove with my shoulder. "After our last surprise outing to the gypsy encampment, I wouldn't put anything past you."

"Now you are just being ridiculous," she chided. "Didn't you have fun?"

Giving Ella a sideways glance, I tried to look stern, but couldn't help but smile when I remembered Caspian teaching me how to dance like a gypsy. "Alright, I admit it, I had a good time learning to dance and watching everyone else swirl around the bonfire."

"Isn't Madam Sabina marvelous?" she stated pensively. "Hey, you never did tell me what she said to you. Has anything come true yet?"

Giving her a suspicious look, I asked, "Are you avoiding my question on purpose?"

"No! Of course not!" she said emphatically, adding, "Why won't you tell me what Madam Sabina really said to you?"

Nervously laughing, I answered, "Because it was all a bunch of nonsense. That's why."

"Really?" Ella questioned. "Because she was spot on with me."

"Maybe you just wanted her to be right and the suggestions she gave you influenced your decisions," I quickly countered.

Shaking her head, causing delicate curls to bounce about her face, Ella flatly denied my statement. "No, I didn't. She told me things about my past, my present and my future—none of which have any influence on my decisions."

"Well good. Now that you have cleared that up for me, maybe you could tell me where we are going this evening."

With a large smile on her lips, Ella lifted delicate eyebrows in a show of excitement. "I don't need to, because we are here," she proudly announced, pulling the small surrey to a stop in front of an establishment with a sign overhead: the Silver Slipper Dance Hall.

Looking around with bewilderment and then pointing, I asked with an accusatory tone, "Why are we going in there?"

Slapping my hand down and sounding embarrassed by my sudden shift in demeanor, Ella quickly looked around to see if anyone was staring at us. "Didn't your mother teach you that it is impolite to point?" she chastised under her breath. "And to answer the obvious question, because it will be fun," she said, climbing down from the carriage with a heavy sigh. "Well, are you coming?"

Still mystified by my friend's behavior, I obediently followed behind her as we entered the Silver Slipper. The place was filled to capacity with people mingling about, talking with one another, and dancing.

The dance floor stretched across the center of the hall, ringed by tables where guests lingered over drinks and conversation with both familiar and unfamiliar faces.

At the far end, five people stood on a raised stage playing their style of lively tunes. Two men played fiddles, another played a mandolin, someone was beating on a drum held between his knees, and one woman sang. There was so much going on that I didn't know what to look at first.

Once the initial shock of standing in the middle of a dance hall had worn off, I noticed the different smells. There were so many, it was

like wandering through freshly hung laundry on a clothesline sitting in the sun. My senses came alive. It was Friday night and people had found the time to wash up and dress, many of them wearing their Sunday best.

Taking my hand, Ella pulled me through the crowd, saying, "Excuse me," along the way until we came to a refreshment table. "Isn't it marvelous?" she gushed.

"It is quite something," I remarked with a smile, trying to be encouraging without fully committing to her brand of craziness.

"Oh, you and my brother deserve each other!" Ella remarked emphatically. "You are both such sticks in the mud."

"Oh, now that's just not true," I grumbled. "I can be a lot of fun—"

"Prove it!" she challenged.

"How?" I cried.

With a twinkle in her eye, Ella said, "You say yes to the first man that asks you to dance." Then she continued as she suddenly had another brilliant idea and defined the rules a little more. "Better yet, you dance with any man who asks you to dance, the entire night. That is how you prove to me that you are no stick in the mud," she stressed by poking me in the arm.

"Ouch! That hurt," I whined, giving her a cross look. "What if—?" I began to say when Ella shook her head and wagged her finger in the air.

"No! You either take the challenge or admit to me and the whole world that you are an old stick stuck deep into the mud."

At that moment, two large men approached us both and bowed. "Please to introduce myself," one said in his broken English. "My name is Alexander Petrov, but you may call me Xander. All my friends do. This is good friend, Ivan Kozlov. You may call him Ivan."

Ella immediately stuck her hand out in greeting. "It is a pleasure to meet you, Mr. Petrov," she said, shaking the large man's hand.

"Please, you call me Xander, I insist."

"All right, Xander. I'm Elizabeth Brown and this is my good friend, Rosaline Mulvaney, but everyone calls her Rosie," she asserted, then extended her hand to the other gentleman. "Mr.—I mean Ivan. What do the two of you do for work?" Ella asked boldly, smiling up at Ivan.

"Shipyard," was the only thing he said, his face sporting a large grin as if that one word was a big accomplishment for him.

Looking slightly abashed, Xander interjected, "Ivan no speak so good a English as me. Perhaps you teach him word or two as you dance," he suggested to Ella.

"It would be my pleasure," she said, placing the emphasis on the word *pleasure* with a wink in my direction.

I smiled and chuckled awkwardly, "Make sure you teach him only good words, El…err…Elizabeth," I advised before she took hold of Ivan's hand to lead him onto the dance floor.

Offering his arm, Xander asked, "Will you do me great honor?"

Taking hold of his arm, I pasted a smile on my lips and replied, "Of course," then muttered under my breath as he led me onto the dance floor: "Wouldn't want to be mistaken for an old stick in the mud."

"Do you say something?" he asked, pulling me closer as we began to dance.

"No, nothing of importance," I answered with a stiff smile and a shake of my head. "And you should say instead, *did you say something?"* I added, "as long as we are giving grammar lessons."

Chuckling to himself, Xander mumbled, "You are very smart girl. No?"

Feeling myself loosen up somewhat, I chuckled as well. "Yes, Xander, some might call me a smart girl."

Alexander Petrov and I danced for exactly two songs before Ella stepped in, telling him and Ivan that they needed to give the other men an opportunity to dance with us. Then she promised that we would say good-bye to them before we left.

It was like a high society social without the dance cards. And in many ways, it was better because we could dance with anyone we

wanted to, with complete anonymity and without the pressure of making a good match. We were just there to have fun and dance.

This process of introductions and dancing for a couple of songs with different partners went on for a couple of hours. I was having so much fun that I began to lose track of time. Ella and I were having the time of our lives when I noticed someone staring at me from the shadows. He stepped forward as I made another turn around the dance floor with my gangly partner by the name of Nathaniel. Then I recognized him. I nearly came to a complete stop right there in the middle of all the dancers. It was Jamie O'Brien standing along the edge of the dance floor staring at me.

The moment the song ended, I made my excuses and stepped to the edge of the dance floor, desperately searching for Ella. I was not yet ready to revisit all those painful emotions from the other day, and I definitely was not ready to face Jamie.

I spotted Ella on the other side of the room, conversing with a very handsome, tall young man that she'd danced with earlier. They were conversing with a group of his friends. She turned, smiled, and waved me over before turning back to continue her conversation. Just then the band began to play another song and people stepped out onto the floor. I frantically searched for a direct path to Ella but was forced to stop and allow a group of people to cross in front of me. As I was about to take a step, I felt a strong hand take hold of my arm. Turning to see who the offending hand belonged to, I came face to face with the one person I didn't wish to see right now—Jamie O'Brien.

"Please," he simply said, gazing down at me with his pleading blue eyes.

Sighing heavily, I relented and allowed him to lead me to the back of the room, away from the throngs of prying eyes.

Letting go of my arm once we had reached a quiet table near the back and close to the door that led to the back of the building, he tipped my chin up, forcing me to look at him. "I know I be the last person ye want to see tonight, but I had to know ye were alright, Lara. I was a worryin' meself sick," he explained with a groan. "The way ye left, I was no' sure—"

I was paying little attention to his words as I looked around, planning my escape. That's when Jamie placed a finger beneath my chin again. "I was no' sure you ever wanted to see me again."

"I just need time to process it all, Jamie," I whispered. "Your news was unsettling and I…I…honestly don't know what to do with it," I stammered.

"I understand," he added stoically.

"Do you?" I asked defensively. "Because I can't really see how on Earth you could understand."

"Ye have a new life, now. One that does no' have anythin' to do with the old one and ye are worried—"

Shaking a finger in his face, I scolded, "Jamie O'Brien, you have no idea of what you speak, so you should stop talking. It has nothing to do with being worried—"

"Oh, no?" he interrupted angrily. "Then maybe ye could explain it to me, in very simplistic terms, since I am just a simple-minded canal worker."

Confused by his sudden change in attitude, I took a step back. "This has nothing to do with you being a canal worker."

Looking hurt and offended, Jamie took a step forward. "Then tell me why ye tried to avoid me, Miss Lara High-and-Mighty Flannigan."

Punching Jamie hard in the arm just like I used to do when we were children, I nearly laughed out loud when he recoiled and cried, "Ouch!" like a little boy. "Why'd ye do that?" he groaned.

"Because, Jamie O'Brien, ye are still an idiot and ye have no' changed, even after all these years. Still think ye know it all, don' ye?" I grumbled. "Ye still believe ye can read my mind and know what's in my heart. Ye silly boy," I rattled on in my Irish brogue, showing him that I was still the same Lara Flannigan he once knew so well. "But time has no' made ye smarter for it. 'Name's Lara Ann Flannigan Roscoe, and I'd thank ye to remember it. To be sure!"

Sweeping me up into his arms, Jamie twirled me around while giving me a tight squeeze. "I don' much care what ye be calling yerself

these days, just as long as yer still be me Lara," he cried. "Ye can call yerself, Rosie Mulvaney, for all I care."

Stunned by his words, I gasped, "What did ye just say?"

"Tell me that's no' the name ye been goin' by tonight?" he grinned and winked. "I know because I checked."

I began to laugh out loud at the same time Jamie pulled me closer and kissed me on the lips. Stunned and caught off guard, I allowed his lips to linger a moment longer before pushing him away and protesting, "Jamie—"

"Miss Roscoe!" came a stern, loud voice behind me. "If you could tear yourself away from your companion for a moment, I believe it's time for us to leave. Now!"

Jamie hadn't loosened his grip on me when I turned to see the disappointed face of Roman Blackthorn as he glowered down at me. And what's more, Ella stood behind her brother, sheepishly peeking out at me from behind him. She was partially hidden from view by his ever-present, ever-looming self. I was struck by the sudden and unexpected feeling that he would make a wonderful father someday. He showed just enough anger to be intimidating yet had enough restraint to keep from tearing a person's head off. I was thoroughly impressed while at the same time terrified as my knees began knocking together.

Awkwardly, I disentangled myself from Jamie and stood up tall, looking directly at Roman. "I will be along momentarily, Mr. Blackthorn." I managed to spit out the words while holding my ground as he narrowed his eyes at me.

"I would prefer that we all leave together," he insisted.

"And I would prefer to say goodbye to my oldest and dearest friend, Jamie O'Brien, whom I haven't spent any time with since I was a child," I smoothly lied. "If you don't mind?" I insisted, controlling the sudden flash of anger I felt.

"Very well then, we will wait for you in the carriage. Please try to leave this place with your dignity intact." He punched out the last words as an insult before turning and dragging Ella along with him.

I saw the flash of worry in Ella's eyes as they disappeared into the crowd.

"Is he yer boyfriend?" Jamie asked.

Turning back around to face Jamie I saw the shadow of jealousy flicker in his eyes before he blinked. Denial was the only answer I was prepared to give before I realized where my loyalties truly laid. "We are strictly business partners."

"Are ye sure? Because that was a man stakin' a claim, if ever I saw it," Jamie argued, pulling me close again as if he intended to kiss me once more.

This time without hesitation, I pushed against his chest. "Jamie O'Brien, let go of me, this instant. I don't know what you were thinking, kissing me—and if you try it again, I will clobber you. I mean it!" I warned.

Looking startled at first, Jamie continued to try to pull me close. "Ye don' mean that."

"I most certainly do, you imp! You are my oldest friend. Why would you kiss me?" I questioned flatly. "Of all the stupid—" I began to say as I turned to leave.

Grabbing hold of my wrist, Jamie pulled me to a stop. "What do ye mean?" he asked, bewildered by my reaction. "I've been in love with ye for as long as I can remember, Lara Flannigan. I'd do anythin' for ye." Then, when he saw the look on my face, he corrected himself sarcastically, "Oh, forgive me, Lara Roscoe." Then, in a milder tone, he added, "My point is, ye will always be me Lara, and I will never stop lovin' ye."

Clasping his face between my hands, I pulled him close. "I will always love you, Jamie, and by that, I mean the boy I knew so many years ago who played make-believe with me on the beach. But let's face it, that boy isn't here with me now!" I sighed. "Just as that girl you knew so long ago is gone. She died years ago with her mother, father, and brother on the cliffs of Dunmore Head in Ireland." Tears of pain swam in my eyes, making it difficult to make out his face any longer.

"You have to let her go. She is in the past, Jamie O'Brien! Move forward with your life. The girl ye be lookin' for is gone forever!"

Then, sadly, I gently kissed his lips to say farewell, turned, and walked out of the Silver Slipper Dance Hall with my head held high. I never looked back, despite Jamie's pitiful pleas from behind me, "Wait, Lara, wait."

I truly believed the words that I had spoken to Jamie that night. I felt that a part of me had died with my family in Ireland. I heard Jamie calling out to me as I climbed up into the waiting carriage and took a seat next to Ella. I struggled to hold back the brimming tears and intense emotions that squeezed at my heart, fearing my heart would truly stop altogether.

The three of us rode in complete silence with Roman's horse tied to the back of the carriage. Ella placed a delicate hand over mine, trying to comfort me, but her attempts to heal the rift that had begun between the three of us was of little consequence. I could feel Roman's anger from where I sat on the opposite side of the seat. He sat as still as a statue, brooding to himself. I truly had my work cut out if I was ever going to fix the rift between the two of us.

As he stopped the carriage to drop me off, my heart sank even lower when there were no niceties. He didn't even bother to step down and see me to the door, but instead, waited for me to step clear of the wheels before slapping the reins and heading down the road. Miserable, dejected, and hurt, I watched as the two of them disappeared around the corner while I stood there staring after them on the sidewalk.

How could I explain to Roman that Jamie was my best friend growing up and that I saw him more as a brother, rather than a love interest? That the kiss he'd witnessed between us was nothing more than a terrible misunderstanding.

No, I believed that the dye had been cast and my fate was sealed. Roman Blackthorn would never again see me in the same light that he had once before and I would end up an old spinster, alone, with only the servants and a few cats to keep me company. Somehow, I knew that the past was not yet through rearing its ugly head with me and that Madam Sabina's predictions would continue to manifest themselves in

ways that I wasn't sure I was prepared to deal with. There was a faint feeling of dread that still gnawed at my soul. Something was coming and I had a feeling that it would be bad—like the feeling Mr. Green gets when the weather changes and his knee gives him fits because a storm is coming. I could feel it in my bones—all of my bones.

Shivering violently, I hugged my arms around myself, walked into the house, and marched up to my room without checking in on Mother and Father. My mind was too full of dreadful thoughts to convincingly carry on small talk.

22

MAY 15, 1852
WEDNESDAY

Age 19
Ella Returns from Exile

Ella and I were severely reprimanded for the incident at the dance hall. Truth be told, Ella received the harshest punishment of all. Her parents were so outraged at her for the incident that Ella was shipped off to Mrs. Blackthorns' elderly, widowed aunt who was as straight and pure as they come. She lived in Albany, New York, and was rumored to attend church nearly every day of the week. Sometimes she even attended twice on Sundays, so I was told.

My parents merely called me into Papa's sick room and gave me the whole *we are very disappointed with your behavior* speech, which didn't have much effect on me until I looked in their eyes and saw the hurt and heartbreak I'd caused. I had let them down and couldn't live with myself for doing so. I felt terrible for causing them grief while Papa languished in his sick bed. I vowed then and there that I would never again do anything to cause them to look at me in that way.

It took Roman nearly three weeks to forgive me enough to even look at me. Then it took another three and a half weeks for us to find a kind of balance that allowed for us to communicate with any kind of civil accord. Yet, every so often, I could still feel his anger over the matter.

Now we had gotten to the point that when he needed to speak with me, he no longer sent someone else to deliver the message, but would come upstairs to the office and call me by my surname, "*Miss*

Roscoe." In return, I would grit my teeth and bite my tongue, replying in a pleasant tone, "Yes, how may I help you, Mr. Blackthorn?"

Yet today, nearly seven months later, I'd heard that Ella was coming home any day now, following her seven months of exile. I was anxious to see my good friend and wondered if she had changed much.

I was standing in the office gazing out of the window at the people and traffic going by, when Roman unexpectedly walked in and cleared his throat. "I beg your pardon, Miss Roscoe, I didn't realize you were in," he blurted out.

Without turning around, I asked, "When are you going to stop punishing me for something that happened over half a year ago? And it wasn't even as it appeared."

Stammering slightly, he responded, "Why, I'm certain I don't know what you mean, Miss—"

"There! Right there," I pointed out, turning from the window and taking two steps toward him. "That's exactly what I mean. If you call me Miss Roscoe one more time, I think I will scream bloody murder!"

Acting as if he didn't have the foggiest idea of what I was talking about, Roman shook his head. "But it's your name, isn't it?"

Clenching my hands at my side, I growled, "You have got to be the most infuriating man. You have judged me on circumstantial evidence, rather than anything concrete," I argued as I advanced on him. "Jamie O'Brien was my best friend growing up. He was my whole world—"

"Then perhaps you and this O'Brien fellow should announce your intentions," he angrily retorted, cutting me off.

"Bloody hell!" I swore under my breath. "You didn't let me finish."

"Then maybe you should come to the point. I have a lot of orders to fill today," he snarled.

Softening my tone, I took another step closer. "If you had let me finish, I would have said that Jamie *was* my whole world, but that was so many years ago and I was just a child at the time. I didn't want him to kiss me that night," I added with a sour look. "He was like another brother to me, not someone I was in love with. Although that does not

negate the fact that I will always love him," I clarified, "like I will always love my brothers Colin, Micky, and Michael."

Whistling between his teeth, Roman looked somewhat shocked. "That's a lot of brothers. You've never told me anything about your family before."

"Well, you've never asked," I pointed out. "Yet had you asked, I still may not have told you," I said saucily.

Taking a step forward, closing the gap between us, he tipped my chin up towards him with one finger, forcing me to look directly at him. "And why is that?"

Swallowing the large lump in my throat, I explained, "Because it can be painful to remember all that happened to me."

Staring down into my eyes, Roman looked at me as if he were trying to learn the shape of me—slow, deliberate, every blink a question. His eyes warmed, and something in his jaw softened, as though all the hardness I'd seen of late was being smoothed away. I felt the room shrink to the space between us. His breath feathered across my cheek, mine came quicker in answer, and my heart tapped a frantic rhythm. He tilted his head, a small, almost shy motion, and then lowered his face until his lips brushed mine—tender at first—before the kiss deepened.

My heart skipped a beat and butterflies fluttered in my stomach. Leaning into him and placing the palms of my hands against his chest, I could feel his heart pounding wildly through the coat he was wearing, and it thrilled me.

We heard someone step onto the landing and Roman pulled away first, clearing his throat loudly as he took a step back. Turning, we saw Ella smiling.

"Speaking of the Devil," he said louder than necessary.

"Were the two of you discussing me?" she cried as she rushed into the room, hugging us both at the same time. I must have looked startled because Ella then added suspiciously, "Did I just interrupt something?"

"No!" I interjected too quickly, stepping back a step, causing Ella to become even more suspicious.

"The old Eloise would have jumped all over that lie and wormed the truth out of you eventually," she informed me. "But the new Eloise will let this one go. I have some very exciting news to share with you both," she said, removing her day gloves and putting them in her coat pocket before pulling out the hat pin and removing her hat.

Rubbing his hands together as if he were a co-conspirator in a plot, Roman quickly pulled up another chair so the three of us could sit together. "Are we going to hear how you intend to make up for lost time? Oh, let me guess, you want to tell us all about bottling applesauce with Aunt Prudence and the latest gossip from Albany!"

Looking at her brother disapprovingly, Ella slapped his arm. "No, dummy, I have real news and I wanted the two of you to hear it from me first."

Leaning forward and placing my hand on her leg, I gave it a squeeze. "Ella, I have truly missed you. I never got the chance to tell you that I was sorry that you found yourself in so much trouble."

"I know, dear. I really missed you too," she said with a dramatic sigh. "But my banishment was my own doing and I never got the chance to tell you how sorry I was for dragging you into that entire mess."

"I agreed to go. No one put a knife to my throat," I bantered.

Looking abashed, she admitted, "To tell the truth, you didn't really have much of a choice. I did ambush you, after all."

"I could have refused to go inside," I insisted.

With a wicked smile, Ella winked. "But you are a better friend than that. You would have never let me go inside by myself and I exploited that—"

"I'm a big girl Ella, I could have talked you out of it."

Interrupting our mutual self-deprecation, Roman said impatiently, "Please, tell us your news. You can go over who is to blame for everything later."

"Oh, Roman, you can suck the air from the room faster than anyone else I know," Ella glared at him, then suddenly perked up. "So, my big

news. I'm glad you are sitting down because I'd hate to pick you both up from off the floor."

"Well, don't keep us in suspense any longer," I demanded.

Shoving her right hand out in front of her, Ella cried, "I'm getting married!"

Roman and I simultaneously yelled, "What?!" as we looked at each other.

"To whom?" he bellowed.

"Roman Alister Henry Blackthorn, don't you take that tone with me!" she snapped. "I don't know who you think you are!"

"I'm sorry, but he's right Ella," I interjected. "You go away for seven months then return and announce that you are getting married?"

Becoming suddenly defensive, Ella stood up abruptly and walked over to the large window to gaze out onto the street below. "I need the two of you to be on my side just now," she whined, quickly turning around to face us. "I don't have a choice in the matter."

Jumping to his feet and taking three long strides, Roman closed the gap between them as he took his sister into his arms and shook her. "What do you mean you don't have a choice?"

"Ouch, Roman, that hurts," Ella complained, brushing him off. "I don't mean it like that. I'm not in the family way," she insisted.

"That's a relief," he groaned, letting out a heavy sigh. "For a moment I thought I was going to have to hurt someone."

Patting her brother's chest, Ella pushed him away and turned to me. "Mother and Father have made arrangements. So, I need the two of you to help me through this..." she hesitated, "or I am afraid I will fall apart."

Coming to Ella's side, I hugged her to me tightly, "Oh, Ella, I'm so sorry."

Squeezing back, Ella buried her head in my neck. "Don't be sorry, Lara, it's really a good match," she murmured.

"It doesn't matter how good of a match it is if you aren't in love with the man," I pressed.

"Let's just make the best of a bad situation," Ella insisted. "That is the only way that it will be palatable."

Wrapping his arms around the two of us, Roman was beside himself. "We'll figure it out."

"What's to figure out? Father has already made arrangements."

Stepping towards the window, Roman ran his hand through his hair as he stared out of the window onto the street. "That can't be it!" he said emphatically. "That just can't be the end of it."

"I told you, I have no say in the matter."

"Who?" he demanded, turning away from the window to face her. "Who is it?!" Roman demanded angrily.

Shyly smiling, Ella raised her chin. "Theodore Cramp."

"Not the youngest son of the shipping magnate Cramps?" he questioned.

Nodding her head, Ella confirmed, "The very one. It's a good match, Roman," she insisted, a defiant gleam in her eyes.

Watching the exchange, I felt I needed to step in before matters got out of hand. "Roman, leave her alone," I pleaded.

Looking at me defensively, he challenged, "I will not. This is my sister and she is making a big mistake."

"Who says she is making a mistake?" I questioned. "Maybe she is happy about the match. Are you happy about the match, Ella?" I questioned.

Nodding her head unconvincingly, I could see tears forming in her eyes. "Of course. It's a very good match," Ella challenged, turning away from us both and dabbing at her eyes.

"You just say the word and I will kidnap you and take you away from all of this," Roman assured her, grasping her by the shoulders and turning her to face him again.

Shaking her head, she sniffed, "No, Roman! This is a good thing. Mother said so."

"Oh, well, then, if Mother says so," Roman added sarcastically, throwing his hands into the air. "I still think you're making a mistake."

"Then it is mine to make, Roman Alister Henry the III!" Ella fired back, blowing her nose into a handkerchief.

I wrapped my arms around my friend. "You're not helping, Roman. So, stop badgering her and just let her speak," I said, holding her to me protectively and stroking her hair. "You tell me how this came about."

"It was conditional that I agree to marry if I wanted to return home," Ella sniffed. "And to tell you the truth, Aunt Prudence can really grate on my nerves."

I looked up and saw Roman nodding his head as he turned towards the window.

"Go on," I encouraged.

"Well, as you can well imagine, after being tied to Prudence's hip for seven months, I would agree to just about anything to make my escape."

"Aha! There it is! You were under duress," Roman pointed out.

"Well, of course I agreed under duress," she sniffed, "the entire, last seven months I've been under duress. What did you think had happened to me?"

"I just figured that you would have a little vacation, then be back," he replied.

Shaking her head, she snapped, "I was with Aunt Prudence, you dolt. I wouldn't call that a vacation. You could have rescued me, but you didn't. I had to rescue myself!"

Patting her back, I redirected her again. "So how did you make your escape?"

"Our parents made a promising match with William Crump to marry me to his youngest son, Theodore. I understand he needs some taming as well," Ella explained. "We meet this evening, but I had to

come by and let you know that I was back home. I missed you so much, Lara. I wanted to write, but I wasn't allowed to."

Giving her a patient smile, I said, "That's all right, Ella. I knew something was up when you weren't even allowed to say good-bye. At least you're home now, and everything will work out as it should." I tried to sound reassuring while feeling less than confident about the matter myself.

"I know," she said tentatively, looking to Roman for understanding. "I'm fine, Roman. Please don't worry."

"This is an outrage," he swore under his breath. "I will speak with Father!"

"Please, don't," she cried. "Really, I'm fine. I truly am!"

Roman and I locked eyes and neither one of us believed her, but he reluctantly nodded, and Ella looked relieved.

"You'll see. Everything will work out just fine," she smiled. "I actually heard he is a nice man."

"Well, he better be or he will have to answer to me," Roman threatened. "You hear me, Ella. I will break his nose if he hurts you."

"Stand down, Roman," she cautioned. "And I love you too, big brother," Ella said, and then cringed when she heard the grandfather clock in the hallway chime. "Oh, dear. I'm late. I'd better be off. I will be fine, Roman, really. You'll see," she assured us both, giving us each one last hug before rushing out the door. "Stop worrying!" she shouted over her shoulder as she flew down the stairs.

"Can you believe my parents?" he murmured, raking his fingers through his hair as he turned to the window to watch Ella climb into the family carriage and drive away.

"I can believe just about anything," I retorted, stepping up to the window next to him. "I've lived through—" I added, before thinking better about opening up to Roman about my past. "Never mind."

"No, please, tell me. What is it that you have lived through?"

With a shake of my head, I said quietly, "It doesn't matter."

"But it matters to me."

"It isn't important. Didn't you come up here earlier to tell me something?" I said, changing the subject.

"Oh, yes. I need to run out and pick up a load of lumber that is ready," Roman said, looking distracted as he pondered his sister's unexpected news. Then, turning to me, he smoothed his hair back with his hand. "But I think I will send Eric instead. He isn't busy."

"What are you going to do instead?"

With a faraway look in his eyes, Roman shook his head. "I need to have a word with someone," he answered as a slight smile formed on his lips as if he had just come up with a plan.

"But…but, you heard what Ella said," I stammered. "She told you to leave this matter alone."

"I can't," he murmured, then walked out of the room, leaving me standing there with my mouth hanging open.

23

JULY 4, 1852

We Meet Again:
Madam Sabina

Ella's sporadic visits in the past two weeks had been understandable since she was preparing for her upcoming nuptials to Theodore Cramp, the youngest son of William Cramp, the Philadelphian shipbuilding tycoon. Yet Roman, on the other hand, was a different story. After our shared kiss, he had become aloof, running errands and disappearing at odd hours of the day, leaving me feeling quite alone in the running of our business.

Papa's health had taken a turn for the worse in the last few days, and I felt the need to spend more time at work making sure that orders were filled on time and bills got paid.

Mother never left Papa's side as of late, so I felt doubly obligated to keep things running for them both. I was comforted by the fact that I could look across the street and see Mother sitting next to Papa in the sitting room reading to him or mending something to keep herself busy.

Being the Fourth of July, it was a holiday, but I'd come into the office anyway, determined to get ahead of the bills and organize my calendar for the rest of the week. That's when Roman walked into the office and took a seat across from me.

Making a high-pitched whistle through his teeth, he said glibly, "You certainly are dedicated. Don't you ever stop to have fun anymore?"

With a sharp snap, I shut the check register and fixed him with a cold glare. I stowed the ledger in the desk, turned the key, and slipped

the keys into my pocket. My white scooped-neck dress with three-quarter sleeves was cinched by a navy ribbon at the waist, the bow resting neatly against the small of my neck.

I stood up, sliding my chair back, making a scraping noise as the back legs slid off the carpet and onto the wooden floor. "Someone has to be accountable for the running of the day-to-day affairs," I stated flatly, folding my arms over my chest as I stepped to the window to check on Mother and Papa.

Silently walking up behind me, Roman turned me around in his arms. "You're right of course and I owe you an apology and an explanation. I realize I haven't been around much in the past few days—"

With a derisive scoff, I pushed against his chest, taking a step to the side, just out of his reach. "Have you now? I hadn't really noticed," I replied as if I could care less. I was feeling petulant and didn't care if I was being rude.

"As I was saying…" he continued, taking a step closer, closing the gap between us and trapping me against the bookshelf. "I'm sorry, Lara. Truly I am. And if there were some way to make it up to you—"

Turning to face the window again, in essence giving Roman the cold shoulder, I said, "How about you show up when you are supposed to, or maybe you could try putting in a full day's work so that I can help out at home more."

Stepping up behind me, he stood like that for a long silent pause. I could feel the heat from Roman's body as he towered over me. We were both looking across the street, into my home. "I heard he took a turn for the worse yesterday," Roman finally said.

I turned on him, "And where were you? I could have really used some help or just a friend to talk to, but you were gone. Again!" I admonished as tears sprang to my eyes.

Pulling a clean handkerchief from his pocket and handing it to me, he said, "I truly am sorry, Lara. I've been very selfish as of late."

"Yes, you have!" I sniffed, wiping my eyes. "I thought we were partners."

"We are," Roman replied adamantly. "It's just that, well, Ella's news threw me for a loop."

"Ella's news threw us all for a loop," I scoffed. "But that's no reason to shirk your duties." I blew my nose, then tucked the handkerchief into my pocket, deciding that I would wash it and return it to him later.

Gently forcing my chin up, Roman gazed down at me as stormy blue eyes regarded me somberly. It was then that I saw him clearly for the first time in months. He was going through something too. An emotional storm was happening behind those piercing blue orbs, and I needed to be patient.

"I truly am sorry for neglecting my duties…and you, Lara. Truly I am," he said, tipping his head at a slight angle before leaning down and placing a gentle kiss upon my lips. The passion behind the kiss melted any resolve I had of staying mad at him. Reluctantly ending the kiss, he pulled me even closer, tightening his arms around my shoulders. "I hope you know I wouldn't hurt you for anything in the world."

"I know," I murmured against his shoulder, hugging his waist. "Just don't abandon me again or I will have to throw something at you."

"And you would be well within your rights to do so," he chuckled. "I doubt that I would even bother to duck."

He made me laugh despite my resolve and I pushed him away again so that I could retrieve the handkerchief from my pocket and blow my nose once more. "Just don't do it again."

"I swear it," he answered, raising his right hand in the air. "Could I talk you into having dinner with me this evening?"

Looking over my shoulder, unsure whether or not I should leave Mother and Papa alone, I hesitated. "Well—"

"I promise not to keep you out late. We could see the fireworks and then I would take you directly home," he insisted, cocking his head to one side and giving me a wink.

With one last look over my shoulder, I turned back around. "That would be lovely," I replied. "I haven't been out of the house for a while except to attend work."

"Excellent. I will call upon you precisely at 8 o'clock."

"I'll be ready."

After checking on Papa and kissing both my parents goodnight, I walked down the stairs as the clock chimed eight. Upon hearing someone wish Emmerson a boisterous good evening, I smiled to myself, knowing that Roman had arrived right on time.

I'd changed into a white, gauzy, button-down blouse with a high collar, and a navy-blue skirt that swished when I walked. I felt very feminine and pretty as I descended the staircase.

Roman stood in the entryway, looking devastatingly masculine, as always, but he was not alone.

"I hope you don't mind, but I took the liberty of inviting Ella to join us," he said, overly jovial. "After all, she will be a married woman soon with little time for the likes of us," he laughed, sounding less than thrilled with the prospect of his sister's upcoming nuptials.

Throwing my arms around Ella's neck, I squealed, "Oh, this is marvelous news." Then I turned to face Roman. "And just for the record, Roman, even when she does become an old, boring, married woman, I will always be happy to see her."

"Hey, this is me we are talking about," Ella added, trying to sound insulted by our playful teasing. "I will never be boring or old!"

Raising a skeptical eyebrow, Roman teased, "We'll see," for which Ella promptly punched him in the arm.

"Ouch! Why did you do that?" he moaned.

"You didn't see that coming now did you?" she pointed out. "That seals it then. I will never be boring or old and I will always be just unpredictable enough to keep you on your toes, Roman Blackthorn. Married or not!"

"Might I suggest we leave before something gets broken and blood is spilled on mother's carpet," I quipped, taking Ella by the arm and leading her out of the front door. "Besides, I am famished and could eat my weight in food. Where are we going tonight?"

"I thought the two of you would enjoy a picnic in the park, followed by a fireworks display," Roman answered, rushing ahead to help usher us both up into the carriage he'd parked at the curb.

"That truly does sound like a lovely evening," I exclaimed, taking hold of his hand as he offered to help me up first. He allowed his fingers to linger a moment longer than necessary and I smiled to myself.

Roman sat between Ella and me on the bench seat with a satisfied grin on his face. "What are you smiling about?" Ella asked, elbowing him in the ribs.

"Oh, nothing. It's just nice to have the two prettiest ladies in the county sitting on either side of me," Roman explained.

Giving his sister a wide, toothy grin, he nodded his head to someone he knew traveling in the opposite direction on the street. Then, lifting his hand to wave to someone else on the sidewalk who'd called out to him, Roman slapped the reins against the horses' rumps and looked very pleased with himself.

"Well, aren't you the little social butterfly tonight, big brother," Ella teased before waving to someone she knew who was passing by and called out to her.

"I'd say that you were both equally social this evening." I smiled and waved to Mr. and Mrs. Chantry as they stood in the doorway of their tea and pastry shop, Harriet's Tea Room. "There are certainly a lot of people mingling about tonight," I acknowledged.

Twenty minutes later, Roman pulled the carriage to a stop. "Here we are," he announced as he set the brake and jumped down. "I thought the park would be the perfect place to view the fireworks from," he added, helping Ella climb down first before reaching up to grasp me by the waist and lift me down to the ground.

We could hear a band playing in the center of the park and people were mingling about, going from one blanket to another, chatting with friends and acquaintances. The park crawled with activity and I found it all very exhilarating.

I was lost in thought when I realized that Roman had said something to me several times, trying to engage me in conversation. "What?…I'm sorry, Roman," I exclaimed, "I was just so taken by all the activity."

"Don't concern yourself," he chuckled. "I am easily distracted myself," he replied, retrieving a basket and two large blankets from the back of the carriage.

"It's true," Ella teased. "I can attest to that."

"All right, that's enough from you, young lady," Roman admonished. "Don't make me sorry I invited you to tag along with us."

Taking ahold of my arm, Ella laughed, encouraging me to hurry along as we left Roman behind.

"Hey, now," he called out, rushing after us to catch up. Ella giggled even more.

We searched about for a few minutes to find the perfect spot to spread out our blankets. We didn't want to be too close to the trees so that we could have a full view of the Wharf. Roman lit the lantern, setting it near the edge of the basket, while Ella began to pull out the food and spread it out before us. We dined on fried chicken, watermelon slices, cheese wedges, grapes, pickles, and sweetened lemonade, and we topped off our delectable feast with a slice of peach pie. The evening couldn't have been more perfect. Our conversation never stopped as we watched the activity move around us. I felt so alive and invigorated that just for a few moments I was able to relax and forget about all my cares.

Children ran around laughing as they chased after one another with sparklers. Older boys lit strings of firecrackers, laughing when women cried out in surprise. The band never missed a beat and continued to play on despite all the chaos.

"Fortunes told. Get your fortunes told," a young gypsy girl called out as she weaved her way through the crowd, careful not to trample on anyone's blanket. "Madam Sabina tells your fortune. Get your fortunes told!" she cried.

Ella smiled and clapped her hands excitedly. "Yay!" she cheered. "Young lady, can I get one of those flyers?"

"Certainly, Ma'am," the young gypsy answered, handing Ella a piece of paper. "Madam Sabina is waiting to speak with you, just over there," she pointed. "And there doesn't appear to be a line if you go now."

Jumping up, Ella grinned widely. "Now I can tell her that everything worked out exactly the way she said it would," she announced.

"Ella, Ella!" Roman called out but was ignored as Ella disappeared into the crowd. "Bullheaded…" he grumbled under his breath.

"She'll be back," I assured him, swallowing the last of my lemonade just as a singular test firework was fired into the evening sky.

Just as the fireworks show began, Roman asked, "Would you like more?" holding a mason jar out to me.

"No, thank you," I responded, staring up at the sky and making an '*awe*' sound along with everyone else. I felt Roman's eyes on me after a few minutes and slowly turned to find him studying me. "Why do you stare at me when the fireworks are up there?" I pointed.

"Because the real attraction of the evening is right in front of me," he announced, taking my hand into his. "There is something I've wanted to say to you for a while now—" he began to say.

"Lara, Lara!" Ella shouted, landing on the blanket next to me with an unladylike plop. "You have to come with me," she insisted breathlessly while pulling at my arm. "Madam Sabina has asked for you."

"How could you have possibly located Madam Sabina and come back to get me so quickly?"

"I ran," she said, getting to her feet and reaching down to pull me up. "I'm not making this up, Lara. She really wants to see you. She says that she has something important to tell you."

A puzzled look crossed my face as I glanced at Roman. He only shrugged, but his eyes crinkled and he gave a quick, encouraging nod.

"Come on," Ella insisted, pulling anxiously at my arm.

"Can't it wait until the fireworks display is done?"

"NO! She told me that it was urgent that she speak with you. Or maybe she said it was dire. I can't remember. Either way, it's important so stop lollygagging, Lara. We need to hurry," Ella insisted, taking hold of my hand as she led me quickly through the crowd of people and blankets, zigzagging her way.

Coming up to the edge of the park where the gypsies had set up camp, I recognized many of them as they stood around enjoying the fireworks. They barely acknowledged us as we passed by on our way to Sabina's trailer.

Madam Sabina stood on the steps of her wagon as if she were watching for us. When she saw us approaching, she entered her wagon ahead of us. I hadn't realized that Roman was following behind us until he touched my shoulder, startling me just as I reached the wagon steps.

"Roman, what are you doing?" I cried.

"I just wanted you to know that I am here for you, and you don't have to do this alone."

"You worry too much," I challenged, knowing in my heart that I was glad he had followed. My stomach clenched tightly at the memory of my last visit with the fortune teller. Everything Madam Sabina had told me before was etched upon my mind. So many of her words had come true and I was afraid that she had more bad news to tell me.

Giving my hand a squeeze, Roman smiled. "I wanted to be here for you regardless."

Nodding my head with gratitude, I climbed the steps and entered the small trailer. Two lanterns hung in the small room, illuminating the interior as they had before. But this time the curtains were securely drawn, ensuring that outsiders could not see in through the windows. The gypsy woman sat at her table, gesturing for me to take a seat opposite her. Sitting down in the chair across from her, I looked over my shoulder and watched as Roman quietly closed the door. He and Ella stood silently in the one corner of the room that was not touched by the light of the lantern, like two flies on a wall.

Clearing my throat before speaking, hoping that she couldn't tell I felt apprehensive about being called to her trailer, I began, "I understand you have something of some urgency to tell me."

Madam Sabina smiled patiently, placing her hand upon the table. "Yes," she purred, "but first spirits of the ancestors must be satisfied," she declared, waiting with her hand palm up and opened upon the table.

At first I didn't understand what she was asking of me, until Ella discretely stepped forward, reached into her pocket, and produced two coins, placing them into Madam Sabina's hand. The old gypsy woman grinned, felt the weight of the coins, and then pronounced, "The ancestors have been satisfied."

"I thought you said she summoned me," I demanded, turning to look up at Ella.

"That doesn't mean that the ancestors don't need to be made happy, Lara," Ella scolded before stepping back into the shadow of the darkened corner.

"Oh," I murmured, turning back around to face the old gypsy woman.

Reaching across the table to me, Madam Sabina insisted, "Give me hands. I had a dream and knew that we would soon cross paths again," she announced dramatically. "Now, you concentrate on family who has gone before you. They come to Madam Sabina and wish me to tell you something important."

Feeling as if I'd just been duped, I started to pull my hands away when the old gypsy grabbed my wrists tightly. She was determined to deliver an important message. "You doubt Madam Sabina. Yes?" she questioned. "But what I told you before came true. Yes?"

Hesitating a moment, then looking over my shoulder at Ella and Roman, I took a deep breath and sighed, "Yes."

She grinned even wider before narrowing her eyes. "So, you know Madam Sabina tells truth. Yes?"

Reluctantly, I answered, "Yes."

"So, now you give me hands. We will see what ancestors wish to tell Madam Sabina that is so urgent."

Barely able to breathe, I slowly turned my hands over on the table, giving myself over to the gypsy woman as my curiosity outweighed my common sense.

Taking my hands into hers, Madam Sabina silently studied them for a moment. "You will have very long life," she said with a sigh. "That is curious. I see two men in your life—" She paused before looking up at me and then cast her eyes towards the darkened corner where Roman stood. Then, nodding her head as if she suddenly understood something that she hadn't before, she tipped her head forward again to gaze at my hand and continued, "There will be children, and you will be very happy," she exclaimed, looking up into my eyes. "But only after you learn to forgive the past," she added pointedly. "You understand what Madam Sabina mean by that?"

Pulling my hands back quickly and placing them in my lap as if someone had just scalded them, I clutched my fingers together, trying to stop them from shaking. The gypsy woman smiled with understanding and stood up, turning toward an old trunk she kept behind her.

I couldn't stop myself from staring after her with curiosity as she carefully pulled an object from the ancient trunk, setting it in a wooden cradle in the middle of the table in front of her. She lovingly removed the dark cloth that covered it to reveal a crystal ball. "I use this for special people," she informed me.

I wanted to be skeptical, get up, and walk out of her trailer and chalk it all up to the rantings of a crazy woman, but I couldn't. I found myself drawn in by her spell, even leaning forward to get a better look at what she was seeing when she gazed into the orb. Her hands gracefully floated over the crystal ball while she stared wide-eyed into its depths. She was quiet for a moment, seeming to absorb whatever it was the ball was telling her. I held my breath as she looked up at me and began to speak, curious as to what she might tell me next.

"I still see the pain that has not yet left you, child. It runs deep. So deep!" she said, shaking her head and clicking her tongue at me as if

it were all a huge shame. "She wants you to know that you must let go of past or it will weigh you down, like anchor around neck."

"Who is this *she* you speak of?" I asked, looking into Madam Sabina's eyes, which now appeared strangely opaque in color, rather than the dark, rich brown shade I remembered them to be. "Who are you talking about, Madam Sabina?"

"Shh, child," she responded, staring again into the ball. "The past is not yet through revealing itself to you. There is another who will come to you, like ghost from past. Don't be afraid," she warned, "you are strong enough."

I couldn't help feeling apprehension as I took several steadying breaths, digging my fingernails into the palms of my hands to remind myself that this was all real and not some dream I was having.

Suddenly, her hands froze in place and a strange expression contorted her face. The gypsy woman vigorously shook her head, the way one does when attempting to dispel a bad thought.

"What is it? What did you see?" I cried, grasping her hand with mine. Her eyes began to clear, returning to their normal, rich brown color. She continued to look down, then shook her head, refusing to answer my question at first.

"Please, Madam Sabina, what did you see?" I begged.

"You will lose someone very dear to you this night," she replied hesitantly as she slowly looked up, sympathetic tears shimmering in her eyes. She looked so sincere that I almost believed that she cared. "I'm very sorry child," she said, grasping my hand as I tried to pull away, "but your ancestors feel it important that you know that they watch over you. You are not alone."

"Who is the *she* that you mentioned before?" I questioned angrily.

"You know in your heart who I speak of," she assured me. "You have always known and felt her with you, giving strength to you when you need it most. Yes?"

Unable to stop the tears that began to trickle down my cheeks, I nodded my head.

Scooting back her chair so that she could come around the table and pull me to my feet, Sabina placed her strong arms around me. "She will be with you this night," she assured me with a final embrace. "Always know that Madam Sabina is here for you," she added, gently guiding me towards the door. "If you need me, I will find you. No worries."

Wordlessly I stepped through the door as Madam Sabina opened it. Looking up into the night sky where the fireworks display was just concluding, I marveled at their beauty and hoped that Madam Sabina was right and that my mama was truly by my side to help me. I could feel that the heartache that was coming my way was going to bring much sadness. I could feel it in my bones, because I knew the moment the words had left her mouth, *you will lose someone close to you this night*, that she could only be talking about one person: my papa was dead.

24

JULY 9, 1852

Saying Goodbye to Papa

"We need to get home—Now!" I hissed to Roman as we spilled out of Madam Sabina's trailer. We didn't pause to gather the blanket or the basket—leaving them like careless things on the grass—and I practically ran for the carriage, heart banging so hard I thought that everyone around me could hear it.

Roman stopped a man he knew and spoke in two clipped words. The man's face went tight, he swallowed, and Roman was at my side again, following Ella and me without another word. The wheels creaked; the road blurred under the hoof beats. I mouthed a prayer between breaths, fingers clamped so hard in my skirts they ached, while a cold knot uncoiled from my chest and settled in my stomach.

By the time we pulled up, my breath had gone thin. Doctor Sheridan's horse and buggy stood there in front of the house like an accusation. Just looking at the door, I knew. He was gone! The certainty hit me like a blow; my body went rigid until Ella's hand landed on my arm and steadied me.

I jumped down from the carriage before Roman had come to a complete stop, running up the steps of the porch with a cry of anger and frustration frozen in my throat. I threw the door open wide before Emmerson could let me in and ran toward the stairs. The air felt different somehow—as if it had been sucked from the entire house and replaced with something heavier. Thicker.

Doctor Sheridan looked startled as I ran past him coming down the stairs. "It was his heart," he called after me as I raced past him without

a word of greeting. I could hear his cries for me to wait, but I ignored them.

The pitiful looks on the faces of the maid, cook, and houseboy as I slowed down, passing each of them standing at the top of the stairs, told me that my worst nightmare had just come true. Quickening my steps down the hallway to my parents' room, I slowed when I reached the bedroom door that stood open. I felt a sob catch in my throat.

The scene before me broke my heart. Mother laid across the bed, her head resting upon Papa's chest, softly crying.

Martha, the housekeeper, stood just inside the doorway, helplessly holding an empty cup in her hand. Her pleading eyes turned to me when I entered the room. "Doctor Sheridan tried to comfort her. He even gave her a sedative," she whispered, holding the glass up as evidence. "But nothing has helped. She has been like that for almost an hour now. I don't know what else to do," she fretted.

"It's alright, Martha, I'm here now. You may go," I said, touching her arm, assuring her that we would be fine.

Martha hesitated a moment before nodding her head and quietly closing the door behind her.

I felt the stoic defenses I'd developed from early childhood sliding into place, like a shield between me and the overpowering heartache of loss that threatened to consume me. A hardness curled around my heart, shielding me from the pain like a sheet of iron—strong and impenetrable. I knew this feeling well. It was the only defense against the utter destruction of my very being. It seemed that I always ended up in this position, no matter how hard I tried to avoid it. This was the place I turned to for solace when all else failed—the only thing that had saved me from a life of utter disappointment and hurt. It would get me through this moment as well.

"Just breathe in, breathe out, move forward," I whispered to myself.

Kneeling down beside mother on the bed, I gently touched her hand and waited for her to acknowledge me. Tears spilled over her red-rimmed eyes as she slowly turned towards me.

"It was his heart. It just couldn't fight the…the—" she stammered helplessly. "He's gone," she finally cried with disbelief etching her words. "He's gone, Lara."

I could feel my heart constrict even tighter as I swallowed hard to hold back my own grief. He was lying there, so quiet and still. "I know, Mother," I whispered in her ear. We held tightly to one another as she cried her bitter tears. "I know, and I'm here now."

The next five days leading up to the funeral were a blur and passed by quickly as we made preparations. Roman and Ella refused to leave either one of us, hovering over us, making sure that we wanted for nothing.

Doctor Sheridan stopped by several more times during the week to check on Mother, giving Martha a goodly supply of sedative powder to slip into Mother's tea, which helped her to sleep.

As the somber day of Papa's funeral drew closer, I found Mother sitting in a chair, dressed in her simple black dress, staring blankly out of the window as if she were in a trance.

"Mother, Doctor Sheridan is here," I softly spoke, jolting her from her own thoughts as I kneeled down beside her, taking her hand into mine. She felt so cold to my touch and I grew concerned. "Martha brought you some hot tea and a fresh roll, fresh out of the oven."

Shaking her head, she turned to look at me. "I'm not hungry."

"But you have to eat something to keep up your strength, Mother," I pleaded, holding the cup of tea out to her. "Please, Mother. At least drink this."

She waved it away, turning up her nose. "I don't want it," she insisted.

"Charity, you must eat something," Henry Sheridan admonished, coming up behind me. "What would Zane think if I allowed you to blow away with the first strong breeze?"

Mother looked at her old friend as if she just realized he was in the room. "What on earth are you doing here again, Henry? Don't you have other patients to attend to?"

"I was visiting a patient down the street and stopped in to see how you were doing," he lied. "Please, Charity, you must try to drink something," he insisted. "Martha, I will take a cup of tea and one of those lovely rolls. My good friend and I are going to eat something," he said flatly as if his stopping by was a normal occurrence.

Mother opened her mouth to protest, but then shut it again when she saw the look in Henry's eyes.

"Martha, do you have any of that delicious marmalade you are so famous for? Charity loves marmalade, as I recall," he said as he spread butter onto his hot roll. "As I remember, she would eat just about anything as long as it had marmalade on it," the good doctor teased, with a wink at Martha.

"I will fetch it straight away, sir," Martha replied, hurrying from the room.

"I will see that she eats something," he said, turning to me and nodding his head. Then, with a smile, he patted Mother's hand and placed a cup of tea between her fingers. "I fixed it just the way you like it. Good and strong."

With a look of resolve, Mother picked up the cup with a heavy sigh and brought it to her lips, taking a sip and savoring the warm liquid as it slid down her throat. Giving us both a stiff smile, she said, "I would appreciate it if the two of you would stop hovering over me as if I were going to faint away any minute."

"We will, just as soon as you start eating again. You have had us all very worried about you, Charity." A compassionate smile accompanied Henry's words. "Lara has already lost one parent this week. It will never do for her to lose you as well."

Mother looked startled by his words and turned to me with tears in her eyes. "I swore that I would never leave you, Lara, and I intend to keep that promise. You have been so strong for me these past few days when it should have been me being strong for you."

"I know how grief can make you lose yourself, Mother," I softly said, wiping a stray tear away with a finger. "But Doctor Sheridan is right, you have to eat, for my sake."

"I will. I promise."

When we arrived at the church on the day of the funeral, somber mourners were quietly mingling before falling silent as Mother and I entered the chapel. It was gratifying to see the number of people from the community who cared enough to pay their respects to Papa. My heart swelled with pride even as it was breaking with his loss.

Roman spotted us coming in and came over to greet us. Taking Mother by the arm, he led her down to the front of the chapel to say her farewells to Papa.

I wanted to fall to my knees and cry like a little child, not caring who looked on and yet, somehow, I managed not to give in to the pain. I found myself looking heavenward, praying for strength as I waited for Mother to take her seat. Then I approached the casket to say my last goodbyes to Papa. I moved forward despite myself, touching his cold, stiff fingers as I remembered all the times he had held my hand and taught me how to live again when I was at my lowest point. "I miss you, Papa, and I don't know how Mother and I will ever endure without you," I whispered. "I will never forget how you loved me as your own. Oh, Papa," I quietly sobbed and swallowed hard, "what will we do now?"

The simple acts of kindness that he'd shown to friends, neighbors, and complete strangers were reflected in the faces of everyone who'd showed up that day and I decided in that moment to live my life in a manner that would make Papa proud of me, even if he wasn't around to tell me so himself.

Bending over to kiss his cheek, I signaled to the two men waiting patiently beside the casket that it was time to close and seal it up. I looked to the priest and signaled to him that it was time to begin the services before I took my seat between Mother and Ella.

I couldn't help but notice that Papa's death caused a ripple effect because of the many lives he'd touched—tear stained faces of people standing side by side—yet still I wondered if loving someone was worth the pain it caused when they were gone.

Papa's younger sister, Matilda—known as Tilly—sat in the front row beside her sister Clarissa, who was next to Ella and me. Mother's brother, Uncle Gideon, sat in the second row with the Blackthorn family, longtime friends of the Roscoes.

As Father Joseph began to speak, the chapel fell silent once again except for the occasional loud sniffle of someone blowing a nose. He began reading from Psalm 23. "The Lord is my Shepherd; I shall not want." Suddenly my mind wandered back in time to a different place and time, long ago, when Father Timothy recited those very same words at my mama's funeral and I felt so alone. Stifling a sob that bubbled up from my throat, I felt that I'd endured far too much loss for one so young. My heart was feeling so heavy that I feared that my eyes would never be dry again.

Papa's service continued, but I could feel myself slipping back in time, getting lost in my own thoughts. After the service, people stopped by to shake my hand and tell me what a loss Zane Roscoe would be to them. I responded politely, nodding my head at all the appropriate times, pretending to listen to their words of condolences, but I was far away in my mind, mourning the loss of another. Memories haunted me and I felt darkness penetrating my soul.

Mother hovered at my elbow, touching my hand or arm from time to time; those quiet gestures steadied me, and I was grateful.

The line of carriages seemed to stretch on forever as we all drove back to our home. People were coming back to our place for a light luncheon prepared by friends and staff who stepped in to arrange everything. Everyone who stopped by to pay their respects was served a light fare of soup, bread, preserves, pie, and lemonade.

When the crowd eased up, Mother retreated to the sanctuary of her bedroom across the hall from the one she had shared with Papa, claiming that the memories were still too raw for her to sleep in their marital bed.

I escaped to the front porch with Ella and Roman, letting them chatter on while I offered an occasional, "Yes, of course," or "You don't say." Eventually Ella rose to leave and Roman followed. Suddenly, I was all alone, with only my morose thoughts for company.

Days passed and I thought I would go out of my mind. Mother barely left her room and I'd begun wandering about the house at all hours of the day and night, staring out of windows for entertainment as I watched people pass by. I'd finally reached my breaking point one afternoon when I couldn't stand the solitude any longer. Walking across the street and up the stairs to my office, I found several large, messy piles of paper sitting in the middle of my desk waiting to be entered into the ledger and then filed. I felt relieved because I would finally have something to distract me from the pain and grief I'd been going through.

I dove into the stacks, working through them pile by pile, until Thomas Barns—a shy fourteen-year-old—wandered into the office with a pot of tea. He set the tray down on the corner of my desk. I forced a smile and thanked him for his troubles, but he only stopped long enough to give me a shy smile, then left without saying a word.

I sipped my tea while finishing up the ledger work, then stood to file the receipts away in the filing cabinet behind me. I was feeling good about the work I'd completed, humming a somber tune to myself, when I heard someone enter my office and clear his throat. "I'll be right with you in just a moment," I called over my shoulder, dropping several receipts into the proper place in the file drawer before shutting it with a satisfied but resounding bang.

Turning around, I was expecting to see Roman standing in front of me but it wasn't him at all. I froze mid-step and was now face to face with a living ghost from my past. Lord Henley stood before me. I nearly swallowed my tongue.

"Good day, Miss Lara Flannigan," he addressed me, his tone menacing. "I dare say, you're looking quite well today. I didn't have the heart to approach you at your…father's funeral the other day. I'm guessing by that odd look on your face, you never expected to see me again in this lifetime," he chortled, a wicked grin playing across his lips.

"Mr. Henley, what an unexpected occurrence this is," I exclaimed, trying to sound as normal as possible. "Funerals never stopped you from saying your piece before. So what unpleasantness brings you to my doorstep today? I would have thought that after our last encounter you would be a bit more cautious in regards to secluding yourself alone with me in an office," I challenged back with a wicked grin of my own.

I sank heavily into my chair before my legs gave way and sent me to the floor.

Chuckling and wagging his finger at me, Lord Henley removed his hat and placed it on the chair next to him before taking a seat. "I always knew you were a special girl, Lara, my dear. I would never have guessed that you had such a wicked sense of humor. But then again, we never had much time to really get to know one another."

"Lara Roscoe," I corrected. "My name is Lara Roscoe, and I'm certain that there are a lot of things you don't know about me, Mr. Henley," I countered. "Although I doubt that we will have the opportunity to get better acquainted, since I'm going to have to insist that you leave my office this instant."

"Lord Henley," he quickly countered by correcting me.

"Are you certain?" I asked skeptically. "Judging by the shabby appearance of your once finely tailored suit and the fact that you now reside in America, it would seem that you have been addressed as Mr. Henley for some time now," I admonished. "See, I've heard that many of the well-to-do back home didn't fare so well after the great famine debacle and that many of you lost your lands and titles because you were unable to pay the taxes. Or did I hear wrong?"

Jumping to his feet, he pounded a fist upon my desk. "You owe me, you little chit," Henley ground out between clenched jaws before flipping back a corner of his hair that had fallen out of place. Self-consciously Henley quickly sucked in air, turning red as he made sure that he'd adequately covered up the four-inch scar on his forehead.

Without thinking, I picked up a letter opener and stabbed it into the desk between his fingers, missing his hand by a mere half an inch. "Don't you ever attempt to intimidate me again, Mr. Henley, or next time I won't miss," I growled back. "Now, take a seat!" I ordered, seeing the startled look on his face.

"You owe me," he reiterated, sounding slightly petulant, but much more respectful this time.

"And how do you figure that I owe you?" I questioned.

"I struck a deal with your father," he said, pulling a tattered piece of paper from his vest pocket.

Taking the paper from his hand, I read the hastily scribbled words, written so long ago. The well-worn piece of paper was faded and frayed at the corners with water spots marring the ink as words ran together, making it difficult to read. But there was no mistaking the intent of the document. It was clearly stated, in black and white for all to read:

I Rory Flannigan agree to sell my youngest daughter, Lara Flannigan, into bondage, in lieu of payment of back rent on property, parcel number 4493.

The hand that wrote those words was not my Da's, but at the bottom of the page I recognized the wobbly mark of my Da's signature, Rory Flannigan, and my mind flashed back to the day of my mama's funeral when I watched my Da from a distance as a piece of paper was shoved at him by the man on the road. I now realized the writing instrument I had seen was a fountain pen.

Feeling the sting of tears in my eyes, I quickly inhaled, trying to dispel them before they could be seen. I neither had the time nor the inclination to travel down that treacherous road of useless emotion and revisit the long-ago wrongs done to me by my Da. "So now you have come to collect on the debt, is that right?" I said, leaning back in my seat, giving him a narrow look while gripping the arm of the chair so tightly with my left hand that my fingers ached.

"Yes," he answered with a grin from ear to ear. "As is my right."

"I must confess, I am just a bit surprised by you, Mr. Henley," I purred, forcing a smile to my lips while slowly sitting forward in my seat.

"Why are you grinning at me like that, girl?" Henley shifted uneasily in his chair. "And I will caution you to remember your place and address your betters by their proper title—"

"I tell you what, Mr. Henley," I uttered, quickly cutting him off as I accentuated the title *Mister* just to see him cringe again. "There is nothing like forgiveness to resurrect one's soul, and my mama always told me that life was too short to go around being angry all of the time." I said each word slowly, distracting him from my true intent. Folding up the worn piece of paper which I still held in my hand, I continued, "And nobody, not even me, deserves to be made to feel like less than a whole person. So, I am going to forgive you, Mr. Henley, and the things that you did to me and my family all those years ago. And please, don't think in your small, little mind, that I do this for your benefit, because I don't. I'm doing this for mine," I added, lifting my chin up just a bit higher as I slowly pulled out an ashtray and fancy flint lighter from my desk drawer. I watched with pleasure as his eyes suddenly grew larger. "Because we all have the right to be made whole again, don't you think?" I sweetly asked with a wicked grin. "See, I've allowed what you did to me years ago to govern my life for far too long, now. But, enough is enough." Lighting the paper on fire, I added, "Wouldn't you agree?"

Jumping up from his seat, Henley tried to grab the paper from the ashtray before it turned to ashes and was rewarded with a hard, sharp thump to the back of his hand from the heavy metal handle of the letter opener I quickly picked up from off of the desk in front of me.

"Ouch!" he yelped, quickly pulling his hand back and vigorously rubbing it. "This does not excuse your debt!" he bellowed loudly.

"Oh, but I think it does!" I answered, quickly coming to my feet. "No paper, no evidence. Besides, you wouldn't want it to be known that you, Mr. Henley," I gestured a hand towards him, "have a misguided propensity towards young girls, now would you? Why, they would crucify you here in America. It isn't at all like Europe where they turn a blind eye to such things just because you hold a title." I wrinkled my nose up at him and shook my head. "By the way, how did you happen to track me down?"

"I saw a picture of you and your new daddy in the newspaper. It really is a shame that he died so young, leaving you and your new mama alone and defenseless," Henley taunted.

Determined not to show my agitation, I dug my nails into the edge of the desk and continued in a steady voice. "Very well, *Mr. Henley*. I'll tell you what I'm going to do for you, *Mr. Henley*—"

"Lord Henley! And you still owe me!" he snapped.

"Mr. Henley!" I calmly ground out the words between clenched teeth, trying to control my utter dislike and revulsion for this man. "I am going to allow you to leave here. Simply walk out of my office and never darken my doorstep again."

"And if I refuse," he challenged.

"Then," I said, pausing for emphasis as I leaned forward, "I will contact my wealthy friends, of which I have many, and have you run out of town for the disgusting, loathsome, odious deviant that you are!" I screamed. "And if you ever make the mistake of crossing paths with me again, I assure you that it will not bode well for you. Now, get out of my office!"

"Is everything alright?" Roman asked, rushing into the room, out of breath from his run up the stairs.

Lord Henley angrily got to his feet, retrieved his hat, and huffed in disgust. "This is not over," he warned, before turning to leave. "I will have recompense. One way or another," he called over his shoulder as he went.

Without thinking, I picked up the hot teapot next to my hand and threw it, narrowly missing his head by an inch as it smashed against the door jam. I saw his ear begin to bleed where a shard of porcelain cut him. "If you are truly as smart as you think you are, Mr. Henley, you will never show your hideous face here again!" I screamed.

Looking startled, Henley touched his neck where the hot tea had scalded him, not realizing that his ear was bleeding. Then, with a glare, he brushed the liquid from his coat with the back of his hand. "You are crazy, Lara Flannigan, and someone should put you away."

"Get out, get out, get out, get out!" I screamed at the top of my lungs while picking up the cup and saucer in front of me and chucking them at him, whereupon he ran all the way down the stairs.

Taking three long strides to my side, Roman took me into his arms. "Are you alright? Did he hurt you?" he questioned, looking me over carefully as he swore under his breath before turning to go after Henley. "If he did—"

Startling Roman, I grabbed his sleeve, stopping him in his tracks and burying my face in his chest. "Don't leave me," I wept.

"I won't," he assured me as his anger dissipated. "What happened, Lara? Who was that man?"

"My past came back to haunt me and I stood up to it, Roman," I sniffed, swiping a hand across my face. "I stood up to him!"

"What does that mean?" Roman questioned, holding me at arm's length as I clung to him for support, unsure that I had the strength to stand on my own two legs.

"I don't want to talk about it just yet, please," I begged, badly shaken. "Take me home, Roman. I need to see Mother. Please, Roman, I just need to go home."

"All right," he relented, placing a protective arm around my shoulder and leading me toward the stairs. As we passed Thomas rushing up the stairs to see what the commotion was about, Roman called over his shoulder, "Thomas, get a broom and dustpan and clean up Miss Roscoe's office if you wouldn't mind. She had a little accident with the tea set. That's a good lad. Oh, and I'm taking Miss Roscoe home. I shouldn't be very long."

"Why won't you tell me who that man was?" Roman questioned again when we reached the street and were waiting to cross.

"I told you. Someone from my past."

"Yes, I heard you the first time. But who was he and why did he upset you so badly?"

"His name is Lord Horatio Henley. At least that's who he was back home in Ireland. He was our landlord," I answered pensively as an involuntary shiver shook me when the memory of Henley's face flashed across my mind. "Does one lose their status and titles if they are forced to leave Europe in disgrace?" I asked.

"Why are you asking me? I wouldn't know about titles and such things. And why won't you answer my question? What did he say to upset you?"

"There really isn't much to say about Henley," I lied, "but that he is a very bad man and he took advantage of my family at the worst time in our lives. Nothing more."

"But what did he want with you now?" he asked, looking confused by my overly simplistic explanation.

"He saw the newspaper clipping of me and Papa and thought he could come by and collect on an old debt he felt he was owed," I explained, sugar coating it. "And that is the last I care to discuss of Mr. Henley," I said bluntly. "Ever!"

"All right, all right. I have received the message loud and clear," Roman said, lifting an eyebrow at me and conceding. Taking a moment to look up then down the street to check for traffic, Roman pulled me off of the sidewalk with him.

"If he is a smart man, he will never show his despicable face around here again," I quietly added under my breath.

"Somehow, Mr. Henley didn't appear to me to be all that bright," Roman concluded, then mused, "I doubt that we have seen the last of him. Perhaps I should look this gentleman up and have a word with him.

"No!" I blurted out, shocking myself by the ferocity of my words. "I mean...he is no gentleman and I'm certain that I have handled the matter," I argued, forcing a stiff smile to my lips. "Thank you for walking me across the street," I added, resting my hand on the doorknob. "I will be fine, now. Really."

Trying to get around me, Roman took another step as if he intended to come inside. "I want to say hello to Mrs. Roscoe," he reasoned.

"She isn't yet receiving visitors," I confessed, hoping that my simple explanation would be enough to discourage him further. But when he persisted, taking another step towards the threshold as I opened the door, I was forced to stop him by placing a hand on his chest. "She won't see you, Roman. She won't see anyone except me and

occasionally Doctor Sheridan. Even Martha and the rest of the staff have been forbidden from stepping foot into her room at the moment."

Looking down into my eyes, Roman rested a sympathetic hand upon my shoulder. "That must be rough."

"Yes, it has been. But I hold out hope that I will bring her around, sooner rather than later," I added as I turned and entered the house.

I exhaled when I heard Roman close the door behind him and watched him cross the street and slip into the carriage shop. Relief warmed my ribs for a heartbeat, then the house's hush pressed in and I knew I had to go upstairs. My feet found the familiar rhythm on the worn steps; the banister was cool beneath my palm, the stair-ends whispering beneath my weight. With each tread my chest tightened—part dread, part a stubborn hope I kept carefully folded away.

Mother's door was ajar. I paused, smoothing my skirts as if that small ritual could straighten the ache in my voice, then pushed it open and slipped inside. She sat by the window with the same faded shawl wrapped around her shoulders, a half-finished embroidery hoop abandoned in her lap. Her hair, once meticulously dressed, had come loose at the temples; her eyes, when she turned toward me, were the pale gray of a sky after rain. She looked smaller than I remembered, not because she had shrunk, but because grief had hollowed the familiar kindness from her face.

"Lara," she said, her voice thin as lace. She tried a smile and it fell away before it could warm the room. "I do not know how to be without him."

I crossed the room and sat on the edge of the bed, close enough to feel the faint tremor of her hand when I settled. I reached out and covered her fingers with mine.

"We'll find a new normal," I told her, and meant it with everything that steadied me. "Just you and I—we'll learn it together."

She blinked, and for a moment the grief in her eyes softened into something like recognition. Her hand tightened around mine—not yet a comfort, not yet a return, but a beginning. Inside me, the ache did not vanish, but a small, fierce resolve took root: I would not let her sorrow become our permanent shape.

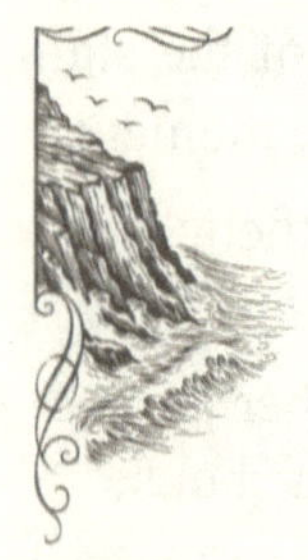

25

OCTOBER 18, 1852

Ella's Wedding Day

Although Mother finally relented and came out of her room, she had not yet left the house and would not attend Ella and Theodore's wedding with me.

The day began like any other day. The sun was up and the sky showed signs that it might rain later in the afternoon, but it did not dampen my desire to make the day perfect for my best friend. I'd spent the night with her at the family estate, keeping Ella company while trying to quiet her shaky nerves. She was anxious over her impending nuptials and had been for weeks. I blamed it on nerves—the bridal flutter that comes over many brides-to-be as they worry about what their new life will be like when, at last, the day arrives and they are asked to say 'I do.'

I saw the transformation begin the week before. The normally infectious sparkle that had drawn me to my friend from the very beginning of our friendship was gone. That certain special spark that said to the world, "Look out everyone, here comes trouble!" was missing. It had been replaced with a sort of dullness as if, somehow, something inside of her had died.

There had been so many preparations to attend to before the wedding since the official announcement of the Blackthorn-Cramp merging in June that Ella had not had much time to think about life after the nuptials, let alone be worried. But now that the day had arrived, she was in a somber mood. I could tell by the way she constantly fidgeted the night before, never staying still, not even for a second.

We had sat up the better part of the night talking, but there was no real substance to our conversation. I needed to do something to change her mood. *But what could I do?* I asked myself, and then I got an idea.

"Ella?" I began, as I got out of bed, rubbing the sleep from my eyes with a big yawn.

I couldn't tell how long she'd been sitting in the window seat, staring at nothing in particular. "Hum?" she absently answered, not bothering to turn her head to look at me.

"I think we should run away. Just the two of us," I said with a capricious tone.

"What?!" she perked up, spinning around in her seat to face me.

"I'm serious!" I asserted, climbing out of bed and padding my way across the room to join her. "We could go far away from here, where no one knows us, and begin a new life," I grinned.

"Oh, Lara, you have truly lost your mind," Ella argued, touching my forehead to check for fever as she allowed a heavy sigh to escape her lips. "I could never do that."

"Why not?" I questioned enthusiastically.

A sad smile marred her face as she took my hands in hers. "Because I am neither brave nor strong like you are," she said wistfully. "I saw it in your eyes the first time we met. Remember? You were sitting in the corner of the room all by yourself while all of those snotty girls swirled around you. Then I came over and introduced myself."

"I remember."

"I decided there and then that you and I were going to be the best of friends," Ella said lovingly as she slid a thumb along the edge of my chin before she dropped her hand back into her lap and gazed back out of the window.

"But how could you decide such a thing when you didn't even know anything about me?" I cried.

Bringing her eyes back around to look at me, Ella smiled pleasantly. "Because, Lara, everything I needed to know about you was right there in your eyes when I looked at you," she concluded as her eyes

welled up with tears. "I could tell that you were kind, loyal, and strong beyond your years. I also knew that you would never betray me."

"Eloise Blackthorn, I believe you are teasing me," I snapped. "How could you have possibly known all of that, simply by looking into my eyes?"

"Because, Lara Ann Flannigan Roscoe, you are an open book. You are so strong." Several tears trailed down her cheeks. "Everything you are is right there, visible for the world to see. Besides, I was right."

"About what?" I asked, confused and taken aback by her words.

"You have always been the most loyal friend and companion a girl could ever have asked for," she pointed out. "Why, even now you are willing to risk everything and whisk me away, just to save me from a life of unhappiness, even if it meant that you would be a social outcast for the rest of your life."

"That's because I've already been a social outcast," I confessed with a wink. "And it really isn't that bad."

Ella giggled through her tears, wiping them away with the corner of her shawl. "I knew I picked you to be my best friend for a reason. I love you, Lara. You are so dear to me. You always have been and you always will be," she interjected, leaning over to hug me tightly.

"I will always be here for you, Eloise Blackthorn, and don't you forget it," I added fiercely. "And the offer still stands if you change your mind. I will take you away from all of this," I vowed.

"I know, but that won't be necessary," she replied as I felt the wetness of her tears run down the back of my neck as she hugged me. "That is why you are my best friend."

"Do you think he really expects you to change your name to Cramp?" I teased, trying to lighten the mood, but instead, my words caused Ella to cry even harder.

"I will be promising for better or worse," she whispered.

"Not yet, you haven't."

"Don't you ever abandon me, Lara." Her tone sounded adamant as she pulled away to wipe her cheeks and blow her nose.

I scoffed at her with a sniff, "You couldn't chase me away with a stick, Mrs. Cramp," I assured her.

She punched my arm just as she often did to her brother. "I don't think I will ever get used to that name," she squealed and shuddered, causing me to laugh.

Ella wore a beautiful white silk and Brussels lace gown. The skirt was two-tiers of concertina pleats that were scalloped at the hemline. The matching bodice tucked into the skirt and had a rounded neckline with three-quarter length sleeves. A large lace sash around her middle was tied into a bow in the back. This exquisite work of art had taken three seamstresses a total of sixty-eight hours to sew together as they added tiny, delicate pearls to the neckline and along the edges of the sleeves and hemline. Her train and veil of lace gracefully trailed two feet behind her on the floor.

The veil was shorter in the front, resting gracefully over the back of her hand and brushing to the ends of her fingertips. It was fastened to a delicate crown of dainty white silk blossoms. The slightest hint of lavender was woven through her headpiece to add just a bit of color.

As Ella's maid-of-honor, I was responsible for seeing that she was properly dressed and to the church on time. Her father, Levi Blackthorn, paced a hole in the carpet downstairs while waiting for us.

Levi was a tall, thin man, an older version of his son, and always carried himself with a restless kind of ambition. I had overheard enough from my own father and from whispers at gatherings to know that Levi had built his fortune as much through marriage as through business. He had put money into banks and shipyards, yes, but his true stroke of genius—or luck—had been marrying Roman's mother, whose well-heeled family, the Cramps, opened doors he alone could not.

I remembered once, years ago, lingering at the edge of a parlor conversation when someone mentioned the Cramp shipyards. The name carried weight, and I'd tucked away the story: William Cramp, a German immigrant's son, had turned a modest beginning into an empire along the Delaware River. Two presidents had walked the

planks of his shipyard within five years—that detail had made me straighten in surprise when I first heard it. His family was a dynasty of shipbuilders, each son drawn into the business of steel and rivets, and by marrying into that world, Levi secured a place at their table.

That was why he beamed whenever the Cramp name was mentioned—why he practically preened when speaking of his daughter's marriage, which would ensure the legacy of the Cramp and Blackthorn union would continue through many generations. But where Levi saw triumph, Ella only saw sacrifice. Her back was too stiff, her eyes too guarded for a girl on her wedding day. She was loyal to a fault, bound by duty to a match her father prized more than her happiness.

I reached for her hand in the carriage, giving it a gentle squeeze. She didn't speak, and neither did I. Her lashes were clumped from the tears she'd already shed, and I feared that if I said anything at all, I would only cause her to cry again.

The carriage pulled up in front of the grand steps of the towering church steeples and I heard Ella stifle a sob. Her father stepped out of the carriage without a word and reached up to help her down.

"I will strong arm the driver and commandeer the carriage if you want," I whispered in her ear.

Tears welled up in her eyes again as she turned to me. "I know, but that won't be necessary. I'm a big girl now and I've made a promise," she whispered back, wiping her nose with a handkerchief that she'd hidden away in her sleeve. "Now, take Daddy's hand and proceed with me into the church. And whatever you do, Lara, for heaven's sake, walk slowly. We wouldn't want to appear too anxious," she added with a feigned smile, shoving the hanky back into her sleeve. "Now, go!"

Disappointed that I couldn't talk Ella out of what I felt was the biggest mistake of her life, I finally relented and somberly stepped down from the carriage. Turning, I waited while Ella carefully gathered the pleats of her gown as she, too, stepped out of the carriage. Then, picking up her veil and train, I followed her to the church entrance and gently spread it out again.

Entering the building's foyer, the three of us proceeded to the chapel doors in silence. I watched as Ella's eyes stared unblinkingly, never deviating from the doors before her. When she did bring her eyes around to look at me, I tried to smile at her before accepting the two bouquets of flowers from the best man, who was waiting in the foyer for us to arrive. Placing the larger arrangement of white mums with delicate pink roses in Ella's hands, I handed Mr. Blackthorn my bouquet so that I could straighten out her train and veil one last time. Then I retrieved my flowers and gave Ella a final glance before slipping through the side door to take my place on the second step near the base of the altar. After a short wait, the music began, signaling that it was time for the bride to appear.

Two minutes passed, then four, and still no bride. People were beginning to look around anxiously. I was beginning to question whether Ella had changed her mind when the music paused, then began again while the enormous doors opened wide. Ella and her father walked down the aisle slowly towards us. As they drew nearer I could tell that she had been crying again. The hanky was no longer up her sleeve but was now clutched in between her fingers as her father lifted her veil to kiss her farewell. As she handed her bouquet to me, I noticed that Ella's hand was shaking uncontrollably and wondered if she was about to faint.

"Just breathe in and breathe out," I whispered in her ear as I leaned in to give her a customary hug, symbolizing my well wishes for her nuptials. "Don't forget to breathe."

Wordlessly, she turned to Theodore, placing her hand into his as she looked over at me one last time. I gave her a reassuring smile before she turned back to the bridegroom. I knew she was scared and unsure of her decision. I saw the turmoil in Ella's eyes—the same misgivings we'd whispered about in the days before. Her fingers fidgeted at the edge of her glove and her mouth went thin as she glanced at me, as if searching for counsel. But, it was too late to bow out gracefully; the hour for changing one's mind had passed. The ceremony would bind them in the eyes of the community and before God. Only death could undo the vows spoken between them today.

The Priest droned on and on as I stood there helplessly watching my best friend's hand shake uncontrollably. It was almost as if I was in a fog as the words were spoken and gold bands were exchanged. Theodore leaned over, lifted her veil, and chastely kissed her cheek.

The deed was done, the vows were completed, and my best friend Ella was now a married woman. I felt somehow unmoored, set adrift, and a little lost.

"I present to you, Mr. and Mrs. Theodore Cramp," the Priest announced as the smiling couple turned to face their family and friends.

Stepping up to hand Ella her flowers back, my hand rested upon hers for a brief moment and I gave her hand a squeeze. Her fingers felt like ice despite the warm day. She looked at me for a split second with a forced smile. Then she turned to walk alongside Theodore down the aisle, shaking hands and exchanging hugs from well-wishers as they went.

The wedding party filed out of the church, following the couple to the front steps where the photographer gathered us together for a group photo. I stood in for a few more portraits at the church doors, smiling dutifully beside the bridesmaids, before slipping away as the photographer's assistant busily arranged more small groups for further photos.

I knew that I'd be missing the special moment when the crowd pelted the bride and groom with uncooked rice before the couple stepped into the waiting carriage provided by Ella's father, but I just didn't want to be a part of the procession of carriages that would carry the wedding party back to the Blackthorn home for the wedding reception festivities, so I chose the closest carriage and told the driver to take the quickest way there. I had just arrived when I heard the sound of thundering hooves behind me.

Turning around, I watched from the front steps as the men from the church crowd came tearing down the lane—a cloud of dust, leather and horseflesh—shouting and whooping as they lunged for the gate. I had heard the men talking earlier, hushed and eager: the prize was a bottle from our homeland, they said, a bottle worth as much as a

week's wages. That explained the recklessness; it explained the shoves and the careless elbows as each man strove to be first.

Fletcher Kane rode like a mad thing, chest forward, spurs flashing. He struck the gate with a cry, tumbled from his saddle, grabbed the prize, and staggered to the door. I saw, out of the corner of my eye, poor Eddie Coltran go sprawling in the dust and Jacob—Fletcher's brother—follow suit, both knocked clean off their mounts. Fletcher laughed then, a high, triumphant sound, brandishing the bottle like a trophy. The label glinted in the sun: Irish whiskey, imported from my homeland. My throat tightened with a sudden, absurd swell of pride.

He stood in the doorway, chest heaving, grin split wide across his face as he boasted of how he had outwitted them all. Eddie picked grit from his sleeve and spat, but there was no real anger in him—only the rough good humor that comes after being thoroughly beaten. Jacob rubbed at a grazed knee and, when Fletcher promised to open the bottle and share a glass after the reception, both brothers laughed and clapped him on the back. The sound settled over the yard, forgiving and loud, and I could not help but smile despite myself.

The house staff had been busy for days, decorating the foyer, great hall, and dining room with evergreens, oranges, and red ribbons. The table groaned under the weight of the finest pastries, cold pheasant, finger sandwiches, white cakes, dried fruits, and mulled cider and wines laid out for the guests' delight.

The reception began with the usual toasting of the bride and groom by the parents and best man as everyone ate. Then bride and groom and three couples from the bridal party began the dancing with a cotillion—a popular European dance. Four couples formed a square, facing inward, then rotated around, moving their feet while partners held hands in the front and behind. Then they came forward, exchanging one partner for another until they cycled through and returned to their original partners. The women came to the center and turned in a circle with a man holding each woman's hand. Reversing the circle, the men interlocked fingers and the women were now on the outside of the circle. I enjoyed watching the intricate movements as more couples joined by forming their own squares.

Roman approached me as I watched the dancing. "Are you enjoying yourself?" he asked nonchalantly, turning to face the dancers.

Smiling, I turned, admiring his profile a moment before replying. "They are quite lively. Don't you think?"

"Yes. Lively indeed," he chuckled, looking at me out of the corner of his eye. "How is your mother these days?"

"Still melancholy, but getting better with each day that passes," I replied. "I'm sorry that I haven't been around very much. The foundation and Mother keep me rather busy."

Turning to look at me, he replied, "There really is no need to concern yourself. I really have become adept with the books."

"And by adept, you mean you have left piles of receipts all over my desk, of course," I laughed.

"Of course. What else would I mean?" Roman countered. "Do you care to dance?" he asked, offering his hand.

Nodding my head, I placed my hand in his as the music ended and looked him in the eyes. "But of course. I thought you would never ask."

He walked me onto the dance floor as the music switched to a minuet. The men bowed and the women curtsied and then the dance began. When the minuet was followed by a Scotch Reel, Fletcher Kane cut in asking for the next dance. True to custom, Roman withdrew, and a steady stream of partners rose to take my hand each time the music changed.

All the while, games abounded as young men attempted to steal the bride's slipper. Those who were successful ransomed the shoe back to Ella for an innocent kiss on the cheek.

The highlight of the evening came when those same young men whisked the bride away, keeping her secluded in another room while they ransomed her back to the bridegroom for one hundred dollars. Theodore was forced to dance with women and perform funny antics to earn the money to get his bride back. At the end of the evening the money was gifted to the bride and groom to start their new life together.

Ella's new father-in-law gifted the happy couple with a home to live in. It was a lavish seven-bedroom home on Little Poplar Street—between Fifth and Sixth Streets—a very desirable area to live.

Despite my concerns, I was happy for my friend and pulled her aside just before ten o'clock to wish her well. "Ella, I want to give you something before you go," I said, shoving an envelope containing a personal note and thirty dollars into her gown pocket.

"You don't have to do that," she insisted after reaching into her pocket and realizing what I had done.

"I know, but take it anyway. A little something just for you," I whispered. "Save it. Share it. It is up to you."

She hugged me tightly. "You are my best friend, Lara Roscoe."

"I know," I hugged her back. "And you are my best friend, Eloise Blackthorn *Cramp*," I teased, emphasizing her new last name.

Giving me a sour face as she leaned in with a conspirator's grin, looking around first to be sure that no one else was listening, she whispered, "I will always be a Blackthorn at heart."

"I know," I assured her, giving her one last hug just as Theodore Cramp approached us to reclaim his bride.

"Are you ready, my dear?" he asked, taking her arm and gently pulling her through the crowd of well-wishers as they worked their way to a waiting carriage.

"Wait, I want to say goodbye to my family," Ella said frantically.

Patiently, he replied, "They are waiting to say their goodbyes at the front of the line. Let's skip the crowd and go directly to your parents. If we don't leave soon, we'll still be here when the sun comes up."

"I love you, Lara," she called over her shoulder as she was dragged away.

"I love you too, Ella," I replied under my breath.

Gathering my cape, I made my way to the back door, stepped into my own waiting carriage, and left the Blackthorn home well before the bride and groom managed to wade through the sea of inebriated guests.

The frogs croaked and the crickets played a happy tune as my driver pulled out of the driveway and drove me safely home.

26

Age 20
Finding a New Normal

I was frustrated by Mother's refusal to rejoin society after Papa's death, and I was becoming concerned. Not to mention, it was beginning to wear on me.

I missed Papa too, but I missed the sound of Mother's laugh and her positive attitude even more. The months of isolation and turning away friends were taking a toll upon her as well. She would wander through the house, not caring whether she was properly dressed, even if it was two o'clock in the afternoon. She frequently used the excuse that she was not yet ready to socialize, which wore thin. I was concerned that her melancholy moods would become permanent.

I had made it my number one mission, starting on New Year's Eve, to pull my mother, Charity Roscoe, from her entrenched behavior, deciding that I would make it impossible for her to say no to me any longer. I was going to force her to care about life and living again if it was the last thing I did. So, just as she had done for me years before when she and Zane found me lying in a filthy alley and I'd hit rock bottom, I was determined to pull her up by her bootstraps.

I had set that vow on New Year's Eve, but I let it smolder through the frozen months while I waited for the right moment to take definitive action; when April finally came, and the sun was brighter in the sky, I determined that it was time to wrench Charity Roscoe back to life by any means necessary.

"Martha, Mother will be accompanying me on my outing today," I began as I informed the outspoken cook of my plans for getting Mother to leave the house.

"Good luck with that," Martha sighed. "She has not budged yet."

"Not only will I get her to leave the house, but I will be attempting to get her to leave the all-black wardrobe behind as well."

"Oh, you are an ambitious girl," Martha added cynically. "I suppose next you will be telling me that you intend to take over running this household while keeping your Papa's business running."

"I refuse to be baited by you, Martha," I said, tweaking her cheek and snitching another handful of raisins from the counter as she prepared raisin scones. "You have such a negative attitude."

"I prefer to see it as being a pragmatist if you please," Martha qualified.

"Well, pardon me," I asserted, popping raisins into my mouth as I left the room.

"I will believe it when I see it with my own eyes," she called after me, stepping to the kitchen door.

"Then keep your eyes opened wide," I replied before climbing the stairs. "Because it will happen."

It was a fight, but in the end, I got my way. Mother relented when I approached her, insisting that only one person died the day Papa passed away, not two. I told her that I missed her and that her friends missed her and that the time had come for her to get out of bed and do something useful again.

I knew from personal experience when I was trying to get beyond my own heartache that it was very important to serve others. My plan was to not only involve Mother in my Laurel's Helping Hands Foundation, but to immerse her in it.

A ship was due in port at ten-thirty from Ireland, my homeland, and I was anxious to get down to the docks to greet the new arrivals. Mother and I left the house at ten-fifteen on the dot with two carriages filled with sandwiches and sweet tea to feed the new arrivals.

Mother and I both wore black skirts, white button-down blouses, and aprons to protect our clothing. I could immediately tell that the beautiful spring day was like a wonderful balm to Mother. I watched as she turned her face towards the morning sun, basking in the warmth, sighing several times as we made our way to the wharf. There were six volunteers that had taken up the cause and they were waiting for us near the spot where the new immigrants exited through the gate when they were found acceptable.

Jake Whitlock, a widower in his mid-fifties, tall in stature and beginning to gray around the temples, was one of my best workers. He had always had the kindest brown eyes and an easy smile despite the loss of his wife of thirty-one years just two years prior. Instead of brooding over the matter, he'd decided to give back to his community by volunteering. I always found him to be a very kind man and was delighted when he told me that he wanted to help with my foundation. At first, he donated a few dollars from time to time, but after his wife passed away, Mr. Whitlock became more involved by giving of his time as well. I was happy to see him today and hoped that he would somehow bring comfort to my mother during her grieving process.

I was first introduced to Mr. Whitlock years ago when Papa took me with him to pick up an order from his shop. He had been a wheelwright by trade, a craftsman who built and repaired wooden wheels. Over the years I had watched as he made the wheels for our carts and wagons by first constructing the hub, called the nave, then the spokes and then the rim or felloe segments. Then he assembled them all into a single wheel by working from the center of the wheel outward. Finally, the wheel was straked with iron by nailing an iron plate onto the felloes to protect the wood against uneven wearing, which also helped bind the wheel together.

Mr. Whitlock seemed to instinctively understand the needs of immigrants and I often had him instruct the new workers on proper etiquette when it came to people coming over from Europe and Ireland.

Another volunteer I'd come to rely on was Edith Newman. She was the daughter of one of my biggest financial contributors. Mr. Newman felt it important that his over-indulged only daughter, Edith, learn how

to give back rather than always taking. So, he made his contributions conditional on the fact that I would take Edith under my wing and show her how to be a contributing member of society. And although I will admit that Edith and I had a few dust-ups in the beginning, we eventually came to a mutually beneficial agreement: I was the boss and she worked for me. Once she understood the importance of working as a team for the benefit of others, she became one of my hardest working volunteers.

I introduced Mother to Edith Newman and John Whitlock, who had arrived before us and set up the tables. And although she hadn't been exactly enthusiastic about leaving the house, she soon fell into a comfortable rhythm that appeared to lighten her melancholy mood.

As she handed out sandwiches and sweet tea, along with much-needed advice about where to go and how to get there, Mother began to smile. I was thrilled when I saw her put her arm around a woman who was clearly overwhelmed by the vastness of Philadelphia and told her that it would all work out in the end. Seeing that simple act, I knew she was on the mend.

Standing on the dock by the gate, I took on the role of director. I pointed people to our table and handed out cards for services that were available to them. I also gave instructions as to how they could get to the various neighborhoods.

Irish-Scottish immigrants and some English immigrants had settled along Canal Street and the Kensington mill district. Then there was Germantown, which consisted of the Northern Liberties and Kensington areas, which had expanded into certain parts of the north and northeast segment of Philadelphia.

A large community of Irish skilled workers and middle-class families had developed west of Broad Street near South Street, but that was by no means a predominantly Irish area. In this area there were no Irish or German ghettos, but instead a group of people coming together to form a new society, free from the restraints of their European counterparts.

In addition, a social revolution was taking place with a group of people who refused to be placed into an ethnic hole. Some Irish

businessmen and professionals had moved to the suburbs while others, who were helped by Philadelphians who provided work for their less fortunate relatives and friends, lived downtown in the traditional style of the wealthy.

When Papa had been alive, I remember him telling me just how many souls now poured into Philadelphia, with ship after ship docking at the port as if the whole of Europe had decided to uproot itself. He said more than a hundred thousand had arrived since the late '40s, and I believed it, for the streets seemed fuller every year with new voices and unfamiliar accents.

Papa liked to speak of the ships by name, as though they were old acquaintances—the *Tonawanda*, the *Tuscarora*, and the *Wyoming*—each of them sailing from Liverpool, taking nearly seven weeks to reach our shores. I remembered him telling Mama that passage cost five to seven pounds a person, more money than most families could easily spare, yet still they came.

By the time I was grown, everyone was talking about the new steamships. I first learned of them when a neighbor showed me a broadside announcing the Liverpool and Philadelphia Steam Ship Company. It had been started by William Inman and his Quaker partners, and their first vessel, the *City of Glasgow*, made the journey in just ten days. I could scarcely imagine it—ten days across the ocean instead of two months. Since then, more ships had joined her— *Manchester*, *Baltimore*, and *Philadelphia*—and though a steerage ticket cost over eight pounds, nearly a laborer's whole season's wage, the company's piers were always crowded.

Standing at the gate directing people to our table, I was enjoying the sound of my native tongue spoken by many of the new arrivals. Groups of immigrants—whether Irish, Scottish, Italian, or German— often disembarked together, which made it easier to identify them and extend help.

Since beginning my little organization, I had managed to assemble many volunteers who represented all the many factions of Europe. Whether the immigrants were wealthy or poor, it didn't matter— when stepping off of the large ships into their new society, many were overwhelmed by the large, bustling city of Philadelphia. That was where our true work began. We identified the needs of each person who sought our help and directed them to where they needed to go. That is, if they didn't already have family anxiously waiting just beyond the gates for them.

That afternoon, as a wave of Irish immigrants streamed past, my gaze caught on a plump woman trying to manage too much at once—a baby balanced against her shoulder while a restless boy tugged and tangled himself in her skirts. She stumbled several times, the child's sharp yanks nearly pulling her off her feet, and her face flushed with equal parts exertion and embarrassment. The din of voices and the press of bodies made her struggle all the more frantic. When she finally stepped aside to steady herself, I slipped through the crowd toward her and offered my help.

"May I be of assistance to you, ma'am?" I offered, bending down to give the young boy a piece of hard candy from my pocket.

The child simply stared at my hand, unsure whether he should take the piece of candy presented to him. We both looked up at his mother at the same time to see her nodding her head. Suddenly I realized that I knew the woman. It was Mrs. O'Keefe, my mama's midwife. She was a little older, less plump, and even more haggard and worn out than the last time I'd seen her, but it was the same woman.

Recognizing that she had no idea of who I was, I slowly stood up, straightened my skirts, and cleared my throat. "Mrs. O'Keefe, what a pleasure to see you again," I said pensively, waiting for her to take a good look at me.

Her plump cheeks seemed to fall as she stared into my eyes a moment. I could see that she was confused and then it hit her like a bolt of lightning out of the sky. "Lara? Lara Flannigan? Is that you?" she gasped, looking as if she had just come face to face with a ghost as the color drained from her skin. "Why, you look just like your mama, child."

I smiled, and Mrs. O'Keefe threw a plump arm around my neck and hugged me to her so tightly I thought I would suffocate. The baby began to cry and she turned loose, quickly placing the baby in my

arms as she bent down to pick up her younger son. "I thought ye were dead," she cried, following me as I stepped away from the gate.

"No, I'm still alive and kicking," I assured her.

"Oh, child, I'm so sorry 'bout yer Da and Micky," she said tenderly, sniffing loudly as she wiped away the tears of joy mingled with sorrow from her eyes with a well-worn handkerchief that she kept tucked in her shirt. "Yer family looked high and low for ye, child—though ye be no' a child any longer," she added, looking me up and down with a discerning eye.

"Well, you found me," I said, sounding slightly cynical.

"Ye would no' believe what a beauty li'l Gracie has turned out to be," she sighed, "and Alana has three babes and another on the way."

"Where are the rest of your children, Mrs. O'Keefe? Is there anyone to meet you?" I asked, quickly trying to change the subject.

Waving her arm wildly in the air while looking beyond where we stood, she dropped the large bundle she carried on her back. "They are here!" she squealed, dashing toward a group of young men and women rushing down the dock, not even bothering to retrieve the baby still in my arms.

"Mama! Mama!" two young girls shouted, running into their mother's arms and burying their faces in her neck. An older son stood behind the two girls, patiently waiting for his turn to join in on the happy reunion.

I felt my heart swell, yet at the same time, I couldn't help feeling cheated somehow by the fact that my own family was thousands of miles away, across the ocean.

Mother saw the commotion and stepped over to see if she could help. "Is there something wrong, Lara? Who is that woman?"

Momentarily caught off guard, I stammered, "Ah, well, she is… was my mama's midwife…the day…" I mumbled as a lump stuck in my throat, preventing me from saying any more.

"Speak up, Lara. You're not making any sense," Mother insisted. "Do you know her or not?"

"Yes," I whispered as my lip began to tremble.

Looking at the woman in question, Mother stood with her mouth half open, ready to say something to Mrs. O'Keefe as she came back to retrieve her baby and belongings.

"Mrs. O'Keefe, this is my mother now, Charity Roscoe," I said quickly, hoping to smooth over what could easily become an awkward moment. "Mother, this is Mrs. O'Keefe. I don't know who this handsome lad is or I would introduce him to you as well," I said, handing the baby back to his mother.

"It be a pleasure to meet ye, ma'am," the plump woman said, bobbing her head in acknowledgment. "I've known Lara Flannigan since before she was born. Oh, and what a bonnie lass she has turned into. It was a shame what happened to her sainted mama and Da. A downright shame, it was," Mrs. O'Keefe announced, shaking her head.

"Roscoe," Mother corrected. "She is a Roscoe now."

"Begging yer pardon, ma'am," Mrs. O'Keefe said, looking embarrassed.

Quickly intervening to ease the tension, I asked, "Would you like a sandwich for you or your child before you go, Mrs. O'Keefe? I know the trip must have been long—"

"Oh, no, Lara. I thank ye much for yer kindness, but me kids and I have enough to eat."

"Are you sure? There is plenty and it wouldn't be any trouble at all," I added, smiling graciously, trying to defuse the awkwardness.

"I'm sure. But I thank ye."

"You take care of yourself, Mrs. O'Keefe, and look me up if you ever need anything," I said in all earnestness.

I watched as each of her older children helped her with her burdens as they all walked away, arm-in-arm. "Mrs. O'Keefe was my mama's midwife and she was there the day my mama died giving birth to my youngest sister, Grace," I noted, still staring after the O'Keefe family.

I felt Mother put a comforting hand upon my shoulder, but I simply turned and walked away, back to the gate, resuming my duties as if nothing had happened.

How could I explain to her what I was feeling? How could I tell her that I missed my family when, as far as she was concerned, she was my only family. I felt my heart harden slightly that day and I didn't know why.

Had I possessed the courage that day, I might have unburdened myself to Mother—laid bare the tangle of my life and confessed that I still had brothers and sisters in Ireland who believed me long buried. Yet I held my tongue. Honesty seemed too sharp a blade, one that would cut too deep, and so I cloaked myself in half-truths and silences. It was easier, at least for a time, to play the part expected of me, though every omission made me feel a little more like an imposter in my own skin.

Which, I was beginning to realize, was the same as living a lie!

27

The Abduction

Mother continued to press on, as we found our new normal, helping me with my foundation during our busiest immigration period, which lasted from April to October.

I had my hands full with the carriage shop: balancing the books, taking orders, and making sure that we had the inventory to produce the carriages that we had outstanding orders for.

Then, of course, there was the ongoing need to raise funds to feed the less fortunate immigrants coming to our shores and finding housing, work, and clothing for their ever-growing families.

By June, my head was spinning with all the little details that needed to be completed in any given day just to keep everything up and running. I was ready to pull my hair out.

It was on this particular day that my best friend, Ella Blackthorn Cramp, as she liked to be addressed, who had been too busy with her new role in society to continue her help with the charity, paid me a visit. She swept into my office with her brother close on her heels, like a whirlwind blowing through town. "Lara. Lara!" she shouted until she finally noticed me crouched down filing some paperwork in a bottom drawer in the corner of the office. "Oh, there you are. Do you have any sweet tea? Preferably, cold, sweet tea," she asked.

Looking up from my crouched position, I pointed to a pitcher on a tray. "There. The glasses are in the cabinet below," I replied, closing the drawer and standing up. "And to what do I owe this momentous honor?"

"What in the world are you—" she began, then started to giggle. "Oh, you mean, why am I here?"

"I can't remember the last time you graced me with your presence since your wedding."

Bringing three glasses over to the sitting area, Roman set them down as Ella put her hat and gloves on the corner of the coffee table and reached for one of the glasses.

"She claims that she has something important to tell us, but she refused to give me a hint regarding the matter until we were all together," Roman interjected.

"You know you needed an excuse to take a break, brother. So, stop sounding so put out," Ella argued. "Besides, it isn't every day that I come to visit. Try to pretend that you are pleased to see me."

"Of course he's pleased, Ella," I answered, picking up a glass of cold tea and pressing it to my forehead to cool myself as I sighed. "And even if he isn't, I'm thrilled that you are here," I added cheerfully, plopping down on the cushion next to her. "If I have to file one more piece of paper, I think I might scream."

"You poor dear," Ella said, brushing back a stray hair and tucking it behind my ear as she gave me one of her well-practiced pouts. "When are you going to settle down and stop working yourself to death?" she asked, looking straight at her brother while nodding her head towards me.

I brushed her hand aside. "My papa would say marriage is an important and sacred decision to make, one that affects your entire life, and that it should never be made by anyone too early in life or there could be disastrous consequences," I related, rather embarrassed by Ella's prying question. Narrowing my eyes, I countered, "You act as if marriage is the answer to every woman's prayers."

She cheerfully replied, "But it is, darling. I have never been happier. Do you have any biscuits or shortbread laying around?"

"In the cabinet," I pointed, "there should be a tin of shortbread."

"I'll get them," Roman insisted, jumping up to retrieve them.

"I've been so hungry lately," Ella explained.

Roman cleared his throat. "Here we go ladies," he said, shoving the open tin of shortbread cookies at his sister.

"You are such a wonderful brother," Ella gushed, taking three cookies and placing them in her lap on a napkin he'd handed her. Then, biting into the first shortbread, she moaned. "Oh, these are the best."

"So, we are together," I prodded. "What is your big news?"

"Yes, Ella, what is it you came here to tell us?" Roman inquired, offering the tin to me next.

Taking a cookie and a napkin, I suddenly remembered that I had missed lunch, and took another. "Thank you."

Leaning forward, Ella smiled broadly. "I'm going to have a baby," she blurted out.

Surprised and caught off guard, Roman began choking on the cookie he'd just popped into his mouth. Reaching over to grab his glass of tea, he guzzled it down while Ella and I stared at him.

"Are you all right, Roman?" Ella inquired. "One might think that you were just delivered shocking information."

"I think you just surprised him, Ella," I interjected, rushing to his side to hand him another napkin. "That is wonderful news!" Turning to look at Roman, I added, "Isn't that wonderful news, Roman?"

"Incredible," he choked out, sounding somewhat dubious regarding the matter. "Just…incredible," he added after I punched him in the arm.

Ella, unfazed by her brother's reaction, defended him. "I realize that this is a shock and that it has happened quickly. Teddy and I have discovered that we have a lot in common, and well, we have really hit it off," she concluded, her cheeks turning a dark shade of red.

Roman stood up quickly, looking embarrassed by the subject matter, and cleared his throat. "That is my cue to leave," he announced, placing his glass upon the table. As he walked away, he called over his

shoulder. "I'm really happy for you and," he stopped, turned, cleared his throat again, and added with a wink, "Teddy."

Ella turned an even darker shade of red. "Oh, go on now," she exclaimed, looking as if she wanted to throw something at his head.

"You ladies have yourselves a lovely chat," Roman said in a wry tone as he stepped through the doorway.

This time I picked up one of the pillows from the couch and threw it at him. He easily dodged it as he rushed from the room. Ella and I could hear him laughing all the way down the stairs.

"Men!" Ella exhaled.

"Don't allow him to spoil your wonderful surprise," I sighed, taking a seat next to her and placing a comforting hand over hers. "I for one am thrilled by your news, Ella. When is the baby due?"

"Late November." She looked up at me nervously, fiddling with the glass in her hand before leaning forward to place it down on the table.

"Ella, whatever is the matter?" I questioned. "Surely this is wonderful news. You and Theodore are happy over the baby, right?" She nodded, looking up at me with tears in her eyes.

"Then what is the matter?" I asked, feeling apprehensive.

"I'm scared, Lara. What if something happens and—"

"Nothing is going to happen, Ella," I assured her. "Everything is going to be just perfect. You will have a beautiful little baby, and you and Theodore will be wonderful parents. What could be better than that?"

"What if I...what if I die?" she stammered as tears began to roll down her cheeks.

"Oh, Ella," I soothed, pulling her into my arms. "Everything is going to be fine. You will have the best care possible. I will be by your side the whole time if you want me to."

Hugging me tightly, Ella sobbed, "You promise?"

I squeezed her back fiercely. "I promise. I won't leave your side."

"Oh, Lara, that makes me feel so much better. You're my best friend in the whole world." She cried even harder.

"Nothing bad is going to happen to you, Ella. I won't let it."

After drying her eyes and blowing her nose, Ella perked up again, reverting back to the old, confident, sassy Ella that I knew. We chatted for another hour and arranged a time that we would meet to discuss everything that needed to be done before the baby came.

The entire time we talked, I never let on that I was scared for her, nor did I tell her the story of the first birth I ever attended. There was nothing to be gained by scaring Ella with my sad tale of woe.

I walked Ella downstairs and saw her safely on her way in the carriage driven by a seasoned driver her husband had hired. His sole purpose in life was to drive Mrs. Ella Cramp any place she wanted to go.

Standing on the sidewalk waving farewell, I decided that I was tired and hungry and needed to go home. I turned towards the carriage shop doors to let Roman know that I was done for the day and was headed home to rest, when a man I'd never met before stopped me on the street.

"Excuse me miss, are ye Lara Roscoe?" he inquired, smiling pleasantly at me, showing off a row of stained, rotting teeth.

Confused by his question for a split second, I stopped and stammered, "What? Well…who is asking?"

"No one of real import, ma'am," he grinned, stepping in front of me as I tried to step around him. "Do not struggle. I hate it when they struggle," he muttered, shoving me toward the street as a closed carriage pulled up.

Still confused by his brazenness, I tried to step past him as he pulled a rag from his pocket. "Stop it!" I screamed, "Let me go this instant! Help!" I yelled, frantically looking back over my shoulder at the shop.

"Help!"

Grasping me by my waist, the large man picked me up and placed the rag over my nose at the same time. I heard someone shout, "Stop!

Unhand her!" but it was too late. I felt my limbs go numb and my head get foggy. I couldn't think or move. I could only watch in horror as the carriage door swung open and I was thrown through the opening into the waiting arms of another large man whom I didn't know. Then the carriage lurched forward before the door was even closed and I was staring into the face of my worst nightmare, Lord Horatio Henley.

He sat across from me on the bench seat of the carriage, smirking. "I told you I would have recompense, one way or the other," he snarled, and brutally pinched my cheek before nodding to the man who held me captive. That's when everything went dark, and I succumbed to the vapors from the filthy cloth that was placed over my nose again.

28

Imprisonment

The first thing I recall is the feeling of heaviness, like the time my brother Micky pushed me from a fifteen-foot cliff into the cold ocean water below. The shock was so great, it took my breath away, and I struggled to swim to the surface before Micky had reached down and pulled me to safety as I gasped for air.

But now, my head felt foggy and my limbs felt like large logs of wood; I couldn't tell if I was moving them or not. I moaned and tried to see, but there was something covering my eyes and the taste of an old rag filled my mouth.

Panic is the next thing I remember. That's when I began to struggle. Unable to control my movement, I thrashed about, trying to get free. I heard footsteps running away and a few minutes later I heard voices and the loud echo of footsteps returning.

"I see that you have deemed to grace us with your presence," Lord Henley remarked as he tore the blindfold from my eyes. "I was beginning to think we'd killed you," he said off-handedly, as if it wouldn't matter to him if he had killed me.

I saw that I was tied to a cot in a large warehouse and struggled to look around as Lord Henley removed the gag from my mouth. The windows near the ceiling were dirty and caked with dust as if they hadn't been cleaned since the day they were installed. Yet the dirt-encrusted windows allowed filtered light in. Boxes lined the walls on two sides and shelves with mechanical parts lined still another.

"Why have you done this?" I managed to croak out even though my mouth was so dry that it hurt my throat to speak.

"I told you I would have recompense one way or another." He leered at me while folding his arms across his large barrel chest. "Too bad you are so old or I would take it out in trade. As it stands, I have a friend that needs to restock his brothel on the corner of Bedford and South Street." He sneered and winked. "You will be in demand with your high and mighty attitude. You know that the working class all dream of having themselves a real lady." Henley laughed derisively.

The infamous Bedford Street was a deplorable, disgraceful district—a hot-bed for all the lowest, vice driven, degenerative people in the great city of Philadelphia—which, by common consent, was left out of the pale of all Christian missionary efforts.

"I will be missed," I cried, even though the pain of speaking was acute. "They will be searching for me."

"Who? Your family? That fellow you work with?" he scoffed, turning his back to me. "They will never find you in time," he added, turning to slap the young man's back who stood next to him as if he'd just told a funny joke. "You will be used up by the time they track you down," he snickered.

"You are pure evil!" I cried out, licking my dry lips.

"So I've been told by my wife," he answered. Then grunted, "It truly is a shame you've gotten so old. I've been watching you since you were very young."

I couldn't stop the involuntary shiver of revulsion I felt before I barked, "You are despicable!" my voice cracking as I strained my dry vocal cords.

"You are too kind, my dear," Henley crooned, taking a step closer and placing his face a mere inch from mine. "But please, save your judgment until the end, because I am just getting started. You haven't seen the depths of my depravity yet."

My blood went cold and I felt sick all the way to my core when I realized just how vulnerable I really was at this moment. My mind flashed back to my days on the streets of Ireland, when I was forced

to fight daily for every mouthful of food I ate. At the same time, I realized how sheltered I had really been. Nothing in my life thus far had prepared me for this situation. Lord Henley was right. I didn't know the depths of his depravity. How could I?

"You're looking a bit pale all of a sudden, my dear," Henley taunted. "Is everything all right?" he laughed again, then turned to the others in the room. "Untie her boys and let her use the loo over there in the corner," he ordered. "Then get the old girl something to drink and I'll have something sent around to eat. We can't have her weak and fainting on us when Reynolds comes to view the merchandise, now can we?"

I could hear his snide laughter echoing throughout the building as he left. My seething revulsion was like a cankerous sore in my belly and I wished that I could go back in time and hit him in the head several more times and finish him off.

The two henchmen doing Henley's bidding dragged me over to the darkened corner which contained a filthy metal pail. I merely stared at it with disdain and then at the two men waiting for me to do something.

"The boss says we can't leave you alone, on account of you're a tricky one," the taller man said.

"You could at least have the decency to turn your backs and give me some privacy," I insisted.

The two men looked at one other and again the taller one spoke. "I'm not sure that would be a good idea."

Tears of frustration and fear welled up in my eyes as I began to cry uncontrollably. "Please," I begged them, "I just need a moment."

The other man, who had freckles across his nose, elbowed his companion. "Come on, Joe. We can give her a moment," he argued. "What harm can it be?"

After a pause, Joe relented as he muttered, "Fine! But don't you go making a fool of me and Jimmy or you will be sorry."

Drying my tears with the back of my hand, I sniffed loudly. "Thank you, Joe. You are a real gentleman."

"Yeah, Yeah. Just be quick about it. If Henley comes back and sees us not doing our job, he'll have both of our heads," Joe confessed as he looked towards the door.

Then, looking back at Jimmy, Joe pulled a finger under his chin from ear to ear as a sign of what would happen to them if they got caught, followed by making a gruesome noise. "You know I'm right, Jimmy," he winked. "This be on ye."

I was grateful for the few minutes of peace they had given and I returned to the cot, sitting on the edge. "Could I have a chair to sit on instead of this filthy bed?" I asked sweetly.

Jimmy ran to the opposite side of the warehouse and retrieved a chair, bringing it to me as quickly as possible. "Here you go, Miss."

"You are a true hero, Jimmy," I concluded, trying to form a bond with him. I was hoping that I could come between the two men and get Jimmy to help me when the time was right.

"Don't go getting no crazy ideas that we work for you, li'l Missy," Joe warned. "We already got us a boss, and he's a mean son of a—" he blurted out, then thought better of finishing the sentence when Jimmy elbowed him in the ribs. "Sorry, ma'am. Sometimes I forget meself," he added sheepishly.

"That's quite alright, Joe," I answered demurely. "I suppose I will hear worse than that when Lord Henley has his way," I sobbed, ducking my head and frantically reaching into my pocket, searching for the handkerchief I always kept there.

"Now, don't start crying on us again," Joe groaned, reaching into his back pocket and pulling out his own dirty handkerchief, shoving it towards me before I produced my own. "I can't stand to hear a pretty girl cry," he helplessly muttered.

Jimmy quickly went to fetch me a glass of water, patiently waiting until I'd finished blowing my nose. I took a sip and then handed it back to him before plopping down in the chair, dejected and hopeless.

"Is it possible that all hope is lost to me?" I whispered to myself.

"Now, don't go being like that," Jimmy encouraged, squatting down to my level. "It's never that bad."

I looked into his brown eyes. "How can you say that to me? You're not the one being sold to this Mr. Reynolds," I pointed out.

Joe hit Jimmy in the back of the head. "Look alive, Jimmy, I hear a carriage pulling up. Henley promised to send us some food. Go take a look," he ordered. "And you need to stop playing to Jimmy's softer side," Joe interjected, pointing an accusatory finger at me, "or I will have to gag your mouth again.

Recoiling from his anger, I glared at his back when he stepped away to check on Jimmy and dinner. Then I quickly looked about for anything I could use as a weapon if I got the chance.

I had spotted some tools sitting on a shelf just a few feet away from me as I was returning from using the 'facilities.' Cautiously standing, I quickly ran to the shelf and grabbed the first thing I saw—an eight-inch adjustable metal wrench. Shoving the tool into my pocket, I also grabbed a wood-handled screw driver at the last minute, just for good measure, as I ran back to the chair. I felt like my heart was beating as loudly as a war drum in the night as I dropped into my seat, accidentally clanking the tools against the wooden chair in my haste. I cringed, trying to breathe normally while making a note to myself to be more careful when I moved.

The two men came through the door at that precise moment. Joe carried a basket in his hand and quickly looked suspiciously in my direction. I prayed that they wouldn't notice my dress was weighed down by the tools or the guilty look on my face.

I put my head down and coughed, wrapping my handkerchief around the wrench head in my pocket to keep it from rattling.

"Jimmy, bring that table over here," Joe directed, still looking at me suspiciously. "What was you up to while we were gone?"

Slowly looking up, I pointed out, "Am I not in the same spot I was when you left?"

"That's not the question I asked, now is it?" Joe said crossly. "You look guilty."

"Leave her alone, Joe," Jimmy insisted, dropping the table in front of me, cutting off his friend before he could interrogate me further. "Ain't she been through enough?"

Looking up at them both through my lashes, I held my breath and reached into my pocket, wrapping cold, stiff fingers around the handle of the wrench.

"Why you got to be so suspicious all of the time?" Jimmy continued. "Can't you see she's scared?"

Dropping the basket on the table, Joe turned towards Jimmy and for a split second I thought he was going to punch him in the face. But then he looked at me again, dropped his hand, and walked over to get another chair.

"Always got to be the bully," Jimmy muttered and shook his head as he pulled up a chair.

Looking like he was forcing a smile to his lips, Jimmy opened the basket and pulled out a covered dish wrapped in a towel. The heavenly smell wafted my way before he removed the towel. I was starving and almost anything would have tasted like the very finest prepared meal by this point.

My stomach loudly gurgled and my cheeks turned crimson as I said, "Excuse me."

"I take it that you're hungry?" he grinned. "You're in for a treat, because Mrs. Brown makes the best pottage. Now look at what we have here, Joe, she even gave us a whole loaf of bread," Jimmy cried with delight as he pulled the warm loaf of bread from the basket. "Mrs. Brown must be feeling generous today."

I hoped that the vegetable stew had some meat in it.

"Enough talk," Joe grumbled as he plopped down in his chair. "Pass the food already. I could eat the side off a cow, I'm so hungry."

Shifting the pocket containing the wrench in it across my lap, I breathed a sigh of relief and reached for the piece of bread Jimmy tore off of the loaf for me. I hadn't eaten in so long, I could have eaten the side off of a live cow myself.

After we'd eaten our fill, Jimmy brought over a bowl of fresh water and the cleanest rag he could find so that I could wash up. I forced a smile and thanked him for his kindness. I hadn't given up hope that he would do the right thing, but I also wasn't going to hold my breath. I figured Jimmy was more afraid of Joe and Lord Henley and what would happen to him if he got caught helping me than he was of the authorities.

The enormous warehouse was beginning to grow darker as the sun set. Joe lit a few lanterns so that we could see, but not enough to draw attention to the building, since it was long past working time.

Being confined to the cot in the middle of the room where they could keep a close eye on me, I laid there pretending to be asleep so that they might relax and slip up. It wasn't long before they began to talk and I overheard them agreeing to take two-hour shifts. Joe said that Henley would be returning before first light with a Mr. Reynolds. I saw Jimmy looking towards me with this strange look of regret on his face, almost as if he was sorry for getting involved in the nasty business of kidnapping in the first place.

"Are you sure about this, Joe?" he questioned. "It just don't feel right."

"Shut yer mouth and do as yer told before ye gets us both killed," Joe blurted out angrily. "Henley promised to pay us well for helping him and I needs the money, Jimmy. My lady is due with the babe any day, and I won't disappoint her!"

"Alright, Joe," Jimmy exhaled, throwing his hands up in the air as he took a step back. "You don't need to get yourself so riled up."

"Don't mess this one up for me, Jimmy," Joe threatened, balling up his fists at his side.

"Alright, alright, Joe," Jimmy cowered. "I just don't think it's right. That's all," he grumbled as he retired to the far end of the warehouse and fell asleep quickly.

I continued to lay there with one eye open, waiting for an opportunity to make my move, but none came. Joe was like a caged animal. He never stopped moving, even when it was Jimmy's turn to stand watch.

Instead of sleeping, Joe took a seat at the table and pulled out a deck of cards. And when it was time to switch again Joe put the cards away and began to roam the warehouse restlessly while Jimmy laid in his cot staring at the ceiling.

My eyes grew heavy watching him pace back and forth and I must have fallen asleep, because the next thing I knew, someone was coming through the side door.

"There she is, just as I promised," Henley crooned, grabbing a lantern from the table as he advanced on me. "Well, get her up boy, so Mr. Reynolds can see what he's buying."

Joe grabbed my arm and yanked me to my feet. "You heard the man, girly. Get up."

I reached for the pocket with the wrench in it so it wouldn't clank around as I was pulled to my feet. "What's a girl got to do to get some decent sleep around here?" I protested loudly to cover up any noise the tools might have made in my pocket.

Joe raised his hand as if he meant to back hand me, and I flinched.

"Don't damage the merchandise, good man!" Henley yelled. "I will take any damage you cause to her out of your pay."

Slowly lowering his hand, Joe yanked hard upon my arm instead and I stood up, pushing stray hairs out of my eyes. Then, stomping on the top of Joe's foot with the heel of my boot as hard as I could, I gave him a frosty glare, daring him to do his worst.

He cursed under his breath and squeezed my arm viciously. I retaliated by kicking him in the shin.

Quickly, Jimmy stepped between us to save his friend from doing something he would regret later. "Here, let me," he said taking hold of my arm.

Joe stepped back with a forced smile. "But of course," he muttered. "By all means."

"Didn't I tell you she was a rare jewel?" Henley proclaimed proudly. "She has spunk and apparently kick as well."

Reynolds stood there assessing me as if he were looking over a prized mare at a public auction. "She does have kick," he mused. "But has she been tamed?"

"Why don't you take a step closer and I'll show you just how tame I am," I threatened, trying to yank my arm free.

"Settle down there, little miss," Jimmy soothed. "No sense in showing everything you can do all at once."

Turning on Jimmy, I tried to deliver a kick to his shin, which he dodged as if he were expecting it. "Don't make me get out the smelly cloth again," he insisted.

"You bloody well wouldn't dare," I responded.

"Only as a last resort," Jimmy sighed. "Now behave and we will all get to go home."

"Not me. I won't get to go home," I cried, tears of frustration filling my eyes.

"Well," Henley prodded. "What do you think? Is she everything I promised?"

"Perhaps more, my friend," Reynolds surmised, stroking his chin as he walked around me.

Reynolds was a tall, thin man who wore all black except for his stark white shirt, which accentuated his darker features. His dark salt and pepper hair was slicked back, emphasizing his long, thin nose, reminding me of a bird's beak. He stood back, fingering his chin and narrowing his eyes down to beady, little slits as he analyzed me.

"Maybe, my friend, she is too much woman for any one man to handle," Mr. Reynolds surmised as he stood back, folding his arms across his chest.

"If you are trying to renege on our agreement, dear man, let me assure you that I have three other buyers lined up behind you," Henley added confidently. "In fact, I believe I hear one of them pulling up right now."

"Now, hold up, old friend," Reynolds cajoled. "I didn't say that I wasn't interested—" he stammered, hearing several carriages pull up outside.

Cutting him off, Henley quipped, "I merely gave you first chance at her because we are such good friends."

Taking a deep breath, I knew this was my last chance. Any minute now, men would be coming through that door and I would be done for. While they argued, I reached my hand into my pocket and pulled out the wrench. I whacked Jimmy across the knuckles and he jumped back in surprise. I knew Joe would be directly behind his friend so I bent low, smashing the wrench into his knee, whereupon he dropped to the ground like a ton of bricks. Joe screamed, grabbing his leg as he rolled around in agony.

"That will teach you," I scolded, "you greedy so and so."

Henley and Reynolds stood frozen in place, not daring to come near me, fearing my wrath in the form of an adjustable metal wrench.

"Grab her, you useless piece of meat," Henley frantically shouted. At the same moment the warehouse door swung open and uniformed men, dressed in navy blue trousers and matching button-down coats, rushed in.

I heard Henley and Reynolds gasp in unison as I turned to find Jimmy sneaking up behind me with a rag in his hand. "If you take one more step closer to me, you will pay dearly with your life, Jimmy," I warned, "because I will smash you in the head this time."

I was so focused on Jimmy that I didn't hear the men shouting orders. "Get down on the ground! That's an order! Do it, now!"

Someone stepped up behind me and I swung with my wrench. "Stay back!" I shouted, turning around and swinging at anything that moved.

"Whoa!" Roman yelled. "It's me, Lara," he said calmly when he saw the wild look in my eyes. "It's me!"

It took me a moment to recognize him, but when I did I dropped the wrench to the ground and leapt into his arms. "You found me! You

found me," I wept, squeezing his neck tightly. "I can't believe you found me," I whispered, pulling back to look at him.

"By the looks of it, I think we actually needed to save those men from you," Roman chuckled. "Are you hurt? What's this?" Roman questioned, pulling the wooden handled screwdriver from my pocket.

I looked at the object in his hand. "My back up," I confessed with a smile.

"You are amazing," he insisted.

"Right now, I don't feel very amazing. I just want to go home and see Mother and have a bath. I feel like my skin is crawling."

"Miss, I'm Constable Franklin. We need to know what happened here," the officer said.

"Miss Roscoe has been through a terrible ordeal. Can you round them all up for now and put them in a cell?" Roman asked the officer. "We will come down later after Miss Roscoe has had a chance to clean up and get some rest."

"Very well, sir," constable Franklin replied. "As you wish."

"Wait," I yelled, pushing away from Roman's protective grasp. "I need to talk with him," I pointed at Jimmy.

Constable Franklin shouted, "Bring that one over here."

"I know that you didn't truly want to go along with everything, but you still chose to," I said sullenly, looking into Jimmy's eyes. "I will plead leniency on your behalf, but you still chose to do what you did."

Jimmy lowered his head, and tears came to his eyes. "I know it was wrong, and I should have been stronger when I realized what was happening," Jimmy cried. "I'm sorry for what we done to you," he added, looking me in the eye. "I deserve what I get."

"Alright, take him away," Constable Franklin ordered. "We will wait until you are ready to make a statement."

"Thank you, Constable Franklin. I will make sure she gets down to the station as soon as she is able," Roman responded, tightening a protective arm around my shoulders.

29

JULY 15, 1853

The Proposal

I was home, surrounded by my mother who did her best to reassure me, and yet I still couldn't relax. Nightmares haunted me every time I closed my eyes, flashing back to the day I was abducted. I repeatedly woke up screaming in terror, night after night. Mother had taken to sleeping in my bed so that she could quickly awaken me and assure me over and over again that I was safe.

Doctor Sheridan prescribed a mild sedative to help me rest but I found the medicine reminded me too much of being drugged by my captors and that made me even more anxious.

I hadn't been to work in over a month and I was imagining my desk piled high with invoices, receipts, and paperwork. Roman assured me everything was being handled and that my desk would be as neat and tidy as the day I left it, but I didn't believe him. I wanted to see for myself, yet I was too afraid to leave the house.

Lord Henley and his henchmen had stolen more from me than a few hours. They had taken away my sense of security and well-being.

The entire incident had been kept out of the papers and as quiet as possible in the attempt to preserve my good name and reputation. An unchaperoned woman was as good as ruined in the eyes of society. People would imagine all sorts of unscrupulous events taking place, either with or without my consent, and then my ability to make a good match and marry someday, if I chose to, would be impossible.

The trial of the four men was kept all very hush-hush and a deal was struck with Mr. Edward Harper, the newspaper man who wanted

to interview me years earlier, giving him exclusive rights to my life's story when I was recovered enough to tell it. In exchange, Mr. Harper would bury any story that might have been whispered in polite society and quash any rumors from his end. There would be nothing printed in the newspaper or bantered around in hushed tones on the street about my abduction. Mother and Roman saw to that. The judge was a close family friend, and he handpicked the jury himself. The entire matter was settled in a matter of two days, rather than two weeks.

I pleaded for leniency on Jimmy Slater's behalf and the judge gave him two and a half years hard labor in the Pennsylvania Penitentiary system, in what was commonly known as the separate system. The other three men were given much harsher sentences.

I had heard whispers of the place long before I ever set eyes on it. The penitentiary stood on a hill to the northwest, in the Fairmount neighborhood, its looming walls rising like some dark cathedral. Papa once pointed it out on a carriage ride, explaining that it had been built to replace the Walnut Street Jail. He called the old jail a "school of crime" where men, women, and even children were all thrown together until their trials. I never forgot the disdain in his voice.

This new prison, he told me, was meant to be different. An English architect, John Haviland, had designed it so that no prisoner would ever corrupt another. Each man was shut away alone with nothing but a narrow cell, a rudimentary toilet, and his work—shoemaking, weaving, chair caning—to fill the hours. They were forbidden to speak, even in the exercise yard. Ministers sometimes walked the corridors to deliver sermons, but otherwise, the prisoners were left to their solitude. Papa said they were even forced to wear hoods when moved about so they would remain faceless shadows to one another.

I could scarcely imagine such silence. To live twenty-three hours of every day without a voice to hear or a face to see—it was no wonder people said the walls themselves drove men mad.

Joe Bartlett, Horatio Henley, and Sam Reynolds each received ten years for their part in my abduction and imprisonment.

Although their convictions were harsh, it was of little consolation to me at night when I closed my eyes and saw their faces in my

nightmares. I was confident, however, that I would eventually work past the horrors of that day and move on with my life.

I was in the upstairs sitting room, enjoying the perfect light as I attempted to needle point an intricate design on the cuff of a shirt, when Martha escorted Roman into the room.

"What a pleasant surprise," I gushed enthusiastically, sounding a bit more chipper than I was actually feeling.

Clearing his throat and waiting for Martha to take his hat and walking cane and leave, Roman looked up hesitantly. "I was on my way back from a meeting with the Mullen brothers when I had the sudden urge to see how you were doing."

Laying the needle work aside, I stood and stretched my back. "Please, sit." I indicated a place on the couch, then took the seat next to him. "I'm terribly glad you did. Was it a productive meeting?" I inquired. "Oh, should I have Martha bring us up some tea and cookies?" I asked, jumping to my feet before he could answer. "She baked them fresh this morning. The cookies, I mean. Not the tea."

"No, thank you. I've recently eaten," he answered, pulling on my hand to stop me from reaching for the tasseled cord that hung near the hearth—a simple tug would send a bell ringing in the servants' quarters and bring Martha at once. "And yes, to answer your question, the meeting was productive. I believe we have a new source of leather. Their prices are better than our current suppliers and the quality was comparable."

"That's marvelous," I raved, "you must tell me every little detail."

Smiling broadly, showing off his beautiful white teeth, Roman took a deep breath. "You have been cooped up in this house for far too long if you want to hear every little detail of a boring business meeting," he bantered. "But I wasn't completely honest when I said I was just passing by, Lara."

"You weren't?"

Looking serious now, Roman shook his head as he scooted closer to me. "No, I wasn't," he admitted. "I've been meaning to discuss a matter with you for several months now—"

"Oh, my, this does sound serious," I teased, trying to lighten the mood.

Chuckling slightly, Roman shifted, taking my hands in his as he gazed into my eyes. "I spoke with your father," he began, then cleared his throat uncomfortably before continuing, "before he passed. He advised me to wait until you reached the age of maturity and could make an intelligent decision for yourself."

"Oh," was all I could say.

He took another deep breath and shifted in his seat again. "Now you're going to make me lose my nerve."

"I'm sorry, Roman. Please, do go on," I encouraged. "I promise not to interrupt you again."

"I spoke with your father, and he gave me his blessing. I feel it important to tell you this first."

"Alright?" I said, feeling puzzled and a bit apprehensive.

"Lara, would you do me the great honor of becoming my wife?" Roman blurted out.

I sat very still for a moment, then got quickly to my feet and walked over to the window to look outside, waiting for the shock of his question to wear off. "Have you completely lost your mind, Roman Blackthorn?" I gasped, crossing my arms over my chest. "I can't even go outside this house or cross the street by myself without breaking out into a cold sweat. I'm broken!"

Coming up behind me, Roman turned me around to face him, gently resting both his hands on my shoulders. "We are all broken, Lara. Let me help you through this. Please!"

Looking up into his clear, indigo eyes, I saw warmth and compassion, but most of all, I saw honesty. "Yes, but why would you want to saddle yourself with someone who has been crippled by life's experiences?"

"Because when I look into your eyes, I don't see someone who has been crippled by her experiences. I see someone who has overcome them and become stronger because of them. You are the strongest, most resilient person I know. I could tell that about you the first time

I met you, Lara. This is just a bump in the road," Roman assured me. "You will get through this. We…we will get through this."

"How can you be so certain?" I pushed him away, not allowing myself to hope for such happiness.

Taking a step back, Roman combed his fingers through his hair as he turned his back to me for a moment. I thought he was going to walk away. Then suddenly he turned back around, embraced me in his arms, and kissed me. "Because I know you," he whispered. "I know you, and I love you, Lara Ann Flannigan Roscoe," Roman fervently declared. "With all of my heart, I love you."

"You should really hang your hat on someone else," I quietly answered, halfheartedly pushing against his chest.

Refusing to turn me loose, Roman held tightly, but gently, forcing me to look up at him. "I don't want anyone else, Lara. Not since the day we first locked eyes," he added with a sigh. "Not even when I went away to school. I couldn't stop comparing every woman I met to you. To you, Lara! No one else!" he emphasized. "Then when I came home and learned that you and my sister had become best friends, I somehow knew that it was fate that had brought you and me together."

"But how can you be so sure that I am the one you love, Roman?" I whispered, my gaze unsteady, my eyes shimmering with emotion. A fragile part of me longed to believe him, even as the fear of disappointing him twisted inside me. There was so much about me that he did not know anything about, starting with my large family still residing in Ireland.

Giving me a patient smile, Roman exhaled, "Because, darling, you are the first person I want to share my accomplishments with when they happen, and you are the only person I think of when I imagine myself growing old," he confessed. Growing even more serious, he lowered his head and kissed me again on the lips, then my left cheek and then my right. "I see you in my dreams, I feel you with each breath I take." Gently forcing me to tip my chin up he continued, "And you are the only person I couldn't live without for the rest of my life."

Our lips touched again, gently at first, like two halves of a whole, perfectly carved and polished to fit together.

He lifted his head to gaze down at me. "And you are the only one I want to bring children into this world with," he passionately whispered, bending down on one knee as he pulled out a small red velvet pouch from his pocket. "I have been carrying this ring around in my pocket for over a year," he said, pulling an emerald ring out and presenting it to me. "From the moment I saw this ring in Schumacher's window, I knew that it belonged on your finger. Will you consent to be my wife, Lara Ann Flannigan Roscoe?"

My heart skipped a beat and then another. I could barely catch my breath. Tears of joy ran down my cheeks and I nodded my head. "Yes, Roman, I would be deeply honored to become your wife."

Slipping the ring upon my finger, he stood and took me into his arms. "You have made me the happiest man alive."

Sighing contentedly, I whispered, "There is only one thing in this world that could make this day even better," while pulling back to look into his eyes.

Looking puzzled, Roman's brows knitted together. "And what could that possibly be, my love?"

Smiling confidently for the first time in over a month, I was feeling stronger already, knowing that Roman loved me. "First, we need to find Mother and tell her the good news. Then we can sit down and talk," I added mysteriously.

"What have you got up your sleeve, my little Irish rose?"

"You will have to be patient and wait."

"I believe I have already proven that I am a very patient man," Roman quipped.

I smiled. "Yes you have, my love. But I wish to beg your indulgence for a little longer."

30

APRIL 27, 1854
PHILADELPHIA WHARF

Lara is 21
The Reunion

This brings me back to the very beginning of my story—Roman and I are standing on the wharf, waiting for the City of Glasgow to sail into Philadelphia Harbor. The salt air stings my nose, mingling with the sharp cries of gulls circling overhead as I pace the length of the wooden dock. Every step echoes too loudly in my ears, a steady reminder of my nerves. Somewhere on that ship are the faces I once thought I would never see again in this lifetime—my family.

Mother, Edith Newman, and John Whitlock are busying themselves behind the gate arranging tables with five other volunteers ready to greet the newly arrived passengers. Their calm order only sharpens my restlessness. Months of planning have led to this day—letters that crossed the ocean and back, arrangements made and remade through delays, passages secured—all while I held my breath and prayed. And now, after endless waiting, the moment has come. The ship is in the harbor. My family is nearly here.

Mother gives my arm a reassuring squeeze as I wring my hands together, waiting for the passengers to disembark and make their way through the inspection queues. I think of how many times I've stood where Edith is standing right now, stationed at the exit gate, directing immigrants to their first meal on American soil, or giving them directions to aid them on their way in this foreign land.

I'm so filled with anticipation I swear I could walk on air, but then I begin to worry. "What if I don't recognize them?" I cry, furrowing my brows together, still staring at the gate. "What if they walk right past me and I don't even know my own flesh and blood!?"

Placing a comforting hand around my shoulder, Roman squeezes it reassuringly. "Stop worrying yourself sick. They will know you the second they lay eyes on you. I promise."

"But what if they don't?" I add frantically, searching each of the faces that comes through the gate.

Mother puts a loving arm around my waist. "I have taken care of that," she says, pointing behind me.

Two of the volunteers are holding up a large sign that reads, 'Welcome to America, Flannigan Clan,' in large eight-inch, black letters.

"Oh, Mother, you do think of everything," I squeal and throw my arms around her. "How would I ever survive without you?"

"I shudder to think of it," she teases.

"Darling, do you recognize that person standing over there?" Roman asks, directing my attention to a dark-haired man standing several feet away from us who has stopped to stare at the sign.

"Colin," I whisper at first, then I scream, "Colin, COLIN!" Running towards him, I throw myself into his arms and he drops the satchel slung over his shoulder. "Is it really you?" I whisper next to his ear.

He sweeps me up and swings me around in a full circle. "Aye, little sister. 'Tis I," his voice cracks. "I thought I'd never see yer face again."

"And I yours, dear brother," I exclaim as he puts me on the ground facing a lovely, blond haired woman with three children by her side. I estimate their ages to be five, four, and two.

"Lara, this is me wife, Jenny, me sons, Micky and Jacob, and me daughter, Lara. Lara, me love, meet yer aunt and name sake," Colin exclaims.

I stare up at Colin, unsure that I've heard him correctly until he nods at me in the affirmative. Then I stoop down to little Lara's eye level and extend my hand. "It is a pleasure to meet you, Lara Flannigan," I say formally.

Shy at first, little Lara places her hand in mine, peering up at me through her lashes. Then I turn to each boy, shaking their little hands. Reaching into my pocket, I pull out a bag of hard candies and give it to the oldest child, Micky. "Just a little present from your Aunt Lara," I say, choking back tears of joy. "I mean for you to share this with the other children," I warn, watching closely as his eyes light up with excitement.

"Thank ye, Aunt Lara," he smiles, immediately taking a piece and popping it into his mouth before handing out the candy to his siblings and rejoining them at his mother's side.

I stand again and look up, noticing several more people gathered around us. "Alana?" I gasp, "is that you and Newel? Oh, I can't believe it. It is you," I cry, throwing my arms around them both at the same time.

"I want ye to meet yer sister," Alana says tentatively as she reaches over, pulling a beautiful young woman from out of the group. "This is Grace. But we all call her Gracie."

Tears of joy and pain fill my eyes at the same time as I remember back to the last time I'd seen my youngest sibling. Looking into her green eyes, I can see Mama there. The pain is quickly replaced with an overwhelming feeling of joy and love when I realize that I no longer blame her for Mama's death and that I had been a fool to do so in the first place.

Gracie is the first to step forward, embracing me. "Sister," she sighed, "I've heard so much about ye. I'm so happy that I finally get to meet ye."

"I was there the day you were born, sweet Gracie. I was one of the first to hold you," I correct. "So, you see, we have already met, many years ago."

Alana pulls another child from the group—a young boy around six years of age. He has strong, striking features and dark eyes fringed with dark lashes. "This is my oldest," she proudly announces. "Rory, meet your Aunt Lara."

Sticking his hand forward, he greets me very properly as if he had practiced it beforehand. "It is a pleasure to make your acquaintance." Rory pronounces each word clearly, trying to sound like a proper Englishman.

"He practiced that accent the entire journey over, trying to imitate the English passengers," Alana chuckles, causing young Rory to blush profusely.

"Oh, Mama…"

"I am rightly impressed by the effort, Master Rory," I say encouragingly. "Why, I do believe you will blend in with the American yanks in no time at all."

Pulling a face at his mother as if to say, *I told you so*, Rory turns back to me. "Thank you, Aunt Lara. Ye, I mean…you are most kind. Most kind indeed."

"Well, la-di-da," Caitlin chimes in as she comes up behind us. "Aren't we Mr. High and Mighty," she teases, ruffling Rory's hair as she steps forward to pull me into her arms. "I will say, ye've changed some since I last saw ye," she exclaims as she embraces me.

When my eyes settle fully on her, a jolt of shock goes through me. The years have left their mark—her once-vivid hair is now faded and streaked with gray, her face is drawn and weary, and her eyes are hollow, as though they still carry every hardship and horror she has endured. Yet beneath it all, she is still my sister. *"Sister!"* I breathe, flinging my arms around her neck. "I have missed you so dearly."

"Look who's lost her accent," Caitlin scolds. "One would never know that ye come from the cliffs of Dunmore Head."

"Oh, how I've missed the sound of our native tongue spoken," I lament, tears of joy rolling freely down my cheeks. "Did you ever marry?" I ask.

A sad smile crosses her lips, not really reaching all the way to her eyes, as Caitlin lets out a heavy sigh. "No, dear sister. It was not to be."

I rub a sympathetic hand up and down her arms. "I truly am sorry, dear Caitlin. But perhaps…it isn't too late."

"Aye!" she sighs. Then, with a glint of sass in her eyes, reminding me of the Caitlin I knew, she perks up. "I'm no' dead yet."

I laugh at her bluntness as someone else comes up behind me and taps me on the shoulder. Turning, I squeal with delight, "Michael, is that truly you?"

"Aye! Who else were ye expecting?" he adds with a hint of mischief.

"Come here and give us a hug," I insist, pulling him to me. "How have you been?"

"I can no' complain. My baby sister is a proper young woman and I find myself standing on America soil, courtesy of her," he points out joyfully, pulling me back into an embrace and squeezing me even tighter this time.

I find myself wondering how I ever believed that I could live the rest of my life without my family. Taking a step back, an overwhelming feeling of joy washes over me and I can't stop grinning as Mother and Roman come up beside me.

Roman clears his throat loudly, "I'm Roman Blackthorn, by the way, Lara's fiancé, and this is Charity Roscoe, her step-mother," he announces, causing everyone to stop and gawk at them both.

Awkwardly, I smile and clear my throat just as Roman had done. "There is, of course, food on the tables here if you are hungry right this minute. But I want to assure you that Martha has prepared a feast for us all back at the house. We have carriages waiting to transport you and all of your belongings." I point to the eight carriages lined up just beyond the tables. "And, of course, anything you might need, please don't hesitate to ask."

Stepping over to the volunteer table, I thank everyone for their hard work and notice some of the children from our group getting sandwiches before they follow their parents to the waiting carriages.

Mother climbs into the lead carriage and leaves for the house with part of the family while Roman and I remain behind, seeing to everyone's needs and making sure that no one is left behind.

As luggage is unloaded at our house, I have my family identify their belongings to the extra help I've hired. Then their things are whisked away to their respective new family locations.

Colin and his family, along with Alana and her family, will reside across the street in the carriage shop housing above our business. Caitlin and Michael will be staying in the main house with me.

Most of our employees are married now, with homes of their own, so they no longer need the housing, and the one who isn't is being given nice accommodations in a boarding house two blocks away. My brother and sister's families will have plenty of room to spread out while still being close, which is what matters to me.

A feeling of unadulterated contentment washes over me as my family enters the dining room with their spouses and children. The noise and clatter that comes with a joyous gathering is like music to my ears and I am reminded of another time in my childhood when I was secure in the knowledge that I was loved and cherished by my family.

Epilogue

MAY 15, 1854

Lara's Wedding Day

Stepping down from the carriage, I take Colin's arm and we begin to walk up the steps when I pause to look up at the beautiful steeple of the church. I'm reminded of a time when I'd childishly vowed to never step foot in a church again. Suddenly, it feels like a lifetime ago. So many things have changed in my life since that day, long ago. So many lessons have been learned since then as well, and yet, I still find it difficult to let go of all that has happened to me, even on a day like this. My vow to avoid all churches had been a foolish one.

"Are you ready?" Colin asks patiently as he gazes down at me.

I nod and smile up at him as the memory begins to fade from my thoughts and I mentally prepare to stand before friends and family and take vows of a different kind, with the man I have chosen to spend the rest of my life with.

"It's funny," I murmur, "there was a time in my life when I could never have imagined any of this for myself."

"And why is that?"

Looking up with a sad smile, I confess, "Because I thought Da would give me away on my wedding day. I also imagined that I would live and die in the very place I was born."

"There would no' be much adventure in such a thing, little sister," Colin said with a hearty laugh.

"None, indeed," I agree, continuing up the steps and into the church. "I am truly grateful you are here."

"Aye, me too," he replies with a wink. "Now, let's see if we can pull the wool over young Roman's eyes and get ye two wed before he realizes what he has done," Colin teases.

Elbowing him in the ribs, I giggle when he makes a very ungentlemanly sound just before the doors open and the wedding music begins to play.

We begin our walk down the aisle and I smile at all of my friends and family who have traveled so far to be with me on this special day. We pass Ella's husband, Theodore Cramp, proudly standing there holding his daughter, Charlotte, who is now six months old. She is such a pretty child with her dark curly hair and rich brown eyes that sparkle with mischief. Her smile lights up the room as I pass by.

I told Ella when Charlotte was first born that she was going to be a heartbreaker when she grew up, to which Ella replied, "Well, I would certainly hope so."

Ella gleefully agreed to be my maid-of-honor without any hesitation when I asked her months before.

Now my eyes lock with Roman's and everything and everyone else fades away as he smiles at me. Colin lifts my veil and kisses my cheek before placing my hand into Roman's with a nod and a solemn, "Treat her well."

Staring up into Roman's shimmering eyes, I can see the emotion and love reflecting back at me and realize just how fortunate I am. Not only did I survive my fair share of hardship, but I thrived and grew stronger because of it, discovering in the process that I am the architect of my dreams and the designer of my destiny. Fate may have had a hand in what happened following the death of my mama, but I learned to never give away my right to choose for myself which path I will travel in this life. It is true that the death of Mama, Da, Micky, and Papa left me with a large hole in my heart that will never completely heal, but I am stronger for it.

Father's words come back to me from the last time I saw him. "Lara, me love, I don' wan' ta send ye away. But I have no choice. I truly hope that one day ye can find it in yer heart ta forgive me."

I can still keenly hear and feel the pain in his words as he clung to me that last time. Those were the last words my Da would ever say to me, and I hope that he realized in the end that I did forgive him. And that I now feel at peace with the decision that was made. I will never be able to wish him ill will or hold a grudge for a choice made with such anguish so many years ago.

I now remember him fondly—his kind eyes, gentle hugs, and hearty laugh. That is how I will always remember him—with love.

New beginnings come to us, not all at once, but over time—a delayed gratification of sorts. We may never know how our lives will conclude, and yet, joy is not held by the receiver with any less enthusiasm because it has been delayed for a while, as in my case. Rather, we embrace it and revel in the joy of it, because we have known the sorrow of hardship.

There will always be bumps, pot holes, and blind curves in the road for each of us to contend with. No one is exempt from them. For love grows when nothing else is expected, and if you are lucky enough to find love on your journey, and the presence of mind to recognize it for the blessing that it is, hold on to it with both hands. For when fate and fortune smiles upon you, love will endure any hazard that lies ahead.

Every question begins with a quest for answers, and every testimony of what is true begins with the test of one's resolve. And if we face outwards with our heads held high, being honest and true to ourselves, it is possible to be made whole again by that same love, as I have been by my family, my mother, and Roman.

True and Interesting Facts

The Irish Potato Famine: A Natural Disaster Compounded by Agricultural Practices, Greed and Neglect

A natural disaster can have ripple effects that last for generations. Such was the case with The Irish Potato Famine, which was partially caused by the limitations the geography of the countryside placed on the people who lived there. The Irish landscape includes some regions with rich, fertile soil, but much of the land is rocky and lacks the nutrients many crops need to grow well. People living in those areas during the 1800s eked out an existence often on the edge between survival and starvation. Potatoes became the staple food supply because they grew well in this climate and could be stored and eaten over the winter.

One particular variety, known as the Lumper, seemed to thrive better than the rest, producing plentiful crops. More and more farmers turned to this crop since it was easy to grow and the high yields provided much needed food for their communities. And then, disaster struck.

In 1845, farmers started to see whole fields of potato plants wither and die, creating a terrible stench in the process. Unknown at the time, an airborne microorganism, later identified as Phytophthora infestans, spread rapidly through the fields, turning up to half of the crops into rotting, wilted wastelands. The lack of genetic variety in the seeds that were planted across the country, coupled with the damp, rainy breezes common in Ireland, made it easier for the disease to spread from farm to farm in one season.

At first it was thought that the next year would bring healthy crops again, but even more of the potato crop failed in 1846. People who had sold their belongings and livestock to buy food and who had found bits of work opportunities to piece together a living, now had nowhere

to turn for work and no resources left to sell. Starvation became a too common reality as year after year, disease ravaged the fields, and then devastated the population of weakened, poverty stricken individuals and families.

The famine lasted from 1845 to 1852. People were left with a grim choice: stay and likely die, or emigrate from their homes to another country, hoping they would survive the journey to begin new lives. Many fled to America in overcrowded, unsanitary ships that came to be known as "coffin ships" since so many passengers lost their lives on board. Those who survived the trip faced new challenges in their new home.

https://learnodo-newtonic.com/irish-potato-famine-facts

http://www.historyplace.com/worldhistory/famine/begins.htm

Land Use and Political Policies Contributing to the Famine's Impact

The long lasting effects of the famine caused by the potato crop failure was intensified by a variety of factors both before and during the famine. Land use and political policies before the natural disaster hit influenced the enormity of its impact. One reason Irish families became so reliant on the potato harvest for their food supply was that some farmers used fertile land to raise grain crops such as wheat, barley, oats, and oatmeal which they sold to the British, rather than to the communities in their homeland, in order to generate enough cash to pay their rent and taxes so they didn't lose their farming livelihood. This practice was often dictated by British landowners who bought the grain from the Irish at low prices and sold it in Britain at a profit. The British also enjoyed the beef which was sold and shipped to them from Irish farmers who raised cattle on fertile lands to meet expenses rather than using the land to grow food crops that could diversify the food supply in their regions. These circumstances led to a situation in which nearly half of the population depended largely, and sometimes solely, on potatoes to survive before the blight took hold on the country.

Government policies, often influenced by land owners, also contributed to the desperate situation. Laws tended to favor landlords, providing few if any rights of redress for tenants whose labor was often exploited. Rent prices were such that after paying rent, many families didn't have enough left to feed their families, much less keep up with other expenses.

Some attempt was made by government leaders, particularly British Prime Minister Sir Robert Peel, to address the threat of starvation, but long-standing British economic laws worked against his efforts. The Corn Laws, which enacted heavy tariffs on all imported grain, served to artificially keep British-grown grain prices high. Prime Minister Peel proposed repealing those laws in order to provide more affordable grain to the Irish; however, politicians and English gentry alike rejected the idea, putting their own economic interests above taking any steps to provide relief for what they considered a temporary problem that would fix itself.

Prime Minister Peel managed to arrange for the purchase of two shipments of Indian corn (maize) from America, but problems with mills not being outfitted with equipment that could grind the hard grain to a usable texture, peasants who didn't even have enough money to purchase it at cost or had difficulty digesting the unfamiliar grain, and people developing scurvy due to the corn lacking vitamin C, rendered this effort temporary and incomplete at best.

Further complicating matters was the policy of laissez-faire (let it be) that leaders of the time thought was the best course of action. So, ships full of grain continued to sail from Irish shores leaving behind a starving populace, food aid was kept to a minimum in order to protect private businesses and English landowners' profit margins, and high interest money lenders and other opportunists were allowed to take advantage of a grim situation as they exploited the desperate plight of millions of Irish citizens.

The Irish Potato Blight Famine of 1845 to 1852 changed not only Ireland's course of history, but that of the nations receiving its people as immigrants, including the United States. The ripple effect of a tiny

pathogen on a nation's potato crop is still felt to this day, even if it has been forgotten by many.

http://www.historyplace.com/worldhistory/famine/begins.htm

Workhouses: A Harsh Answer to Poverty

The roots of the workhouse system date back to the Statute of Cambridge 1388. That law was created to address labor shortages following the outbreak of the Black Death in England. It aimed to prevent workers from relocating in search of better pay and gradually shifted the responsibility of caring for the poor onto the government.

The Poor Relief Act of 1601 proposed relief in three different forms. The able-bodied were expected to work in a house of correction. Housing was to be constructed for the old and infirm and those classified as impotent poor. However, many were assisted through a program called outdoor relief which provided food, money, and necessities to those who remained in their own homes. Since this method was usually less expensive than housing the poor in facilities, and each parish was responsible for the poor within their boundaries, this was usually the chosen way relief was provided. A tax on the wealthy residents in the parish provided the funding.

By the early 1800s, the cost of providing for the poor was escalating. After the Napoleonic Wars ended in 1815, thousands of people found themselves out of work. Adding to the unemployment crisis was the rise of machines that replaced farm laborers as well as several bad harvests. The old system of helping the poor could no longer keep up.

In 1834, the government passed what became known as the New Poor Law. It was meant to cut costs and discourage people from relying on public assistance. Under this new law, assistance was only provided to individuals who were willing to enter a workhouse. Essentially, if you needed help, you were expected to go to the workhouse or receive nothing at all. These places weren't designed to help people thrive—they were designed to be tough. The idea was to make life inside so unpleasant that only the truly desperate would turn to them for help.

Some local officials even attempted to profit by utilizing workhouse inmates as cheap labor. The problem was, many of the people sent there didn't have the skills—or the health—to do much. They were often assigned to mindless, grueling tasks, such as breaking stones, crushing bones for fertilizer, or picking apart old rope (called oakum) with a metal nail, which might be where the term "the spike" originated.

Conditions inside were grim. The buildings were stuffy, poorly lit, and overcrowded—more like prisons than places of care. A dozen beds might be crammed into one room, making it easy for disease to spread. Ventilation was almost nonexistent, and filth, vermin, and terrible smells were part of daily life. Outbreaks of smallpox, measles, or fever could wipe out dozens in just a few months.

In more rural areas, however, some local parishes devised workarounds to the law. They put the homeless in rented rooms or offered small amounts of support to struggling families in their own homes. Even with the 1834 law in place, the responsibility of helping the poor still fell on local taxpayers. Many communities continued to find that providing support outside the workhouse was actually more cost-effective.

In 1844, the government passed the Outdoor Relief Prohibitory Order, aiming to shut down any workhouse exceptions for the poor who were determined to be able-bodied. However, records show that hundreds of thousands of able-bodied poor relied on outdoor relief, despite the government's attempts to end it altogether.

https://en.wikipedia.org/wiki/Workhouse

Shane's Confectionery: A Sweet Slice of History

Believe it or not, Shane's Confectionery in Philadelphia is one of the oldest continuously operating candy shops in America—and it's still going strong. It all began back in 1863 when Samuel Herring opened a small candy business at 110 Market Street. At the time, Philadelphia was full of confectionery shops, thanks to the city's booming sugar trade, but Herring's store stood out for one simple reason: he made really good candy.

Over the years, the shop passed through several hands, but in 1910, Edward R. Shane bought it and truly made it into a local treasure. Thanks to his high-quality chocolates and handmade treats, the store not only built a devoted following but also managed to survive two world wars and the ups and downs of the surrounding neighborhood.

For nearly a century, people have lined up around the holidays—especially at Christmas and Easter—to get their hands on Shane's famous buttercreams. It's a Philly tradition, and one bite makes it easy to see why.

Today, the shop is owned by brothers Ryan and Eric Berley, who have lovingly restored it to its old-fashioned charm. Walking into Shane's feels like stepping back in time. So, if you're ever in Philadelphia, treat yourself to a bit of history (and a lot of sugar). Stop in, say hello, and let yourself be transported by the sights, smells, and sweet tastes of the past.

https://shanecandies.com/

https://secretphiladelphia.co/shane-confectionery-philadelphia/

The Lazaretto: One of America's First Quarantine Hospitals

The Lazaretto Hospital, built in 1799 in Tinicum Township, just outside Philadelphia, holds the distinction of being the second quarantine hospital in the United States. However, the story really begins a few years earlier, during one of the darkest periods in Philadelphia's history—the Yellow Fever Epidemic of 1793. That outbreak claimed the lives of nearly 5,000 people, wiping out about a tenth of the city's population. It got so bad, the national government—which was based in Philadelphia at the time—packed up and temporarily left the city.

In the aftermath, the state of Pennsylvania realized something had to be done. In 1798, they established a city-run Board of Health with absolute authority, including the power to raise taxes to support public health. Just a year later, the Lazaretto was built on a 10-acre property along the Delaware River, about ten miles south of the city. The idea was simple but critical: stop disease before it could spread.

The Lazaretto wasn't just a hospital. It was a fully functioning quarantine station, with offices, living quarters, and a warehouse. Any ship arriving in Philadelphia had to stop there first. If passengers showed signs of illness, they were kept at the hospital. Suspicious cargo was stored until cleared by the health board.

Philadelphia's Board of Health managed the Lazaretto for nearly a century, until the state took over quarantine enforcement in 1893. After its days as a hospital ended, the site found a new purpose—this time in aviation. But its legacy as a pioneering step in American public health lives on.

Sarah Worthington King Peter:
A Woman Ahead of Her Time

Sarah Worthington King Peter (1800–1877) was no ordinary woman. Born into wealth and privilege as the daughter of Ohio's sixth governor and first U.S. senator, Thomas Worthington, Sarah could have chosen a quiet, comfortable life. Instead, she dedicated herself to helping others—especially women, the poor, and the sick—at a time when very few did.

She was well aware of the brutal realities that others faced. During her travels through the U.S. and Europe, she visited prisons and saw firsthand how inhumane the conditions were. Imagine the jails of the 1800s—men, women, and children crammed into filthy cells together, often not even separated by gender or age, let alone the severity of their crimes. Male guards ran everything, and abuse was not uncommon. Sarah had deep compassion, especially for the women trapped in these horrifying places.

Her personal life wasn't easy, either. Her first husband, Edward King, was a gambler who left her in serious debt after he died in 1836. She was left to raise their two sons, Rufus and Tom, on her own. To support them, she took a job as a housemother while they attended Harvard—a far cry from the life she was born into. But instead of giving up, Sarah used her hardships as fuel. Once her sons graduated,

she moved to Philadelphia, where she married William Peter, the British consul. The marriage wasn't a happy one, but Sarah remained with him until his death in 1853.

Through it all, she remained deeply committed to the arts and to service. In 1848, Sarah established the Philadelphia School of Design for Women from her own home on 3rd and Spruce Streets. Her mission was simple: teach young women practical art skills—drawing, design, engraving—so they could support themselves and contribute to American industry. It was one of the first of its kind, and it helped open doors that had long been closed to women.

After her husband's death, Sarah returned to Cincinnati and founded the Ladies' Academy of Fine Arts, inspired by her Philadelphia school. That effort eventually evolved into the Cincinnati Academy of Fine Arts, helping to lay the foundation for what would become the Cincinnati Art Museum. Her travels through Europe had also led her to collect a vast array of art, all of which played a role in shaping the city's artistic heritage.

Sarah's influence went far beyond education and the arts. She brought three Catholic sisterhoods to Cincinnati—the Sisters of the Good Shepherd, the Sisters of Mercy from Ireland, and the Sisters of the Poor of St. Francis from Germany. With them, she helped establish St. Mary's Hospital in the West End in 1859 and St. Elizabeth Hospital in Covington in 1861.

When the Civil War broke out, Sarah didn't hesitate to act. In 1862, she hired a steamboat—called *The Superior*—out of her own pocket. Alongside a doctor and the Sisters from St. Mary's, she traveled to the site of the Battle of Shiloh to treat the wounded from both the Union and Confederate sides. Back in Cincinnati, she visited Confederate prisoners, offering them paper and pens so they could write letters to loved ones. She even taught them how to make tents, canteen covers, and other essential items.

She never stopped pushing for better treatment of women. In 1863, thanks to her efforts, Cincinnati opened its first women-only prison—the Cincinnati Female Prison—run by the Sisters of the Good Shepherd.

Sarah passed away on February 6, 1877, in her home, which she had turned into the Convent of St. Clare. She was surrounded and cared for by the very sisters she had brought to Cincinnati. Though she was just one person, her impact was enormous. The *Cincinnati Enquirer* wrote that there had never been such a turnout for the funeral of a private citizen. Church leaders praised her for her saintly generosity and tireless devotion to the people of her city.

She may have been born into privilege, but she used her life to uplift those who had none. Sarah Worthington King Peter left behind a legacy of compassion, vision, and lasting change.

http://www.adenamansion.com/wp-content/uploads/2017/02/Sar-ah-Ann-Worthington-King-Peter.pdf

https://en.wikipedia.org/wiki/Sarah_Peter

The Great Exhibition:
A Glorious Showcase of Progress

The Great Exhibition of the Works of Industry of All Nations—more commonly known simply as the Great Exhibition—was one of the most spectacular events of the 19th century. Held in London's Hyde Park from May to October 1851, it was the very first of what we now call World's Fairs. People across Britain and beyond were buzzing with anticipation, and it truly lived up to the hype.

The centerpiece of it all was the jaw-dropping Crystal Palace, a massive glass and iron structure that shimmered in the sunlight. Designed by Joseph Paxton and built in record time—just nine months—it was unlike anything anyone had ever seen. Stretching over 1,800 feet long and more than 450 feet wide, the building itself was a marvel of modern engineering, crafted almost entirely from materials produced in Birmingham and Smethwick. From inside, the soaring ceilings, towering trees, and classical statues gave visitors the overwhelming sense that mankind had conquered nature and wrapped it in elegance.

The exhibition was the brainchild of Prince Albert, Queen Victoria's husband, who, along with Henry Cole and a team of forward-thinking leaders, set out to prove that Britain was at the forefront of global industry and design. The French had held a similar event in 1844, and the British weren't about to be outdone. In fact, this was their chance to show the world just how far industrial progress could go, especially in the hands of British ingenuity.

And they succeeded. Countries from around the globe participated, but Britain took center stage with impressive displays in ironwork, machinery, steel, textiles—you name it. Anything that spoke to durability, strength, or cutting-edge design was there. More than just a show of power, the exhibition was meant to inspire hope. After decades of war and political unrest in Europe, Britain wanted to lead the way into a better future—one shaped by innovation, cooperation, and industry.

Famous figures of the day walked through the grand halls of the Crystal Palace, including Charles Darwin, Charlotte Brontë, Charles Dickens, Lewis Carroll, George Eliot, Lord Alfred Tennyson, and even Samuel Colt, the inventor of the Colt revolver. The royal family visited three times, and music filled the halls, carefully coordinated under the direction of leading composers of the day.

The Crystal Palace itself was so beloved that after the exhibition ended, it was dismantled, relocated, and rebuilt (even larger!) in Sydenham Hill, South London. This neighborhood was named after the building. Unfortunately, the grand structure was eventually lost to a fire in 1936, but its legacy lives on as a symbol of a moment in history when people came together to celebrate the best of what humanity could create.

https://en.wikipedia.org/wiki/The_Great_Exhibition

William Cramp:
The Iron Visionary of the Delaware

To the people of Philadelphia, the name "Cramp" didn't just mean ships—it meant pride, precision, and power. William Cramp wasn't born into industry or privilege. He was the son of German immigrants, raised in a city that pulsed with possibility. At just 23, most young men were still finding their place in the world, but William had already cast his anchor. In 1830, with a bold vision and the financial backing of his family's humble shad fishery, he laid the foundation for a shipyard on the banks of the Delaware in Port Richmond.

Back then, the river was crowded with competing yards. Dozens of smokestacks puffed into the sky, craftsmen shouted over hammer and flame, and ships rose from wooden skeletons into mighty hulls. But something about Cramp's operation was different. He wasn't content to follow old models. He embraced innovation, pushing his yard to transition from traditional wooden ships to the iron and steam vessels that would define a new era. Where others hesitated, he charged ahead.

The Cramp shipyard quickly became one of the most respected in the world. At a time when Harland & Wolff in Belfast were building the *Titanic* and John Brown & Company in Scotland were crafting the *Lusitania*, Philadelphia had Cramp—and his reputation stood proudly alongside them. His sleek clipper ships sliced through the seas with unmatched speed, and soon, governments were taking notice.

By the 1890s, Cramp's yard was buzzing with the labor of over 5,000 workers, many of whom lived just blocks away in the gritty Kensington neighborhood. These were men with calloused hands and soot-streaked faces—fathers, sons, and immigrants who, like Cramp, believed in building something that would last. The clang of steel, the hiss of steam, and the deep rumble of ship engines became the heartbeat of the neighborhood.

Cramp's company didn't just build ships—they built symbols of American strength. In 1890, they delivered four major warships to the U.S. Navy: the *USS Indiana, USS Massachusetts*, the armored cruiser *USS New York*, and the protected cruiser *USS Columbia*. These weren't just machines—they were floating declarations of American ambition. When three of those ships sailed into the 1898 Battle of Santiago de Cuba, helping crush the Spanish fleet and marking America's arrival as a global power, Cramp's legacy rode the waves with them.

Even across the ocean, eyes turned to Philadelphia. In 1899, the Imperial Russian Navy ordered a top-of-the-line cruiser—the *Varyag*—from Cramp's shipyard. Imagine that: a Philadelphia-built warship proudly bearing the Russian flag, cutting through the cold northern seas. That kind of confidence from a foreign power said everything about the quality of Cramp's work.

But beyond the battleships and steel hulls, there's something quieter and more profound about Cramp's legacy. His yard represented the American dream in full force—a dream powered not just by vision, but by grit. He gave thousands of workers the chance to earn an honest living, to build ships that mattered, and to stand tall knowing that what they created could change the world.

William Cramp died in 1879, before his yard reached its peak. But his sons and grandsons carried on his legacy, and his name remained etched into the iron ribs of every ship that slipped from the docks into the Delaware.

Today, though the shipyard is long gone, the echoes still remain—in the stories of families who worked there, in the pages of naval history, and in every American ship that proudly charts a course across the sea.

https://en.wikipedia.org/wiki/William_Cramp_%26_Sons

https://www.globalsecurity.org/military/facility/cramp.htm

https://www.phillyhistory.org/blog/index.php/2012/04/william-cramp-sons-ship-and-engine-building-company/

The Philadelphia Penitentiary System:
A Grand Experiment in Silence

The Eastern State Penitentiary wasn't just a prison—it was an idea, a symbol of reform, and, in time, a haunting reminder of how good intentions can go terribly wrong. When it opened its massive doors on October 25, 1829, in the heart of Philadelphia, it was hailed as the world's first full-scale penitentiary. Designed by architect John Haviland, it was as grand as it was grim, built with high stone walls,

soaring arches, and a fortress-like presence that seemed to whisper punishment before anyone even stepped inside.

What set it apart wasn't just the architecture—it was the radical philosophy behind it. Known as the "Pennsylvania System," the model focused on complete isolation. Prisoners lived, worked, ate, and even exercised alone. No contact, no conversation. Inmates wore hoods when moved through the halls so they wouldn't see or be seen by other prisoners. Solitary confinement wasn't just part of the sentence—it *was* the sentence.

This concept of silence and solitude didn't emerge from nowhere. In fact, it began decades earlier, in the 1790s, at the Walnut Street Jail, located between Fifth and Sixth Streets, behind what is now known as Independence Hall. Back then, men, women, and even children were thrown into the same standard rooms, regardless of age, crime, or gender. Conditions were so chaotic that the jail earned a reputation as a "school of crime" rather than a place of justice.

After the American Revolution, reformers began to question the old methods of punishment—whippings, brandings, public shaming—and pushed for something new. The idea was to shift punishment from public spectacle to private reflection. In 1789 and 1790, the state passed laws turning a section of Walnut Street into what they called a "penitentiary house," where serious offenders could serve their time in silence, meant to encourage repentance and spiritual awakening.

Initially, this experiment appeared promising. Reformers believed silence and labor would lead to inner change. But overcrowding, poor management, and rising mental health issues quickly made the limitations of that system clear.

Eastern State Penitentiary took those early ideas and amplified them. The prison was built to embody the belief that solitude, combined with honest labor, could reform even the most hardened criminals. Each inmate lived alone in a cell with a skylight—referred to as the "eye of God"—and spent their days weaving, caning chairs, or making shoes. Meals were brought to the cell, and exercise happened in tiny outdoor yards, one prisoner at a time. No visitors were allowed, except a prison chaplain or a member of the prison society. The Philadelphia Bible

Society provided Bibles, and as the population of German-speaking inmates grew, the German Society provided Bibles in their language, too—though many prisoners, sadly, couldn't read them.

Over time, the cracks in the system began to show. What was meant to be a path to redemption too often turned into a slow descent into madness. Prolonged isolation took its toll. While prison officials believed they were encouraging quiet reflection, many inmates suffered from emotional breakdowns and profound loneliness. What reformers had once believed would heal, in many cases, ended up doing more harm than good.

By the 1970s, Eastern State had been abandoned. Today, its crumbling cellblocks and echoing halls have been preserved as a museum—both a monument to the past and a sobering reminder of how even well-meaning ideas can carry dark consequences.

http://philadelphiaencyclopedia.org/archive/eastern-state-penitentiary/

https://en.wikipedia.org/wiki/Eastern_State_Penitentiary

The Tradition of Throwing Rice at Weddings

There's something sweet and a little chaotic about the tradition of throwing rice at newlyweds—it's one of those long-standing customs that's both symbolic and fun. While it may appear that guests are simply tossing grains for the sake of the spectacle, the act actually has deep roots. For centuries, people have showered couples with everything from oats to barley to dried corn as a way to wish them prosperity, fertility, and good luck in their new life together. Rice just happened to win out over the years as the go-to grain of choice.

But then came the myth that nearly ruined the party. At some point, a rumor began to spread that if birds ate the tossed rice, it would expand in their stomachs and cause them to die. Cue the panic. Many venues even banned the tradition out of concern for the poor birds. The truth? It's simply not true. Birds eat rice—and all sorts of dry grains—in the wild all the time, and somehow, we've managed to avoid any headline-worthy bird explosions. So, unless someone's out there chucking cooked risotto at the happy couple, the birds are safe.

In the end, whether it's rice, rose petals, or bubbles, the tradition is less about the substance and more about the sentiment. It's a joyful little ritual—a symbolic send-off into a future filled with abundance, love, and a few lucky grains caught in your hair for good measure.

http://www.celticjewelry.com/celtic-culture/throwing-rice

http://mentalfloss.com/article/18915/bizarre-origins-8-wedding-traditions

A Little Something Extra

Classic Western and European Wedding Traditions

1. **Something Old, New, Borrowed, and Blue**
   A Victorian-era rhyme meant to bring good luck. Each item symbolizes a blessing: continuity, optimism for the future, shared happiness, and fidelity.

2. **The White Dress**
   Popularized by Queen Victoria in 1840, the white wedding dress represents purity and celebration, not necessarily virginity, as many assume.

3. **The First Look**
   Originally, the groom wasn't supposed to see the bride before the ceremony—just in case he got cold feet! It's now often turned into an emotional pre-ceremony moment.

4. **Carrying the Bride Over the Threshold**
   Rooted in ancient superstition, this tradition was intended to protect the bride from evil spirits that were believed to lurk on the floorboards.

5. **The Veil**
   In ancient Rome, veils were believed to ward off evil spirits. In arranged marriages, it also kept the groom from seeing the bride until the last possible moment!

6. **Throwing the Bouquet & Garter Toss**
   Single women used to rush the bride to touch her for good luck, so she tossed the bouquet as a decoy. The garter toss is a cheekier version of the same idea.

7. **Tying the Knot**
   This phrase originates from Celtic handfasting, where the couple's hands were literally tied together to symbolize their union—hence its origin.

8. **Wedding Cake Cutting**
   Once a fertility ritual, today it's a sweet moment symbolizing
   the couple's first act of service to one another.

Unique & Cultural Wedding Traditions

1. **Jumping the Broom (African-American Tradition)**
   With roots in West African culture and the era of slavery in
   America, couples jump over a broom to symbolize sweeping
   away the past and starting fresh together.

2. **Breaking the Glass (Jewish Weddings)**
   A glass is smashed underfoot to mark the fragility of life
   and the seriousness of the vows. Guests shout "Mazel Tov!"
   (Congratulations!)

3. **Henna Night (Middle Eastern/South Asian Weddings)**
   The bride's hands are adorned with intricate henna designs to
   bring luck and protect her from evil spirits.

4. **Money Dance (Various Cultures)**
   Guests pin money to the bride or groom as they dance, to
   help fund the honeymoon or start their new life.

5. **Crowning (Greek Orthodox Weddings)**
   The couple wears crowns (called **stefana**) joined by a ribbon,
   symbolizing the unity of their souls and the blessing of God.

6. **La Hora Loca (Latin American Weddings)**
   Translating to "the crazy hour," this late-night dance party
   includes costumes, props, and a carnival-like vibe to energize
   the reception.

7. **Red Dresses & Door Games (Chinese Weddings)**
   Brides often wear red for luck and prosperity, and the groom
   must "win" access to her by playing silly or challenging
   games at her family's door.

8. **Sake Sharing (Japanese Shinto Weddings)**
    Known as **san-san-kudo**, the bride and groom take three
    sips from three different cups of sake, representing unity and
    family bonds.

https://www.brides.com/tying-the-knot-meaning-history-8302631

https://www.theknot.com/content/favorite-wedding-traditions-from-around-the-world

About the Author

Diane Merrill Wigginton was born in Riverside, California in 1963. Her family moved to San Diego near the end of 1970, where she grew up in the newly developed community of Mira Mesa. She would spend portions of her summers each year in Burly, Idaho with her mother's parents, Florence and Orval Merrill. There she developed a love of animals and a respect for the land. It was during this time on the farm riding horses, herding cattle and taming the wild kittens born between the haystacks that Diane also developed a love of storytelling. She dreamed that one day she would become a published author and would be able to tell her stories to the world. In February 2018, she and her husband made the move from Northern California to Kalispell, Montana to retire. Now she is able to pursue her passion of writing books full-time. "I am thrilled and elated to be doing what I love."

Love is not what you say, love is what you do.

So give this hard-working Author a hug and a little bit of love by following me on my websites and leaving me a review at

www.dianemerrillwigginton.com

https://www.goodreads.com/author/show/8355606.Diane_Merrill_Wigginton

https://www.amazon.com/author/dianemerrillwigginton

https://frankly.franklinpublishers.com/v2/preview/8cJRD9R69n1K=kS8mtEeBr

https://twitter.com/wiggintondiane

www.ingramcontent.com/pod-product-compliance
Lightning Source LLC
Chambersburg PA
CBHW030607170726
48283CB00002B/507